But I am, after all, an immature idealist.
Occasionally, I'd like to die ~~together~~ with my ideals too.

CW01510026

VOL.04

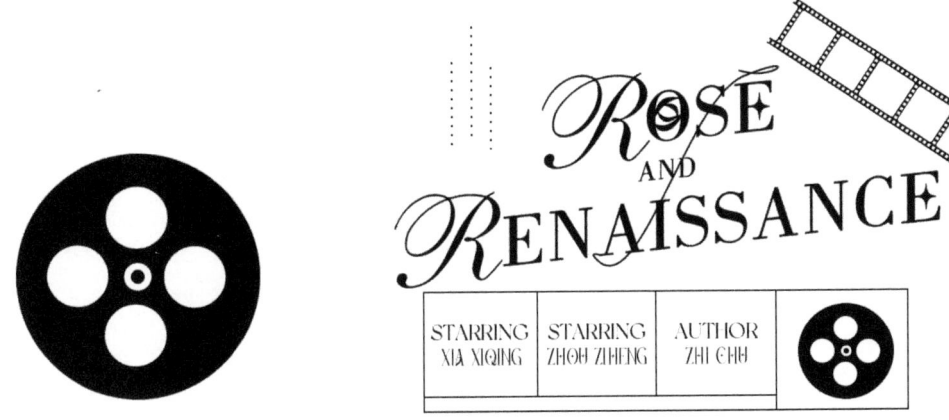

ROSE AND RENAISSANCE

STARRING	STARRING	AUTHOR	
XIA XIQING	ZHOU ZHENG	ZHI CHU	

But I am,
after all, an immature idealist.
Occasionally, I'd like to die together with my ideals too.

Rose and Renaissance

An imprint of Via Lactea Ltd.

Copyright © ZHI CHU

Author: Zhi Chu
Translator: MS; XiA; Meiling
Editor: Michaela M

CONTACT:
Customer Support: info@vialactea.ca
Wholesale & Distribution: market@vialactea.ca
Other Cooperation: https://vialactea.ca/pages/cooperation
Discord Channel: https://discord.gg/vialactea

Follow us on Twitter/Instagram/Facebook: @ViaLactea_Ltd
Official Website: www.vialactea.ca

ISBN: 978-1-77408-361-1(pbk)
Printed in Canada

LOCATION:
Shops At Waterloo Town Square
#27, 75 King Street South, Waterloo, ON
Canada
N2J 1P2

Via Lactea

Rosé and Renaissance

I'm also drunk on oxygen.
From the very first day I met you, I've been drunk.
To this day, I've still yet to recover from it.
What am I to do? You have to save me.

Only roses match you.

ROSE AND RENAISSANCE

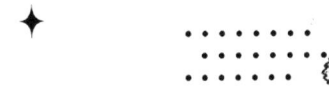

THE MOVIE STARTS

CONTENT

E.03

Three Pieces of Advice

After Xu Qichen's repeated invitations, Xia Xiqing brings Zhou Ziheng to Xia Zhixu's house on the day of the Lantern Festival. Xu Qichen just happens to be making glutinous rice balls when they arrive. Xia Xiqing puts down the red wine he's brought along and starts to tease him.

"Chen-Chen, aren't you a little too much like a virtuous wife? You even make your own glutinous rice balls."

"The ones made outside don't taste good." Xu Qichen looks down and pulls off a piece of glutinous rice dough. "To be honest, I just wanted to try making them according to the recipe."

Zhou Ziheng sighs. "When will I ever get to eat a meal Xiqing makes for me?"

Xia Zhixu gives him a look. "Anytime, as long as you aren't afraid of getting food poisoning."

Both men high-five behind Xia Xiqing's back.

"Who was the one who told me back then that using these

hands of mine to cook is a waste of heaven's gifts?"

Xia Xiqing kicks at Zhou Ziheng's leg, and Zhou Ziheng grins broadly as he makes to pull him. Xia Xiqing tells him to go away, and walks over to the dining room where he sits beside Xu Qichen.

"Let me help you."

"I'm not going to eat what you make. Put it aside." Xia Zhixu disses him and pulls Zhou Ziheng to the living room. "I've developed a new game lately; do you want to give it a try? It's a VR game, a first-person shooter. Chen-Chen doesn't like it, and there's usually no one at home to play with me."

"Sure." Zhou Ziheng's interest is piqued when he hears Xia Zhixu mention that it's a shooting game.

Xia Zhixu takes out two sets of equipment and passes one set over to Zhou Ziheng. Then, he says to some hidden microphone, "0901, open the map."

"Who's 0901?"

Zhou Ziheng puts on a black vest equipped with sensors. The instant he puts on the glasses, the living room before him completely vanishes and turns into a smoke-filled battlefield. After adjusting the headphones, he can no longer hear Xu Qichen's and Xia Xiqing's voices in the living room. All around him is the thunderous roar of gunfire, then a flat and emotionless voice speaks up.

"Hello, Mr. Zhou. Happy Lantern Festival. Nice to meet you. I'm your AI manager, serial no. 0901. I will act as your game management system and guide you in this experience."

Zhou Ziheng is suddenly fired up with enthusiasm, but he also has some doubts. "Then what about Zhixu's system?"

"I'm also the administrator's system. Please rest assured. My parallel operation process is able to execute commands for up to two hundred people simultaneously."

"That's so cool."

"I will now help connect you to the administrator's signal, and you will become squad-mates. Good luck."

From where he's sitting a distance away in the dining room, Xu Qichen can't help but smile as he watches the two guys turn into high school students as soon as they start to play the game. "Fortunately, the living room is big enough. Otherwise there wouldn't be enough space for them to play."

"It's over. Zhou Ziheng is truly going to turn into an internet addict now that he's been led astray by Xia Zhixu." Xia Xiqing follows Xu Qichen's example and closes the glutinous rice ball in his hands. But no matter how he does it, the filling keeps spilling out, so he just rolls it into a ball in his palm and abandons himself to despair as he sets it aside on the plate. "Oh man, I really don't have the talent to cook."

Xu Qichen laughs. "You can make them without fillings. Those are delicious too."

"Forget it." Xia Xiqing takes over the large bowls filled with peanuts and red bean sugar fillings. "I'll help you roll the fillings into tiny balls so you can wrap them right away."

The two of them chat about recent events as they work, and midway through, Xu Qichen suddenly says, "Oh right. There's something I've been pretty curious about."

"What?" Xia Xiqing is focused as he balls up the sugared fillings.

"Between you and Zhou Ziheng..." Xu Qichen lowers his voice. "Who tops?"

In a moment of nervousness, he ends up flattening the sugared filling in his hands. He turns to look at Xu Qichen. "W-why do you ask?"

Xu Qichen smiles, a little embarrassed. "I'm just curious.

Weren't you always a top in the past...?"

Xia Xiqing gets stuck for a moment, but he feels as though he's being too dramatic, so he sighs and admits to it outright. "He's on top."

"Really?" Xu Qichen clenches his fist in inexplicable glee and whispers, "Yes!"

"What are you happy about?" It immediately dawns on Xia Xiqing. "You weren't placing bets on me, were you?!"

Xu Qichen smiles sheepishly, "We wondered for a very long time. At first, I also thought that you're unlikely to...be the one at the bottom."

Xia Xiqing puts down the sugared filling in his hands and flops over the table with hands outstretched in front of him. He lets loose a long sigh. "Surprising, huh? Who would've thought that I'd come to this?"

Xu Qichen stifles a laugh. "Nah, I just find it a pity that there's one less top in the world." Very quickly, he adds with a solemn expression, "How did you come to an agreement? I thought it would also work if you took turns or something."

"Forget it." A strand of hair is sticking out from the back of Xia Xiqing's head. He doesn't notice it himself, but it swings around when he speaks. His expression as he lowers his voice is also comical. "Goddamn, it's too fucking painful. I almost couldn't get out of bed the first time, both of my legs were trembling. I couldn't even sit. So if a sturdy guy like me who's used to pain would hurt to such an extent, think about it..." Xia Xiqing shakes his head. "Never mind, forget it. I'll do it, Zhou Ziheng probably can't take it."

Xu Qichen is a little shocked. "So you're willing to bottom because you don't want him to hurt?" He's not just a little shocked, but greatly astounded. "Goodness me..."

"It's not too bad, actually, as long as you're used to it. I'm already used to it anyway, so there's no need to let him try again. It doesn't matter who's on top or bottom."

Xia Xiqing would've never said such words in the past; Xu Qichen knows better than anyone just how proud a person he is. He exclaims in a soft voice, "So there really are people who are willing to bottom in the name of love..."

Xia Xiqing sits up straight. "You're not allowed to tell Xia Zhixu." He adds, "Or Zhou Ziheng."

He washes his hands, then takes out his phone to check Weibo. Xia Xiqing will habitually click into a fan's profile when he sees an interesting comment, and sometimes he will follow the links into another Weibo profile and keep going. He can even end up scrolling like this for an entire evening.

Xu Qichen is just about to say something to him when he sees Xia Xiqing's somewhat contorted expression, so he leans in curiously. "What are you looking at?"

Xia Xiqing looks at him with a puzzled expression. "What's a clay sculpture?"

"Clay sculpture?" Xu Qichen shakes his head. "Shouldn't you know that better than me?"

"But I feel like this..." Xia Xiqing's expression turns even stranger. "...Is not the clay sculpture I understand it to be."

"What is it?" Xu Qichen leans in to look at his phone screen. It's a Weibo post. He reads out the accompanying text at the top of the post, "The heart of a stunning beauty is bound to be cold, along with her snow-white complexion, eyes obscured by lace, and slender, delicate fingers—they are all frosty. But her lips are as vibrant as roses, so beautiful and exquisite in their fragility that one can't help but..."

He lets out a cough, unable to read on. The picture attached at the bottom is the inside spread of Xia Xiqing and Zhou Ziheng lying in the rose-covered bathtub from the last

time they had a duo photoshoot for a magazine. Xu Qichen
raises his head awkwardly and looks Xia Xiqing in the eyes,
his face full of question marks.

"Is this...is this a porno book?"

"How would I know?" Xia Xiqing exits the thread and
frowns as he thinks about the description in that post.
Goosebumps break out all over him. "What's wrong with
little girls these days...?"

Xu Qichen has always known that Xia Xiqing doesn't like
it when people associate him with feminine descriptions.
He's so pretty that it was the subject of frequent discussion
ever since he was a child. Although he says he doesn't mind,
Xia Xiqing still can't figure out why someone would make
a Weibo post like that. What's more, there are many people
sharing and commenting below.

@XXQOnlyHusbandOnline: only a face of this caliber is
qualified to be modeled into clay sculpture k. Muacks<333 my
babe.

There are countless comments like this one, some even
more exaggerated. He's feeling a little curious, so he looks up
what a clay sculpture is, only to learn that a clay sculpture
fan, or a *nisu* fan—based on the homophone for "reverse
Mary Sue"—is a type of fan that likes to reverse the genders
of their idols.

"As a man who..." Halfway through, Xia Xiqing corrects
himself. "As a man who was a top for twenty-five years, how
can I have so many *nisu* fans? This makes no sense at all!"

Xu Qichen can't help but burst out laughing. "Go look
into the mirror, and see if it makes sense."

Xia Xiqing purses his lips and makes a sound of disdain.

"Let me just say, in all honesty..." Xu Qichen fearlessly
adds fuel to fire. "That photo of the little girl in the white

dress really is very pretty." He struggles to hold in his laugh. "Very ethereal."

"Ethereal, my ass!" Xia Xiqing is speechless. "You're not allowed to bring up my dark past."

"Hey, Zhixu's mom brought over that dress of hers along with that pile of odds and ends. She said you're the only one who's worn it, and there's no one to wear it even if she leaves it lying around. Why don't you..."

"Shut up."

Xia Xiqing promptly covers Xu Qichen's mouth with his own hand, and the dining room suddenly falls silent. In comparison, the living room is bursting with noise.

"Left, to the left! Fuck, I'm running out of bullets, give me some!"

"Dang, how is this game is so realistic, it hurts where I got shot!"

"Here, gauze!"

Desperate for a reason to escape the insinuation maniac that is Xu Qichen, Xia Xiqing stands and says, "I'll go take a look. They make it sound so fun that I feel like playing too."

Just as he walks over to Zhou Ziheng's side...

"Get down!" Wearing his VR headset, Zhou Ziheng suddenly drops to the ground. Beside him, Xia Zhixu does the same, giving Xia Xiqing a fright.

"What the..." Xia Xiqing sits on the sofa that has been shifted to the side and remains still as he folds his arms and watches the busy Zhou Ziheng. The more he looks at him, the more he finds him fascinating and childlike.

The game seems to end after ten minutes or so. Both men are panting as they take off the headsets. Zhou Ziheng turns his head and immediately notices Xia Xiqing sitting on the sofa. He's so tired that he falls straight onto him; the impact is so hard that Xia Xiqing finds it hard to breathe.

"Oh fuck...You're crushing me to death."

Zhou Ziheng lets out a mischievous chuckle, then hugs Xia Xiqing's head and kisses it loudly. "I won!"

"Yes, yes, you won." Xia Xiqing says half-heartedly, like an empty shell of a man. "Get off me."

"Tsk." Xia Zhixu casts a glance at them in disdain. He was going to say that there's no love in E-sports, but he forgets all about it when he sees the lovable Xu Qichen sitting in the dining room making glutinous rice balls. He takes off his vest and runs over to him.

Zhou Ziheng rolls over and lies beside Xia Xiqing, gasping for breath. "That vest can simulate pain. I got shot earlier, it hurts!"

Xia Xiqing shoots him a glance. "Where did you get shot?"

"Here." Zhou Ziheng grabs his hand and puts it on his chest. "It hurts here."

Xia Xiqing lies next to Zhou Ziheng. "Then why didn't you die?"

"I almost died. Almost." Zhou Ziheng activates his story fabrication mode. "Then I felt a strong sense of conviction that sustained me and led me to victory."

Xia Xiqing snorts. "Immature."

Zhou Ziheng turns to look at Xia Xiqing's face. "Why aren't you asking me what the conviction is?"

Xia Xiqing is helpless when it comes to him. "What is it?"

"Love!" Having said that, Zhou Ziheng grabs him and showers him with a stream of fervent kisses until Xia Xiqing can't even open his eyes. He pretends to push him away, but in truth, he isn't using any force at all, but merely putting on an act playing the immature kid with him.

"Let's play a round together."

"Sure." Xia Xiqing wipes his own face and gives him a look. "I'll fuck you over."

After the meal, the two of them get ready to return home. Xia Zhixu still wants to gift a set of gaming equipment to Zhou Ziheng, but Xia Xiqing stops him. What is he going to do if Zhou Ziheng actually gets addicted?

Xu Qichen also takes out a bag and says, "These are mini buns and biscuits I baked yesterday, as well as lotus root meatballs that Zhixu's mom fried. I already packed everything, take them home to enjoy."

Xia Xiqing accepts the food, but in fear of Xia Zhixu launching into his promotion spiel again, he drags Zhou Ziheng away and flees. They drive back home, and in the elevator, Zhou Ziheng says with a smile, "The glutinous rice balls I ate all had fillings bursting from the seams."

"Why did you eat them, then?"

"I liked them; the ones with busted fillings are sweet. "

"Go away."

Xia Xiqing heads straight for the bathroom after arriving home. It's freezing cold outside, and he plans to take a hot shower to warm himself up. Zhou Ziheng sits on the sofa for a moment before it occurs to him that he should put the food Xu Qichen gave them into the refrigerator, so he takes the bag into the kitchen.

When Xia Xiqing emerges from the bathroom after his shower, he finds the living room empty. He calls out for Zhou Ziheng, but there's no response, so he has no choice but to head upstairs to check if he's in the en-suite bathroom. Xia Xiqing only just opens the door to the bedroom when he's dragged in. He doesn't even have time to catch his breath before Zhou Ziheng pins him to the bed. He's also taken a shower, and his hair is still dripping wet.

Xia Xiqing says with a confounded expression, "What's with you? Pinning me several times a day."

"I *do* want to pin you several times a day."

All at once, the dialogue falls into a certain kind of philosophical fallacy.

The water droplets on Zhou Ziheng's hair drips onto Xia Xiqing's face, and he starts to lecture, "Your hair is so wet, go blow-dry it."

"No." Like a puppy after a bath, Zhou Ziheng shakes his head from side to side, flinging water droplets everywhere.

"You're so annoying." This is what Xia Xiqing says, but his expression says he's holding back laughter. He shoves Zhou Ziheng. "Get up, or do you really want to crush me to death?"

"I'll get up, but you have to agree to a request of mine."

Xia Xiqing raises his eyebrows. "What request?"

"First you have to agree."

"First you have to tell me."

And so both of them remain in this stalemate for such a long time that half of Xia Xiqing's body goes numb. He thinks, *whatever, what request can he possibly have, it always comes down to the same old stuff*, and so he steels himself and relents, "Okay, okay, get off me first."

"Really?! You can't go back on your words." With a swoosh, Zhou Ziheng pulls out a garment from under the pillow.

Fuck.

Fuck. Fuck. Fuck.

After getting a clear look at what it is, Xia Xiqing just wants to perish on the spot. Isn't this the white dress that Xia Zhixu and Chen Fang forced him to wear before?! To think it actually ended up in Zhou Ziheng's hands! What the hell is this plot development?!

"I'm going to sever all ties with Xu Qichen. Now. Right away. Immediately!"

"Come on, be good. Wear it first before you cut ties."

Xia Xiqing, with half of his body numb, is coerced into stripping naked. To be honest, Xia Xiqing has always liked a face like Zhou Ziheng's, but he never expected such a huge contrast between the man's appearance and his personality. However, it still excites him to see Zhou Ziheng do such a debauched thing as forcibly stripping him bare.

He suddenly feels as if he's awakened some weird kind of attribute in him. *But Zhou Ziheng is really too damn sexy.* Xia Xiqing lies in bed and exclaims this every time he catches sight of him. He marvels about his own great taste, to have gotten with such an extraordinary little wolfhound. With that face and that figure, who wouldn't be turned on by just looking at him?

Horny for a moment, high for a time; horny for always, high all the time.

A mentally satisfied Xia Xiqing suddenly forgets all about the fact that he's been forced by Zhou Ziheng to wear women's clothing. Plus, Zhou Ziheng's kisses as he strips Xia Xiqing have him completely disoriented. Xia Xiqing wraps his arms around Zhou Ziheng's neck and sits up of his own accord.

Although Xia Xiqing's head isn't entirely clear, Zhou Ziheng is very clear-headed. He's not only sober, but also extra worked up. He tentatively holds the dress above Xia Xiqing's head and prepares to slip it over him. It's a sleeveless, round-necked strappy dress with a long, large skirt. The fabric isn't cotton, and it feels a little smooth to the touch. But when Zhou Ziheng forcibly tries to pull that sleeveless dress over him, Xia Xiqing suddenly starts to regret it and struggle.

"I don't want to wear..."

But the more he resists, the more fired up Zhou Ziheng becomes. He simply has to make him wear it, "Just wear it once, please. Just once." Looking into Xia Xiqing's eyes, he drops kisses on Xia Xiqing's pursed lips and puts on a pitiful pleading face. "Just this once."

After a long stalemate, Xia Xiqing ultimately gives in. He really can't say no to Zhou Ziheng. Zhou Ziheng is so happy to get his nod of approval that he almost leaps for joy. Despite Xia Xiqing's unhappy look, he still pulls the white dress over him as though he's dressing a child.

"It's a little tight." With Xia Xiqing in his arms, Zhou Ziheng moves his hands behind him to help him zip up, but it doesn't go smoothly. With his humiliation already reaching a max, Xia Xiqing lowers his head on Zhou Ziheng's shoulder and says in a muffled voice, "No shit, Sherlock. I'm a man."

Although Xia Xiqing is tall, he doesn't have a large frame like Zhou Ziheng; instead, he has a thin and lean figure. Putting the dress on didn't present much difficulty, but there's no way the zipper will reach all the way up.

"Just leave it." Xia Xiqing lifts his head. He looks very embarrassed, and his ears are bright red. "Stop pulling..."

This pitiful look strikes Zhou Ziheng right in his heart. It seems as though the little girl in the white dress who's been on his mind for so many years is now right before him at his mercy.

Perhaps Xia Xiqing really doesn't like to be the passive one, or perhaps he wants to use some other emotions to cover up the shame of being forced to don women's clothing. Either way, he charges ahead, wraps his arms around Zhou Ziheng's neck, and kisses him on the lips.

"Hurry...cut the crap."

Zhou Ziheng wraps Xia Xiqing's bare legs under the skirt around his own waist, then holds Xia Xiqing's thighs and lifts him from the bed to press him against the glass door between the bedroom and balcony, where he kisses him fervently. With the wide hem of the skirt sliding down to cover his legs, Xia Xiqing wraps his arm around Zhou Ziheng's neck and lifts his face. Zhou Ziheng's tongue reaches into his mouth, stirring up a heat that spreads all over his body. Zhou Ziheng's hot, wet breath touches his face, like a mist of aphrodisiac that renders Xia Xiqing delirious and dazed.

"Zhou Ziheng...you gotta stop seducing me..." Xia Xiqing shoves him. With his head leaning against the glass door, he opens his mouth and lifts his head to catch his breath. This look in Zhou Ziheng's eyes is nothing short of bewitching—he's spellbound.

"Who's seducing whom? Look at you right now."

The body wrapped in the pristine white dress heaves with every gasp. The depression of the collarbone is deep, beautifully accentuated by the neckline of the dress. Zhou Ziheng can't help but bend to lick and kiss his collarbone. His hands grab hold of the pliable, slender waist, and his wet and hot kisses leave red marks all over Xia Xiqing's long neck. As he kisses him, he starts to hear Xia Xiqing groaning in a nasal tone. Xia Xiqing's long fingers latch onto the back of Zhou Ziheng's head and caress it hard—this is his favorite thing to do when he's in the throes of passion.

"Hurry..."

Zhou Ziheng's pace remains cruelly steady. With his arms around Xia Xiqing, he lifts him by the waist forward and upward, arching Xia Xiqing's chest up, then he lowers his head to lick and bite him through the fabric. Under the wave of lust, the tips of his nipples stick out until they are visible at a glance.

"Don't lick there..." Xia Xiqing is a little resistant. "It's...it's not like I'm a woman..."

"I know." Zhou Ziheng kisses his lips to soothe him. "I just want to make you feel good."

With that, he continues to lick and nibble on Xia Xiqing's nipples. The cloth has already been completely soaked through, becoming translucent. His tongue circles its target, and Xia Xiqing can't help but shiver. He can't describe the feeling—it isn't unpleasant, but it doesn't feel great either. It's more like sinful torture borne out of a blend of shame and thirst.

With his fingers, Zhou Ziheng squeezes a nipple that has hardened from his attention and listens as Xia Xiqing is caught off guard and lets loose a groan.

"Ah..."

This quivering, gasping sound is rather different from that seductive lift in his voice when he speaks; it carries a tinge of the fragility of one who's just been bullied into humiliation. The heat rushes to Zhou Ziheng's head on hearing it. The hot sweat on Zhou Ziheng's back glues his pajamas to his body, so he strips them off and tosses them to one side. He grabs the lubricant from the bedside table and holds Xia Xiqing as he gives him another deep kiss. He thrusts his tongue all the way in and brings it out again, simulating the movements of sexual intercourse. Xia Xiqing feels absolutely wretched as he sucks Zhou Ziheng's tongue and refuses to let him leave.

"Mnn...hmn..."

There's so much saliva that it spills from the corner of his mouth. Xia Xiqing is leaning his head against the door and panting heavily when Zhou Ziheng kneels on the floor, then lifts up the hem of the skirt and burrows inside.

"You! What are you doing...? Ahhhh..." His sense of shame almost overwhelms him. Xia Xiqing wants to push him away, but Zhou Ziheng grabs hold of his cock hidden in the skirt. Xia Xiqing has been hard for a while, and being grasped like this almost makes him come.

"What you have down here really is pretty." Zhou Ziheng's voice drifts out from underneath the skirt. "As pretty as you."

"Cut the crap...Ahhh..."

With his own manhood suddenly enveloped by a warm, moist mouth, Xia Xiqing instinctively bites his lips, but a moan escapes nonetheless. Zhou Ziheng is holding the base of Xia Xiqing's shaft with both hands while ruthlessly toying with his scrotum. Wave after wave of pleasure assaults him, and he almost suffocates. His arms drop limply at his sides as he grabs hold of Zhou Ziheng's broad shoulders.

"Ha...ahh...Ziheng..."

Zhou Ziheng slides his mouth up and down Xia Xiqing's shaft, but he doesn't want Xia Xiqing to come so quickly, so after every few rounds of in and out he pauses for a while. Such a way of toying is driving Xia Xiqing insane.

"Damn you...hurry up..."

Meanwhile, Zhou Ziheng is kneeling underneath the skirt and looks on as Xia Xiqing rubs his legs together. His stiff cock swings gently along with his movements. It's a scene so enchanting that Zhou Ziheng could come just from watching.

Zhou Ziheng squeezes the lube onto his hand and smears it over Xia Xiqing's rear entrance as he licks and kisses Xia Xiqing's groin. "Be good...try to relax..."

Xia Xiqing tries his best to relax the muscle around the entrance to allow Zhou Ziheng's fingers to reach in. Zhou Ziheng has squeezed out too much lubricant, and his opening feels so sticky that it's almost unbearable. When two fingers are moving in and out with ease, Zhou Ziheng adds another finger to thrust into the hot, wet passage. Xia Xiqing almost gives up all effort at struggling and repression. Each time Zhou Ziheng's fingers thrust in, he cries out in a trembling voice and an unrestrained moan with his head tilted back.

"Ah...ahh...ahhhh...! ...You can stop now...come in...hurry up..."

It's stuffy and hot under the skirt. Zhou Ziheng is having a hard time of it, and has broken out in sweat. Hearing his lover cry out so wantonly, he finally reaches his limit and stands. He turns Xia Xiqing around, presses him against the glass and, holding his cock, jabs at that slippery hole a few times. Xia Xiqing starts to cry out from the jabs alone.

It's still a little difficult in the beginning; Zhou Ziheng has only just pushed the gigantic tip of his cock in when Xia Xiqing starts groaning in pain. The lower entrance contracts subconsciously. Zhou Ziheng takes Xia Xiqing's face and kisses him until he goes soft all over, then the moment Xia Xiqing relaxes, Zhou Ziheng goes all the way in.

"Ah...So full..."

"It'll feel better in a while, baby." Zhou Ziheng puts his hands on Xia Xiqing's waist and pushes in slowly, enduring the intense desire, he unhurriedly slides in and out of him. The white skirt is like a veil that hides the privacy of both men's union, yet it sends Zhou Ziheng's heart into overdrive. He can feel that hot, wet tunnel beginning to suck in his manhood. Xia Xiqing's voice also starts to veer from grunts of pain to one of insatiable greed for more.

"Ah...ah ahhh...Zhou Ziheng...fuck me faster..."

"Your words." Bestial desire takes over his mind, and Zhou Ziheng thrusts his cock inside with all his might. The wet slapping sounds reverberate in the quiet bedroom, along with Xia Xiqing's unbridled screams.

Zhou Ziheng licks and kisses his ear from behind, extending the tip of his tongue. His voice is husky from lust and desire. "Xiqing, you're so hot and wet down there, like a woman."

"Shut...Shut up...I won't let you off easily...AH—" Before he can finish his tough talk, Zhou Ziheng ruthlessly thrusts all the way in, almost to the deepest depths. Xia Xiqing's voice suddenly turns shrill. "Ahh...too deep...it's too deep..."

Seeing Xia Xiqing wants to evade, Zhou Ziheng holds him by the waist and drags him into a kneeling position on the floor. He spreads Xia Xiqing's legs from behind and places them on either side of his knees so that Xia Xiqing's entire body is pressed against the glass door. The shaft that has slipped out during the change in position is now once again pressed against Xia Xiqing's hole. Zhou Ziheng breathes hoarsely into his ear.

"Xiqing, sit down."

Already feeling dazed and dizzy, Xia Xiqing doesn't even have an ounce of energy left in him to resist. He attempts to sit and take in Zhou Ziheng's impressively sized cock little by little.

"Ha...ha..."

His breaths condense into a white cloud on the glass door. Zhou Ziheng grabs his thighs and begins to thrust up hard, fucking into Xia Xiqing so thoroughly that Xia Xiqing's face scrapes up and down against the glass, smearing the white cloud of condensation that didn't get to stay for long.

"Too much...This position, ahhh...! Ah...ah...I can't..." Xia Xiqing cries out in a muddle.

He's being fucked so hard that the tender flesh of his hole

is about to turn inside-out. *Too deep. It's really too deep.* He clings to the glass and attempts to move up and escape, but Zhou Ziheng yanks him back in one fell swoop, and he lands back heavily on that frightening girth.

"Ah—"

"No escaping."

The bead of sweat on Zhou Ziheng's temple slides down his chin. He grabs both of Xia Xiqing's arms, forcing him to arch his back. In the struggle, the zipper on the back of Xia Xiqing's dress falls to his waist. Zhou Ziheng bends to lick and kiss his back, leaving love bites all over. With this position, Xia Xiqing has almost no chance of escape. Zhou Ziheng's lower body ruthlessly pounds into Xia Xiqing's bottom, each thrust burying Zhou Ziheng's cock up to the hilt. The most terrifying thing is that Zhou Ziheng is still whispering explicit sweet nothings he's never uttered before into his ear.

"You know, the first time I jerked myself off, I was only fifteen years old, and I was thinking of you. All I could think of was the way you looked wearing this dress... Hng... It was always you every time..."

"Ah...ah..." Xia Xiqing is trembling. Zhou Ziheng's fucking is messing with his ability to say a complete sentence; the drool coming out his mouth is slurring even his moans. "Ahhh...Ziheng...Hah..." He can't help but squirm with his waist, it's the only thing he has control over. Completely under the control of lust, he lets himself go wild as he writhes and squirms like an animal in heat. That hard scorching object jabs at his prostate. "Ah! Ah—"

Not even two thrusts later, he cries out and comes. Like a gorgeous fish on the verge of death, his entire sweat-drenched body is overcome with spasms, while the hole below rapidly contracts, and he loses himself in the lingering afterglow of the orgasm.

But Zhou Ziheng's not letting him off so easily; instead, he takes advantage of this interval of Xia Xiqing's weakness to thrust up hard and pound into him with increasing speed.

"So good...Xiqing..."

His heavy, husky gasping is Xia Xiqing's aphrodisiac. It turns him into a tottering flower bud on the verge of collapse. He can only moan powerlessly and writhe along with Zhou Ziheng's movements.

The incessant humping persists for so long that he feels as if it was about to catch fire down there. Xia Xiqing finally senses Zhou Ziheng's hands, which are holding him in an embrace, are starting to tremble. The sound of panting grows more and more urgent, and heavier. Xia Xiqing squeezes forcefully, and with scarcely any breath left, he turns his face, sweat-soaked hair sticking to his temples.

"Come inside me..."

"But..."

"Hurry..."

The way Xia Xiqing looks when he frowns is entirely too alluring. Zhou Ziheng dazedly kisses the side of his face as he holds Xia Xiqing's waist and rams hard a few dozen times, before he finally climaxes and sends sticky semen into that hot, wet passageway.

He embraces Xia Xiqing from behind, leaning on his shoulder as he pants and says with a smile, "Begging me to come inside you...so that you can bear me a child...?"

Xia Xiqing seems to be both laughing and gasping for breath as he turns his head to kiss Zhou Ziheng on the bridge of his nose. His sweat-soaked eyelashes lift feebly, revealing a pair of glistening eyes that are tender with desire, along with a hint of alluring contempt.

"Is that likely...just from this one time?"

Thanks to word-of-mouth marketing, *Stalking*'s box office continues to soar until it breaks the record of previous films with heavy subjects. It becomes a phenomenon discussed by a majority of netizens. The two main characters, Jiang Tong and Gao Kun, become new targets for transformative works in fandoms. Many legendary fan-artists also produce a great number of fan-comics.

Xia Xiqing, whose job is also to draw and paint, goes online every day to look at the fanarts. He finds it interesting, but he hasn't forgotten his mission. After holing up at home to paint for a whole day, he finally finishes that fan giveaway gift he promised. Xia Xiqing then posts a raffle draw on his Weibo account and attaches a photo of the painting. Everyone goes wild sharing the post, regardless of whether they are solo stans of Xia Xiqing, Self-Study shippers, or movie fans. In just a matter of minutes, the share count breaks ten thousand. By the day of the draw, the Weibo post has been shared more than a hundred thousand times.

"Say, do you think I should frame the painting myself when the time comes? I'm afraid it'll be hard to ship if it's framed." Xia Xiqing takes the glass of kiwi juice Zhou Ziheng hands him. He's only just taken one sip when he frowns. "It's sour, god, it's so sour."

"Let me taste it." Upon hearing this, Xia Xiqing promptly hands the glass to Zhou Ziheng, but Zhou Ziheng suddenly pulls him by the collar of his sweater and kisses him. He's been kissed out of the blue again. Xia Xiqing seriously feels that he's about to be dethroned from his Casanova title.

"It's sweet enough." Zhou Ziheng holds back a smile next

to Xia Xiqing and leans against him.

Xia Xiqing wipes his mouth with the back of his hand. "Such a large sofa, but you just have to squeeze next to me. Are you trying to give me a hard time on purpose?"

The more he speaks, the more enthusiastic Zhou Ziheng is. He reaches out to take Xia Xiqing into his arms and holds him tightly. "No, not a hard time; we are going to spend a lifetime together."

His words make Xia Xiqing's face burn. Xia Xiqing shoves him once but fails to push him away. So out of laziness, he lets him keep his hold. "Aye, did you hear what I said earlier?"

"The raffle for the painting?" Zhou Ziheng pouted. "Aren't you spoiling those fans a tad too much? When are you going to spoil me too?"

Have I not spoiled you enough? I already became the fucking bottom in the name of love, okay?

"I won't frame it, then." Xia Xiqing leans back into Zhou Ziheng's embrace and rests his head on his collarbone, reclining comfortably against him as he plays with his phone.

"I want to go on a trip." Zhou Ziheng suddenly says. "We've never gone traveling together."

Xia Xiqing replies as he looks through comments, "There are people everywhere we go. We'll be watched and photographed like monkeys the moment both of us step out of the house. I don't wanna."

"We can go overseas." Zhou Ziheng gently pinches the tips of Xia Xiqing's ears with both hands. "What about Tahiti? Do you like the sea?"

Xia Xiqing doesn't answer him. He's still looking at his phone with a serious expression. This makes Zhou Ziheng a little unhappy. "Stop looking at the phone." He reaches out both hands to cup Xia Xiqing's face and forces him into lifting his head. "Look at me."

This posture inadvertently causes Xia Xiqing to think of the time when Zhou Ziheng entered during the livestream and kissed him. He feels something stir in his heart, and remains in this way as he stares upside-down into those deep eyes of his.

Zhou Ziheng sees Xia Xiqing blink and is about to say something, when Xia Xiqing stretches his neck to give him a kiss. Then he rolls over to lie down on the end of the sofa, his smile saccharine sweet. "I can take you to a place."

He said "take you to a place," and not "go with you to a place." Zhou Ziheng finds it a little strange. "What kind of place?"

"A good place." With a wicked smile, Xia Xiqing pressed his bare feet against Zhou Ziheng's chest and even bent his legs to take a couple of steps. "Wanna go?"

Zhou Ziheng doesn't say anything to stop Xia Xiqing, so Xia Xiqing steps with even more gusto, with a smile like a wicked fox. Zhou Ziheng grabs hold of Xia Xiqing's ankle and caresses it twice, kneading the smooth, round bone through thin and fair skin. Xia Xiqing watches him grab his foot and lift it, so still smiling with his head resting on his hand, he straightens out his leg and hooks his toe under Zhou Ziheng's chin.

With this one move, the soft smile on Zhou Ziheng's face finally dissipates. He grabs Xia Xiqing's foot and yanks hard, pulling Xia Xiqing down until he's lying on the sofa. By the time Zhou Ziheng releases his hand, Xia Xiqing's knee is already on Zhou Ziheng's shoulder.

Zhou Ziheng's hand slides down his thigh. He looks at Xia Xiqing with a shadow of a smile. "I like this posture."

Xia Xiqing smiles too from his prone position, "I seem to have found your switch."

The switch from little pup to wolfhound.

During his vacation, Zhou Ziheng cooked up a storm making delicious food in various ways for Xia Xiqing every day. At first, Xia Xiqing would make his way into the kitchen to help him. But ever since he beat the eggshells into the bowl with the eggs three times in a row, Zhou Ziheng never let him enter the kitchen again.

"Oh, the raffle is about to start." Xia Xiqing mutters to himself as he walks into the dining room, pulls out a chair, and takes a seat to check the raffle result on Weibo.

The raffle platform on Weibo has automatically released the winners list. The ID selected as the winner is a little strange.

"I hate Lenz's law...what the hell is with this ID?"

He can't have drawn a fake fan as the winner, can he? Xia Xiqing frowns as he clicks into the profile of that ID. At first, he didn't think anything of it, but he freezes when he sees the avatar.

This avatar... He clicks on it to display the enlarged picture. The photo is that of fingers joined together. There's a black rose drawn with a black marker on the inside of the ring finger. *How, how is this possible...?*

All at once, he lifts his head and leans over the table to look at Zhou Ziheng in the kitchen. This was drawn in passing by him back then; Zhou Ziheng is the only person who could've taken a photo of it.

Fuck. This can't be Zhou Ziheng's side account, can it...?

Was this raffle platform blessed by a Buddha? He sets the phone on the table and pulls his legs up on the chair. He mulls over it anxiously for a minute, then decides to delete the Weibo post and pretend that nothing happened while he draws a new winner and makes a new announcement post.

Right. Let's do this. When Xia Xiqing opens Weibo again, there are already more than a thousand comments below this winner announcement post, which also has almost a thousand shares. Without even reading them, Xia Xiqing quickly deletes it and proceeds to the second round of raffle draw without an explanation. Fortunately, it's an ordinary fan who got picked this time. The ID is "XXQandZZHsmarriageWHEN"—clearly a shipper.

Xia Xiqing, who's gone through a roller-coaster of emotions in just one minute, quickly posts this winner announcement.

@Tsing_Summer: Congratulations! Please send me a private message with your address and contact details. Thank you all for your participation~

Very quickly, the comment section is overrun.

@boxofsweets: That's not right, Xiqing-*gege*. She wasn't the one who got drawn first!

@junkman replying to @boxofsweets: Yeah! I saw it too, I even took a screenshot! Why was it deleted? [shared image]

@GANBATTEselfstudygirls: Another salty day for me...but still, congrats! This little angel is so blessed.

@GirlNamedMingJi replying to @junkman: That person's id is so cute hahaha. Why hate Lenz's Law? Are they a slacker? Hahaha.

@SelfStudyTodayAgain replying to @junkman: This avatar...seems familiar to me?

@MUMU replying to @junkman: OMGGG this avatar! I remember there's also a rose like this on Ziheng's hand at an event! Lemme find the photo! I've seen it before!

@SeaSaltMilkFoamOvaltine: *whispers as a Ziheng

fan* psssssst, seems like there's also a small rose like this on Ziheng's hand, on the ring finger, palm side.

@MOMU: OMGOMGOMG I FOUND IT!!! That's the rose! Mommyyy look at what I found! [shared image]

@98Kforyou replying to @MOMU: Whoaaaaaaaaaaaaa! Is this a tattoo? It IS a tattoo, right?!

@ManmanLoveSelfStudy replying to @MOMU: Gosh this tattoo is exactly the same as the avatar but in a different color! One is black, the other is red.

@FLYSelfStudyGirls replying to @MOMU: Sis, you found a clue!!! So, can this account be Ziheng's...

@SelfStudyGirlsNeverConcedeDefeat replying to @FLYSelfStudyGirls: Sis, same brain cell!! That's why Xiqing-*gege* deleted the winner announcement post right away. If not, why would he delete and not even give an explanation? It must be because he realized the winner is the side account of his own husband!!! Does my reasoning make sense?!

@mochen replying to @SelfStudyGirlsNeverConcedeDefeat: Brilliant!! Have a seat please!!

@FangXiaoxiaoSmiles replying to @SelfStudyGirlsNeverConcedeDefeat: I just took a look at that account. The birthday on the profile is October 20, and the location is Beijing. One of the posts seems to come with a location tag for Peking University. Also, the account made a lot of physics-related posts. It's a 99% match with Zhou Ziheng!

@OutstandingSlingshotPlayer replying to @FangXiaoxiaoSmiles: You're amazing, sis! I'm going to stalk the side account now, bye!

@YisntSelfStudyMARRIEDyet replying to @FangXiaoxiaoSmiles: OMG SCREAMS! IS IT RLY HENG-HENG?

And that's how Zhou Ziheng's side account, which he kept securely hidden for three and a half years, ends up being exposed by this raffle draw snafu. There are more than eight hundred posts in the side account, and a third of them are about his university life and academic research, with a portion of them also talking about current affairs, as well as rants about things he encountered during filming. It isn't just the netizens reading it, even Xia Xiqing joins in.

@ihatelenzlaw: Day 2 after the basketball match. Can't lift my arms.

@ihatelenzlaw: What the hell? None of the equipment worked as planned today. Don't tell me the Pauli effect has found me??? [Are_you_kidding_me_politecat.jpg]

@ihatelenzlaw: If I can get the ppt presentation for midterms done today, I'll reward myself...nvm, it'd be a miracle if I can get it done in time.

@ihatelenzlaw: Tbh physicists are all quite handsome (when they were young), but every time I see their photos when they are old, I worry a lot about my own hair. I've always had a thick crown of hair, but who doesn't know the saying that physics makes people ugly? This strengthens my resolve to never make a living with my looks. [ganbatte.jpg]

@ihatelenzlaw: The moon is bound by the Earth's tides—unrequited love. Pluto and Charon are mutually bound by each other's tides—mutual love. To sum it up, Earth is playboy scum.

What the...? This little guy is too adorkable. Xia Xiqing glances at the dates as he scrolls back from the oldest posts. These were all posted by Zhou Ziheng when he was eighteen years old. Just looking at the text alone, Xia Xiqing can imagine how Zhou Ziheng was like back then.

@ihatelenzlaw: Is it considered greedy to have so many dreams? It shouldn't be considered as such if one works hard for it, right?

As expected, he's always been greedy. Xia

Xiqing smiles as he scrolls until he comes to
a post with just a picture and no text.

@ihatelenzlaw: [shared image]

The photo is of a bouquet of origami roses in a flower
vase. Xia Xiqing looks up at the dining table—exactly the
same as the photo. So he already moved into this place when
he was a sophomore in university.

@ihatelenzlaw: Met a very scary person. [HomerSimpson-
BacksIntoBushes.gif]

@ihatelenzlaw: Late-night soul-searching—why are there
people whose personalities are so at odds with their appearances?

Hmm? Xia Xiqing looks at the date:
March. *Is he talking about me?*

@ihatelenzlaw: Don't understand why everyone will do
a complete 180 from what they originally said. Is it really as
mystical as Murphy's Law?

@ihatelenzlaw: Most of my brain cells are dead after
recording a TV show. But this isn't what's important. The
important thing is that I have, once again, fallen for the trap. A
fall into the pit, a gain in your wit—experience is the mother of
all wisdom.

@ihatelenzlaw: I suddenly get the need for the existence
and development of art. There's no doubt that science is the
driving force for the continued exploration and development
of the world, but art is the instinctive pursuit of the beauty that
comes from deep within the hearts of mankind. If we just focus
on expanding our exploration and broadening our knowledge
of the external world, but overlook the inner entreaties of the
heart, then human beings will just become a carbon-based
creature that is all hollow inside, won't they?

To think he'd even have such enlightenment. Xia Xiqing can't help but laugh out loud. Zhou Ziheng really is too cute.

@ihatelenzlaw: So it seems that I also have my moments when my heart wavers.

There are no posts for a long time in between. From the timing, it was probably after the recording for the first episode of *Survive and Escape*.

Were they deleted? Xia Xiqing scrolls further and freezes when he sees the next post.

@ihatelenzlaw: Became an accomplice.

*Accomplice...*He looks at the date, it was after the recording for the second episode of *Survive and Escape*. He vaguely remembers Shang Sirui calling them to drink together and play Truth or Dare...

@ihatelenzlaw: The little prince couldn't stand the willfulness and haughtiness of the rose, so he left his planet. The Earth was full of blooming roses, none of which were the one he wanted. When he realized this, he went back to look for the one. But the abandoned rose had waited until it withered. Don't let yourself regret it. It takes patience to embrace a rose.

@ihatelenzlaw: I feel so sad just by reading this script, but I'd be even sadder if he didn't act in it with me.

@ihatelenzlaw: Why does he look so good in everything he wears? How strange.

@ihatelenzlaw: The local food in Wuhan is really delicious, the Yangtze River Bridge is very beautiful, and Wuhan's national architecture is truly marvelous. Most importantly, the way xxq looks as he speaks the Wuhan dialect is so lively. Forgive my insufficient vocabulary.

@ihatelenzlaw: For every action, there's an equal and opposite reaction. The same must go for feelings. As long as I give enough, I'll definitely get something in return.

As Xia Xiqing reads on, his vision suddenly blurs. He only

has to wonder at Zhou Ziheng's state during that time and he would feel terrible. Frankly, he was also in agony then. He didn't want to harm him or drag him into the mire, but he wallowed in his tenderness all the same, unable to walk out. Selfish. And cruel.

@ihatelenzlaw: !!!!!!!!!!!!!!!!!!!!!

Before he can snap out of his sorrow, the next post suddenly turns into a series of exclamation marks. There are several comments too. In the earlier posts, he's been merely amusing himself on his own. Out of curiosity, Xia Xiqing clicks into the post and realizes that it's still Zhou Ziheng talking to himself.

@ihatelenzlaw: I'm going to remember this day!

@ihatelenzlaw: How do I rein in this exuberant feeling? head over heels in love; no motivation to work.

@ihatelenzlaw: Why were his scenes completed so quickly...I want to go back to Beijing...

@ihatelenzlaw: Going back to Beijing tomorrow!!!

Xia Xiqing feels warm and fuzzy all over. A Zhou Ziheng who talks to himself so surreptitiously is simply too adorable.

@ihatelenzlaw: The theorem that says you will eat your own words hasn't failed me.

@ihatelenzlaw: Not in the mood to study even as I sit in the self-study room. Everyone around me is in a frenzy tackling practice questions and I only want to go home. I must focus on studying tomorrow.

@ihatelenzlaw: So did ZZH focus on studying today? Nope.

@ihatelenzlaw: First class in the morning is hell! I don't want to get up. xq in the morning is so soft and warm to hug. I don't want to go to school!!!!

@ihatelenzlaw: Rooftop is freezing my ass off. Why is it so hard to take a photo? Holographic projection is so hard to work, but still not as hard as xxq.

"Right back at you..." Xia Xiqing mutters to himself.

Just then, Zhou Ziheng suddenly walks into the dining room holding a pot of stewed casserole beef in both hands. "What are you talking about?"

"Huh?" Xia Xiqing sheepishly puts down his phone. "Nothing, it's nothing. Is the meal ready?"

"Almost."

Xia Xiqing doesn't know how he should tell Zhou Ziheng about the fact that everyone is gawking at his side account. But then again, he can't put it off forever; sooner or later, he will have to deal with it. Furthermore... He stares at Zhou Ziheng's face and links him to the little cutie from the side account. Finding it both adorable and hilarious, he can't help but stand up and wrap his arms around Zhou Ziheng's neck to give him a few kisses on his face.

Zhou Ziheng can't stop himself from grinning as he places both hands on Xia Xiqing's waist. "What's with you? You're so happy today."

"I'm not." Xia Xiqing attempts to suppress the corners of his lips, but they still curve up into a broad grin.

"You clearly are." Zhou Ziheng lowers his head to nip at Xia Xiqing's lips. "Are you going to tell me?"

"I'm really not."

"Spit it out."

"Uh..." Xia Xiqing's eyes shift for a moment as he lets go. "About that, Ziheng..."

He hesitates for a long time over his wording, but he still doesn't know how to explain it to him. So he sits back in the chair, calmly scoops up a spoonful of beef into his mouth, and says in a mild and casual tone, "I guess you should go check it out on Weibo yourself. To clarify in advance, this has nothing to do with me."

You were the one who had to use your side account to share the post and join the raffle.

Zhou Ziheng sits across from him in confusion and takes his phone from his pocket. He opens Weibo and reflexively goes to look at the trending list.

"Oh, fuck..."

This must be the first time he's heard Zhou Ziheng cuss this badly.

@**HaveYouGossipedToday:**Zhou Ziheng's side account has been dug out by netizens. Everyone come look at just how adorable this big boi is! Rants à la STEM geek version. I don't want to go to school. How very relatable!

@**anuprightwalkingcamel:** Absolute legend. I'm not a fan. I just find guys like this cute, not at all the persona of the #1 alpha in showbiz.

@**b_l_a_d_e_s:** Oh wow this id is so cute to me for some reason, what kind of super lovable little angel is Zhou Ziheng?!

@**selfstudygirl:** Scroll his posts from back to front and you'll obtain a little cutie who went from wholeheartedly reading physics books to being smitten by love with each passing day! Today I cry again for their beautiful love!!

@**richcutie:** "Earth is a playboy scumbag" lmfaoooo this is a lame quip that only a science baby can say. He's cute and hot at the same time, this man is a legend.

@**luobeiluobei:** omg I'm so salty. What is this stem bf déjà vu. It's so sweet toward the back when he becomes more and more besotted I'm crying!

@**starrymoon:** He's really too sweet when he said Xiqing-*gege* looks good no matter how he looks at him. So jelly T___T and oh his bio—I have a little rose. He's referring to Xiqing-*gege* right? wtf why is Heng-Heng so sweet ahhhh.

@SelfStudyGirlsNeverConcedeDefeat: Noooooo how can this be so sweet?! A process in which he gradually came to eat his words (TдT) Zhou Ziheng really loves Xia Xiqing.

@jieyiyiyi: Don't wanna go school and not in the mood to study—That's so me. But I don't have a soft and warm Xiqing-*gege* on my bed I'm so salty.

@LordKunlun: I noticed from his posts that there's a period when he seems downhearted. That's probably when he couldn't get what his heart desired? The use of Lenz's Law as his id is so intriguing too. Doesn't Lenz Law refer to the law in electromagnetism in which changes in magnetic flux induce currents in a direction that opposes the change that caused it, that is, "repelling when coming together and retaining when parting ways"? Taking all his posts together, he probably wants to say that he hates the tug-of-war feeling of 'wanting to reject yet still welcoming it with open arms' when one is in love? When I think of it this way, I feel that he must really like Xia Xiqing. Also, about his avatar...is it possible that Xia Xiqing drew him the flower, and he later tattooed this flower pattern on his hand? Just a guess.

@Petition4SelfStudyToGetMarried replying to @Lord-Kunlun: Dude that's impressive and I'm crying!! Zhou Ziheng is really awesome! Who wouldn't fall in love with him?? What kind of divine love story is this?!!!

@HengHengSuperAlpha: "physics makes people ugly," "I must never make a living with my looks," "The theorem that says you will eat your own words hasn't failed me." BWAHAHA-HAHA how can Zhou Ziheng be so deadpan silly?? And he still has the cheek to say "why are there people whose personality is so at odds with their appearance." Please take a good look at yourself!

@ShowbizNo1Alpha replying to @HengHengSuperAlpha: LOOOOOL Zhou Ziheng please open your eyes and take a good look at yourself.

@iamMrsZhou replying to @ShowbizNo1Alpha: Sis, you should change your name to ShowbizNo1Cutie lmao

@SelfStudyinHeaven: The best part is that the way he got exposed is also very silly lmfaoooo. To think this handsome dude used his own side account to share his own boyfriend's raffle post, and he fucking ends up winning the prize roflmao. And just like this, the side account he's been keeping secret all this while was accidentally exposed by his own boyfriend hahahahahaha. This is enough to keep me laughing for a year.

@ShipSelfStudySisterhood: I suppose Heng-Heng is jealous. He doesn't want to see Xiqing-*gege*'s art end up in other people's hands! He even shared the raffle post dozens of times lmfao help I'm dying

@icanXiqinggege: Y'all, go look at his likes. All the posts he liked are shipping posts of him and Xiqing-*gege*. He even liked a post that dissed Xiqing and Sirui's ship. LOL what's with this Lord of Jealousy lololol. Now look where your jealousy got you!

Zhou Ziheng slams his phone screen down on the table. "Oh no, I'm done for..."

His lifelong reputation, ruined. Who would've imagined that his persona would fall apart in such a bizarre way? Who could've imagined this?

Xia Xiqing is in stitches from holding back his laughter. He props himself up with the table and moves over to Zhou Ziheng's side, then leans over his shoulder and laughs. Zhou Ziheng feels miffed and embarrassed. It's really too humiliating now that everyone knows all the things he's done.

"Stop laughing." Zhou Ziheng looks up at the ceiling and sighs. He's so full of regret that he just wants to bang his head against the wall. "Can you stop laughing already?"

"Okay, okay, no more laughing." Xia Xiqing pats his own cheeks and tries his best to adjust his expression. He reaches out a hand to turn Zhou Ziheng's face, but just as he turns it toward him, he can't help but crack up. "BWAHAHA-HAHA..."

"You..."

"Sorry, sorry." Xia Xiqing holds his stomach and apologizes to him with tears in his eyes. "You're too cute, really. How can you be this cute?" He repeats the words in Zhou Ziheng's side account. "Met a very scary person, huh? Am I that scary? Hmm?"

"Stop it." Zhou Ziheng can't look at him in the eyes. Xia Xiqing moves up to him and gives him a kiss.

"So, to the little angel who hates Lenz's Law, do you like being my accomplice?"

Here it is again. This playful tone. Zhou Ziheng feels as though he's gone back to the time when he first met Xia Xiqing.

"Why are you such a little puppy?" Xia Xiqing wraps his arms around Zhou Ziheng's neck and keeps on laughing. "Every day you don't want to go to school, but every day you still take your backpack and diligently attend class. No wait, I'm going to laugh myself to death. You're really too cute." He starts to laugh again.

"You think I'm childish, don't you...I *am* childish sometimes."

The five-year age gap has always been a sore point for Zhou Ziheng. He tries his best to smooth out the age disparity in all aspects between them, he also tries his hardest to be more mature, but time is objective and independent of man's will.

Xia Xiqing cups Zhou Ziheng's face and presses his forehead against his. The expression in his eyes is gentle.

"Others say that you should never grow up with a boy. It's a waste of time, a waste of affection, and you will end up doing all the work just to benefit someone else, much like sewing a bridal gown for another."

His voice plunges into Zhou Ziheng's heart like an ice cube that has fallen into the champagne.

"They're lying." Very slowly, Xia Xiqing blinks. His eyelashes flutter lightly. "I should have stolen you away when I met you in the park at eleven years old. Oh, how I regret it now."

From the moment his side account got exposed, the phrase "Zhou Ziheng's Persona Falls Apart" never left the Weibo trending list. More and more people are coming to gawk at his side account. Zhou Ziheng is in such a panic that he even skips classes.

Jiang Yin is both miffed and amused when she finds out about this matter. She calls him up and gives him a scolding. "Do you know how hard it was for us to impress your alpha persona so deeply in everyone's mind? I really have to hand it to you. Really."

"It's not like I did it on purpose... Besides, I didn't want this persona in the first place."

"If you don't have it, then you'll always remain that child star in everyone's mind, you'll always seem like a child." Jiang Yin helplessly let loose a sigh. "Forget it. Fortunately, everyone is just having a laugh at your expense now."

Fortunately?! Is having a laugh at my expense a good thing now? Zhou Ziheng feels greatly humiliated.

Jiang Yin adds, "On our end, the company will help you keep an eye on it. Don't update your side account for the time being. Delete all the relationship-related posts, just in case."

"I don't want to delete them."

Zhou Ziheng frowns. He hears movement outside, so he gets off the sofa and walks to the foyer, in time to see Xia Xiqing who's just returned. The cold has reddened his nose. Without a word, Zhou Ziheng goes up to him to hug him while pressing his own warm face against Xia Xiqing's. Xia Xiqing sees Zhou Ziheng holding his phone like he's on a call, so he says nothing and simply lets Zhou Ziheng cup his face.

"Then give me your account. I'll delete it for you. Nothing good usually happens after a celebrity's side account is exposed. Too easy for it to be used by others."

Xia Xiqing vaguely hears the word "side account" and can't help but crack up again. He grabs Zhou Ziheng's shoulders and leans on him as he keeps laughing. Zhou Ziheng feels that his dignity as a top is completely non-existent now.

"Didn't you prepare a vlog earlier? Go ahead and post it now. I'll buy a spot on the trending list and bump it up to suppress the matter of the side account. As for the account, I'll discuss a follow-up plan with the team again. Just leave it there for now." Jiang Yin sighed. "Can you just stop giving me problems for once?"

Zhou Ziheng pouts in silent protest. Xia Xiqing, who's laughed enough, comes up to him and pecks him twice on the lips. He imitates Jiang Yin's tone and mouths, *Can you just stop giving me problems for once, huh?*

After hanging up the call, Zhou Ziheng stuffs the phone into his pocket and picks up Xia Xiqing in his arms.

"Whoa, what are you doing?!"

"How dare you laugh!" Zhou Ziheng holds him and spins

around a few times, then walks over to the side of the sofa and puts him down before he presses down against Xia Xiqing's body. "Still laughing?"

Xia Xiqing isn't afraid of him at all, so he continues laughing. "What's wrong with laughing? All the more I want to laugh."

A crestfallen Zhou Ziheng pins Xia Xiqing down, like a giant stone slab crushing him until Xia Xiqing can't breathe.

"Get off me, or am I supposed to smash boulders on my chest as a performance?"

Hearing that, Zhou Ziheng can't bear for him to get hurt, so he rolls over onto the woolen rug.

"Hahahaha, what are you doing?" Xia Xiqing sits up and gives a little kick to Zhou Ziheng, who's sprawled out on the rug like a corpse. "It's okay. If the persona falls apart, then so be it. It's not a big deal."

Zhou Ziheng presses his face into the floor. His muffled voice drifts out, "I've really embarrassed myself big time."

Look at how aggrieved he is. Xia Xiqing very nearly loses it again. He stretches out his foot to step gently on Zhou Ziheng's back. "Nah. Everyone thinks you're adorable." Jiang Yin's words earlier come to his mind, and Xia Xiqing hurriedly diverts his attention. "Oh, right. Didn't your sister-in-law ask you to post the vlog? Go ahead and post it. Don't dilly-dally here and forget all about it later."

Zhou Ziheng reluctantly heads upstairs to his study and brings down his laptop. Xia Xiqing is on the phone with the curator, so Zhou Ziheng sits by himself on the sofa and posts the vlog he's already edited to his main account on Weibo, then shares it also on Bilibili.

"You're going to the Awards Ceremony later, right?" Xia Xiqing hangs up and walks to pick up the coffee for a sip.

It's then that Zhou Ziheng remembers. "Oh, right. We have to go and get styled."

He was planning to take a peek at the comments first, but there's no time now. As for the content of the vlog, it's really nothing special. The main topic is "A Day In The Life Of Zhou Ziheng," and is footage of one day of his life from morning to night. The content of the vlog is also chosen by Jiang Yin. He's signed an endorsement deal with a top-tier luxury brand earlier, so in order to do some subliminal publicity for this endorsement when the vlog is released, Jiang Yin has specifically asked him to schedule the vlog on the day he goes to shoot a brand advertisement commercial.

There are so many comments on Bilibili that they almost cover the whole screen. The first scene in the video is a shot of the bedside alarm clock going off. Zhou Ziheng reaches out to turn it off, then retracts his hand to cover his face. He turns to hug a huge bundle of "quilt" with both arms and legs and remains there for a few minutes before sitting up.

> Kyaaaaaaaa that must be Xiqing he's hugging!!

> omgomg candy right at the start!

> Does Xiqing like to sleep with his head covered?

> Who knows? Maybe Zhou Ziheng hid him under the quilt because he's taking a video

> lololololololol hid him under the quilt too funny I can't

> So sweet hnnnnnnn why is my Self-Study so sweet hnnnn-ngnggg

The next shot shows Zhou Ziheng standing in the bathroom to wash up. Several strands of his hair are sticking up. With his head lowered and eyes closed, he brushes his teeth carefully for a long time. After washing his face, Zhou Ziheng picks up the video camera and looks into it, then says in a very small voice, "Why is my hair so...messy?"

> His real form comes with the ahoge hahaha

> Xiqing also had a small wisp of hair sticking out during his livestream last time. Super cute.

> Ahoge husbands hahahaha

It's only when he walks out of the room that his voice becomes louder. "Hello everyone, I'm Zhou Ziheng."

> Did he speak so softly earlier because he was afraid of waking Xiqing-*gege* up?

> I'm crying that's so sweet, Heng-Heng spoils him so much

> Self-Study is so sweet I can hardly stomach it all really

He heads down the stairs while still pointing the camera at himself. "To be honest, this is my first time doing a vlog. It's a gift that I promised everyone for reaching the one billion goal." He occasionally glances at the ground for fear that he would miss a step. "It's now..." He squints his eyes at the clock in the living room. "Six-fifteen AM. I have a class later at eight. Yeah."

> Hahahahaha class again hahahaha

> Wahahaha Zhou Ziheng can't escape from school

"First class in the morning is hell! Xiqing in the morning is so soft and warm, I don't want to go to school!" spams the entire screen.

> Lmfaooooo Heng-Heng gonna cry if y'all keep spamming

At this time, Zhou Ziheng in the video has already walked over to the dining room while muttering to himself. "I usually make my own breakfast in the morning. Breakfast is important." After saying that, he looks straight into the camera and repeats, "Breakfast is really important, understand? You have to have a proper breakfast."

> What kind of daddy tone is this kyaaaa so cute!

> The seamless synergy of a mommy fan and a daughter fan. I LOVE ZHOU ZIHENG!!

"I have to go prepare the ingredients." He covers the camera lens with his hand.

When the screen lights up again, Zhou Ziheng is already standing before the kitchen counter cutting bacon. After cutting six slices, he puts the rest of the bacon back into the Tupperware container and takes out an avocado.

"Do you know how to cut this? I can teach you." He holds the avocado in one hand and places a knife on the center with the other hand. "Cut it open along this median line." Very quickly, he asks himself in confusion. "Median line?"

> HAHAHAHAHAHA What the hell is median line, STEM major!

> Median line lmfaooooo help

> Zhou Ziheng is the most adorable STEM major I've ever seen. Too cute.

Oh, whatever. Zhou Ziheng slices around the entire avocado and puts down the knife. "Then hold both halves and twist. See, the pit in the middle is now out." Then he puts the avocado on the chopping board and cuts it into slices with a knife. As he slices, he mumbles in a small voice to himself, "Frankly, I don't really like this. Besides..." He turns his face to the camera. "The nutritional value of the avocado isn't that high either. I've seen avocados included in plenty of online recipes for reduced-fat meals, and at the time I thought..." His neck feels a little sore, so he raises his head and lowers it again. "It'd be a miracle if this thing can help you lose weight."

> Famous line lololol a miracle

> It'd be a miracle if I can get it done in time hahaha reminds me of Heng-Heng in his side account.

> I don't like avocado either, but the way Heng-Heng slices them is so pretty~

> Why do you eat it if you don't like it?

> Because a certain someone likes it!

> Oooooohhh damn right! Sis, you hit the nail on the head!!!

Zhou Ziheng starts rambling again. "The fat content of avocado is higher than that of durian, and there's nothing special about its nutritional content. The reason for its popularity is all due to marketing hype. They gave it a low-fat and high-nutrition...fruit-sona." Zhou Ziheng seems to be quite satisfied with the word he's newly invented. He smiles happily. "Anyway, this marketing was so successful that it made the once unmarketable avocado popular all over the world. It's comparable to the diamond hoax of this century."

> Look at how serious he is dispelling myths lmao

> Earth is a jerk, avocado is a liar lolololol

But he quickly grouses under his breath, "Oops, that's an insult to diamonds..."

> Hahahah did he just?? What kind of net addict is he?? hahaha!

> Looool this is some fandom lingo why does he know this XD

> Avocado Anti-fan—Zhou Ziheng

"Every time I start to explain myths I get scolded for not being romantic enough." Zhou Ziheng looks up and smiles as the water in the other pot starts boiling. He stirs it with a spoon until there's a whirlpool in the center and cracks an egg into it. "This is a poached egg."

> Must have talked about it to Xiqing, only to end up getting disdained by the little artist roflmao

> Little artist: I like avocados, what can you do? Heng-Heng: Yes, yes, you like it. We'll eat it, okay?

> I can see it in my mind hahahaha

There's a chime as the toasts pop up. Zhou Ziheng takes

out two slices and puts them onto two plates, then lays three slices of crispy bacon on it. The soft eggs wobble when he adds them, with the yellow yolk center visible among the white tenderness. He then arranges the avocado slices and a pair of cherry tomatoes which have been cut into half onto the plate before sprinkling a thin layer of pepper over them. Finally, he puts the washed blueberries and diced strawberries into the yogurt he poured earlier.

> Omg to think I'd feel hungry just by watching a celebrity day-in-the-life vlog.

> So hungry, I'm gonna go make instant noodles

> WHO WOULD BELIEVE ZZH IS ACTUALLY THIS GOOD AT COOKING?!?! HE'S THE ULTIMATE BOYFRIEND!!

"Done. This is breakfast." Zhou Ziheng picks up one of the plates and puts it on the table. "When I don't have time, I'll just cook noodles or have oatmeal. But I have a vlog to make today, so I have to make it a little more impressive."

> Lmfao this kid is so candid!!

> XDXDXD It's impressive, very impressive!!!

> What about the other plate?

> The other plate must be for Xiqing-*gege*!!!

> I remember Xiqing-*gege* once said "the one who makes breakfast was almost late" the last time during his livestream. Hahaha he must be talking about Heng-Heng.

> Crying, I'm so jelly. What kind of world-class boyfriend is this sobs

When the scene changes, Zhou Ziheng is already putting on his jacket. "It's seven-twenty-eight in the morning now. I'm getting ready to leave." He picks up the bag placed on the cabinet in the foyer, and the thermos bottle at the side falls off. Zhou Ziheng rushes to catch it and puts it back. "This is coffee. Listening to lectures in the morning makes me sleepy, it's easy to fall asleep."

> hahahaha sameee

> Can't go to school without coffee lololol

> This bag has a cameo role during the livestream the last time!!!!

The next scene is of Zhou Ziheng coming out of the driver's seat. He carries the bag on his back and closes the door. "I actually don't like driving to school, but I tried to take the subway once, and it was so awkward to be recognized. My height really is too recognizable."

> There are very few average ppl who are 6'4" tall lol

> Who would've known that this little buddy with the height of an alpha male dreams on the sly of not wanting to go to school every day LOL

Upon entering the classroom, Zhou Ziheng automatically sits in the back row and puts the video camera on a corner of the desk. He fishes out a spectacle case from his bag, takes out the black-framed glasses inside, and puts them on.

"I usually don't wear glasses, but I have to during class."

> Such a good boy!! He looks like an obedient little kid in black-framed glasses!!

> omg this coursework looks so hard...look at those obscure texts

> Look, Heng-Heng! Your professor is bald!!!

> Hahaha damn girl! Heng-Heng still has lotsa hair!

The entire portion of the class is sped up in the video, taking only about one minute in all.

"Class is over." Zhou Ziheng looks at his watch. "I have to rush to the photoshoot venue now. I'm doing a new endorsement for a brand that wants to take a series of promotional photos. When the time comes, I may have to fly overseas to shoot a video too. I think it's New Zealand, but it's not decided yet. I shall see y'all in a while then."

Once again, Zhou Ziheng covers the screen with his palm. The camera scene changes. Zhou Ziheng is already done with her hair and makeup.

"It's a quiff style today. All blown up."

> KYAAAAAA SO HANDSOME!!!! The universe #1 Alpha!!!

> Damn, he even knows of a quiff style??? True-internet-addict-youth lmfao

> This is the most alpha hairstyle ever!!!

He touches his hairline, and the hairstylist behind him says with a laugh, "It hasn't receded, no worries there, hahaha."

> Did the hairstylist also peek at zzh's side account?!!

> Now that you've said it...LOL

> Heng-Heng said he mustn't make a living with his looks!! If he's balding then so be it trolololol

In the video, Zhou Ziheng laughs along with the hairstylist. He displays his gray shirt for the camera. "The collar is specially designed to look this loose and relaxed; I'm not wearing it improperly on purpose, okay." The stylist brings over a very slim black tie and hangs it around Zhou Ziheng's neck before tying a simple knot, then puts a pair of gold-rimmed glasses on him.

> WTF SO HANDSOME!!! I LOVE!!!

> I LOVE +2!!!!

> Alpha!!! Of the pure type!!!

> Y'all, think back on his side account rofl do you still think he's pure lmaoooo. I don't want to go to school!!!!

"This is my first style. I might have to shoot five sets later." Zhou Ziheng stands and walks from the dressing room to the studio with the camera in hand. "Doesn't this studio look cool with the red lights?" He goes over to the photographer's side. The photographer this time is a famous photographer from France: a blond man in his early forties. Zhou Ziheng holds the video camera and calls out, "*Hey Lucien!*"

> So manly when he speaks English!!
> It's a British accent!! love it!!!
> Damn, the English accent goes too well with this look. All hail the invincible gentleman!!

"Hey!" The photographer turns to him. Zhou Ziheng flips the camera to selfie mode and walks over to Lucien's side. Both men appear on camera and converse in English for a while.

> Zhou Ziheng's English really is good, his pronunciation is so on point!
> He's from Peking University after all. And he's been getting top grades since high school!
> After all, he's one of those impressive science majors who can bring his comprehensive grade up with his English score!
> Crais, he's so perfect. I heard Xiqing-*gege* is from the Accademia di Belle Arti di Firenze. I want to hear Xiqing-*gege* speak Italian!!
> Omgomg I just visualized it!!! That would be so sexy!!

Zhou Ziheng's chat with the photographer is interrupted by Lucien's assistant.

"In fact, I've always wanted to learn French." Zhou Ziheng walks over to the side alone. The makeup artist is adjusting his look. "But I don't have the time." Someone a short distance away calls him by his name. Zhou Ziheng looks up. "Are we shooting now? Alright."

> Mommy doesn't permit you to learn French! Go learn Italian from Xia Xiqing!!!
> Hahaha Mama Heng's so strict
> lmao at learning Italian!!!

"See you later."

The photoshoot process isn't recorded in the vlog, so the next scene cuts right to Zhou Ziheng sitting in his car eating. His hair isn't quite the same as the previous hairstyle. It now has bangs shaped like brackets.

> WHOA this style makes him look so young and soft!! Little pupper!!

> Heng-Heng, mommy loves you!!! Eat more!!!

"This is my late lunch. There was no time to eat earlier during the photoshoot, since we shot for three and a half hours without breaks." Zhou Ziheng shows his phone's lock screen. "It's now two-thirty."

> You've worked hard, my son!!!

> Fug!! The lock screen!!!!

> What's that on the lock screen?!?!?!

> Looking back, it seems to be someone's side profile. It's too blurry. Looks like it was taken on the plane. It's the airplane's window!

> OMG IT'S XIQING-*Gege*, RIGHT?!! A sleeping Xiqing-*gege* on the plane!!

> The side profile does resemble him! The composition of the photo is so beautiful and the rays of light are particularly gorgeous! A beam just happens to fall upon Xiqing-*gege*'s chest!!

> Heng-Heng!!! Quick, release all the private photos of your mommy's daughter-in-law!!!

In the video, Zhou Ziheng is still having his meal. "I've been working out lately, that's why I'm eating this." He adjusts the camera. Inside the bowl, there's steak that's been cut into pieces, boiled broccoli, hard-boiled egg, chunks of peppered boiled potatoes, and a box of fruits. "Tastes terrible, but I have to finish eating them for my abs."

> Hahaha sonny, didn't we agree not to make a living with

our looks?

> Lmao the man who says one thing and does another!

> He has other uses for his abs okay?!

After the photoshoot ends, Zhou Ziheng, stripped of his makeup, returns to Peking University. "It's now six PM...I'm back in school." Zhou Ziheng is wearing a mask on his face. The night is about to fall, and the streetlights on campus are already lit up. "I'm going to the Second Teaching Building now since I have a course paper due in two days. I've written half of it, and I'm going to finish it up today before I head home."

> This scene is so attractive!!! It feels like a little boyfriend taking us around campus on a tour!

> Wow, he still has to go back to school to study after work.

> Living up to the ship name of Self-Study LOL!

> rofl Self-Study practicing what they preach

> OMG I'm in the Teaching Building 2 right now!!!

Having found an empty classroom, Zhou Ziheng sits alone in a corner without removing his mask and cap. However, wearing a hat obstructs the light way too much, so he takes out a portable power bank from his bag, plugs in a small night light the length of a finger, and aims it at the books. After doing so, he seems to also find it amusing and laughs for a moment before he takes out his laptop.

> lmaooo he comes with his own spotlight XD

> Wearing a cap with a night light wwwwwww why is my son so cute!

> Hnnnnng Heng-Heng is such a baby in his daily life. I wanna cry!!

A line is displayed in the subtitles: "I'm going to study now, maintaining silence in the study rooms is a must-have virtue."

This is another sped-up segment with background music for effect, as there are no lines. Zhou Ziheng spends the whole time diligently flipping through his books and writing his essay. He occasionally stands for a moment in the midst of studying and takes a sip of water before continuing.

> WHOA BGM!!!

> wtf the BGM is "Rhinoceros"!!! Omg I'm gonna cry!!

> Score one for Self-Study girls!!! It's the "Rhinoceros" that Xiqing-*gege* sang before!!!

> Zhou Ziheng definitely watched the livestream many times!! Oh wow, what is this divine pairing I'm shipping?!!

Subtitle: "Two hours later."

"I'm getting ready to go home now, but first I'm going to buy some grilled skewers near my school." Zhou Ziheng walks to the door of a tiny grilled skewers shop. "Boss, ten lamb, five kidneys, and five wheat gluten please."

> LOL feels like I'm watching a food blogger's vlog

> I'm really am hungry now Heng-Heng

"Do you want it spicy, Handsome?"

"Yes, make it spicier." Zhou Ziheng holds up the video camera to film the grilling process. "A little more, please."

> ?????? Zhou Ziheng doesn't take spicy food?!?!?! There was a time he ate spicy food on a show and almost cried.

> ???? So much chili pepper. What are you doing Zhou Ziheng?!

"You really dig spicy food, huh?"

Zhou Ziheng smiles, but doesn't answer.

> AHhhhhh I get it now!! It's for Xiqing!!!!

> OH RIGHT Xiqing-*gege* is a Wuhan native, he has a taste for food with intense flavors!!!

> Omg, I'm so damn jelly. He even buys a midnight snack for his boyfriend on the way home after studying. He's so

well-behaved and he spoils his boyfriend. What is this devoted little puppy dog?!!

> No wonder Xiqing says that Zhou Ziheng is a reality far more beautiful than fiction. The Zhou Ziheng in everyday life is really too adorable and too good.

> Today is another day I shed tears for the beautiful love story of Self-Study

When the scene switches again, Zhou Ziheng is already in the bathroom with his hair dripping wet. "I've just taken a shower and am getting ready for bed. It's eleven-thirty already, but I don't have morning classes tomorrow, so I can sleep in a little longer."

> Kyaaaaaaa Heng-Heng's navy blue pajamas is so kyo-ooooooot!!!

> Baby you gotta blow your hair dry!!

He walks out of the bathroom holding up the video camera and sits on the bed to take a shot of the bedroom. A figure suddenly appears in the doorway, though it dodges out of frame quickly, as if he's been about to come in but exited again. All at once, the comments go wild.

> Fark!!!!!!!!!!

> THAT WAS XIQING-*GEGE* EARLIER RIGHT?!!!!!!!

> SCREAAAAAAAMS XIQING-*GEGE*!!!

> It's definitely him!!! Argh he went into hiding my Xiqing-*gege*!!!

> Xiqing-*gege* I love you!!!

> I heart you Xiqing-*gege*!!!!

The camera cuts off at once, but the comments are still going.

> Is this considered an incident hahahaha

> Zhou Ziheng didn't even cut out this part!!! So cunning hahahaha!

> So, Xiqing-*gege* and Ziheng really do sleep together every day!!!

> No shit, Sherlock. Last poster, are you trying to make me die of laughter ROFL

> Nuuuu I want to sleep between them!!!

The last scene shows Zhou Ziheng lying on the bed holding up the video camera in his hand. "Good night. This is my vlog. The end. It's a wrap!"

A very small voice suddenly drifts out from beside him.

> Kyaaaaaa I heard Xiqing-*gege*'s voice!!!

> Sounds like Xiqing-*gege* said "good night"!

> IM DEAD XIQING-*GEGE*'S GUD NITE!!!

> This vlog is way too sweet!! My teeth are aching, and my heart feels so sore.

As soon as the vlog airs, the amount of shares immediately pushes it onto Weibo's top ranking list. The luxury brand with which he has an endorsement deal also makes an official announcement on his ambassadorship after the release of this video, and releases the first wave of promo photos. But this doesn't suppress the matter of Zhou Ziheng's side account. In fact, the netizens manage to creep from his side account to his Lofter account, and discover that he's followed more than thirty Self-Study RPF fanfic writers on the content platform, along with a bunch of comments that he hasn't deleted in time.

@ihatelenzlaw: Taitai are you still updating?

@ihatelenzlaw: Taitai your writing is great, and the plot is rly good too. Btw, not to ky but I really think zzh is top!

@ihatelenzlaw: Begging for updates! [pleadingface][pleadingface]

@ihatelenzlaw: Can we not add a love rival?? I think it'd be better if these two don't have a love rival, ps: the formula you wrote here seems to be wrong; a polynomial is missing.

@ihatelenzlaw: Sis, no knives pls, I need a HE!!!

At this time, Xia Xiqing and Zhou Ziheng are done with their styling. In order to walk the red carpet, the stylists had the two of them wear suits. Both of them are dressed in haute couture, with Xia Xiqing in white and Zhou Ziheng in black. The assistants carry their coats behind them so they can put them on right after walking the red carpet and the photo and autograph session after.

Together, they walk onto the red carpet, sign their names, and stand still for their photos to be taken. Zhou Ziheng has just put on an aloof expression when he hears a female fan scream at a volume comparable to a built-in megaphone.

"Heng-Heng! Mommy won't allow you to wear so little!"

"Hahahahahaha..." All the reporters and fans start laughing. Even Xia Xiqing, who's standing beside him, can't help himself. Zhou Ziheng laughs too, but a second later he corrects his expression and continues posing.

"Heng-Heng! Study hard! Read fewer fanfics!"

"Hahahahahahahaha, sis, that's brutal!"

Zhou Ziheng is startled. Xia Xiqing has his head down and can't stop laughing. These fans are hilarious.

It's with some difficulty that both of them have their photos taken. Xia Xiqing is still laughing as they leave the red carpet. He keeps making fun of Zhou Ziheng. "This time, you've embarrassed yourself all the way to your granny's home and back, hahahahahaha."

But who would've expected a deafening voice to boom out of the crowd the next second?

"Xiqing! Mother-in-law loves you! My dear daughter-in-law, remember to eat well!"

What goes around comes around. Karma makes us all a clown.

Mother-in-law fan? Why is there even such a thing?! Xia Xiqing finds it laughable and embarrassing at the same time. He finally understands what it means by getting one's comeuppance. His ridicule of Zhou Ziheng these days has ricocheted back at himself.

Zhou Ziheng wants to walk next to him, but Xia Xiqing gives him a small push. "Tell your mommy fan that I'm not anyone's daughter-in-law."

"That's out of my hands. I have too many mommies." Zhou Ziheng smiles smugly. "My mommies have the right to freedom of speech."

They're backstage, where there are a lot of people of all varieties, and all of them are celebrities. Zhou Ziheng has just scored the Silver Bear award, and is a highly popular celebrity with a large legion of fans. All at once, he's become the hot favorite in the entertainment industry. Everyone who sees him wants to greet him affectionately. Zhou Ziheng has his hands full just by shaking everyone else's. On top of which, there are also lots of cameras pointed at them; Xia Xiqing finds it all a pain in the ass.

If this had happened in the past, his first reaction would no doubt be to find a quiet place by himself. But now, he has no wish to do so. He merely stays close to Zhou Ziheng amidst the packed crowd, because he can see that every time Zhou Ziheng makes a bow or shakes a hand, he will subconsciously look back to see if he's still there.

With all the greetings done and over with, they and their assistants find an inconspicuous spot to sit down and wait to enter the venue. Taking advantage of the chaotic crowd, Zhou Ziheng quietly takes Xia Xiqing's hand.

"Your hands are cold." He rubs it twice. "Are you cold?"

"I was earlier, but I feel much better now." Xia Xiqing

leans back in his chair and looks up at the ceiling. "It's so tiring to be a celebrity."

Zhou Ziheng puts Xia Xiqing's hands into the pockets of his overcoat. "You can decline next time. That is if you don't wish to come out."

Xia Xiqing turns to look at him. "I'm talking about you. I'm not a celebrity." He wrinkles his nose and, with his hand still in his pocket, jabs at Zhou Ziheng's waist. The expression in his eyes is gentle, but at the same time, it also carries a tinge of mischief. "Our Heng-Heng is so exhausted every day."

He hardly ever calls Zhou Ziheng this. It isn't an unfamiliar word to Zhou Ziheng; his fans call him that every day, so he doesn't feel anything special about it anymore. But Xia Xiqing calling him Heng-Heng coupled with such an adorable expression makes Zhou Ziheng's heart thump hard.

How I want to kiss him.

What Xia Xiqing doesn't know is that these are the moments when Zhou Ziheng truly feels how tough it is to be a celebrity.

Half an hour before the start of the award ceremony, the two of them enter the venue together. In the process of finding a seat, Zhou Ziheng is called away by the organizer, as he will be presenting the award as the guest of honor for the best newcomer. By the time Xia Xiqing finds his own seat with the guidance of his assistant, the fans have also entered the venue, and they start screaming as soon as they see him.

"Xiqing-*gege*!"

"Xiqing-*gege*, look here!"

One after another, fansite photographers aim their telescopic lenses at him. Xia Xiqing dotingly turns around to smile back at them.

"Xiqing! Mama loves you!"

"Mommy loves you too! Xiqing, put on more clothes!"

"Xiqing! I went to the art gallery yesterday!"

"Xiqing, I love you!"

The fans are truly too enthusiastic. Xia Xiqing lets show a resigned and doting smile, and puts a hand on his chest to bow to them, then finally finds his seat and sits.

"Oh my god, what kind of prince is Xiqing?!"

"How gentlemanly!"

"My Prince Charming!"

"Not yours! But Zhou Ziheng's!"

Internal conflict suddenly arises.

"Zhou Ziheng's little rose!"

"Kyaaaaaaaaaa, little rose!"

The exposure of this title is all thanks to Zhou Ziheng's side account. Xia Xiqing didn't mind it before, but now that it's been called out in public by the fans, it's indeed a little embarrassing. Xia Xiqing turns around and makes a hush gesture at them. The fans dutifully cover their mouths. Xia Xiqing makes a heart with his hands and playfully raises his eyebrows in passing.

Xia Xiqing hasn't turned around for long when he hears the fans again. It isn't loud, but it's audible.

"Xiqing-*gege*, turn around!"

They call out to him in succession many times. Xia Xiqing can't bear to play dumb, so he turns to see a dozen fans holding up their phones with the screens displaying over-sized words—Little Rose, as if they're homemade electronic handheld banners. Rose-colored words flash at him, looking especially eye-catching.

He really has to hand it to these girls. Xia Xiqing lowers his head and smiles in resignation.

The fans, however, are on cloud nine, thinking that

they've successfully teased Xiqing-*gege*. But to their surprise, not five minutes later, Xia Xiqing turns around and holds up his own phone. A phrase scrolls across his screen, with each character filling up the screen: **Be good. Call me *gege*.**

"KYAAAAAAAAAAAAA!"

"Oh my god, ahhhhhh, Xiqing-*gege* is such a tease!"

"*Gege*! *Gege*, I HEART YOU!"

Even fans of other celebrities can't help but lament, "Goddamn, look at their idol. Oh my gosh, he really is too good at this."

Xia Xiqing puts away his phone, but now the fans in the other direction are starting to call his name.

He looks up and hears them ask, "Xiqing-*gege*, are you aware that Heng-Heng reads fanfics?"

Xia Xiqing shakes his head with a smile.

"Really?"

Xia Xiqing lets out a cool and adorable smile. "He always reads them behind my back."

"Hahahaha..."

After chatting with the fans, Xia Xiqing lowers his head to straighten his tie. Zhou Ziheng is coming down from a corner of the stage and looking around. Xia Xiqing doesn't see him, but the fans behind him do, and they yell out one louder than the other to catch his attention.

"Heng-Heng! Your wife is here!"

"Over here! Heng-Heng!"

Under the guidance of the "enthusiastic cues" from the fans, Zhou Ziheng walks to Xia Xiqing's side with a smile. He doesn't sit right down, but stands on the side to speak to him. As he speaks, he reaches out to squeeze the back of Xia Xiqing's neck. It isn't that much of an intimate gesture on its own, but the fans become extremely excited as they hold up their expensive cameras to click away.

Another celebrity walks toward them from behind. Zhou Ziheng turns aside to let the person pass before he sits himself.

"When is the Newcomer Award?" Xia Xiqing looks at Zhou Ziheng.

"Hmm...the sixth." Zhou Ziheng is a little tired and, without thinking, leans over to put his head on Xia Xiqing's shoulder.

"Hey, there are people watching."

"Then let them watch." Zhou Ziheng is not in the least bit concerned as he smiles. "I came out of the closet just so I can put on a public display of affection, lest they can't see it."

His tone is extremely childish, like a kid throwing a tantrum, but Xia Xiqing feels very happy nonetheless. A joyful feeling fills up his heart, like a little loaf slowly rising in the oven.

"I want the whole world to know that you're mine." Zhou Ziheng's voice is steady as he says this, then he suddenly smiles. "I didn't mean for my side account to be exposed, but in terms of consequentialism, it's not a bad thing either." He lifts his head and turns to look at Xia Xiqing. "At least now, many people know just how much I like you."

These tender words of love drift into his ears like a tiny spark floating down to ignite a fiber of emotionally charged nerve. A little embarrassed, Xia Xiqing leans forward over the seat in front of him and buries his face into his folded arms. He takes a moment to recover before he turns and looks at Zhou Ziheng with a sly smile, like that of a fox.

"But your side account really is hilarious."

Sweet revenge.

Once the award ceremony starts, they both stop their

joking banter and sit upright in their seats, waiting for the awards to be presented. This award ceremony isn't considered to be of importance or value domestically, but because of their collaboration with Weibo, plenty of celebrities turned up, thereby cranking up the heat.

When it's time to present the Newcomer Award, Zhou Ziheng walks onto the stage as the guest of honor. The one presenting the award with him is Feng Cheng, an actor in his early forties who made his name in comedies and has excellent interpersonal skills. The disparity between their images is huge.

Zhou Ziheng has only just arrived at the podium and is adjusting the microphone when Feng Cheng jokes, "Upon a closer look, Zhou Ziheng and I really do look quite similar."

A burst of laughter and applause erupts from the audience, and Zhou Ziheng laughs along.

Feng Cheng adds, "Everyone says I'm the Zhou Ziheng of the comedy world."

"No, no, sir, you are so much more handsome than I am." Zhou Ziheng smiles modestly.

"True that!"

Another burst of laughter from the audience.

"We are going to present the Newcomer of the Year Award today." With one hand behind him holding the envelope, Feng Cheng asks Zhou Ziheng, "Well, Ziheng, do you still remember how you felt when you were a newcomer?"

Zhou Ziheng thinks for a moment with a smile, and eventually shakes his head. "Afraid I don't."

A fan below yells, "He was only six years old!"

"Hahahahahahaha..."

Everyone laughs along. Zhou Ziheng smiles and licks the corner of his lips, looking rather helpless.

"Then, do you have any advice for newcomers?" Feng Cheng throws out a remark to get the ball rolling. "If you ask me, I think for a newcomer, it'd be best not to rush. The more impatient you are, the more aged you'll look." With that, he points to himself. "Like me, hahaha."

Zhou Ziheng purses his lips and says in all seriousness, "I have three suggestions. First, do not establish a persona for yourself."

"Hahahahahahahaha..."

"Second, do not create a side account."

"Hahahahahahahahahahahaha..."

This self-deprecating humor amuses the guests and audience so much that they can't stop laughing. It's more entertaining than a crosstalk show.

Zhou Ziheng clears his throat. "Third, do not use your side account to reblog a raffle draw."

"Hahahahahahahaha!"

"What a man, hahahahahaha."

The camera turns to Xia Xiqing, who can only lower his head and hold back a laugh as he claps, keeping the last of his poise and composure when he looks up.

Feng Cheng leads the applause beside Zhou Ziheng. "It's been a long time since I've heard such constructive suggestions." He then takes out the envelope. "Now, let us give the award."

After handing out the award, Zhou Ziheng straightens the lapels of his suit and strides back to his own seat, where he leans into Xia Xiqing and they have a little whispered conversation. As soon as both of them draw close to one another, the fans behind them can't keep themselves from screaming. It can't be helped. Their own ship is handing out eye candy with this PDA; they'd be letting their ship down if they don't lap it all up.

When the ceremony ends, Xia Xiqing and Zhou Ziheng come out together. Due to the special nature of the venue, the celebrities' nanny vans can't stop directly outside the building. Fans who've long gathered outside the venue swarm around them the moment they emerge. Four bodyguards separate both men from the fans, but the distance between them is still very close.

A fan jokes, "Heng-Heng, you are even taller than the bodyguards. Who's protecting whom? Hahaha!"

"Hahahahahahaha..."

Another fan yells, "Heng-Heng! Didn't mommy tell you to put on more clothes?! Don't wear so little just to look handsome!"

Xia Xiqing can't stop laughing, and imitates the mommy fan's tone to lecture Zhou Ziheng, "You hear that? Don't wear so little just to look handsome!"

He hasn't been smug for ten seconds when another fan shouts, "Xiqing! You have to listen to mother-in-law too!"

Zhou Ziheng bursts out laughing loudly. He even gives the fan a thumbs up. "Bravo!"

Xia Xiqing elbows Zhou Ziheng.

"Aye, why is my daughter-in-law such a tsundere?"

"Hahahahahaha, a tsundere bottom!"

Xia Xiqing's forehead twitches twice. "I'm not the bottom..."

The fans all laugh. One of them suddenly shouts, "Right, you're o!"

A kind and genial smile materializes on Xia Xiqing's face. "This batch of fans is really too hard to please."

"I think they know to play the game pretty well." Right after saying this, Zhou Ziheng's words come back to bite him in the ass.

"Zhou Ziheng, the fanfic writer took a screenshot of your comment and posted it! She said it was precisely her intention to reverse the ship!"

"Hahahahahahaha, she said she doesn't like to have a childish kiddo as the top!"

"Hahahahahaha, childish kiddo top, I'm dying!"

Zhou Ziheng says cold-heartedly, "Kick her out of the fan club!"

"Says who?" Xia Xiqing laughs like a rascal. "No dismissal allowed."

"Kick her out!"

"Nope."

"Hahahahahahaha, how is it that my ship is still so sweet even when they're quarreling?!"

Suddenly, a male fan's voice emerges from the crowd. It sounds extremely familiar. "Xiqing-*gege*, I love you!"

Zhou Ziheng recognizes it at once and looks toward the voice, and it's as he expected. "You again?!"

"Hahahahahahaha, what's meant to come will still come."

Then, in English, someone yells, "*Not you again!*"[1]

The dude in a blue sweater who wildly professed his love at the roadshow in Beijing last time swings his head ostentatiously. He continues to shout with a what-can-you-do-to-me expression, "Xiqing-*gege*, look at me! I can be bottom! I can be top! For Xiqing-*gege*, I can keep going on!"

"Hahahahaha, it's the cuckold dude!"

---

1 Originally, this was a reference to a Chinese meme. The Chinese equivalent to the phrase "Why is it always you?" can be transliterated, word-for-word, to "How old are you?" This latter phrase of Chinglish has since become a meme, and it is the English phrase "How old are you?" that was in the original text in place of "Not you again!"

"Hahahahahahahaha, this little dude is killing me!"

Zhou Ziheng pretends to fly into a rage. With a furious expression, he rolls up his sleeves and makes to charge forward. "I'll see if you can keep going on..."

The dude shrieks in a loud, shrill voice. "Bodyguards, please stop him!"

"The bodyguards exist to stop Zhou Ziheng, hahahahaha."

Xia Xiqing laughs all the way to the car before he finally catches a breather.

"Xiqing-*gege* is mine!"

This sentence finally touches Zhou Ziheng's sore spot. "I'll show you whose he is!" He childishly reaches out to hold Xia Xiqing's head and smooches him loudly on the cheek. Xia Xiqing is so stunned by this sudden attack that he freezes in place and glares at Zhou Ziheng in wide-eyed disbelief.

"Oh damnnnnn! He kissed his face!"

"Kyaaaaaaaaa, I'm dead!"

"AHhhhhhHHhh!"

Xiao-Luo pulls the car door open. "Ziheng, Xiqing, get in. It's cold outside."

Zhou Ziheng grabs Xia Xiqing's hand and pulls him into the car with him. Then he waves to the fans, and the car door promptly pulls shut. The cuckold dude is still putting up a last-ditch struggle, looking just like a screeching chicken that is being trampled in a stampede.

"Arghhhh, Xiqing-*gege*, look at me! Zhou Ziheng is way too childish!"

The car is about to leave, but the window slides down a little to reveal a pair of smiling peach blossom eyes. Amidst the screams and shrieks of the fans, a slender, fair hand holds a phone up to the opening. A line of text scrolls past:

I like how childish he is.

E.04

⋮

Idealism

After the various public displays of affection during the award ceremony are uploaded online by the fans who were there, the popularity of the Self-Study ship continues to rise with each passing day, topping all the other couples in the shipping world. Zhou Ziheng's self-deprecating speech at the award ceremony, in which he gave "three suggestions for newcomers," is also uploaded to the internet. After shedding his alpha persona, Zhou Ziheng has a sudden influx of new fans, and his popularity soars yet again.

During the preparation for the second season of *Survive and Escape*, the official Weibo account of the show is overrun with comments from fans of the show and the guests. The last live broadcast of *Werewolves of Millers Hollow* was very popular and well-received. In order to meet fan expectation, and to build up the hype for the second season, which is still in the works, the program crew decides to go ahead with a second live broadcast of *Werewolves of Millers Hollow*.

@PlainofWater: omg, so does this mean it's going to be serialized?!!! So excited!!!

@comekissme: yaaaaaaaay werewolvessss!!!!

@sweetshrooms: Looking forward to it!! Live broadcast noww!!

The program crew contacted the nine guests to arrange the schedule. After a few days of coordination, the second live broadcast of *Werewolves of Millers Hollow* finally starts at seven sharp on a Saturday night.

In order to save time, everyone has their styling done before heading over to the live broadcast studio. Due to traffic on the way there, Xia Xiqing and Zhou Ziheng are the last to arrive. However, the moment they enter the studio, the live broadcast's comments section burst into life.

> AAAAAAAAAAH I SEE SELF-STUDY!!

> Oh fack!!! Xiqing-*gege*[2]!!! Heng-Heng[3]!!!

> Hold up!! Xiqing-*gege*'s and Heng-Heng's sweaters!! Seems like a couple set!!

> You with those sharp eyes!!! You're awesome!!

The dark gray sweater Xia Xiqing is wearing actually does belong to Zhou Ziheng. It's a high street brand from abroad, but it's a little narrow at the shoulders for Zhou Ziheng, so Xia Xiqing took it. Zhou Ziheng ordered another one the next day, but as dark gray was sold out, he could only get a black one. The pattern, however, is the same as the one Xia Xiqing is wearing.

> When is Xiqing-*gege* going to have long hair again? He's

2 "Ge(ge)" is an honorific title or suffix that is used any boy or man of the same nominal generation as the speaker, occasionally even for those who are slightly younger than the speaker, especially if they have some other form of seniority over the speaker. Literally, it means "older brother," but it is used regardless of familial relation and also sometimes regardless of relative age.
3 In Chinese, this method of reduplicating characters is often affectionately used to make diminutive nicknames.

sooo pretty with long hair!!

> Xiqing-*gege* will have long hair whenever he gets too lazy to cut his hair hahahahaha

> Ziheng's shoulders!!! His broad shoulders are so manly!!

All the guests take their seats in the same order as the last session of *The Werewolves of Millers Hollow*: Player 1, Xia Zhixu. Player 2, Xu Qichen. Player 3, Ruan Xiao. Player 4, Yang Bo. Player 5, Xia Xiqing. Player 6, Shang Sirui. Player 7, Zhao Ke. Player 8, Xia Xiuze. Player 9, Zhou Ziheng. Everyone faces the camera and greets the audience in their respective order. While Ruan Xiao is talking, Xia Xiqing catches Xia Zhixu giving Xu Qichen a handful of *Wang-Zai* milk candy. With a grin on his face, Xia Xiqing raps his hand on the table and makes eyes at Xu Qichen.

> OMG Xiqing's little gestures!!

> xxq looks so handsome every time he raises his eyebrows!!!!!

> Xiqing-*gege* wants candies?? I have some here!!

Xu Qichen sees Xia Xiqing's hint and is about to toss a candy to him when beside him, Xia Zhixu throws one right at Xia Xiqing's head. Fortunately, Xia Xiqing is quick to react and leans back, as he grabs the candy with his hand.

Very soon, it's Xia Xiqing's turn to say his greetings, so he has no time to teach Xia Zhixu a lesson. He smiles, waves at the camera, and says, "Good evening! I'm Player 5, Xia Xiqing."

After Xia Xiqing is done, he catches a glimpse of Zhou Ziheng as he gives Xia Zhixu's shoulder a pat. With a severe expression, Zhou Ziheng says, "You're not allowed to bully my wife."

> Whoa fuck!!!!! Heng-Heng awesome!!!

> Why is my wittle son so stronk today!!!

> AAAAAAAAAAAH DID I JUST HEAR THE WORD WIFE?!?!
> Yes!!! Officially his wife!!

Xia Xiqing throws a candy at Zhou Ziheng, hitting him on the head. "What the hell are you spouting?!"

Beside him, Xia Xiuze imitates Xia Xiqing, "Yeah, what the hell of a truth are you spouting?!" After that, he even stands up and trades a high-five with the Milk Candy Victim, Zhou Ziheng. *"Yeah!"*

"Seriously..." Xia Xiqing is rendered speechless. *Why is everyone standing on that little brat Zhou Ziheng's side?*

It's only after they horse around for a while that the game officially starts. After everyone confirms the card they've drawn, the familiar voice-over of the program's narrator rings out.

"Night falls. Everyone, please close your eyes."

Chilling background music plays, and all the lights turn a dark red.

> The music from Survive and Escape and Escape from Werewolves Town is especially spine-chilling
> Right, right. I don't even dare to watch Survive and Escape at night! It's obviously not a horror reality show, but I feel so panic-stricken watching it!
> I always watch it with all my roommates hahaha

"Cupid, please open your eyes."

Ruan Xiao opens her eyes and extends a hand.

> Whoaaa bark bark it's Xiao-Xiao!!!
> Omgomg lil sis Ruan is Cupid!!

"Cupid, please choose two players to pair up as the lovers."

Ruan Xiao carefully studies everyone, who still have their heads lowered. She hesitates for a moment, then gestures a 9 and a 2 to the camera.

> What??? Heng-Heng and the screenwriter-*gege*???

> Are Xiao-Xiao and Zhao Ke the ship-sinkers lolololol

All of a sudden, Ruan Xiao signs a cross with her fingers to the program crew to signal her intent to reselect her choices. Two seconds later, she gestures a 9 and a 5.

> WAHHhhhh Self-Study are the lovers!!!!

> Self-Study is real!!! Self-Study are really the lovers!!!

> Ruan Xiao is truly Self-Study's Number 1 Chief of Fans loooooool

> Ruan Xiao knows the game!!!

> Human-werewolf pair, human-werewolf pair, please let it be human-werewolf pair, please, please, please. Jade Emperor, Queen Mother, Goddess of Mercy, Great Immortals, I want to watch a human-werewolf pair in action hnnnnn

"Cupid, please close your eyes." The narration pauses. "Lovers, please open your eyes."

Xia Xiqing feels a staff member pat him on his shoulder, he's a little excited. He can have some fun now that he's been paired up with a lover for this round. But who would've guessed? The moment he opens his eyes, he sees Zhou Ziheng. His expression right then is worthy of being made into a meme.

> lmfaoooo Xiqing is so funny

> Cupid: Hehehehe didn't expect this, did you?

> Xia Xiqing: don't tell me the production team was asking the REAL lovers to open their eyes???

Zhou Ziheng is a little surprised too. Not only that, but he's also a little excited. Unable to contain himself, the corners of his mouth rise as he breaks into a wide grin.

> Heng-Heng is dying of joy lmfaooooo

> Heng-Heng: hot damn, how do you expect me to act like this? I've been paired up with my wife

Once both of them have confirmed, the narration starts

again, "Lovers, please close your eyes. Werewolves, please open your eyes."

Xia Xiuze, Zhou Ziheng, and Yang Bo raise their heads at the prompt and open their eyes.

"Werewolves, please confirm your associates."

> Fuq, Heng-Heng is a werewolf this time!!!

> Heng-Heng and baby bro are werewolves!!! The angel team is all werewolves!!

> If only the screenwriter-*gege* is the third werewolf, then we'll have three angel werewolves hahahaha

> Oh fk! Zhou Ziheng is a werewolf!!! So it's really a human-werewolf pair this time!!

> HOW EXCITING XDDDDD

"Werewolves, please choose a victim."

Yang Bo takes the lead and signals a 5. The way he sees it, Xia Xiqing is a great variable as long as he isn't his companion. Just like Zhou Ziheng said, an intelligent person like Xia Xiqing who doesn't play by the rules is the greatest uncertainty in every game. If they want to win, they have to eliminate this uncertainty. But this move is opposed by Xia Xiuze. He shakes his head vehemently and signs a 2—Xu Qichen.

> LOL baby bro is too much of a loyal hound

> Baby Bro probably: even if my big bro deceives me, I can't let him be the first victim!!!

> Heng-Heng is thinking, I don't have to worry with younger bro here hahaha

> Two-third of the werewolves team are diehard fans of Xia Xiqing lmfao! At this rate, can the game still continue? xD

The two can't come to an agreement. Zhou Ziheng signals a 1, wanting to kill off Xia Zhixu. Xia Xiuze glances over and compromises. In any case, as long as his big bro doesn't die, everything else is negotiable. Yang Bo considers it for a moment, then thinking that Xia Zhixu is a pro at this, he agrees to kill off Player 1.

"Werewolves, please close your eyes."

> Zhixu that poor thing rofl

> Xia Zhixu...betrayed by his auntie and tiny uncle. I'm crying lmfao

> Wtf? auntie??? LOOOOOOOOL

> Hold it right there with the auntie!! Did you just switch my ship around?!

"Witch, please open your eyes."

Upon hearing the prompt, Xu Qichen raises his head and rubs his eyes.

> Holy crap!! Screenwriter Xu is the witch!!

> All the identity cards this time is awesome!!

> This witch will definitely save him hahahaha

"He's the one who died last night."

Xu Qichen is a little taken aback when he sees the director's gesture, he's surprised to see that the one who died is Zhixu.

> Hahaha Screenwriter Xu is shocked

> My hubby is dead????

"Witch, you have a bottle of antidote; would you like to use it?"

Xu Qichen turns it over in his mind. Xia Xiqing has already played the trick of killing himself last time, so it's unlikely Xia Zhixu will repeat it. It also doesn't seem likely in terms of the program's watchability. Besides, killing himself has never been Xia Zhixu's style. He's the classic werewolf who's always on the offensive.

Guess I should save him. Xu Qichen nods his head at the program crew.

> I can't believe the screenwriter-*gege* didn't save him right away lmaooooo

> He even thought about it for a long time hahaha poor Zhixu-*gege*

> If you compare it to how baby bro saved Xiqing last time, baby brother truly is a faithful hound who acts with no regard to gameplay hahaha!

"You have a bottle of poison, would you like to use it?"

Xu Qichen shakes his head and closes his eyes.

"Seer, please open your eyes."

Xia Xiqing raises his head and quirks his lips at the camera.

> Hot damn!!!!! Xiqing-*gege* is the seer!!

> This time the Cupid camp is wild!!! A special character-werewolf pair!!!

> Omg!! I've already thought of a plot for a 100k fic!!! What kind of divine setup is a special character-werewolf pair?!!!

"Seer, please check the identity of one person."

Without hesitation, Xia Xiqing signals a 9.

> As expected, he's going to check the identity of his lover hahaha

> Xiqing is always so cool every time he plays a game!! I love watching him play!!

> Yeah!! Does the rich heir really have no thoughts of forming an e-sports squad?? If not, how about being a game streamer??

"His identity is—" The crew holds up the werewolf card to Xia Xiqing. "This."

On seeing the information, a meaningful expression instantly comes over Xia Xiqing's face.

> xq is thinking, I always knew my hubby is a wolf

> Your hubby is the *real* wolfhound hahaha

"Seer, please close your eyes. It's now daytime."

The lights come back on, and all the players open their eyes. "The sheriff's election campaign will now begin. Players who wish to run for sheriff, please press the round button in front of you."

A number of players press the buttons, especially Xia Xiqing, who smacks hard on it.

> Hahaha Xiqing-*gege* sure goes all out playing
> "I carry my hubby this round!"
> Oh dang, three special characters and two werewolves!!

"The players in the running are: Player 2 Xu Qichen, Player 3 Ruan Xiao, Player 4 Yang Bo, Player 5 Xia Xiqing, and Player 9 Zhou Ziheng. Please make your speeches now, starting from Player 2."

With a calm expression, Xu Qichen adjusts his mic before speaking up.

"To keep it short, I'm a strong special character who can self-verify my identity. If there's more than one person after me claiming to be the seer, you must give me the sheriff's badge. Special Character, over."

> Why do I suddenly find Screenwriter Xu so cool too hhhh
> Screenwriter Xu has the kind of personality where he's a little cold and indifferent when he gets all serious. But when he's gentle, he's super-duper gentle. Especially when he's with Xiqing, sooo cute
> While Xiqing-*gege* is wickedly and adorably cool!

"Player 3, special character." Ruan Xiao takes over. "Here to guard against multiple players claiming to be the seer. You can consider giving me the sheriff's badge; over."

> Ruan Xiao-*jie*⁴ is also so succinct hahaha

---

4 "Jie(jie)" is an honorific title or suffix used on any girl or woman of the same nominal generation as the speaker, even those who are slightly younger than the speaker if they have some other form of seniority. It means "older sister," but is used regardless of relation and sometimes regardless of age.

> Xiao-Xiao has the Cupid card in her hands. As they say, she who talks much errs much. It'll be easier for her to expose herself, so she definitely can't say too much right at the start. If she continues talking, Screenwriter Xu might even think that Xiao-Xiao wants to pretend to be the witch

Yang Bo follows right on Ruan Xiao's heels with a smile on his face. "I'm finally not an eye-shut player this round—I'm a seer. I checked Xiqing's identity yesterday." With that, he turns around to smile at Xia Xiqing.

Xia Xiqing props up his chin with a hand and turns his face to smile at Yang Bo.

> HAHAHAHA right off the bat he claims to check the seer hahahahaha epic!

> xxq be like, Let's see how you're going to play the part. Kiddo, you checked my identity? With what?

> Having an omniscient POV is too much fun lmaooooo

Everyone's attention is on Xia Xiqing and Yang Bo. Xia Xiqing even raises an eyebrow at him, leading everyone at the table to burst out laughing. Yang Bo places both of his hands on the table and holds in a long breath.

"He...has a good identity. Hahaha. A shame I didn't ferret out a werewolf, but it's a good thing for us good guys that Xiqing is a confirmed good guy. At least we'll have a pro teammate." After saying that, Yang Bo begins to make his statements. "Next round, I will check..." He looks at the other people running for sheriff. "Qichen and Xiao-Xiao are both claiming to be special characters, so I'll choose one to check—I'll check Qichen. If the witch can still save me for another round, I'll check Ziheng's identity after that. To reiterate, I'm the seer. This round, I verified Xia Xiqing to be one of the good guys. You must give me the sheriff's badge; over."

> Yang Bo's speech is surprisingly steady~

> True, but making the move to verify the good guy identity of the real seer is really a bit of a riot hahaha

> Xiqing's expression is so handsome ahhhhh I love, love, love seeing him smile so wickedly like this

Xia Xiqing nonchalantly rests his chin in his hand as he taps his fingers lightly against the side of his face.

"I'm the seer. I checked Yang Bo last night, and I'm telling you that he's, without doubt, a werewolf. Everyone must follow my lead and vote him out tonight. Give me the sheriff's badge, and I'll check the identity of Player 9, Zhou Ziheng, in the next round, and the identity of Xia Zhixu in the round after that." Having said that, Xia Xiqing looks at Yang Bo, the smile on his face is confident and ostentatious. "If I were you, I would self-expose right now. Once you do, there'll be no sheriff's badge this round, and you can all proceed directly into night mode."

> Oh wow, such excitement right at the start???

> Xiqing-*gege*, can you not be so cool, please! He deduced Yang Bo's werewolf identity from his speech, right???

> This countermove is too savage!!! Xiqing-*gege*, I heart you!!!

> xxq (probably): even though I verified my hubby, I'll still declare you a werewolf!

The corner of Xia Xiqing's eyebrow arches slightly, and the corners of his lips quirk upward. His tone is soft and gentle. "So, will you?"

The words have only just left Xia Xiqing's mouth when the comments go absolutely wild.

> xqgg I willlll!!! I'll expose myself, alright?!!! I can!!

> xqgg I'll expose it all for you! For you, I'll even do it with full fireworks in the background!!

> LOOK AT ME GEGE I'VE EXPOSED MYSELF!

Contrary to what one might expect, Yang Bo is bold but cautious. He looks right at Xia Xiqing, showing absolutely no sign of wanting to self-expose. Seeing his lack of reaction, Xia Xiqing shrugs.

"Nice mental fortitude there, I suppose you're thinking of toughing it out?" He lets out a relaxed smile. "Go ahead then. The situation is already very obvious. I even dared to deal a counter-blow to a seer who verified my good guy identity. No one would do such a thing unless they're the seer. We have to vote out Yang Bo this round—he's a werewolf whom I've verified. Give me the sheriff's badge; over."

> Xiqing-*gege* is so cool!!!

> This countermove is really too awesome. It'll be hard for Yang Bo to defend himself now

> The fact proves that when it comes to players like xxq, pretending to be the seer and verifying him as the werewolf is better than verifying his good guy identity hahahaha. If you verify him to be a good guy, he'll counter you with no warning to declare you a werewolf, and bite you to death directly hahaha

It's now time for the last player running for sheriff, Zhou Ziheng, to speak. He doesn't have much expression on his face as he starts to speak in a calm manner.

"Player 9, villager or higher. I'm running for sheriff only for a chance to speak. It's all too easy for players like me to be the first to be verified and killed off. I'm a little worried, so I want to say a few words, and it happens that I'm the last to speak again. I will remind all voting players that the situation is complicated by two people claiming to be the seer, so you must be vigilant when voting. I have a feeling that both people claiming to be the seer are players with identities."

> Heng-Heng is so alpha once he starts playing! Instant Alpha!

> The moment he starts playing I don't even want to call him Heng-Heng anymore hahaha. He's so calm and upright hahaha

> Seriously, this pair is too hilarious, especially when he's pretending not to know Xia Xiqing lolol. Feels like I'm back in the Survive and Escape days~

Zhou Ziheng continues, "The sheriff's badge is very important. This may be a slaughter-of-city round, but if the good guys can't get the sheriff's badge right at the start, they won't be able to out-survive the rate at which they are being killed. What's more, there's still the Cupid as a variable. No matter who gets to be the sheriff, we have to be cautious during their summary speech—it's possible to see if the sheriff is one of the good guys or not from his speech. The good guys must observe carefully in a game as muddied as this, that's what I joined the election to say. I'm not going to go for this sheriff's badge, I'm withdrawing now."

> *claps claps* he really knows how to feign

> Zhou Ziheng is killing it, even as a werewolf he can speak from the perspective of the good guys. His speech is super convincing

> xqgg plays a seer like a wolf on the offensive, while heng-heng is way too convincing as a good guy, what a pair of drama queen husbands lmfaoooo

> Ziheng joins the election to speak out for the good guys but not to win the sheriff's badge, this motive is truly impressive. If I'm one of the players, I'd think that Heng-Heng is the person most likely to be the good guy

The narrator speaks up again, "All players running for sheriff have made their speeches. Players who wish to withdraw, you may press the button before you."

"Player 3 Ruan Xiao and Player 9 Zhou Ziheng have withdrawn from the election and will not be running for sheriff." After a few seconds, the narrator continues. "Players who did not run in the election, please proceed to vote."

"Player 1 Xia Zhixu, Player 6 Shang Sirui, and Player 7 Zhao Ke voted for Player 2 Xu Qichen. Player 8 Xia Xiuze voted for Player 5 Xia Xiqing. Player 2 Xu Qichen is hereby elected sheriff."

> omg baby bro voted for big brother!

> Baby bro is really a little loyal hound hahahaha no matter what I have to vote for my big bro!

> Nah. It's possible baby bro did so to make Yang Bo and himself look like the good guys. If he helps Yang Bo now, he and Yang Bo will both look sus

"Last night was a peaceful night. Next, the sheriff will designate the order of speech."

Xu Qichen points to his left. Ruan Xiao nods and begins her speech. "I dropped out of the election because I think the sheriff needs to be a real special character. It's a slaughter-of-city game, isn't it, so special characters stepping forth to get their hands on the sheriff's badge is the right way to play. The vote will be split if I remain in the running, so I withdrew to make sure that this sheriff's badge landed in Qichen's hands."

> As expected, Xiao-Xiao is claiming to be a villager

> Stay on the scene to muddy the waters. Self-Study girl, fighting!!!

> The most beautiful Cupid in history!!

"It was a peaceful night, so someone probably got saved. I think the identity of that person should be revealed. After all, it's a slaughter-of-city game, and revealing who's been saved by the witch can help the good guys play. I'll focus on listening to Yang Bo's speech this time because I think he's suddenly made a lot of progress in the way he plays this time. As for who to vote out..."

Ruan Xiao sweeps a glance across the room. "I can't really tell much as someone who's the first to speak. But honestly speaking, of the five people running for sheriff, there's a bigger problem with the two seers. I stand with the special character sheriff, because no one else is claiming to be a special character, and Ziheng has withdrawn from the election. My gut tells me that there's definitely a wolf among those who didn't run for sheriff. I'll focus on listening to the speeches of those people next to see if I can identify the werewolf; over."

"Player 4 speaks." Yang Bo takes over. "Not withdrawing from the election is proof that I'm the real seer. I don't know exactly what Xiqing is playing at, but I was pretty happy at first when my check threw up a good guy." He looks at Xia Xiqing. "I know you are a good guy. A good guy should play like a good guy. I don't know what the point is of you smearing me. Don't tell me you've been paired with someone?"

> Whoa Bo-ge is really pro at stepping on others' toes!!

> Yang Bo is right tho, he identified xq as a good guy, he can't challenge his identity or he won't be able to hold on to his seer identity. He can only grit his teeth and admit that Xia Xiqing's a good guy. But what he can do is smear him with Cupid. Yeaaah, this game is gonna be exciting

> xxq is probably like fuck, never mind if you pretend to be a seer too, but you had to expose my pairing, maybe you are the real seer?

> Yang Bo must have his third eye opened this game hahaha, everything he said is true

Yang Bo continues, "I think it's reasonable to suspect that. But he's indeed a good guy. I'm the real seer. I won't be checking the identity of the sheriff tonight. I acknowledge the sheriff as a special character. I'll be checking Zhixu; over."

When it's time for Xia Xiqing to give his speech, he lowers his head, staring at the round button before him, and says in a steady voice, "Yang Bo plays a pretty good game this round." He turns to look at Yang Bo with a smile. "Not bad, did you secretly find someone to practice with after last time?"

He pauses, then looks up and says, "Yang Bo is no doubt a werewolf. I'm the real seer. It's fine if you don't believe me, but think about it. Given his experience with playing *The Werewolves of Millers Hollow*, the fact that he could say all of that is enough to show that he's not just a simple villager. He's definitely a werewolf in possession of classified information. Even if we give him the benefit of the doubt and trust his claim of being a seer, if he verified my good guy identity, why would I turn around and refute it? If I dared to refute it, then that shows that I'm the one who's truly identified the werewolf. He was lying about verifying my identity. His identity is also fake. Simple as that."

> xq is riiight, the speech Yang Bo made is so different from the last time

> xqgg's biggest source of trouble is himself. He's simply too good at playing, and he has too many tricks up his sleeves. Even if he gets a special character card, others will suspect that he's just pretending to be one hahaha

> The torment of being a pro hahahaha

"What's more, he slandered me, saying that I'm one of the lovers. The seer is the most dangerous role, since it's way too easy to end up killed by the werewolves. If I really am one of the lovers, how would I have dared to reveal my seer identity that easily? If I die, it'll take another person with me, no?"

Xia Xiqing leans back in his chair like a little ruffian. "I mean, do you guys really think that I, Xia Xiqing, would make that kind of noob mistake?"

> Because your hubby is a wolf lmaoooo

> Not only your hubby even your younger brother is too lololol

Then Xia Xiqing turns to look at Yang Bo. "You slandered me like that because you have no way to refute my good guy identity. Right, Wolf Bo?"

> LOOL Wolf Bo

> Yang Bo: ???? Sudden name change

"There's also a problem with your identity check. Checking Xia Zhixu? Xia Zhixu hasn't even spoken yet, so I don't understand why exactly you'd want to check his identity. It's obviously a fake seer's move. Frankly, I suspect that your chosen victim last night was Xia Zhixu."

> Damn, Xiqing damn impressive! He really did choose Xia Zhixu as the victim haha!

> xqgg so cool!!

> There's one area xqgg is at a disadvantage. Having claimed Yang Bo to be a werewolf, he can't lay out too much of Yang Bo's werewolf qualities. There's no need for him to analyze since he's already pegged him as a werewolf. You can actually see that there are plenty of things Xiqing-*gege* can say, but to substantiate his claim, he can't voice it. He can only incriminate him

"Alright, I'll stop talking. No one can take the seer identity away from me. It's possible the werewolves team won't choose me as the victim tonight in order to frame me. In that case, I'll still check Ziheng in the second round. Although his speech during the election was pretty well-made, I feel that he can put on a pretty convincing act. The sheriff must vote for the confirmed werewolf. If Player 4 isn't out of the game, I will accuse him every round; over."

Shang Sirui is the next to make his speech. After a few seconds of silence, he suddenly bursts out laughing. As he laughs, he looks at Xia Xiqing and says, "After Xiqing screwed me over and slapped the werewolf teammate label on me last time, I have trauma every time I see him claim to be the seer now, hahaha."

> lmaooo poor san-san

> San-San: ??? Wtf why is xxq the seer again?

> Wahahaha san-san is so adorable

The other players follow suit and laugh, except for Xia Xiqing, who reaches over to hold Shang Sirui's chin and beams. "Don't worry, I won't screw you this time."

The comments promptly go crazy.

> Won't screw you hahahaha. Srsly xxq xD

> Kyaaaaa I still think san-san and xiqing are a good match together. I'm sorry let a girl dream!

> zzh control your expression plssss you're an actor!!

> Why is zzh clenching his fist LOOL, the green-eyed monster zzh!

> no worries, zzh. your waifu screw only you, only you!

"But then again, although Xia Xiqing has cast a shadow in my heart, that isn't the reason I didn't vote for him." Shang Sirui says with a serious countenance. "I'm a villager, so I don't have any info to share. There are two people claiming to be the seer, and generally speaking, one of them will be the real one and the other a fake. However, the possibility that they are two werewolves trying to lynch one another can't be ruled out, especially with a veteran player like Xiqing. In that case, all the more reason that I can't vote for the seer with peace of mind."

> That really is possible looool

> The real seer, Xiqing is also bad to the bone hahahaha

"No one else can lay claim to the special character sheriff's identity at present. Even if those after me claim to be a special character, I won't believe them. Last night was a peaceful night, so the witch used the potion. Actually, I initially thought that it was fine not to save the victim, but I thought about it earlier. The victim is likely to be a formidable player. Moreover, werewolves don't have the advantage in a slaughter-of-city game to begin with. A victory is nearly impossible if they kill one of their own."

> San-san is right in his analysis!

> After listening to San-san, it dawned on me why Screenwriter Xu would use the potion. It's true that the werewolves team really won't dare to kill one of their own. In a slaughter-of-city game, killing your own is tantamount to a lost game

> San-san is still so powerful even with a villager identity!! I <3 san-san!!!

"As for the seer, I think we can keep him around for another round. The good guys have the upper hand at present, and it's not hard to identify the werewolves and vote them out as long as the good guys do their part and speak well. I'll follow the sheriff's vote. I think Screenwriter Xu can carry us through this; over."

On Xia Xiuze's turn, he cups his smiling cheeks with both hands and says, "I voted for my older brother during the sheriff election, and it was not because I'm his little brother."

All the players start laughing.

> It IS because you're his younger bro!

> hahahahahaha bro, you still have the gall to say that?? Hahahahahaha

> His big brother complex is terrifying lmfaooo

"It's like this," Xia Xiuze explains his reason for voting for Xia Xiqing. "I personally think that having the seer as the sheriff is the best for the good guys. The seer gets the sheriff's badge and helps the good guys deduce and vote out the werewolves one at a time, and the witch uses the potion according to the information. I think this is perfect. Furthermore, the reason I believe Player 5 out of these two seers is not because he's my brother. Really."

Although everyone starts laughing at him again, Xia Xiuze continues to explain solemnly and seriously. "Yang Bo-*gege*'s claim to be the seer right at the start gives me the sense that he's pretending. But it doesn't feel serious; it's as if he was just doing it for fun. What's more, my big bro's countermove made me even more certain that Yang Bo-*gege*'s not the seer. No one else claimed to be the seer, and there's no reason for a seer to hide in a slaughter-of-city game, right? My big bro has also pointed out who the werewolf is, so I definitely believe in my brother, which is why I voted for him..."

> Baby bro is pretty smart to play it this way. His logic is entirely consistent

> Baby bro is looking more and more like his big bro. What is with the Xia genes?? Each one of them is so good-looking!! Crais *too engrossed in looking at pretty faces to listen carefully to the speech*

> Younger bro is too cute~ I <3 him~

"I think we can vote Yang Bo-*gege* out this round. Of course, it still depends on what the sheriff says. As for the speeches before, let me cast some doubt on Ruan Xiao. Although she withdrew from the election, I always feel that Ruan Xiao-*jiejie* is a conservative player. If she's really a villager, she wouldn't simply step forth to join the election. Sirui-*gege* should be one of the good guys. His speech paints him in a positive light. That's it. I'm a villager, so don't get influenced by me, guys. I'm merely stating my views; over."

> Feels like everyone is much better at playing than the last round

> Yeah!! It could also be because of the omniscient perspective we have hahaha. We see it all clearly

"My turn." Zhao Ke speaks up. "My reason for voting for Qichen is the same as Sirui. His special character identity is firmly established, and no one else has claimed otherwise the entire round, so I trust the sheriff even more. I have the good identity of a villager or above, definitely a good guy. The way I see it, there has to be one werewolf among the two seers. Since Xiqing dares reject the good guy identity given to him and dares to oust another as a werewolf, I trust him a little more, relatively speaking. However, the way Xiqing plays games is erratic."

The moment he says "erratic," everyone laughs. Even Xia Xiqing can't help himself and laughs too.

"So I think the lovers pair Yang Bo spoke of isn't entirely impossible. And the strangest thing is that no one voted for Yang Bo. At the time, I wondered if he really doesn't have a teammate? Not a single person gave him a helping hand, everyone was just ripping into him, which scares me a little. My suggestion for this round is to keep the two seers around. Of course, it depends on the sheriff's choice. I believe in the sheriff's ability."

After saying that, he shoots a glance at Xia Xiuze. "Earlier, Xiuze cast some doubt on Ruan Xiao. I don't really understand it, as I feel that Ruan Xiao should be one of the good guys. There aren't any major issues with her speech either. It was also because of her withdrawal from the election that the sheriff's badge did indeed land in the hands of a real special character. But this is just my opinion. I'm not in any camp; I stand only with the sheriff; over."

> Zhao Ke's speech seems to have substance, but in truth, it's just some high-level hedging hahaha

> It can't be helped. He's a real villager who has to shut his eyes at night hahaha. It's already good that he was able to say all this

> He even gave Yang Bo a hand. Welp, villagers really have too little information. If it were me, I'd also be suspicious to see everyone gaining up on him

> OMG it's finally my Heng-Heng's turn!!

"Player 9 speaking." Zhou Ziheng speaks up solemnly. "I said it before during the election, the good guys need to be prudent with our considerations, so I carefully observed the pattern of voting during the sheriff election." His gaze falls upon those who voted for Xu Qichen, one at a time. "Zhixu, Sirui, and Zhao Ke voted for Qichen, and Xiuze voted for Xiqing. In my opinion, Xiuze's daringness to vote for one of the two seers at this time makes me think he's one of the good guys. The statements he made earlier also show that he had indeed listened to my suggestion, and has carefully considered how best to play for the good guys."

> Whoa, he really helped him out there www

"I'm more inclined to think that there's a werewolf among the people who voted for the sheriff. There are five people running for sheriff, and chances are slim that all three werewolves would be in the running, so there must be a werewolf among those who didn't run for sheriff. If one of the two seers is a werewolf, he won't dare vote for his own teammate as he pleases, especially when Qichen seemed more likely to get the sheriff's badge. To clear himself of suspicion, the werewolf will definitely follow the popular vote. Then, of these three people who voted for the sheriff, who seems most suspicious?"

Zhou Ziheng's eyes fall upon his childhood friend, Zhao Ke. "I'm more inclined to think it's Zhao Ke. First, he followed Sirui's train of thought, saying things like 'the same,' 'am also,' and so on. This is how a werewolf tends to talk. Secondly, he helped Ruan Xiao out. This is very strange. Xiuze actually didn't kick Ruan Xiao too much. If Xiuze's goal was to vote Yang Bo out, there was no need to speak up for Ruan Xiao. Moreover, even as a good guy, I still can't tell what Ruan Xiao's identity is. Giving her a hand so hastily seems like he's casting aspersions on Ruan Xiao's identity."

> This mudslinging hahahahaha there's no brotherhood in the werewolves of millers hollow

> Childhood friend: ??? What have I done wrong??

"However, given that Zhixu has yet to give his statements, I'll reserve my judgment. It's possible that Zhixu's speech will change my opinion. I'll definitely follow the lead of the sheriff this time. The witch has already used the antidote, so they can't save anyone else. Everyone says that the good guys have the upper hand, but I actually don't think so. Don't forget that there's still Cupid; no one knows if they're good or bad. As I said before, the good guys have to be cautious. Don't get strung along by another player; over."

> No wonder Zhou Ziheng is an actor, he's too good at getting into character. He's speaking completely from a good guy's perspective by pointing out the werewolf and teaching the good guys how to play. If not for my omniscient perspective, I'd think he's a good guy for sure

> The lovers in this round are too damn powerful. As expected of Self-Study hnnnnng

> Omgomgomg it's been a long time since I've seen such an

alpha Heng-Heng!! Mama loves you!!

"My turn. Finally." Xia Zhixu smiles and reveals his fang-like canines.

> Xia Zhixu really is handsome!!! Those fangs are killing me!!

> Why is everyone from the Xia household that effing good-looking?!!

"I'm a villager or above. I may be a special character, I may be a villager. I'll leave it up to you to guess." With a smile, he juts his chin at Xia Xiqing. "I'll be honest. When it comes to Xia Xiqing, I don't trust him at all. He plays so dirty that he has no credibility to speak of in my books. But on the other hand, Xia Xiqing plays dirty in any identity he takes on."

The whole room laughs, and Xia Xiqing spreads out his hand with a smile.

> So damn true hahahaha he's absolutely right!

> He gets accused of being a werewolf even when he's the real seer, you can really see just how underhanded he is

"So, I can't outright deny Xia Xiqing's motive just because he claims to be a seer. Anything is possible when it comes to him. There will never be an ounce of rationality in Xia Xiqing's life."

> HAHAHAHA brutal!!

> There will never be an ounce of rationality in Xia Xiqing's life lmfaoooo. Memorable quote obtained +1

Xia Zhixu changes the subject. "But I do agree with one point he made, and those before me have overlooked it. Yang Bo is definitely not just a simple villager. Otherwise, the way he plays, he would never claim to be a seer."

Having said that, Xia Zhixu points out another issue. "But there's also something else you've overlooked. I don't believe Xia Xiqing checked Yang Bo's identity on the first night. It doesn't make sense—he would never check Yang Bo's identity. He didn't bring this point up either. Perhaps he's forgotten all about it himself, right?" Xia Zhixu winks at Xia Xiqing, and Xia Xiqing smiles back at him.

"I have a reasonable suspicion: it's possible Xia Xiqing is indeed a seer, but the person whose identity he checked on the first night is someone else. A good guy, and so a round of checks was wasted. He deduced who the werewolf was when he listened to the statements later, and accused the person who said he was a good guy of being the werewolf at the last second."

> Damn, he's good. He found the logic behind Xiqing's move!

> He's spot on. No way would Xiqing check Yang Bo's identity on the first night. But Zhixu probably hasn't realized that Xiqing has been paired up as lovers, and that his lover's identity was the first one he checked

> It's good to check your lover first to see if it's a human-werewolf pair or a human-human pair before you can come up with a plan. No doubt Xiqing has been playing as the human-werewolf camp since verifying Ziheng to be a werewolf. That's the only way he can win

"I'd advise the sheriff to keep the seers around for another round, or maybe the sheriff has managed to deduce which of the two is more likely to be the werewolf. I'll use my vote carefully for this round."

And now, it's Xu Qichen's turn. Xu Qichen has a slight frown on his face. He isn't looking at the camera, but is instead staring at a fixed spot before him. Xia Zhixu understands him very well—Xu Qichen is thinking.

"The sheriff speaks now." Xu Qichen says. "After a round of listening, the ones who seem the most likely to be the good guys are Ziheng and Zhixu. Their speeches are open and transparent, and the points they made are all ones that

the good guys have overlooked. They've also been helping the good guys find the werewolves.

"There's a statement Yang Bo made during his election speech that has been bothering me—he said he would check Ziheng and my identities next. There were only five people running for sheriff, which means the safest course of action would be to check the identity of someone who ran for sheriff, followed by someone who didn't. This is how a real seer would play, but Yang Bo decided to check only those who ran for sheriff."

Xu Qichen pauses. "In addition, there's a big difference in Yang Bo's speeches in this game and the first time he played, so he's definitely a special character or a werewolf. As to what exactly, let us deduce it."

> Screenwriter Xu's speech is really very logical, calm, and rational

> Screenwriter-*gege* I <3 you!! He's so my type!!

"If he's the real seer, it's reasonable for him to check Xiqing's identity, since any seer *will* consider checking Xiqing's identity. He checked Xiqing to be one of the good guys, which means they are both good guys. But if Xiqing is a verified good guy, why would he say that the real seer, Yang Bo, is a werewolf? This isn't something Xiqing would do when he's the good guy.

"Even if, as Yang Bo said, Xiqing has been paired up with another as a pair of lovers, there's no benefit to the couple by insisting on incriminating the seer who verified his good guy identity in the first round. He might not even know the identity of his own lover. It's impossible for anyone to act so rashly under such circumstances, especially for pros like Xiqing, who's even less likely to make such a mistake. At this point, the logic falls apart."

> Is Xu Qichen really a liberal arts student? Why is his logic so smooth!

> They really made a good choice with the sheriff!

"On the other hand, we will end up with plenty of scenarios if Yang Bo is a werewolf pretending to be a seer who checks out Xiqing's identity to cement his own as the good guy. The first is that Xiqing is the real seer who just happened to check Yang Bo's identity. That would make Yang Bo a werewolf. But like Zhixu said, it seems unlikely that Xiqing would check Yang Bo's identity in the first round. I think it's more likely that he would check Ziheng, Zhixu, or me first."

> Hahaha the worries of the pros. First kill and first identity check both put them on tenterhooks

"The other option is, Xiqing is the seer but didn't check Yang Bo's identity. Instead, he deduced his werewolf identity from his speech. This is also possible. As for the lovers, I don't actually believe it. It's too easy for a seer to die. If he has a lover, he won't dare step forth like this, or his lover has to be ready to die with him any time in the name of love."

> yoooo @zzh

> Lmfaooooo die with him any time in the name of love

> zzh: I'm actually ready to do this

> Lololol he's Xia Xiqing, okay. You can't use normal human logic to analyze him. It's too normal for him to let his lover die with him in the name of love lololololol

"No matter how I break it down, Yang Bo is more likely than Xiqing to be the werewolf. It's unlikely for fellow werewolves to lynch each other in a game where there are only three werewolves. To sum it up, I think it makes the most sense to vote out Yang Bo. What's more, he's also been slapped with a werewolf label by someone who claims to be the seer. That concludes my speech. Let's vote."

The narrator's voice starts. "The speeches of all nine players hereby conclude. Please commence with public voting."

The players simultaneously gesture the number of the person they wish to vote out.

"Player 1 Xia Zhixu and Player 9 Zhou Ziheng forfeit their ballots. The rest of the players follow the sheriff to vote out Player 4. Player 4 Yang Bo is out. Please say your last words."

Yang Bo frowns and puts on a very puzzled and even angry expression. "Firstly, I have to say that I'm a special character. Do you guys really trust Xiqing? How could he have checked my identity? I happened to be the one before him, and he just so happened to check my identity, which coincidentally happened to be a werewolf." He nods his head twice. "Forget it. I'll 'fess up to it. I was indeed pretending to be a seer, but I'm not a werewolf—I'm Cupid."

> Whoa damn, Bo-ge is truly an actor!

> Will anyone believe him if he pretends to be Cupid now?

> Cupid is originally meant to muddy the water. Might as well pretend to be one in an attempt to create confusion

"Fortunately, I still have last words. I'm still thinking about the identities of the couple I've paired up. I only claimed to be a seer in an attempt to make a grab for the sheriff's badge, because I know no one would vote Cupid for sheriff. But now, before I figured it out, I've been voted out after everyone got strung along by Xia Xiqing. At this point, I can only say that most of you probably can't guess who the two people I've paired up are. That's all, I guess; I'm not even sure of it myself. I'm leaving. All of you good guys have to believe me, ya?"

> He's still thinking of slinging mud at Xiqing, isn't he? Maybe he doesn't know that Xiqing is one half of the human-werewolf pair. He just wants to slander the real seer

> In any case, Xiqing's seer identity is unshakable, it's all he can do to cast doubt on him. Also, Xiao-Xiao won't expose her Cupid identity for the time being either

> But Xiqing is really paired up as a couple. What a close shave in this game!

The players all wear varying expressions on their faces. The narrator's voice starts up again. "Night falls. Everyone, please close your eyes."

After the nightfall music ends, the voice continues, "Werewolves, please open your eyes. Werewolves, please choose a victim."

Zhou Ziheng casts a glance at Xia Xiuze, who's hesitating. By all logic, the best strategy is to kill off the seer, since the seer can check the players' identities. But this sheriff is too formidable, and a special character to boot. In comparison, the seer isn't as credible as the sheriff. Even though Xu Qichen hasn't revealed the identity of the witch or the person the witch saved as others requested, Zhou Ziheng can still conclude that Xu Qichen is the witch.

He signs a 2 to Xia Xiuze. Xia Xiuze nods his head at last and signs a 2 to the camera. No matter what, they can do no wrong in voting the sheriff out.

> Oh no, it's over. The most badass special character of the good guy camp is gone

> Just how badly does Ziheng want to win that he has to be so brutal lmfaoooo

> It all depends if Zhixu-*gege* can carry the good guys to victory now, but at the end of the day he's only a villager...

> If baby bro tries to kill his big bro, he should be able to discover the human-werewolf pair in time. Nevertheless, it's pretty scary to keep a witch/sheriff alive. Baby bro has no choice

"Werewolves, please close your eyes."

"Seer, please open your eyes."

Xia Xiqing opens his eyes and signs an 8 to the camera.

> Wow, Xiqing-*gege* is too good!

> Both times he chose the werewolves. If xq hasn't been paired up with a werewolf, this kind of powerful seer will definitely carry the good guys to victory!

> He's too smart!! He first checked the identity of his lover first to lay out his strategy, then sussed out the last werewolf to determine the positions of all the other players. This way of playing is like he has his third eye opened!

> This couple is truly terrifying hahahahaha

Xia Xiqing already suspected Xia Xiuze during the sheriff's campaign. Xia Xiuze's logic was consistent, but the way Xia Xiqing sees it, he was merely making use of Xia Xiqing to make himself look like the good guy. Yang Bo is no doubt a werewolf, as is Zhou Ziheng. Xia Xiqing just wants to weed out the last one. He only has two suspects, one of whom is Xia Xiuze, and the other, Zhao Ke. Though to him, Xia Xiuze seems the more likely suspect.

As long as he can verify Xia Xiuze's identity, he will have known the identities of everyone in the game. In a slaughter-of-city game, there has to be an order even when it comes to killing people.

"His identity is..." The production team holds up a werewolf prompt. "This."

Exactly as expected. Xi Xiqing nods and closes his eyes.

"Witch, please open your eyes."

Xu Qichen opens his eyes. The production team speaks up without gesturing to the victim. "This is the victim of the werewolves. You have a bottle of antidote. Would you like to use it?"

> Honey, you're the one who died tonight

> Screenwriter-*gege*: Alright, I'm dead

> Screenwriter Xu probably guessed that he would die, right? He looks so calm

> Screenwriter Xu has to use the potion, or it will go to waste. But I doubt he will poison Ziheng. Other than Zhixu, the person he saved, Ziheng has the most convincing good guy identity, at least in Screenwriter Xu's eyes

"You have a bottle of poison. Would you like to use it?"

Xu Qichen frowns and mulls it over for a while. He's hesitating whether or not to use this potion. If he doesn't, then the bottle of potion will be forfeited. Since this is a slaughter-of-city game, it's better to kill an innocent villager than to miss the opportunity to poison a werewolf.

Zhao Ke smeared Xia Xiuze for putting in a good word for Ruan Xiao. Xia Xiuze voted for Xia Xiqing during the sheriff's election, while Ruan Xiao... Ruan Xiao's speech was really quite out of character from her usual self. Xu Qichen is well aware of Ruan Xiao's capabilities. Considering her astonishing scheming, her logical reasoning in *Survive and Escape*, or her performance as a normal villager in the last *The Werewolves of Millers Hollow* game, she should not be playing in such a random, muddled way. If Ruan Xiao isn't a wolf, then she's at the very least Cupid. Xu Qichen signs a 3 and closes his eyes.

"Day breaks."

All the players open their eyes and wait for the narrator to announce the result.

"The one who died last night is Player 2 Xu Qichen and Player 3 Ruan Xiao. No last words. Please hand over the sheriff's badge."

Xu Qichen takes off the sheriff's badge and hands it over

✦ . 092 III

to Xia Zhixu, who's beside him. At the same time, he also gives him a look. The rapport and tacit understanding that comes from ten years of being in love with each other allows the two of them to understand each other from this brief interchange. Xia Zhixu nods his head gently.

> KYAAAAAA THE EXPRESSION IN ZHIXU'S EYES AS HE LOOKS UP AT SCREENWRITER-*GEGE*!

> HIS HAND!!! He touched screenwriter-*gege*'s waist so naturally!!! THEY ARE DEFO LOVERS!!

> Such a perfect couple!! You sure this really isn't a dating show???? It's really not a love show? Exactly how many pairs are there?

> He transferred the badge to his hubby! Yes!!!

> Not to stir up trouble, but I think the screenwriter looks like Xiya-dada[5], if you cover the lower half of his face he looks basically exactly the same!

> Xiya fan sighted!! I'll always love Xiya-dada!!

"The players have left the scene. The sheriff's badge is handed over to Player 1 Xia Zhixu." The narrator paused before continuing. "Next, sheriff, please indicate the order of speeches."

Xia Zhixu raises his chin at Xia Xiqing, and Xia Xiqing rolls his eyes at him.

> Lmfaoooo uncle and nephew are truly nemeses

> Somehow for a tiny little moment I ship uncle and nephew. I'm sooo sorry, Heng-Heng!!

> The one who ships uncle and nephew, have you gone bonkers? This is even worse than normal incest!

"Alright, I'll make my speech." Xia Xiqing slumps over the table with the tip of his chin against his arm. When

---

5 On the internet, "dada" is an honorific title or suffix given to artists and writers who operate primarily online. Literally, it means "big-big."

he smiles, he looks like a delightful yet willful kitten. "I improvised last night and checked Zhixu's identity because I was afraid Chen-Chen would hand the sheriff's badge over to you. If not you, then Zhou Ziheng. He said it himself, to him, the two of you are most likely to be the good guys. To be on the safe side, I have to know if the sheriff candidate is one of our own. Sure enough, I was right, he really did hand the sheriff's badge to you."

Having said that, Xia Xiqing looks to his left. "You guys are all still in the game, and there's at least one werewolf among you, or two." He then looks at Xu Qichen's empty seat. "But there's one thing. I initially didn't want to deduce the identity of the special characters, but Chen-Chen is already dead, so there's no harm in talking about it. The way I see it, Chen-Chen is the witch, but why didn't he claim his role? Why didn't he report who the person he saved was? Was he not afraid of someone else pretending to be the witch? This is what I can't figure out, but it's okay, I'll consider him the witch.

"I'll list out the remaining players whom I think are werewolves. Yang Bo is no doubt a werewolf, while Ruan Xiao is probably a werewolf too. This is not how she tends to play as one of the good guys. As for the remaining werewolf, it's either Zhao Ke or Xia Xiuze. You guys keep casting doubts on each other, while Xia Xiuze voted for me during the sheriff election. So, let's check the identity of one and vote out the other. Whoever is voted out, I'll check the identity of the remaining one. Sheriff, you can choose from these two options." Xia Xiqing then winks at Xia Zhixu. "You can tell, right? There's definitely a werewolf among these two. I won't say any more. Over, I guess."

Xia Xiuze pouts and looks very much aggrieved. "I'm really

a villager. Was it only because I voted for the real seer right at the start? I don't understand why you still want to vote me out when I voted for you during the sheriff election."

Xia Xiqing rests his chin in his hand and turns sideways at him with the entertained expression of one waiting to watch a performance.

> Lololololol your bro was never one of you lolololol
> He won't be on your side even if he hasn't been paired up XD
> Wake up, baby bro!!!

"I'm really one of the good guys." Xia Xiuze explains. "I think it goes to show that I'm not a werewolf since I dared to vote for you during the sheriff election. Although Zhao Ke cast doubt on me, I still have to say this, just because both of the people Zhao Ke has spoken about died, doesn't mean that he's a wolf. Who knows if Ruan Xiao was really poisoned to death? What if she's one of the lovers?" After saying so, his eyes light up. "Maybe Xu Qichen isn't the witch. That's why he didn't tell us who he saved before he left, because he didn't save anyone. It's possible that he and Ruan Xiao are the lovers, possibly even a human-werewolf pair."

Gotcha. Xia Xiqing can't help but lift the corners of his mouth. He turns his head slightly and raises his eyebrows at Xia Zhixu.

> Oh shit. Feels like Xiqing is laying a trap!
> Oh dear me, baby bro has exposed himself with his words, xqgg is really on a roll here laying traps, killing two birds with one stone!

"I'm not quite sure why you keep picking on me. I'm a good guy, a good guy!" Xia Xiuze sighs. "Over, I suppose."

Shang Sirui begins his speech. "I'm a villager, just an ordinary villager, but I think Ruan Xiao is a werewolf. I heard her speech while I was backstage in the last game, and it's all very logical. She feels a bit peculiar in this game, like she has a shady identity. I believe the seer when he said that Yang Bo is a werewolf. In that case, there's only one werewolf left in the game, and I think it's either Zhao Ke or Xia Xiuze. Honestly speaking, Xia Xiuze's earlier speech had no substance, but he spoke up for Zhao Ke, and so I think he's more of a good guy."

He then looks to his left at Zhao Ke. "Hmm...I think you should make your speech carefully later. I'll listen carefully to it; over."

> Feels like a close shave this round. If younger bro is voted out, it'll be the human-werewolf pair vs. the villager team. If Zhao Ke is voted out, it'll be hard for the good guys to win, and the battle will be down to the werewolves vs. the human-werewolf pair

> San-san looks so adorable when he frowns!! KYAAAAAAA!!

It's now Zhao Ke's turn. He seems perplexed and in a dilemma. "I don't understand why mud is being slung in my direction. Don't tell me it was because I spoke up for Ruan Xiao and Yang Bo? No, think about it, guys. If I'm really the wolf, would I dare to help others that way?"

> That's true. At times like these, a werewolf won't dare to speak up for others so casually

Zhao Ke continues, "Even now, I don't think Ruan Xiao is a werewolf. The way I see it, there should be two werewolves remaining in the game. No one opposes Xiqing's identity as the seer, and he verified Xia Zhixu to be the good guy, so both of them are bonafide good guys; I'm a good guy too. My view is that there are two werewolves between Xia Xiuze, Zhou Ziheng, and Shang Sirui. Ziheng's speech is convincing; he doesn't seem to be a werewolf, so I guess it's just down to

Shang Sirui and Xia Xiuze. We have to vote one out among these two today. The lovers haven't spoken up either. I think the situation now is pretty clear. So lovers, if you find out that you're both good guys, step forward and play in the open to eliminate suspicion; over."

> Ziheng's too convincing. There's no one against him even now

> It's truly something else when the best actor plays the traitor werewolf

"My turn." Zhou Ziheng's expression is still composed. It's as if he's an uninvolved player with an omniscient perspective. "I said it before, a good guy should play like a good guy. Yang Bo is obviously a werewolf, so I doubt anyone will believe he's Cupid. Everyone else has already talked about Ruan Xiao, so I won't dissect it any further. She seems very likely to be a werewolf. And if that's the case…" Zhou Ziheng frowns slightly, his eyes cold.

> OH MAH GAWD ZZH'S EXPRESSION IS TOO FUCKING ALPHA!!!!

> How can my Heng-Heng be so alpha and so cute at the same time!! What kind of divine treasure is this!!

> My heart went doki doki the moment Heng-Heng frowned!

"The last werewolf and Cupid are both still in the game, and those whose identities are uncertain are Xia Xiuze, Zhao Ke, Sirui, and me. Zhao Ke and Xiuze are the most likely to be the werewolf. But if I were to choose, I would think it's Xia Xiuze. Everyone was pointing out those they feel could be a werewolf, and you were the only one who was talking about yourself the entire time. You said you're a good guy, but your reason is flimsy."

> Oh ho, he's starting to sell baby bro out!!

> Double Agent Best Actor Wolf Sells Teammate Out LIVE!

> Baby bro: sister-in-law??? How can you do this to me?!?!?!

"I think the lovers are present too. In my opinion, Qichen is the witch. After all, no one has claimed to be the witch so far. Of course, if the sheriff claims to be the witch later, pretend I didn't say anything." With that, he looks at Xia Zhixu, who's fiddling with the sheriff's badge Xu Qichen left him. Xia Zhixu lifts his eyes to look back at him and smiles.

> OooOooOHHHH!! Two alpha facing off each other!! Look at that imposing aura!

> Fangs-*gege* is smiling so wickedly! He was clearly all sunshine earlier! Why is everyone from the Xia family like this?

> I can't with those fangs crais, I'm sorry san-san, lemme just fangirl about another guy for a second!! Just for a second!

"If the sheriff admits to being the witch, then all the earlier deductive reasoning will have to start over from zero. However, I'll still follow the sheriff's lead when it comes to voting. After all, the sheriff's identity has been verified by the seer. But who knows, maybe the sheriff is Cupid. After all, Cupid has still yet to appear; over."

Xia Zhixu knocks on the table twice with the sheriff's badge. "The sheriff speaks. Vote Xia Xiuze out this round."

Xia Xiuze suddenly looks very aggrieved.

> Crais poor baby bro!

> Little *gege* with the fangs is definitely the top. He's really very charismatic

"Let me tell you why." Xia Zhixu turns to Xia Xiuze. "You exposed yourself with your speech earlier, did you know that? You said Xu Qichen isn't the witch, that it's possible that he and Ruan Xiao are the lovers. If you think that Ruan Xiao was a werewolf, then I'd like to ask you this: on the first day, a person verified to be a werewolf left, and there were only two werewolves left that night. If one of them was Ruan

Xiao, whom you claim to be one of the lovers, how could she have allowed the other werewolf to kill off her own lover, Xu Qichen?"

> Damn, this loophole!

> No wonder Xiqing smiled right after baby bro finished his speech!!! I get it now!!!

> Mah gawd, I'm getting goosebumps. Xiqing's speech earlier was done on purpose! He deliberately wondered aloud why Screenwriter Xu didn't reveal his witch identity, but in fact, he was setting a trap for baby bro! Baby bro probably didn't think of smearing Screenwriter Xu as one of the lovers, but the moment Xiqing mentioned it, it planted the idea in baby bro's mind, and he blurted it out without thinking! Which made him expose himself! Mah gawd, xqgg is truly diabolical!

> What's scariest isn't xqgg setting a trap for baby bro, but that he's also screwing his nephew at the same time. If baby Xiuze is voted out now, the only ones remaining will be the human-werewolf pair and the good guys group

> Damn, what a pro move this is to kill two birds with one stone, and he hasn't exposed himself at all!

> And Ziheng is also rubbing salt on baby bro's wound. He cements his good guy identity while pushing out his last werewolf teammate. This husband-husband pair is so OP

Xia Zhixu continues, "I know you panicked the moment you heard Xiqing would check your identity at night. Your speech is so weak it can't withstand a single blow. Of everyone here, you're the only one who didn't attempt to deduce who the werewolves are, and tried to smear Xu Qichen by saying that he's one of the lovers. How could he and Ruan Xiao possibly be lovers?"

> Fangs-*gege*: He's clearly my lover!

> I'm wheezing, can't breathe lmfao, fangs-*gege* fighting for

his lover live!

"He didn't reveal himself as a witch because he wanted to trick another werewolf into exposing his or her identity. Even if no other werewolf claims to be the witch, there will be one who will go along with Yang Bo's train of thought and falsely claim him to be one of the lovers or Cupid. But if *he's* not the witch, then who dares to say they are?" Xia Zhixu laughs, inadvertently revealing his fangs. "Also, you werewolves chose me as the victim on the first night, am I right? The reason Xu Qichen would hand the sheriff's badge over to me is simply because I was the person he saved on the first night."

> Wow, the tacit understanding between fangs-*gege* and Screenwriter Xu

> I'm suddenly obsessed with this ship!!!

> For some reason, that last sentence gave me headcanons enough to fill an entire novel!! Sunny, flamboyant top x calm, introverted bottom! My ship is sailing!!

"Alrighty. Everyone, follow my lead and vote Xia Xiuze out. Anyone who doesn't vote for him, I'll consider that person to be his werewolf teammate. I don't think Ruan Xiao was a werewolf; she's most likely Cupid. Over."

> The four OPs in the game: Zhou Ziheng, Xia Xiqing, fangs-*gege*, and Screenwriter Xu

"Public voting commences. Players, please cast your votes." The production team glances at the voting results. "All players voted for Player 8 Xia Xiuze. Xia Xiuze is out of the game. No last words."

> Baby bro should've self-exposed if he figured out the human-werewolf pair

> I doubt he did. At this point in time, Ziheng can't put in a good word for him even if he isn't one of the lovers. Otherwise,

his betrayals thus far would be in vain

"Night falls. Please close your eyes."

The lighting changes once again. All players close their eyes and wait for the third night to descend.

"Werewolves, please open your eyes."

Zhou Ziheng alone lifts his head.

> Hot damn! This scene is so hot! The one and only werewolf in the game! And he's a double agent to boot!!

> Mommyyyy! The way he lifted his head is so alpha I'm melting!! asdfghjkl heng-heng I love you!!

> Only zzh can make me switch seamlessly between being a girlfriend fan and a mom fan :V

"Werewolves, please choose your victim."

Zhou Ziheng signs a 1 without hesitation.

> He's definitely gonna tear up the badge

> zzh: I'm 1

> You can make a meme with this lolol "I'm 1"

"Werewolves, please close your eyes. Witch, please open your eyes."

The narrator reads out the witch's prompts as usual, then wakes the seer. "Seer, please open your eyes."

Xia Xiqing lifts his head and looks lazily into the camera.

> wtf why is self-study so alpha?!!!

> I'll always love Self-Study in games!!! I can watch them play forever!! They are really soooo charismatic when they are playing games! The charm of high IQ!

> Gosh, this pair are those nocturnal players who survive to the very end. How scary

"Seer, please check the identity of one person."

Xia Xiqing shakes his head slowly. Without signing any numbers, he covers his eyes with his hands.

> xxq: what else is there left to check

> xqgg: it's no fun to be the seer in this game of yours

> That expression is so arrogant and cute!!

"Day breaks. The one who died last night is Player 1. Please transfer the sheriff's badge." Xia Zhixu gestures a cross with his fingers. "Player 1 opts to tear up the badge."

> I knew it. Fangs-*gege* would rather tear it up than hand it to xqgg

> If he gives it to xqgg, the game is over

"Make your speeches now, starting from the left-hand side of the deceased player."

Xia Xiqing sits up straight. "Last night, I checked Zhou Ziheng's identity; he's one of the good guys. That really perplexes me. The game hasn't ended as of now, so there's at least one more wolf still in the game." He looks to his left. "If that's the case, it can only be Sirui or Zhao Ke. Sirui, you've certainly spoken well this game, huh? Is this the betrayal that you're so good at? After all, you were so good at deception in *Survive and Escape*. As for Zhao Ke, I initially thought he wasn't convincing enough, but I've changed my mind now.

"To be honest, I think the werewolves wanted to smear me for being one of the lovers, which is why they haven't killed me yet, since they know there's no point. The remaining players will be voted out through the process of elimination, but leaving a seer behind can help them muddy the waters." Xia Xiqing shoots a glance at Zhou Ziheng. "I'm thinking, is it possible that Zhou Ziheng is one of the lovers? You've been playing so cautiously, so perhaps you've been paired with a good guy? If that's the case, you guys should say it when the time comes so that we don't end up voting you out together. If that happens, the werewolves win. If you won't say it, then I'll consider you as a human-werewolf pair." The corner of Xia Xiqing's lips curls up. "In which case, I'll vote you out."

> Crap, that's some dirty playing hahahaha

> zzh: playing a couple with my waifu is really nerve-racking

"But I'm sure I'll know who the last werewolf is after hearing what these two people have to say. Good one, this game. The werewolf has concealed himself really well; over."

Shang Sirui looks as if he was snapping out of deep thoughts. "I think Xiqing's words make sense, but I really am a good guy. It seems pretty obvious now to me. The seer points out the couple, which means he isn't one of the lovers. He's been playing as the seer right from the start with such zest; he doesn't seem to be someone with a lover. Zhao Ke must be the werewolf, and he's paired up with Zhou Ziheng. Once we vote them out, we good guys will win. In any case, Zhao Ke is the werewolf. Let's vote him out this round, and it'll be a sure win for the good guys."

> He fell for it!! San-san, you've been deceived by Xia Xiqing!!!

> And here I was wondering why xqgg was so flashy while playing as the seer. Turns out he was eliminating other people's suspicions of him being one of the lovers

Zhao Ke's temper is starting to flare. "No, how am I the werewolf now? I don't understand. Must you believe everything the seer says? What if it's the seer who's paired up with Zhou Ziheng? Wait, that's not right." His train of thoughts is derailing. "That would make it a human-human pair, so that means you, Shang Sirui, are the werewolf. Were you planning to vote me out in the daytime, then kill off the lovers at night? Then the end of it, you'll be the only one left in the game. How ruthless of you."

> Oh noes hahahaha Zhao Ke fell for it too. Damn, xqgg's been digging pits the entire time, watching as the good guys jump in one after another!

> Zhao Ke is getting anxious! It didn't occur to him that zzh's good guy identity was given by xxq himself! It'll all be clear once he realizes it!

> Self-Study: I'll just quietly watch you villager pointing the finger at your fellow villager

"Vote for Sirui. He's definitely the last werewolf! Over."

The last one to speak is Zhou Ziheng. He says nothing for a very long time, and dead silence descends upon the set. After a long while, he lifts his head.

"I've indeed been paired with another, but until yesterday I thought we were a human-human pair because the other party really sounds like a villager in his speeches. But now, I'm starting to doubt it. Sirui." He suddenly looks at Shang Sirui, who appears absolutely dumbfounded.

> San-san: what are you doing?! I don't know you!!

> Oh dear me, San-san's so mad he's gonna cry hahahaha

> zzh's two-faced look is too fucking mesmerizing!!! omg i love self-study to death!! 2x the deviousness! double-crossing, dog eat dog!

"You're the werewolf, right?" Zhou Ziheng continues. "I now think you're that hidden werewolf. Oh man, I was in the dark the whole time. To think I've been playing as if I were a human-human pair."

Shang Sirui shakes his head frantically.

> San-san: I'm not! I didn't! You're lying!!

> Wahahaha san-san's style of shaking your head till it drops

"I forfeit the right to vote this round. I've lost the will to fight." Zhou Ziheng leans back in his chair like a deflated balloon. "I really thought it was a human-human pair this whole time. This turn of events has really left me baffled. Oh man, let's just vote."

> Zhou Ziheng, why are you still acting?!! You're too melo-

dramatic hahahaha

> To think xqgg can still keep a straight face and not burst into laughter lmaoooo help I can't stop laughing!

"Public voting commences."

"Player 5 Xia Xiqing and Player 6 Shang Sirui vote for Player 7 Zhao Ke. Player 9 Zhou Ziheng and Player 7 Zhao Ke vote for Player 6 Shang Sirui."

> Loooooooool this voting result!! Zhao Ke looks so floored!!!

> Zhao Ke: Ay, ay, ay, I thought you were all going to vote Shang Sirui?! What's happening?!

> Confusion all around lolololol

> Even Shang Sirui is shocked hahahaha

> Damn, I really wouldn't have been able to understand this game if not for my omniscient perspective. So, zzh pretends that his own lover is Zhao Ke, and he was feigning earlier to slander ssr. xxq pretends that he could tell ssr was being framed, and so he votes for the other person. How are these two so good at acting?

> Can't Self-Study let the two villagers leave in peace? Can't they let them preserve the last of their dignities?

"It's a tie. Player 6 Shang Sirui and Player 7 Zhao Ke, please step up to the PK stage."

> LMFAOOOOO how are two innocent villagers going to PK? They're gonna blah blah blah a bunch of crap, then choose to vote one out. But regardless of the outcome, the special character-werewolf pair wins. All the voting right lies in the hands of the lovers

> The program crew isn't declaring the end of the game yet for entertainment effect, right? They're really evil too!

> Wahahaha villagers on the pk stage with special character-werewolf lovers deciding their fate. What kind of game is this?!

> I feel like Self-Study already knows they've won a long time back, so they are now just toying with these two weak and innocent lives! Truly a pair of homicidal maniac lovers! Hahaha!

> Omg these two terrifying psychos! The more I think about it the more I lmao

Shang Sirui is the first to speak. "No, Zhou Ziheng is for sure framing me. Xiqing, you noticed it too, right? Human-werewolf pair, you guys should concede defeat. Oh wait, no. Xiqing, you don't have a sheriff's badge. But if both of you end in a tie..." Shang Sirui looks at Zhou Ziheng. "Didn't you say you'd forfeit your vote? Why are you so untrustworthy?"

> Hahaha san-san's getting anxious!

> San-san is so cute!! You're so untrustworthy! Child, he's a werewolf

"I don't know. Xiqing believes me for sure."

Xia Xiqing gives Shang Sirui a serious nod of his head.

"We're going to lose if we don't vote out Zhao Ke this round. Xiqing, you must remain firm. I don't know what else to say. Next, I guess."

Zhao Ke is also very confused. "Why am I a pair with Zhou Ziheng? He already said he's paired up with you. He voted for you because he doesn't want to keep playing anymore. He voted for you so the two of you can be booted out of the game together. And then the game will end. Such simple logic. Xiqing, what exactly are you playing at? Vote out Shang Sirui."

> Lmaooooo this is so funny. The program crew might as well tell them right now that the good guys have already lost hahahaha

"Xiqing, you must vote out Shang Sirui. Open your eyes and take a good look. He's the last werewolf in hiding."

> xxq: Nah, my hubby is the werewolf

"Vote out Shang Sirui. Vote out Shang Sirui. Vote out Shang Sirui. Over."

"Public voting commences now."

In unison, Self-Study hold up their index fingers and thumbs to sign a 6.

"Player 6 Shang Sirui is out of the game. Game over."

The program crew takes a deliberately long pause. Zhao Ke slaps the tabletop. "Hurry up, man!"

"The Cupid camp wins!"

> Wow!!! That was a great game! The special character-were-wolf pair is too OP!!!

> OMG having an omniscient perspective feels completely like reading a feel-good story!! How is the pairing I ship so awesome?!?

> Screenwriter Xu and fangs-*gege* will probably cough out blood watching the last segment

"What the fuck? That's impossible." Zhao Ke points at Shang Sirui. "He's not the last werewolf? Then who is?"

Zhou Ziheng stands, sticks his hands in his pockets, and smiles. "Me."

"Fuck." Zhao Ke holds his own head. "So then..."

He's yet to voice it when it suddenly dawns on Shang Sirui. "Holy crap! Xiqing and Ziheng are the lovers!"

Zhao Ke feels goosebumps rising all over him. "Fuck, fuck, fuck...I've been deceived from start to finish."

The other players all come back on set one by one. Xia Zhixu is beyond pissed. "I was about to die of anxiety backstage. You guys should have voted out Zhou Ziheng. You'd have won if both of you voted him out. What's the point of going for each other's neck?! Zhou Ziheng was playing so dirty with his last speech, couldn't you guys tell?! I really have to hand it to both of you!"

> Hahaha as expected, fangs-*gege* is pissed

Chen-Chen smiles gently. "Actually, I realized that something was off after I was eliminated and before I made my way to the control room. Xiqing was playing reverse psychology, all so we wouldn't associate him with the lovers. I missed it."

Yang Bo catches on. "Not just you, even I didn't expect Ziheng to be one of the lovers. I thought the werewolves team would win, I was so naïve. This couple is too formidable."

Shang Sirui clutches Xia Xiqing's neck with both hands. "Arghhh, couldn't you just let me die a quick death? Why make me go on the PK stage at the end?! Xiqing, you're so cruel."

Xia Xiqing can't stop laughing. He cups Shang Sirui's face in his hands and kneads his cheeks. "You two were hilarious at the end, I almost couldn't help but burst out laughing."

Zhao Ke looks utterly deflated and mentally exhausted. "Zhou Ziheng...to think I grew up with you in the same courtyard. We grew up wearing the same pair of pants...and I suffered so many beatings on your behalf...I trusted you... How could you do this...? You liar..."

"Hahahaha...Zhao Ke's lost it."

Ruan Xiao looks smugly at him. "Concede defeat since you've lost. Don't go embarrassing yourself further."

"You really are Cupid!" Zhao Ke abruptly stands up, before clutching his chest in pain. "To think I've been backstabbed by both my buddy and my girlfriend at the same time! Where is the justice...?"

> Dafuq, Zhao Ke and Xiao-Xiao are together???

> Is there a contagious relationship bug spreading in this show??? Zhao Ke!! For snatching my waifu, you and I are now

sworn enemies!!

> My Xiao-Xiao is no longer single???

> Hahaha Zhao Ke-*gege* is so cute~

Zhou Ziheng's hands are still in his pockets as he watches Zhao Ke's antics with a smile. His gaze skips past him and falls upon Xia Xiqing's side profile. Perhaps it's telepathy, but at that very moment, Xia Xiqing, who's chatting with Shang Sirui, suddenly turns his head and meets Zhou Ziheng's gaze. The look in Xia Xiqing's eyes suddenly softens as he gives him a very sweet grin.

> Omggg my Xiqing-*gege* is so sweet!!!

> Look at how adorable his smile is

> zzh may look like the alpha, but when he smiles, his eyes go all curvy like crescent moons. hnnng my ship is too sweet

"Actually, I was also shaking while I played." Zhou Ziheng suddenly speaks up, and everyone looks at him. "Xiqing was being so flashy with his playing, so he could die at any time. I even prepared myself mentally for it."

> YELLS so sweet I'm jelly!!!

Zhou Ziheng walks to Xia Xiqing's side and reaches out to brush aside the bangs that are long enough to cover his eyes.

> Sirui automatically gets out of the way hahahaha the self-awareness of a single dog

"But..." Zhou Ziheng speaks up again. His voice is deep, as if it could drop together with the atmosphere.

Xia Xiqing cocks his head and looks at him, his eyes shining bright and clear as he waits for Zhou Ziheng to continue.

"It's a bit of a pity that I didn't get to die with you in the name of love." Zhou Ziheng bends to Xia Xiqing's ear and whispers in an extremely soft voice, like the fluttering of a butterfly's wings. Yet it stirs up a tremendous tsunami in Xia Xiqing's heart.

"What's there to pity?" Xia Xiqing pretends to lower his head nonchalantly. He can't say why exactly, but his heart is pounding fast. "I only wanted to win with you."

He finally made up for what he didn't manage to do in *Survive and Escape*.

"Winning is great too..." Zhou Ziheng straightens up. His fingers slowly slide down to caress the gentle hill of Xia Xiqing's nape. Extending from the neckline of his sweater, it's covered under a thin layer of skin, and is indescribably sexy. "But I am, after all, an immature idealist."

Xia Xiqing looks at him with a hint of a smile on the corners of his lips and raises his head back mischievously, as if trying to trap Zhou Ziheng's hand back there, so Zhou Ziheng's hand makes its way around and touches his cheek.

"Occasionally, I'd like to die together with my ideals too."

E.05

Soul Mates

P erception of time is relative and ever-changing.
When it's slow, it's like a camera shot in slow-motion where each lingering frame dwells on the senses. But once it picks up speed, it's like quicksand that's impossible to grasp.

The chirps of the cicadas herald the arrival of summer days. As graduation nears, Zhou Ziheng turns down all jobs and devotes himself to writing his thesis at school every day. At first, he felt as if he might be neglecting Xia Xiqing by doing this, but strangely enough, Xia Xiqing has also been busy lately, going out early and returning late every day— even their busy periods coincide with one another.

And so, after a few hectic months, Zhou Ziheng finally completes his thesis defense and gains some free time to catch up on some previous jobs. On the last day of May, Zhou Ziheng calls Xia Xiqing after he returns from shooting a commercial in Koh Samui to ask if he has time to have dinner together that evening.

"Dinner..." Xia Xiqing sounds rather busy on the other end, speaking intermittently. "I may be a little late. How about you book the place first? I'll have time after eight PM. I'll go to you then."

Zhou Ziheng makes a sound of acknowledgment. As he hangs up the phone, he looks at the time in passing—it's already past four in the afternoon. He tells *Xiao*-Luo[6] to help him reserve the seats in a very private Western-style restaurant and makes a trip back home. At seven-thirty in the evening, he sets off for the restaurant and after waiting for half an hour in the private room, he finally sees Xia Xiqing.

Xia Xiqing appears to have rushed. "I'm not too late, am I?"

"No." Zhou Ziheng takes Xia Xiqing's hand and discovers a layer of bandages around the palm. His heart clenches immediately. "What's this? You got hurt? What happened?"

"Just a small wound, it's nothing, it'll be fine after a few days." Xia Xiqing rubs Zhou Ziheng's ear and walks to the opposite side of the table to sit.

"What happened?" Zhou Ziheng asks again.

"Well..." Xia Xiqing looks a little hesitant. "Nothing, really, it was just the exhibition. I accidentally cut myself."

"You should be careful."

Xia Xiqing blinks and says in a light-hearted tone, "I know."

Out of habit, he uses his right hand to prop up the side of his face, but he's only just put up his elbow when he switches to his other hand to gaze at Zhou Ziheng's face.

"You've lost weight." Before Zhou Ziheng can reply, Xia Xiqing adds, "I've missed you so much."

---

6 "Xiao-" is a prefix used for making diminutive nicknames, often used affectionately for children or for someone who's younger than whoever is speaking. Literally, it means "little" or "young."

For a man like him who treats life as a mere game, he rarely uses such sincere and frank expressions, so even Zhou Ziheng can't help but go blank upon hearing this. He's suddenly at a loss for how to respond. He also misses Xia Xiqing very much. He thinks of him every single second of his free time.

The two of them haven't sat down and had a proper conversation in a long time, so they take the opportunity to chat with each other while waiting for the dishes. When the waiter enters to serve, Zhou Ziheng's phone rings—it's a call from his teacher.

"I'm just going to step out for a second, be back soon."

He stands outside the private room and talks on the phone for ten minutes, most of which is about applying for graduate school and the like. After hanging up, Zhou Ziheng heads back inside, only to close the door and find Xia Xiqing slumped over the table asleep, when he'd just been chatting with him.

His face is down, with his left arm serving as a cushion under his forehead and his right hand drooping at the side. He's the very picture of exhaustion. What exactly has been keeping him busy, to be this tired?

Zhou Ziheng treads over softly and slowly to Xia Xiqing's side, and squats to carefully remove the gauze bandage on his palm. Round and round the bandage goes as it comes off, until the wound on Xia Xiqing's palm is finally exposed before his eyes. He seems to have been cut by something, and though it isn't deep, it's still a little inflamed.

Zhou Ziheng feels as if his heart is being clenched by a pair of invisible hands. He wants to re-bandage the wound for him, when he sees Xia Xiqing's fingers twitch. Xia Xiqing is waking up.

His first reaction is to raise his head to look across the table. Seeing the empty chair, he turns his head in a daze and searches around with a dull, sluggish gaze. It's only when he sees Zhou Ziheng crouching at his side that his eyes slowly focus.

"What are you..." When Xia Xiqing is half awake, his voice is much softer than usual. His eyes are misty and hazy, as if covered with a veil of fog.

Zhou Ziheng stands and strokes his head. "Why are you so tired?"

Xia Xiqing says nothing. He merely puts his head against Zhou Ziheng's lower abdomen and wraps his arms around Zhou Ziheng's waist, looking utterly like a child asking to be pampered. Zhou Ziheng strokes the top of Xia Xiqing's head with his broad palm and makes his way down to his nape, one stroke at a time, gentle to the max.

"Why does it feel like you're petting a cat?" Xia Xiqing's voice is muffled with the nasal tone of someone who's still sleepy. Zhou Ziheng finds it extremely adorable.

You're even more adorable than a cat. More adorable than any other critter in the world. He's instantly on cloud nine at the thought that he's the only one who can see such a soft and headstrong Xia Xiqing, unique and so at odds with his usual character. It's one which he's arbitrarily labeled as "Zhou Ziheng Exclusive."

"Let's eat first. We'll go back for a rest later." Zhou Ziheng pats him on the back. He then pulls his chair over to Xia Xiqing's side and shifts his cutlery over. He has long felt uneasy to be so far away from him during a meal.

Xia Xiqing realizes that the bandage on his hand has been unwrapped by Zhou Ziheng, but merely puts his head down and wraps it back in place. Zhou Ziheng didn't ask, so he doesn't explain either.

After the meal, they walk out of the restaurant together. Summer, with its hasty arrival, kicks off with sweltering humidity in this dry city. The two of them walk side-by-side to the parking lot, and just as Xia Xiqing pulls the car door open, Zhou Ziheng suddenly speaks up.

"I'm graduating this Friday."

Xia Xiqing's hand pauses. His face doesn't look surprised, but with his lips, he says, "So soon?"

Zhou Ziheng feels puzzled, but he still circles to the driver's side. "I'll drive since your hand is injured." Xia Xiqing can't change his mind, so he walks over to the passenger seat.

"Feels like you've only just finished defending your thesis." Xia Xiqing pinches the bridge of his nose. "I've been so busy that I hardly remember what day it is."

"I have to go on a business trip to the United States in the next couple of days." Without waiting for Zhou Ziheng to speak, Xia Xiqing continues. "But I'll definitely hurry back before your graduation ceremony starts. Don't worry."

If Xia Xiqing says not to worry, then Zhou Ziheng won't doubt him.

Indeed, he doesn't come home for several days in a row.

On the day of the graduation ceremony, Mama Zhou makes a special trip down to see Zhou Ziheng. It's still early in the morning, and already she's urging him to leave for school. Zhou Ziheng is the one graduating, but his mother is even more excited than him.

"I brought along a camera just to record you."

Zhou Ziheng isn't that excited. He puts his head down and looks at his phone.

"What's with you?" As they wait for the light to turn green, Mama Zhou shoots him a look. "Are you sick?"

"No." Zhou Ziheng turns his phone off and thumps the back of his head against the seat.

"Are you waiting for Xiqing?"

Zhou Ziheng freezes and stiffly turns around to look at his mother. "How do you know?"

"Do you think you can hide from me?" The light turns green, and Mama Zhou steps on the gas. "Xiqing just gave me a call and said he'll come find us later."

"Why didn't he call me?" Zhou Ziheng is like a child as he turns to grab his mother's arm. "What else did he say?"

"He didn't say anything else." Mama Zhou focuses on driving, but something suddenly crosses her mind. "Oh, right."

Thinking it's about Xia Xiqing, Zhou Ziheng immediately raises his head from the backrest of the seat. Seeing how keen her son is, Mama Zhou can't help but laugh.

"It's not Xiqing, but your dean. He called me earlier too. Make a trip to his office later when you arrive, he probably wants to talk to you about something."

Zhou Ziheng sighs inwardly to himself and turns to look out of the window. Sunlight pours from the soft clouds, penetrating the lush trees as it descends from afar to fall upon his shoulders through the glass, baking his black graduation gown until it's hot. He longs so much for Xia Xiqing to witness this day. He's been harboring this thought since a long, long time ago, even though he knows very well that this day is only slightly special in his own heart. To Xia Xiqing, it's at best his lover's graduation day. But graduation day signifies the successful end of a phase in life; it also signifies growth and maturity.

Zhou Ziheng hopes he can graduate in Xia Xiqing's heart. Not for the sake of protecting him, or to be stronger than him. Zhou Ziheng has no expectations when it comes to that, nor does Xia Xiqing like it either. He only wants to become a lover who can evenly match Xia Xiqing in every aspect. Even if there's an age gap that he can't surmount, he wants to be one who's worthy of being called a mature lover.

When they arrive at the faculty, many of the students who are graduating together come over to take photos with Zhou Ziheng. A lot of them are faces Zhou Ziheng isn't familiar with, probably wanting to seize the last opportunity to take a memento with their celebrity classmate. Although Zhou Ziheng always keeps to himself, he isn't someone who can easily turn others down, so he obligingly takes photos with everyone.

Most of the people present are graduating students. Only a few of them are Zhou Ziheng's fans who followed him there. Zhou Ziheng already said in his side account right at the beginning that he doesn't want too many fans to come to his school, for fear that it would affect the other students.

Seeing her son trapped in the awkward predicament of taking photos with the others, Mama Zhou, who's standing at the side, gently reminds him, "Heng-Heng, don't forget to look for Dean Wang."

Only when Zhou Ziheng hears his mother's words does he remember, and extracts himself from the crowd while apologizing.

"Mom, are you coming with me?"

"You go on ahead. I'll wait for you here."

Zhou Ziheng nods and walks alone to the dean's office. He finds it strange. No matter what it's about, the dean shouldn't be looking for him on the day of the graduation ceremony itself. But since it's his mother who's said so, there must be no mistake about it. He lifts a hand to knock on the door.

"Sir, I'm here."

Dean Wang, who's just poured himself a cup of tea, looks up at the doorway. The moment he sees Zhou Ziheng, a smile breaks out on his face.

"Ah, Ziheng's here, come on in."

Zhou Ziheng is about to sit across from the dean, but unexpectedly, the dean stops him. "Ay, hold on. Let's keep it short, so we won't sit and chat. I still have to walk you down shortly."

Zhou Ziheng can't help looking a little puzzled. The dean says with a smile, "You see, you are an outstanding student, and you are also a paragon of virtue who serves as a role model for others. Both the university and faculty have always been proud to have such an outstanding student like you."

"Thank you, sir." Zhou Ziheng smiles politely.

"The faculty is also very grateful for your donation. In fact, it's the first time that an alumni donation like yours has been made just after graduation, but..."

Taken aback, Zhou Ziheng frowns. "Donation? What did you just say, sir? I don't understand."

Dean Wang suddenly laughs. "Ziheng, why are you still playing dumb?" Then it suddenly hits him. "Don't tell me you don't know? That can't be right, your name is written on the document. Never mind, come with me."

With that, Dean Wang leads Zhou Ziheng to the new building. On the way, Zhou Ziheng thinks back to what the dean has just said. *Donation?* He thinks of his mother, who instructed him to look for the dean. Could his parents have secretly made a donation to the school in his name?

"We're here."

It's a rare sight for the open hall on the first floor to be so filled with people. On hearing the dean announce their arrival, Zhou Ziheng snaps out of his thoughts and directs his eyes in the direction where the dean has motioned for him to look. Hanging from the top of the vaulted ceiling in the very center of the hall is a huge white cloth that descends on all four sides all the way to the floor. It looks as though it's been hung to cover something.

"This is?"

"Take a look first. We still have to take a photo together later." Dean Wang disperses the gathered crowd and orders someone to drop the cloth. "The message of this exhibit is excellent and in tune with the vibe of our faculty. I heard from the professor who handled the donation that this piece is a gold award recipient from the recent New York Times Arts Exhibition. The faculty appreciates your donation very much..."

The very instant the word "art" appears, the gears in Zhou Ziheng's brain stop turning. He doesn't listen to the rest of the words. In the blink of an eye, the white cloth drops. Amidst the cries and exclamations of surprise from all around, the mysterious donation that has been concealed within finally reveals itself. The second his gaze falls upon it, Zhou Ziheng's pounding heart almost comes to an abrupt stop.

It's a modernist public sculpture that's about six meters tall. When seen from a distance, the outermost layer is a myriad of tiny spheres of varying sizes, most of which are blue and gold. They glow with a beautiful metallic luster under the intense lighting in the hall. All the microscopic spheres revolve to form a flat ellipsoid, with a tail of light trailing behind each. Light from within spills between the gaps of the particles. These particles seem animated, as if they are simultaneously splashing out, much like...

"The Big Bang..."

All the particles take leave of me and fly toward you.

Zhou Ziheng mutters to himself as he walks toward that massive and magnificent exhibit one step at a time, his feet following the lead of his dimming consciousness. His vision, once obscured by the crowd, gradually clears up, as more of the sculpture fills his vision.

"The Big Bang" is only a shell in the outermost layer. Enclosed within the two scattering halves is a hollow area. There's a palm-sized golden nameplate with the creator's name at the bottom right corner of the outer shell.

"Creator: Antimatter"

Antimatter. This phrase lands a perfect blow to Zhou Ziheng's heart.

"Donor: Zhou Ziheng"

There's also a message engraved below: *"The boundless universe cannot be privately owned, but it can be encompassed in the eyes of those who pursue their ideals."*

It's as if he's entering into the vacuous space as he steps into the center of the "Big Bang." The noisy chatter in Zhou Ziheng's ears instantly ceases and vanishes. His pace slows, and his heart, deceived by a sense of weightlessness, floats.

Inside the shell is a small boy cast in bronze, with a tiny rose in his chest pocket. His two hands are holding a book, the pages of which are connected to two helices spiraling up. One of them is composed of countless white particles, and the other, black particles. They are two completely opposite forces mutually repelling each other amidst their mutual attraction, and blending together in harmony in spite of their antagonism.

Matter and antimatter, intertwining in a dance amidst the Milky Way.

The little boy holding the book has his head raised, so Zhou Ziheng lifts his head too, as his gaze follows these beautiful spirals, inching up a little at a time. Hanging at the center of the Big Bang, where particles of matter and antimatter collide and merge, at the top, is a star. It glows silently in Zhou Ziheng's gentle upward gaze.

"A question for the outstanding graduate of the Faculty of Physics."

A familiar voice rings out behind him. It's the voice Zhou Ziheng thought he would've the lowest chance of hearing before he saw this sculpture.

The radio signal emitting from the vibrant, beautiful space station has traveled billions of light-years through the drifting, resplendent stardust, and barged into his lonely and silent universe. He turns back. His line of sight hitches a ride on the spaceship traveling at the speed of light and lands on a face that is even more beautiful than the nebula. At that smile, his floating heart reaches its destination.

Xia Xiqing reveals his right hand from behind him. The bandaged hand is holding a red rose, which he hands over. He looks up and points at the shining star, the expression in his eyes innocent and tender.

"Why does it shine?"

"When did you create this?" The delight is clearly written on Zhou Ziheng's face for all to see. This kind of youthful, sunny smile is so very precious to Xia Xiqing. He loves the untainted youthfulness of Zhou Ziheng that doesn't come from his external appearance, but from the pureness and steadfastness that radiates from deep within him. After all, in this materialistic world, someone merely embracing his ideals is forced to become a soldier, courageously fighting a lonely battle all on his own.

"I'd been preparing it for quite a few months while you were busy writing your graduation thesis." Xia Xiqing walks up to the little boy and points at the book in his hands. "Look at the details too, STEM boy."

Zhou Ziheng walks over as well and looks down at it. It turns out that there are words engraved on the book too. Inscribed in very elegant calligraphy in the vicinity of the rising storm of matter and antimatter is the story that Zhou Ziheng has once told Xia Xiqing.

"You are truly...amazing." Zhou Ziheng feels as if he's suddenly lost his ability to express himself, like a schoolboy who only knows how to use the most elementary words. However, his eyes are shining brightly, and they speak of indescribable happiness. After saying that, he looks down again and carefully caresses the handwriting in the book with his fingers.

Xia Xiqing stands at the side and fixes his eyes on the man admiring the sculpture. Zhou Ziheng is no doubt dazzling. He possesses the ardent love of thousands upon thousands of people. But it's only when he's facing his dreams that he truly shines. And at this moment, Xia Xiqing is the one and only person in the world who knows why he does.

This work took him nearly four months from design to completion. Xia Xiqing started working on the sketch almost right after Lunar New Year, searching all over the world for suitable materials. Every single particle was made by Xia Xiqing alone in his studio. From polishing to coloring, every process was infused with his passion for art and his love for Zhou Ziheng.

"How many did you make?" Zhou Ziheng looks up and reaches out to touch the tiny black particles and asks the question he's been wanting to ask.

Before Xia Xiqing can reply, Dean Wang brings a junior classmate from the news club, who asks to take a photo with Zhou Ziheng. Xia Xiqing steps out consciously. Zhou Ziheng follows him with his eyes and sees him standing far to the side, where he gestures four numbers to him.

1-3-1-4

—*Forever.*

One thousand three hundred and fourteen colliding particles of matter and antimatter. *Too corny,* Xia Xiqing thinks. He wasn't planning on telling Zhou Ziheng. Indeed, he's gone and done something so cliché. It doesn't matter if it goes against the usual aesthetic of randomness, or if it's just a pretentious and deliberate move—he simply wanted to do it. At the very least, he's gotten the greatest satisfaction of all the moment he sees Zhou Ziheng's smile.

Looking at Zhou Ziheng from afar, Xia Xiqing suddenly realizes that he truly has changed a lot. In the past, he was always reluctant to create public sculptures. He felt that those lonely and dark works of his were not suitable for public exposure. The outcome of being the odd one out was to melt away under all the uncomprehending gazes, to become a puddle of sewage water that drained to some hidden place.

But now, he wants the fruit of his own painstaking labor to be the best that he can do, to be full of goodness and hope so that everyone can't help but stop and be inspired by it when they see it. Only then can he feel reassured enough to label this artwork with Zhou Ziheng's name.

After the group photo, Zhou Ziheng accepts the donation certificate from the dean and bows to him before walking over to Xia Xiqing with a smile on his face.

Leaning against the marble pillar, Xia Xiqing teases, "You're so much taller than your dean that it's really making the job hard for the photographer girl."

"What can I do?" Zhou Ziheng raises his eyebrows at him. With the rose in his hand, he makes his way out of the building with Xia Xiqing, all the while looking down at his own name on the donation certification.

"Do you like this graduation gift?"

Sunlight falls upon Xia Xiqing's face for an instant as he walks down the stairs, causing him to squint his eyes slightly when he speaks—it's adorable.

"Of course." Zhou Ziheng takes Xia Xiqing's hands without inhibition. "Thank you."

How many people in this world can win the favor of such an aloof and prideful artist? Just this alone makes Zhou Ziheng feel incredibly fortunate. When he feels the coarse gauze chafing against his palm that holds Xia Xiqing's hand, Zhou Ziheng's heart begins to ache again. "You got this wound when you were sculpting, didn't you?"

"I was too lost in thought and accidentally grasped the blade end when I wanted to grab it to cut some materials; that's how I ended up getting it."

Xia Xiqing says this breezily, but Zhou Ziheng's heart is aching. He can totally imagine the way Xia Xiqing holed up in the quiet studio to finish up every single detail in silence. He aches for him, and suddenly yearns to embrace him.

"You said you had to go on a business trip these last few days. Did you really go to America?"

Xia Xiqing nods. "Yeah. I went to New York to accept the award."

So what the dean said is true. Zhou Ziheng can't help but find it strange. The way he sees it, Xia Xiqing is never a person who chases after awards. His viewpoint on art has always been independent. He's never taken the initiative to seek out the appraisals and praise of others. Taking the initiative to join award events isn't his style at all.

"Finding it hard to understand?" Xia Xiqing can read exactly what Zhou Ziheng is thinking from the look in his eyes. He laughs. "This is going to be donated in your name after all; I can't just make a random sculpture. I don't think the value of an artwork should be judged based on the so-called awards, but when it comes to the general public, this is the fastest way to make them believe in it and worship it."

"An anonymous creator's work may be unknown, but if it has the distinction of a gold award..." Xia Xiqing turns his head aside to look at him. "...Then it'd still be worthy of our Heng-Heng."

Using such a form of address again. "In that case..." Zhou Ziheng puts his arm around Xia Xiqing's shoulders and walks with him along the concealed atrium path. He lifts his hand to stroke the side of Xia Xiqing's face. "I should thank you, Xiqing-*gege*."

"Good boy."

They walk to the spot where Zhou Ziheng and his mother split up earlier, and see Mama Zhou and Zhao Ke in his graduation gown chatting while standing under a tree. Ruan Xiao is next to them in a red dress. She's the first to see Zhou Ziheng and Xia Xiqing and waves to them excitedly with an outstretched arm.

Mama Zhou is all smiles as she looks at the two of them. "Have you seen the gift Xiqing gave you?" It's only upon hearing her question that it dawns on him—his mother has been preparing him for it since early this morning.

"So you already knew about it." Zhou Ziheng laughs in resignation. "I was the only one kept in the dark."

Zhao Ke laughs like a rascal. "It's a surprise, man. It'd lose its effectiveness if we were to tell you. Say, you really are blessed, a giant sculpture like that." He says, then clutches his chest and shakes his head as he laments, "Today is another jelly day for me."

Ruan Xiao smacks Zhao Ke on the back with her handbag. "What did you say?"

"Nothing, nothing." Zhao Ke wraps his arm around Ruan Xiao's waist. "I'm feeling all sweet now."

"Shameless." Zhou Ziheng roasts him mercilessly.

Mama Zhou has just remembered something. "Oh, that's right. Your sister-in-law called me earlier and asked if you have the time to do a live broadcast. Many of your fans heeded your advice not to come. She suggested doing a half-hour live broadcast so everyone can be happy together."

Zhou Ziheng doesn't really mind. He didn't want the fans to come only for fear of disrupting others, but it would also mean a lot to him to share his graduation day with them. As there's still another collective graduation ceremony later, Zhou Ziheng can only start the live broadcast now. However, he doesn't want too many people to see it, nor does he want this sharing of his life to become a celebrity publicity stunt, so he starts the live broadcast on his Weibo side account.

In less than three minutes, the livestream is already bombarded with comments. After handing the rose to his mother, he puts his phone on a selfie stick and holds it far enough to include everyone in the frame, except his mother who isn't willing to show herself.

"Hello there," Zhou Ziheng smiles at the camera. "It's my graduation ceremony today. I'm sure all of you already knew about it."

> AaAAAHhhhh why is zzh so handsome in his graduation gown?!

> Heng-Heng, congratulations on your graduation! From now on, Heng-Heng will be a fully functional adult in society!

> OMG xqgg!!! I knew xqgg will definitely attend Heng-Heng's graduation ceremony. Why is xqgg so good? Crais I'm so touched

> And Xiao-Xiao and Zhao Ke too! Oh, right. Zhao Ke has also graduated! Grats grats!

> Heng-Heng's graduation! Mama feels so proud! Heng-Heng is the most wonderful graduate there is

> Omgomgomg Self-Study! My xqgg is so good-looking today too! It's truly different when the pairing you ship becomes a reality T^T Self-Study girls are truly a high-risk group for diabetes

"Actually, I was planning on making a vlog." Zhou Ziheng is too preoccupied to look at the camera while he's walking and talking. On the screen, however, it feels as if they are in a video call—it's all very affable. "But the vlog would've to be edited—it's not in real-time, like a livestream is, right?"

> Hell yeah!!! I like livestreams! I can ask questions and chat with you! But I also like vlogs!

> You can also interact in a livestream!

> Heng-Heng! Mama wants to see her daughter-in-law!! Quick, show mama her daughter-in-law!!

> Hahahaha stahp!!

> I wanna see my daughter-in-law too!!!

The comments are too amusing. Zhou Ziheng takes the phone from the selfie stick and practically presses it onto Xia Xiqing's face. "They are all clamoring to see you, these mother-in-law fans of yours."

Xia Xiqing shoots back with a frown. "*You're* a mother-in-law fan."

Zhou Ziheng crooks a corner of his lips and gives him a

smug smile. "I'm the hubby fan."

> omg smexy talk on live!

> hot damn, what kind of sweet-talking wolf-pup top!!!

> Here comes my favorite part hahaha

> Hubby fan!!!!! ZZH OP!! *voice cracks*

Xia Xiqing almost rolls his eyes right before the camera. Looking at Zhou Ziheng now, he can't help but miss the puppy dog from ten minutes or so ago when he had just received the gift. "No, wait. Who was it who called me Xiqing-*gege* earlier?"

> OMG he called him xqgg!!!

> I really don't dare to imagine just how sweet they are in private

> AHHHHHHHHHHH Self-Study drives me crazy!!!

"What's wrong with calling you *gege*?" Zhou Ziheng sees nothing wrong with it. "Will calling you *gege* change the fact that I'm your hubby? No."

> Wellll fuq!!! Zzh wtf why are you so awesome!!!

> Honey, please keep on talking if you're so good at it! Hnnnnngh, zzh you absolute genius!

> Damn, so what I'm watching isn't zzh's graduation ceremony, but a livestream of him F-L-I-R-T-I-N-G with his waifu!

> Noooooo it doesn't change the fact!! You're his husband! It's a fact. A theorem!!!

Xia Xiqing holds back his urge to engage in domestic violence before the livestream audience. He reveals a genial smile and pats Zhou Ziheng gently on the cheek. "You're good with words, huh. Go on, keep on talking."

> Hahahahahaha sexy xq, raging live!!!

> Wow, Xiqing's tone is so sexy!! I just thought of a smutty headcanon!!! Queen bottom!!!

> Queen bottom vs. Alpha Wolfhound top! Who will win and

who will lose??

> Wolfhound I guess, they are beasts when doing the deed
> Roflmao beasts! Girl, are you a werewolf?!
> Helppp I can't breathe!

"My bad," Zhou Ziheng ingratiatingly strokes Xia Xiqing's nape. "I'll shut up."

> Looks like he's still a loyal hound before xxq lmaooo
> xqgg's expression is so seductive even when he's rolling his eyes! Who can resist this?!?!
> Not zzh for sure!!

"Hey, don't stray too far from the topic." Zhou Ziheng points a finger at the screen. "It's game over if the livestream channel gets locked."

Xia Xiqing puts his head down and laughs, then looks up at the fans on the screen and adds, "That's right. The internet isn't a land beyond the reach of the law."

> Lmfao so funny I can't!!
> Ok, ok, ok, I'll send myself to horny jail
> Lmfaoooo why are you like this, girl?!

Zhou Ziheng holds up his phone and walks around the exterior of the faculty to show everyone his classmates, as well as the venue that was set up for the graduates. The whole time, Xia Xiqing walks behind him at a leisurely pace, all the while looking at his back with a smile.

> Younger tops are too good T^T
> Look at that doting gaze in xqgg's eyes. Mah gawd, this is too sweet.
> Why are younger tops so yum??
> "I dressed up, to attend your graduation ceremony."
> Woots! fanfic writers, please write and share asap!!

"Ziheng!" Zhao Ke beckons to Zhou Ziheng from where he's ahead. "Come here. Let's all of us buddies take a photo together!"

"Coming." Zhou Ziheng hands his phone to Xia Xiqing. "I'll be just a minute."

Xia Xiqing nods and walks over as well. He stands next to the red wall where Zhou Ziheng is having his photos taken and glances down at the camera.

> Holy! xqgg's attractiveness is over the charts!! He's so devastatingly gorgeous even at this angle, and up-close!!

> *drools* xqgg I love you! xqgg look at me! I <3<3<3 you!!

> I'm crying, xqgg is so fair that he's glowing under the sunlight. He's truly too gorgeous crais

"Hmm...do you guys wanna keep looking at me, or look at Zhou Ziheng having his photos taken?" An incredibly considerate Xia Xiqing asks their opinions to better decide if he should turn the camera around.

> At you!!!!

> It's been a long time since I last heard xqgg talk!!!

> xqgg, I miss you!! We haven't seen each other for months!!!

"Yeah, it's been two and a half months since I showed my face, right?" Xia Xiqing tends to inadvertently look up when he's thinking. He then lowers his eyes again and smiles. "Miss me?"

> Yes!!!

> xqgg, post more selfies and do more livestreams in the future! I want to see you draw!!!

> xqgg, are you busy with the art gallery?

> Feels like xq lost weight; it's been hard on you! I love you, *gege*!

"I don't think so? It's probably lens distortion." Xia Xiqing turns to look at himself in the camera. "But I've indeed been busy lately. Thank you for going to the art gallery. I've seen the guide and the travel notes all of you posted on the internet. I really appreciate it."

> XQGG I LOVE YOU!!!

> I went to Beijing because I wanted to see the art gallery, and being able to see the works of Xiqing and so many other artists made it all so worthwhile. I still want to go again the next time!

> Thank you xqgg for being willing to give us so many wonderful works! I used to think that art was too distant, that it was not a daily necessity. But now I've totally changed my mind. You are the one who made me understand that art is an indispensable part of a wonderful life

On seeing this, Xia Xiqing suddenly feels his heart welling up with many emotions. He's never thought himself capable of changing anything, much less think himself to be a qualified missionary.

> I've been meaning to ask Xiqing-*gege* a question. What do you think art is to you?

This question is so out of the blue that it stumps Xia Xiqing a little. He's never thought about it before. Living in such a family as his has made him accept it all since he was a child—no, not family. More accurately put, it's the genes he's inherited.

"Actually...I've always felt that art might be considered a kind of sustenance in people's everyday life." His voice is like the warm summer breeze—soft and light. "To me, it is in fact, life itself."

The others have finished taking the group photos, and a few mirthful grown-up boys high-five each other with a laugh. Zhao Ke runs over to his exclusive photographer, Ruan Xiao, to check out the finished photos, while Zhou Ziheng comes over to Xia Xiqing, bringing along with him the dazzling brilliance of mid-summer.

> Then, Xiqing-*gege*, what is your sustenance?

My sustenance... Xia Xiqing looks up and sees, through the phone screen, the man who's flashing him a radiant smile. *A shining star within a silent universe.*

On the small screen, all the fans are waiting for Xia Xiqing's answer, but they don't hear his voice, only the long, drawn-out chirps of the cicadas. After a few seconds, they see the screen flip around. Their line of vision switches from that attractive face to a large patch of green grass, the clear sky-blue summer skies, and the beams of dancing light filtered through the gaps of a dense canopy.

And the man walking toward them, Zhou Ziheng, the tender expression in his eyes reserved only for the person behind the camera.

My sustenance.

"Him."

Firenze

On the first Friday of June, Xia Xiqing suddenly suggests taking Zhou Ziheng abroad on a trip. The long, red, curling peel of the apple that Zhou Ziheng is peeling for him breaks off—a real pity.

"Where to?" Zhou Ziheng takes a bite of the apple. The crisp, juicy sound tempts Xia Xiqing, and he takes the apple from Zhou Ziheng's hand to get a bite too. He answers vaguely, "Firenze."

He's speaking Italian, and this is the first time Zhou Ziheng hears him speak it, which he finds novel and charming. The familiar-sounding syllables promptly register in his mind.

"Florence?"

Xia Xiqing nods. "Haven't you wanted the two of us to go on a trip together? I've been thinking of going back to see my teacher. There are some things I need to ask of him."

Ever since he learned of this plan, Zhou Ziheng has been

in a state of extreme excitement every day. To begin with, he's the kind of person who must spend a lot of time making advance plans no matter what he does. It doesn't matter if it's for his acting or his thesis—that is simply the standard operating procedure of a rigorous science geek. However, Xia Xiqing is the complete opposite. He's laid-back, carefree, and spontaneous, going wherever it pleases him. So he feels both amused and helpless when he sees all the information Zhou Ziheng has collected.

"Oof, you're going to my alma mater with me, not back-packing." Xia Xiqing pokes Zhou Ziheng's head with a finger. "Why are you preparing yourself as if you're gonna be a tour guide? Do you think I don't know my way around, Young Master Zhou?"

Zhou Ziheng catches Xia Xiqing's index finger and pulls it over to his mouth to kiss it, like a hummingbird kissing a delicate flower bud. "I know that, but I also want to know more about the city where you attended school. That way at least I won't be completely ignorant."

"It's okay." Xia Xiqing sits cross-legged before him and deliberately teases him. "It's not like I like you for your inner beauty, anyway."

He's only just finished saying that when Zhou Ziheng pounces on him. Zhou Ziheng rests his head on his shoulder and turns to kiss the side of his neck gently. But finding the kiss not enough, he opens his mouth to nip his skin, even biting down on the faintly throbbing vein beneath the surface.

"Are you a dog?" Says Xia Xiqing, but his arms still wrap themselves around Zhou Ziheng's back.

"Does it hurt?"

"It's alright."

So Zhou Ziheng takes another bite, and this time, Xia Xiqing sucks in a breath from the pain. Cupping Zhou Ziheng's face with both hands, Xia Xiqing pulls him up, rubbing and kneading that attractive face before inexplicably exchanging another kiss with him.

He really, really likes Zhou Ziheng. Xia Xiqing thinks even as he has trouble catching his breath from this kiss.

On the first working day, the two of them discreetly board a plane to Italy. It's in the wee hours of the morning when they arrive in Florence after a flight of over ten hours. Due to the special nature of his work, Zhou Ziheng has never had the experience of traveling abroad alone; Xiao-Luo and the other staff members would follow him every time. No matter where he goes, he always has a large entourage of people tagging along. But it's different for Xia Xiqing. He's a lone wolf who always keeps to himself, even more so when he's abroad.

"Where's our hotel?" After putting the luggage in the trunk of the taxi, Zhou Ziheng climbs into the car to sit next to Xia Xiqing. "Is it close by?"

Very naturally, Xia Xiqing leans on Zhou Ziheng's shoulders. "I didn't book a hotel."

"You didn't?" Zhou Ziheng doesn't believe him. "Then where are we staying?"

"On the streets, I guess."

There's a hint of laughter in Xia Xiqing's voice. The driver is an older Italian man in his fifties; his rotund body can barely fit in the tiny seat, but he has a very boisterous laugh. When he sees the two young men with Asian-looking faces, his first reaction is to speak to them in his broken English with a heavy Italian accent.

However, Xia Xiqing answers him directly in Italian, "You can speak Italian."

The older man is astonished. "You really speak like a local."

"I used to be a student at the Accademia di Belle Arti." Xia Xiqing smiles and lifts his head to tell the driver the address. Coincidentally, this enthusiastic driver lives nearby. They chat for quite a while before the driver finally steps on the gas and drives off in the small hours of the morning toward their destination.

Zhou Ziheng sits at the side and gazes at Xia Xiqing. The way Xia Xiqing looks when he speaks Italian is completely different from when he speaks Mandarin. There are many tiny, vivid expressions on his face, and when he enunciates the words, he always purses his lips swiftly and lightly. Tongue and teeth concealed within those lips collide as he speaks with a playful trill. Sometimes, he would even make some hand gestures with a smile in his eyes.

"The houses here are all beautiful. You've good taste." The driver drops a sincere compliment as they get out of the car.

"I think so too." Xia Xiqing smiles at him.

"Do you have a rental car?" The driver props his arm on the car window as he worries for them.

"No." Xia Xiqing shakes his head. "But I will consider renting a car tomorrow."

Zhou Ziheng stands beside him and watches him in a daze. He finds Xia Xiqing far too adorable when he said the "no." It's not a negative sentence that is straight to the point like it is in English, but instead has a very heavy nasal twang to it. Its primary point of articulation is not the mouth, nor the vocal cords, but the nasal cavity.

His nose wrinkles slightly as his nasal cavity emits a resonance similar to an "em." Then his shoulders shrink a little, accompanied by a gentle shake of his head. Finally, the soft surface of his tongue presses against the roof of his mouth and flits away. All these little details come together to form a tiny "no."

Far too adorable. Like a kitten that refuses to be petted.

"In that case, I hope you have a wonderful time, good-looking boys from the East."

The driver drives off. He dropped them off in a quiet alley lined with charming Italian houses on both sides. A sharp first quarter moon, glowing with luminous grayish-white light, hangs high up in the narrow sky above the alley.

Zhou Ziheng speaks up and imitates Xia Xiqing's tone earlier. "Were you saying no earlier?"

Xia Xiqing's right eyebrow raises as he reveals an astonished smile. *As expected of the ace student.* But he just has to have the urge to tease Zhou Ziheng, so he shrugs, "*Boh.*"

It's another adorable interjection. Zhou Ziheng's heart palpitates restlessly again. The unfamiliar interjections that pop out of Xia Xiqing's mouth are just as lovable as the tiny pansies by the roadside.

"And what does it mean?"

What Zhou Ziheng doesn't know is that "*boh*" is much more of a quip than a simple negative phrase. It means "I dunno," and can be said any time. Xia Xiqing particularly likes to use this word when verbalizing.

"*Boh.*"

"What exactly does it mean?"

Zhou Ziheng follows behind him with the luggage. The two of them walk up the green wrought-iron staircase at the outer side of a beige-colored house, turning back and forth twice up the zigzag staircase before they finally reach the top story.

Xia Xiqing stops before a Paris-blue door and turns around to tell Zhou Ziheng one last time, "*Boh.*"

After that, he sticks out his tongue. Such an impish way of playing cute deals a devastating blow to Zhou Ziheng's heart. Before Xia Xiqing can feel smug, Zhou Ziheng presses him up against the blue door, wraps his arms around his waist, and tightens his grip. Two warm bodies cling together, separated by thin cotton shirts.

The cold white moonlight shines past Zhou Ziheng's ears to illuminate Xia Xiqing's face, softening the crafty smile on his face. Zhou Ziheng lowers his head and brushes the bridge of his nose against the tip of Xia Xiqing's nose. His voice, mellowed by the night, is deep.

"Aren't you little too wicked?"

Xia Xiqing raises his head, his full lips slightly open, and his watery, soft eyes looking into Zhou Ziheng's lowered eyes. His two hands rest loosely on Zhou Ziheng's hip bones as he lets Zhou Ziheng rub against him. It's only when Zhou Ziheng raises his eyes to look at him again that Xia Xiqing opens his mouth and utters words of temptation to him with the kindest, purest expression.

"I'll become even more wicked if you don't kiss me right now."

These words are laced with too many soft, breathy tones that turn Zhou Ziheng's heart into a puddle. Just as he leans down to kiss Xia Xiqing, Xia Xiqing dodges him with a smile. "Too late."

He fishes out the key from the pocket of his jeans and opens the door that hasn't been opened for over a year, then he reaches a hand inside first to turn on the lights. Warm, yellow light instantly floods the small apartment, casting a beautifully warm and inviting glow upon the beige walls.

"What exactly does '*boh*' mean?"

Xia Xiqing expresses helplessness at Zhou Ziheng's need to get to the bottom of everything. He says as he carries the luggage into the room, "I don't know."

"How can you not know?" Zhou Ziheng brings in the larger luggage and places it side by side with Xia Xiqing's luggage in the corner of the room, then immediately takes Xia Xiqing's hand.

"'*Boh*' means I. Don't. Know." Xia Xiqing tugs at Zhou Ziheng's hand and pulls him over to the small sofa in the living room to sit down. The moment his tired body sinks into the soft sofa, he lets loose a contented sigh and leans his head back to look at the ceiling.

The decor of this room is very interesting. The furniture in the living room is all beautifully set in a classical Italian style; even the coffee cups are as exquisite as sculpted works of art. The brick-red ceiling looks as if it's pieced together with planks of mahogany wood, but upon closer look, it looks to be painted on. The crystal chandelier on the ceiling refracts multi-colored light, creating large and small bokeh effects on the small hanging ornaments. But this house has a homely, lived-in vibe too. The beige walls are covered with paintings, some of which are oil paintings with intense colors, but most of them are casual line sketches that are somewhat messily arranged. Then there are the pages that have been ripped off some unspecified books, tacked to the wall with small, silver thumbtacks along with the drawings and paintings.

These finer details of life are completely in tune with Xia Xiqing's own style.

"Is this the house you used to live in while attending school?"

"That's right." Xia Xiqing tilts his head into the side of Zhou Ziheng's neck. "I was still living here at the end of February last year."

Zhou Ziheng has actually assumed that Xia Xiqing was probably living off-campus, but he never expected it to be such a small one-bedroom apartment. But on second thought, he feels it's very much like the kind of place where Xia Xiqing would live.

"Your landlord never rented the house to anyone in the year or so you've been gone?"

Xia Xiqing shakes his head. "The landlord is a very nice granny. I specifically told her to reserve the house for me, and that I would pay her rent regularly. At that time, I didn't think that I'd stay in China for long; I'd have to come back here someday, somehow." As Xia Xiqing speaks, he begins to space out. "That granny is 70 years old. She lives on the first and second floor with her spouse, and they have a very adorable granddaughter. Every morning, the granny sits on a small stool at the doorway of the first floor to comb her granddaughter's hair. When she sees me coming downstairs, she raises her hand at me warmly, *ciao*!" He imitates the way the granny greets him and laughs again.

Zhou Ziheng enjoys hearing him talk about these things. His own limited imagination would suddenly prove effective and useful at this time as he imagines the way Xia Xiqing looks while dashing downstairs with his backpack to greet the granny.

"Her spouse used to be a shoemaker who repaired leather shoes. He's so good at his craft that many people come looking for him, so he often goes around calling on houses with his little toolbox in hand. When he returns, he always brings granny little flowers. Sometimes it's an iris, and sometimes it's a rose. Every time I see him arranging the flowers for granny, I'd think about how nice it is to be alive." Xia Xiqing sighs with a smile and falls over sideways to rest his head on Zhou Ziheng's lap. He looks up at the ceiling, before letting his gaze drift over to Zhou Ziheng's deeply thoughtful eyes.

He stretches out his finger and strokes Zhou Ziheng gently along the prominent bridge of his nose all the way down to the peak of his lips, where he traces its shape like a brush with the gentlest brush strokes.

"Because if you live long enough, you will surely meet someone you can fall in love with." Xia Xiqing mutters to himself.

Zhou Ziheng's heart skips a beat, as if it's been jabbed with this long and slender finger. He leans down and kisses Xia Xiqing's thin eyelid.

After resting in the living room for a while, Xia Xiqing leads him to his former bedroom. The bathroom is large enough, and they both change into oversized t-shirts after taking their bath. Xia Xiqing sits cross-legged on the bed and falls silent while Zhou Ziheng stands by the bed and helps him blow dry his hair, his fingers lightly combing through his hair, gently brushing across his scalp.

"Fortunately, the granny always hires someone to help me clean the house, so we can sleep right away. Otherwise, it'd take all night just to clean the room." Xia Xiqing looks at the wall. "But all this stuff on the wall is too messy."

He's talking about the paintings plastered over the walls of the bedroom. Those can't actually be considered Xia Xiqing's works; they're all semi-finished works he once did in an effort to vent his emotions. Some are just a messy jumble of lines, not even half-finished. Upon hearing this,

Zhou Ziheng turns his attention to the paintings on the wall. Frankly speaking, most of these paintings are very abstract, even dark. Since the day he met Xia Xiqing, he rarely sees him paint in such a style—they are mostly exquisite and elegant classical paintings.

Directly facing the middle of the bed is a very large oil painting that looks much more finished compared to the others. The face on the painting looks like a human face, but broken up by lines into many pieces, like a face reflected in a shattered mirror. The eyes are red, the cheeks are black, while the lips are a pale white. Every fragment is painted in a different color, giving off a rather eerie vibe. There's a black heart under his emaciated face. This is the most realistic part of the whole painting; even the blood vessels connected to the heart are flowing with black-colored blood, like venom flowing through the heart.

Xia Xiqing looks silently at that painting and says nothing. Zhou Ziheng can feel the change in his emotion. He isn't even sure of the underlying principle himself; it's as if their two hearts are tethered together by a thin, red string, which would tug at his heart whenever there's the slightest movement in Xia Xiqing's heart. As if it's saying, "Hey, the person you like is sad."

Zhou Ziheng turns off the hairdryer and tousles Xia Xiqing's hair, then kisses the top of his head. "What's the matter?" He can see Xia Xiqing staring fixedly at that painting, so he probes, "What's the painting about?"

Xia Xiqing's voice is a little flat and devoid of emotions, as if he's merely answering a question about the weather. "My self-portrait." Then he adds, "Past self-portrait."

As if adding this phrase can make Zhou Ziheng's heart ache less. But even he himself can sense that it's a useless effort, so he turns around to burrow into the thin blanket, lies on his side, and closes his eyes.

"I'm so exhausted." Xia Xiqing's voice is soft. "Let's sleep."

Zhou Ziheng lies next to him and pats him on his shoulder gently, trying to lull him to sleep. But a long time passes, and Xia Xiqing still hasn't fallen asleep. His eyelashes cast shadows that flutter nonstop under the light of the bedside lamp. Zhou Ziheng holds him in his arms, trying to give him a sense of security.

"Do you know why I rented this house?" Xia Xiqing's eyes are still closed. He's always inexplicably headstrong in certain aspects.

"Because it's small. A small house won't be too empty."

"Yeah." Xia Xiqing continues, "I pretty much came to Italy to escape from my past. But I realized after coming here that I was on my own again. I was the only Chinese student in the class. My Italian wasn't really fluent back then, and many times when others called me names behind my back, I could only tell from their looks."

Zhou Ziheng frowns. "What names did they call you?"

"Freak, looks like a girl, and so on..." Xia Xiqing sighs. "Actually, I didn't really take that much offense to it. Compared to what happened when I was little, these were nothing. Besides, I went on to become the center of this social circle, which is quite ironic, to say the least. However, my teacher was very worried about me. He thought I had serious psychological issues. If I kept using painting to express my twisted innermost feelings, then I would only push myself into a more precarious situation." Xia Xiqing smiles. "He wouldn't let me paint at one point, and made me travel around Europe for my studies."

Zhou Ziheng thinks of the painting. "So this painting was

painted by you during that time."

"Yeah." Xia Xiqing suddenly lifts his eyes. "I won't lie to you, that's how I was."

Of course, I don't wish for you to see my dark side. Naturally, I hope I can cover up all those scars, all those hideous and ruined parts, and all those lonely times when I was weak and rotten. But how can I say that all those things are not me?

I have so many moments of hypocrisy, but at the very least, I don't want to keep on pretending in front of you. Because you showed up and gave me the love that I never had. You told me that I'm wonderful. Then...I shall believe it for the time being.

Xia Xiqing's consciousness gradually sinks into somewhere soft like the clouds, but much deeper than that. He vaguely feels the person beside him leaving, but he doesn't know if it's a dream or reality. He feels flustered and panicked, but he's unable to reach out and hold him tight in his arms. And just like this, his consciousness disintegrates and lapses, little by little.

The sun already fills the small bedroom when they wake up the next day, spilling over the light green blanket that covers them. The summer breeze, tinged with a waft of rose fragrance, ruffles the curtains, knocking window pane open. Xia Xiqing stirs awake and shields his eyes with the back of his hand. It's only when he gradually regains his consciousness and control of his fully relaxed body that he opens his eyes.

Zhou Ziheng is still sleeping, and his sleeping face is very good-looking. He always gets up in a hurry back home, Xia Xiqing rarely has the chance to see his sleeping face, so he lies on his side and watches for a long time. When Zhou Ziheng is sleeping, every angle on his face turns soft and gentle, like a distant mountain shrouded in mist.

Xia Xiqing muses whether he should buy Zhou Ziheng

some local specialties for breakfast, so he sits up, rolls his neck, and moves to get off the bed to wash up. Strangely enough, he notices a box of colored pencils, along with several crushed balls of scrap papers scattered all over the table beside the bed.

It doesn't register initially, but the moment he looks at the opposite wall, he can't help but freeze in place from shock.

That self-portrait of him is gone. Plastered in the middle of the painting-covered wall is an amateurish and somewhat amusing drawing of a boy with a brilliant smile, colored with the soft colors of the colored pencils. It looks like a child's drawing.

Confused, he walks over and takes a closer look. It turns out that there's a line written at the bottom. The contrast of the beautiful handwriting against the drawing made the drawing out to be even more childish.

"A Portrait of Xia Xiqing—by: Zhou Ziheng"

When Zhou Ziheng wakes up, his first reaction is to reach out his arm. The bed is empty. Xia Xiqing is no longer in the room. The feeling of jet lag is uncomfortable, but to a celebrity like him, it's already a common occurrence. Zhou Ziheng sits up. The sunlight is so dazzling that he can't help but squint his eyes. The drawing opposite is still up there; it seems rather mediocre looking at it now.

Should have enrolled in a drawing class when I was a kid, Zhou Ziheng thinks to himself. He remembers the self-portrait he took down last night, so he gets off the bed and lifts the mattress on his side. Seeing that painting still there, he heaves a sigh of relief. Zhou Ziheng turns around and sees his luggage leaning against the wall.

He wants to take this painting back and secretly hide it

away. With this in mind, Zhou Ziheng puts the canvas away at the bottom of his luggage.

When he emerges again after washing up, he sees a cup of coffee on the small coffee table in the living room. There's also a bread roll wrapped in light brown kraft paper. Zhou Ziheng takes a sip of the coffee, takes the bread roll, and goes to open the door. He's only just pulled the blue iron door open when he hears Xia Xiqing's voice. It turns out that he's downstairs, having a chat with the old landlady.

Zhou Ziheng walks over to the railing and takes a bite of the bread roll as he looks quietly at Xia Xiqing downstairs. He always enjoys these moments of watching Xia Xiqing, especially the way Xia Xiqing looks when he's in high spirits.

The granny looks just the way Xia Xiqing described her. She's wearing a dark green skirt with yellow flower print, and her hair is speckled with silver. When she smiles, she's the picture of benevolence. Xia Xiqing spreads his legs when he speaks to her, with his hands on his thighs and his head tilted, as he looks at the granny with his beautiful eyes. Coupled with his light blue striped short-sleeved shirt and dark blue knee-length shorts, he looks just like an adorable high-school student.

Not long after, a little lass in a pink one-piece dress suddenly comes running out to hug Xia Xiqing's leg, like a little skylark flapping its wings. Xia Xiqing beams happily as he squats to hug the little girl and give her air kisses on each side of her cheeks.

Xia Xiqing really is good-looking. No matter how many times Zhou Ziheng looks at him, he always thinks so. Thinking this gives Zhou Ziheng the notion that he mustn't disgrace himself for Xia Xiqing's sake. He recalls he has some bed hair, so he bites down on the bread roll to hold it in his mouth and frees a hand to press his hair down. He tidies up his own light green t-shirt and lowers his head to pat away the bread crumbs on it.

To his surprise, the little girl in Xia Xiqing's arms suddenly looks up, points at the sky, and yells out in a language Zhou Ziheng doesn't understand. This time, all three of them lift their heads in unison. The granny's astonished expression is truly amusing—she raises her hands to her mouth as she lets loose an adorable sound of exclamation. She then speaks to Xia Xiqing with her head down in a tone that sounds like a query.

Whoops. A flustered Zhou Ziheng takes down the bread he's stuffed into his mouth and smiles awkwardly at the people below. His hand anxiously moves to press down his bed hair again.

Xia Xiqing smiles with his lips pursed. The little girl imitates the granny and asks the same question again. Xia Xiqing pinches the little girl's cheeks and answers in English.

"My boy."

His voice is very gentle, and so, so soft, but the warm June breeze still carries it over into Zhou Ziheng's ears.

For some inexplicable reason, he feels that "my boy" moves him even more than "my boyfriend."

Xia Xiqing looks up and calls to a dazed Zhou Ziheng, "Come on down."

"Oh, right." Zhou Ziheng walks down the stairs and finishes the bread as he descends. He hears the little girl pestering Xia Xiqing in wonky English, "Then...then am I your girl?"

On hearing this, Xia Xiqing purses his lips. "Hmm...how about this? Before you find your boy, you are my little girl."

The little one, delighted on hearing this, runs to the small

potted plant at the doorway of her own house and plucks off
a tiny red rose. She runs back to give it to Xia Xiqing. Xia
Xiqing refuses it, but she insists and even stands on tiptoe to
put the flower above Xia Xiqing's ear.

"Now you are my boy." The little girl says matter-of-factly,
amusing the old landlady standing beside them.

Zhou Ziheng walks over and squats beside Xia Xiqing. He
says to her in English as well, "Even though this guy accepted
your flower, he's still mine, not yours, understand?"

Xia Xiqing bumps Zhou Ziheng with his shoulder and
says in Chinese, "Why are you taking a child's words to
heart?"

Zhou Ziheng ignores him and repeats to the little girl in
all seriousness, "Get it?"

The little girl pouts and thinks about it for a while, then
runs again to pick a little daisy. Standing on tiptoe, she pins
the flower above Zhou Ziheng's ear.

"And you are my boy!"

Xia Xiqing and Zhou Ziheng look at each other and burst
out laughing. The granny, amused to bits, says to her little
granddaughter, "You can't say things like that to every pretty
boy you see, dear."

The two of them chat with the granny for a while, then
Xia Xiqing glances at his watch—it's about time for his
appointment with his professor. He takes his leave of the
landlady's family and leads Zhou Ziheng to the school. Zhou
Ziheng takes down the little daisy beside his ear and holds
the stem between his fingers and twirls it. With his other
hand, he reaches for Xia Xiqing's hand and pulls him close.

Xia Xiqing casts a glance at Zhou Ziheng with a faint
smile and grasps Zhou Ziheng's hand back. The happiness
in his heart can't be contained, like soda so violently shaken

that the pressure pops the bottle cap open and shoots out wild spurts of sweet bubbles. There's simply no remedy. Xia Xiqing feels that the present him has undoubtedly been infected by the Zhou Ziheng virus. He's just like an impulsive teenager, the moment he sees Zhou Ziheng smile at him, he feels pleasantly warm all over, and the urge to embrace and kiss him will overcome him.

He even thinks about how blissful he will be if he can live with Zhou Ziheng in that tiny rental house forever.

Along the way, they come across a boy selling handmade cookies. Zhou Ziheng buys a big box and stuffs the cookies one after another into Xia Xiqing's mouth. Xia Xiqing shakes his head to stop him from stuffing even more, so Zhou Ziheng stuffs them into his own mouth.

The Accademia isn't that far away from the house, and they arrive after a short walk. They've only just walked through the gates when Xia Xiqing receives a call from his mentor. The mentor's office is on the second floor, and there's a small garden downstairs with a bench, where Zhou Ziheng sits alone while he waits for Xia Xiqing.

Back when Xia Xiqing left school and went back to China, it was also at the suggestion of his mentor. This time, he's returned to take away part of the works he's previously left with the professor, as well as to formally bid him farewell.

Professor Bianchi rises to his feet the moment he sees Xia Xiqing, and walks around his desk to give him a hug. "It's been a long time, Tsing." He's a middle-aged man of forty-five who's very particular about his appearance, and wears a different color neck scarf every day.

"It's been a long time. Have you been well lately?"

Professor Bianchi shrugs with a smile. "Of course. But I would probably be better if you were around to assist me."

Italian men are glib talkers regardless of their age. Xia Xiqing is already used to it. He smiles. "God forbid, it'd be better for a trouble-maker like me to steer clear of your path."

After chatting for a while, Xia Xiqing mentions his wish to retrieve part of his previous works, which the professor readily agrees to. He's holding a fountain pen in hand, jabbing it at a blank book, yet his eyes are fixed on Xia Xiqing's face in a stare. Xia Xiqing knows what he wants to say.

As expected, not a minute later, the professor asks, "I've always known that you are popular, but I still can't help but ask: are you in love?"

Xia Xiqing rubs the tip of his nose with his hand. At first, he hums and haws, but he very quickly puts both hands on the desk and shrugs, "Yep."

"Oh, my god." The professor can't believe it. "You've never admitted that before." He shakes his head with a smile. "You've been here for five years, and I've never seen you like this...not even once."

Xia Xiqing lowers his head to stare at a document on the desk. The handwriting on it is extremely pretty. "Yeah. Who would've thought?"

"That person must be an angel." The professor burst out laughing. "How else could you have been charmed?"

Bingo. The tips of Xia Xiqing's ears begin to burn.

"I have to say, you are in a totally different state than you were before. You used to be too melancholic, and even though it was clear you were in a dark place, you still took pains to smile. I was always worried about you." The professor lets loose a long sigh. "But it's all good now. I can see how happy you are. The smile on your face is genuine. I'm truly happy for you."

Xia Xiqing feels a little moved. Back then, he merely locked away all his depressing sides in his heart. By all appearances, he seemed to be popular and fitted in with the crowd, but his paintings could deceive no one.

"Right now I'm...very happy." A small smile hangs on Xia Xiqing's face, like ripples stirred by a breeze. "He's the one who changed me."

Saved me.

"No. You are worth it." The gaze in the professor's eyes is so resolute that it surprises Xia Xiqing. "You weren't saved by someone. It's your tenacity that made you wait until he appeared."

Xia Xiqing feels a lump in his throat. He can't stand his own increasingly volatile emotions and fragile, sensitive heart, but he has to admit that such words do indeed move him.

All of a sudden, he wants very much to introduce Zhou Ziheng to the professor. Even though he feels that doing so is slightly childish—it feels like he's showing off or something—he still hopes that the professor can see how much of a wonderful person Zhou Ziheng is.

After struggling over it for a while, Xia Xiqing stands up. "He's just downstairs. Would you like to see him?"

"Of course."

They walk together to the office window. Looking down on that lush little garden from above, Xia Xiqing can't help but blink at the sight. Still sitting on the bench, Zhou Ziheng has his hand spread out, and three or five white doves have flown onto his hand and are now pecking away at his palm. Another two foolhardy doves have flown onto his shoulders, their tiny claws tightly clutching at his mint-colored shirt.

Zhou Ziheng's face is radiant with a patient and gentle smile. After the doves are done eating, he takes out another cookie from the box, crushes it to pieces, and places the crumbs in his palm. The sunlight brings a soft, sparkling glow to his not-so-dark hair.

"He really is an angel." The professor wears an "I knew it" expression on his face, but very quickly, a comforted smile appears. "Tsing, seeing you like this makes me very glad."

Xia Xiqing turns, his eyes clear and bright. "Thank you."

When Xia Xiqing makes his way downstairs, the doves are mostly gone, leaving only a small one pacing back and forth on the bench, looking busy. Zhou Ziheng stares at that little dove, finding it amusing no matter how he looks at it. He turns upon hearing the footsteps, and stands the instant he sees Xia Xiqing.

"All done?"

Xia Xiqing nods and walks to him. When he sees Zhou Ziheng picking up that empty cookie box, he teases him. "Where are the cookies?"

"Huh? I finished them." Zhou Ziheng wraps an arm around his shoulders. "I thought you didn't like them."

"I didn't like them, so you fed them to the doves?"

Zhou Ziheng is a little astonished to be exposed. "You saw?"

Xia Xiqing points. Zhou Ziheng's eyes follow the direction of his finger and look up. A middle-aged man is standing at the window of the second floor, smiling at them both.

Feeling as though he's meeting the parent of his lover, Zhou Ziheng awkwardly scratches the back of his head, then looks up and smiles back at the mentor.

"You should have said I was going to meet him. I would've styled myself up a bit."

Xia Xiqing casts a glance at him. "Your idol baggage sure is heavy." But quickly, he adds, "Just how much more handsome do you want to be?"

This pleases Zhou Ziheng. He moves his hand from Xia Xiqing's shoulder to his head and kisses him on the side of his cheek. Xia Xiqing feigns a look of disdain as he wipes his face and pushes Zhou Ziheng away, but the smile on his face can't be contained. Just then, a young and tall Italian boy walks toward them. Xia Xiqing isn't paying much attention, but the other person unexpectedly calls out his name.

"Hey, Tsing!"

Xia Xiqing halts in his tracks and looks toward the voice. Before he can say a word, the brown-haired young man trots over, hugs him enthusiastically, and starts going on about how long it's been since they last saw each other, with happy surprise written all over his face.

"It's been a long..." Xia Xiqing's hand is grabbed before he can finish his words, and he turns to look to the side. Zhou Ziheng's expression has suddenly changed. Unlike his sweet and well-behaved look earlier, he now looks aggressive, with hostility on full display on his face, as if afraid the other person wouldn't be able to notice. Now that is truly a wolf transformation out of the blue.

"This is..." The young man looks at Zhou Ziheng, still smiling in spite of the awkward atmosphere.

"Lucas, he's my boyfriend." Xia Xiqing decisively cuts to the chase, then turns his head to introduce the other person to Zhou Ziheng in Chinese. "This is my classmate from when I was doing my masters, Lucas."

Zhou Ziheng greets Lucas in English. Even though Xia Xiqing has already explained, he still doesn't feel reassured, and the expression in his eyes as he looks at Lucas is wary.

"So handsome." Lucas completely overlooks Zhou Ziheng's childish sense of possessiveness as he focuses his full attention on Zhou Ziheng's face of Eurasian beauty and extraordinary figure. "Proportions are great too. Very suitable as a model for live drawings. Is he of mixed blood? Or the same as you?"

Even though his relationship with Lucas used to be pretty good, Xia Xiqing still can't stand Lucas sizing up Zhou Ziheng with such a blatant and brazen look in his eyes. As a student of the arts, he's very clear that they all come with x-ray vision that can see through clothes to the human body, and thinking of it this way makes him uncomfortable, as if his most precious thing has been touched by someone other than him. He never thought he would have such a strong sense of possessiveness.

Therefore Xia Xiqing immediately changes the subject, "Did you just come back?"

"Yeah, I went to the church earlier with two newcomers for some still-life sketching."

Speaking of which. Xia Xiqing looks down at his watch. "I have to be somewhere, gotta go." He pulls Zhou Ziheng by the hand and makes to leave.

"Wanna have dinner together tonight? A decent bar just opened."

"I have plans. Maybe next time." Xia Xiqing waves at Lucas as they walk away.

"Hey! Can I leave my number with your boyfriend?"

"Don't even think about it." Xia Xiqing grabs Zhou Ziheng's hand tightly without even looking back.

Zhou Ziheng can't understand what the two of them have been saying, but something feels odd, so he asks tentatively, "Is he cussing at me?"

Xia Xiqing puffs out a laugh. "Yeah, he said you're ugly."

"I'm not ugly!" Zhou Ziheng rarely cares about other people's opinions, especially their comments about his appearance, but he's extraordinarily bothered by it today. He presses down the bed hair on his head again. "I think I'm better looking than most people here."

Why is he so cute? Xia Xiqing can't stop laughing. He reaches out and strokes Zhou Ziheng's chin. "Not most of them. All of them." Then he adds breezily, "Our Heng-Heng is the most handsome."

As Xia Xiqing leads him out, he keeps checking his watch, as if he's trying to catch something. The sun gradually moves up to the center of the sky, illuminating the whole of Florence: the dark gray roads, the winding alleys that extend in all directions, and the entire city of brick-red rooftops. A tall building stands not far away from them, regal and imposing. Traversing through this city, Zhou Ziheng suddenly finds it kind of romantic in a brash way—it's as if he's barged onto the set of *Roman Holiday*.

As he looks at Xia Xiqing's back, Zhou Ziheng suddenly feels that this is the kind of place that Xia Xiqing ought to be living in. He's had this kind of feeling once before when he was in Wuhan. It doesn't matter if it's a bustling night city brimming with life, or the streets of Florence with a vibrant art scene, Xia Xiqing's presence is always so fitting and natural.

"I was going to show you David at the Accademia. It's the real thing." Still pulling him by the wrist, Xia Xiqing slows down a little. They are almost there. The brick-red dome of the Cathedral of Florence—also known as the Cathedral of Santa Maria del Fiore—is already before their eyes.

"Then why didn't we see it?" Zhou Ziheng follows beside

him.

This Gothic church that is almost a hundred meters high has already captured almost all of his attention. The marble panels on the exterior are magnificently ornate, with creamy white marble, dark green glaze, and ubiquitous classical sculptures everywhere. Truly exquisite, it doesn't look like a church at all, but more like some incomparably valuable and precious work of art.

"The real thing is indeed stunning, but more than that, I wanted to show you this—no, to let you hear this."

Xia Xiqing suddenly stops in his tracks before a towering building. He glances down at his watch.

"What's this place?" Zhou Ziheng looks up at the building. Having done his homework prior to the trip, he attempts to match what he's seen online with reality. "Is this...the Giotto's Bell Tower?"

Xia Xiqing can't help but laugh when he hears this. "Not bad, little classmate Zhou."

"Of course."

Zhou Ziheng is about to say something else when the bell suddenly begins to toll. The thunderous clash of metal on metal resonates loud and clear, giving him a blow to his heart. He feels as though he's not his own master, as the solemn sound of this ancient bell freezes him in place, electrifying him from head to toe. Even his soul is quivering along with the reverberation of the sound waves.

Just as he's stunned in place, Xia Xiqing kisses him. A soft, gentle kiss, like a piece of cloud drifting leisurely onto his lips. Xia Xiqing looks into his eyes. Sunlight pours generously onto his fair face, making him look very much like the meticulously sculpted pure and white angels on the church.

"Actually, I was enchanted by your voice not long after

we first met." Xia Xiqing's eyes brim with tenderness, like a cool mountain stream after the melting of spring snow. "There were so many times I wanted to tell you that I always think of the Cathedral of Florence's bell whenever I hear you speak."

The reason he hasn't told Zhou Ziheng is that it's all too mystical, what's more, this is indeed something he genuinely associates mentally with him. Unlike the other words he utters when he's teasing him, this is subliminal. Telling Zhou Ziheng would be like holding his heart out for him to see.

So dangerous.

So real.

As Xia Xiqing is saying this, Zhou Ziheng's mind wanders to the analogy he made of him back then—Rodin's Kiss. Whether it's a deliberate tantalization on his part or a revelation of his true feelings, Xia Xiqing has always been able to describe Zhou Ziheng using these incomparably precious works of art. It makes Zhou Ziheng wonder if he's deserving of it.

Zhou Ziheng leans down and strokes Xia Xiqing's nape carefully with his palm. His low, magnetic voice resonates harmoniously and beautifully amidst the reverberating tolls of the bell. "Where is the resemblance?"

As the last, lingering chime of the hour trails off, Xia Xiqing answers him in his most gentle voice. "Both...make my heart sing."

On the fourth day of Xia Xiqing and Zhou Ziheng's vacation in Florence, a candid photograph taken by a passerby suddenly begins to circulate wildly on the internet. The photo, set against the backdrop of the stately, majestic Cathedral of Florence, features in the foreground Xia Xiqing leaning forward to kiss Zhou Ziheng on the lips in front of the tall Giotto's Bell Tower. The photographer is just a passerby who happened to be on a trip to Florence. At first, he simply found the appearance of these two Asian men exceptional and familiar, and the visual of their kiss under the tolls of the bell simply too beautiful. And so it was for this simple purpose he took this photo. It's only after he shared it with his friends upon returning to China that he learned that these two young men are the hottest and most popular ship in the country.

@thetravellingrabbit: I thought about it and decided to post this amazing candid shot. Y'all can't imagine just how awed I felt at that moment when I saw this scene with my own eyes. This is probably what love looks like at its best

This Weibo post itself didn't include any tags or names. However, the large base of self-study girls is not one to be underestimated, as is the audience reach of popular, verified accounts that reposted the photo. In no time, there are nearly ten thousand comments under the post.

@dollforevergirl: OMG It's my Self-Study!! I'm crying this is so beautiful! So envious of op!!

@Chalametroye: Heng-Heng and Xiqing-*gege* are in Florence??? Is it too late to book a plane ticket now T___T

@ChillTime: omg I love them so much!! This scene is like a painting

@LilWitchInTheLighthouse: It's like a movie screenshot. These two men's attractiveness and disposition are really off the charts. Even their casual outfits are so refreshing

@Tufted: I LOVE SELF-STUDY FOREVER!!! Why is Xiqing-*gege* so handsome? Why is Heng-Heng so cool?!?!

@idunlikeyou: Just passing by, but this shot really is gorgeous. How can these two look so good together? My eyes are cleansed...@directors of BL adaptations, from now on, please cast your leads according to these beauty standards, ok?

@SelfStudyGirlFighting: I'm crying so much I'm drowning in my tears, crais. I want to see Self-Study LIVE!!!

@IcyBlueDeepSea: So xqgg was bringing Heng-Heng to his alma mater? I'm really lucky to be a fan of such a couple. My life is complete

@athousandautumnsslumber: NO!!! I miss them so much!! I want to see a livestream of their trip! I'm gonna go bang pots and pans on their Weibo!

@pureandvivid replying to @athousandautumnsslumber: Damn girl, you good!! There's no time to lose, let's go right now

@hotspringsauce replying to @athousandautumnsslumber: Hahahahaha you're so cute! You're totally doing that just because both of them spoil their fans hahaha

@snowphoenixinsummer: My Self-Study is undoubtedly the gem of the shipping world! Which other ship in the world can be more compatible and more romantic than Self-Study?

@sss replying to @athousandautumnsslumber: Wait for me sis! I wanna join in too!! (╯ °□°)╯ ︵ ┻━┻

Because of the one fan who took the lead, tens of thousands of Self-Study girls all follow suit and start spamming comments on the Weibo accounts of the two clueless idols with demands to see the livestream of their trip. Zhou Ziheng and Xia Xiqing haven't been on Weibo for quite a number of days, so they are oblivious to the online hubbub until Zhou Ziheng receives a private WeChat message from his sister-in-law.

Sister-in-law: Go on Weibo.

This is such a clear and concise sentence that Zhou Ziheng has to concede ruefully that his sister-in-law is indeed becoming more and more like his older brother. No wonder people say that lovers who've been together for a long time will eventually come to resemble each other.

It's now eleven in the morning in Florence, a time when the sunlight is just perfect. After lazing around for a time in bed, both of them get up to search for food. A pity the restaurant they've chosen is too popular. Zhou Ziheng and Xia Xiqing can only sit with empty stomachs by their window seats as they wait for the food.

"Sis-in-law told me to go on Weibo. I guess something must have happened." Zhou Ziheng says to Xia Xiqing sitting across from him, before opening Weibo on his phone.

As soon as Xia Xiqing hears the word Weibo, he has an ill sense of foreboding. Unfortunately, he's simply too prone to being in a shitstorm; every time he goes on Weibo, he's mired in one controversy or another. "Then I'll look too." With that, he unlocks his phone.

About ten or so seconds later...

"Damn."

"Fuck."

They both cuss out loud in unison and look up at the same time.

"Is your comments section filled with that kissing photo too?" Zhou Ziheng asked.

Xia Xiqing nods and holds up his phone to show Zhou Ziheng. "Looks like it was taken by a tourist who was passing by. There are too many Chinese people in Italy." He looks at his phone again. "They're all clamoring for a livestream in the comments."

"Let's do it then." Zhou Ziheng puts both hands on the table and drums on it with his fingers. "With my side account."

Xia Xiqing feels amused and resigned at Zhou Ziheng's initiative. "But wait, why are you so enthusiastic?"

"Of course I have to be enthusiastic when it comes to

showing off our love." Zhou Ziheng's smile is even more brilliant than the sunshine outside the floor-to-ceiling window.
"Besides, my fans want to see me show off. See, I don't really
have any strengths compared to other celebrities, the only
good point about me is that I spoil my fans."

Xia Xiqing snorts. "Sure, keep on being smug."

Zhou Ziheng laughs mischievously. He swiftly swaps
over to his side account on Weibo and opens the livestream
platform. Xia Xiqing is truly speechless. It usually takes lots
of nagging to convince Zhou Ziheng to post a selfie, but he's
practically rushing to do this.

The moment the livestream room opens, thousands upon
thousands of fans who've been waiting with puppy eyes all
swarm in, causing the live feed to get stuck momentarily on
the slightly-opened collars of Zhou Ziheng's polo tee and
collarbone.

> OMGGGGG WHOSE COLLARBONE IS THIS?!!?!??!?! Hot
damn, eye candy right on entering!!!

> My screen is so wet...

> This is Heng-Heng's, right? Xiqing-*gege*'s collarbone sticks
out more, and his complexion is fairer!

> I can already smell the pheromones wafting through the
screen!

> I can hear sounds but my screen is stuck. I can hear Heng-
Heng talking!

> It's okay now! It's moving!

Zhou Ziheng's face suddenly closes in on the camera.
From the other end of the screen, all they can see is an eye
with fluttering eyelashes. "Eh? Seems like it's working now."
He moves the phone away, revealing his entire face. Zhou
Ziheng, wearing a white baseball cap, waves at the screen.
"Long time no see."

> Kyaaaaaa Heng-Heng looks so, so, so good in this get-up!!!

> Damn, why is my son so handsome!! His bare face is so charming and clean!!

> Heng-Heng!!! Mommy misses you so much!!!

> Heng-Heng! Mama wants to see her daughter-in-law!! Where is my daughter-in-law?

Zhou Ziheng cracks up at the comments of daughter-in-law requests filling up the screen. He flips the camera with a smile. Xia Xiqing currently has his head down while he types out a message to Xu Qichen.

"They want to see you—their daughter-in-law."

"To hell with that." Xia Xiqing shoots back subconsciously. It's only when he looks that he notices Zhou Ziheng is holding up the phone. "Oh, it started?"

> KYAAAAA XIQING-*GEGE*!!!

> Why does xqgg look so good in a pink t-shirt?! He even has a little ponytail!!! Too adorable!!!

> Sobs, my little rose is pink today!

> xqgg is the honey peach walking among us on earth today. xqgg <33333

> Self-Study's outfits today really make it clear who tops and who bottoms, and Xiqing-*gege*'s little ponytail is too kyoot~

> I also want such a sweet wifey like xqgg T^T xqgg I love you!

> I can sing praises of these two's attractiveness a million times. Too damn gorgeous!

Although the livestream catches him off guard, Xia Xiqing still pretty much dotes on his fans. The second he sees the camera, he beams and waves at the Self-Study girls on the other side to greet them, "Oh hi everyone, good evening."

> Ahhhhh Xiqing-*gege* is so warm! He knows it's night here for us so he makes a point of saying good evening!

> xqgg good afternoon!
> What's that on xqgg's ring finger? Looks like a tattoo...
> I think I saw it too. Has anyone with deft fingers taken a screenshot yet?

"We are waiting for food now. They're very slow at serving up the dishes here."

Zhou Ziheng's voice has become background sound. The camera is still focused on Xia Xiqing, but he's oblivious. Seeing Zhou Ziheng talking to the phone, Xia Xiqing assumes the camera has already turned around, so he reaches out to the waiter and asks in Italian, "Excuse me, we have been waiting for a long time. Did you miss our order?"

The blond waiter apologizes and promptly heads away to check.

> Goodness me, an Italian-speaking xqgg is so cool!
> His pronunciation sounds so nice! I'm melting. I want an ASMR clip recorded by xqgg!!!
> Ziheng's voice is lovely too. The super manly voice of a top!
> That waiter is pretty handsome too btw
> xqgg has such a wonderful disposition. He's even gentler when he speaks Italian. Today is another day I want to date an artist!
> Want to date an artist +1
> Want to date an artist +10086!!!

The comments are going in a strange direction, so Zhou Ziheng turns the camera around and holds out a finger to warn the fake shippers who want to date Xia Xiqing, "You are not allowed this kind of presumptuous thinking."

> Lmaoooooo zzh are you a 3yo kid??? How can a celebrity get jelly of their fans?! Wake up!
> zzh is truly the epitome of possessiveness hahaha!
> The liddol kiddo top never fails me

> hahahaha liddol kiddo top! Help I'm dying!!

> Okok we won't fight you for him (as if we can)

> ZZH's daily jelly fit—check

> Jealousy personified Zhou Ziheng, cuckolded by his fans day after day; Green-eyed monster eying them all, jelly and pissed—what a pain!

> Lmfaooo that's so brilliant I can't! Stahp!!

"You girls are insufferable." Zhou Ziheng shakes his head. "I'm not at all jealous." Right at this time, the dishes are served. Xia Xiqing thanks the waiter, pushes the T-Bone steak over to Zhou Ziheng, and introduces the dish to the camera. "This is the most famous T-Bone steak in Florence, his is medium-rare." Then he shows the fans his order. "I got the lobster capellini, I really like this kind of thin pasta."

Zhou Ziheng moves to put down his phone, but if he does, the camera won't be able to see anything. Seeing his dilemma, Xia Xiqing reaches out to pull his steak toward himself and without a word, starts to cut the steak for him.

> Kyaaaaaa why is xqgg so sweet!!! He's the Perfect Boyfriend Material!!

> He's cutting the steak for him, I'm crying I'm so jelly

> Hi everyone, imma tuck in now. [sucks on lemon.jpg]

> Why does xqgg seem to be more of an ideal boyfriend than zzh hahahaha. Zhou Ziheng, you're the 1 ok?!?!? Don't let your mama down!!

> Because ZZH is a pure heart maiden top

> Lmfao pure heart maiden top!!!

> I'm wheezing

> Y'all, keep bullying the little puppy and he's gonna shapeshift into a wolf soon!

"I can't take this, you guys aren't my fans." Zhou Ziheng sets the phone face down on the table. Xia Xiqing pierces a piece of steak on a fork and delivers it to his mouth. Being personally fed by Xia Xiqing like this instantly makes Zhou Ziheng happy again.

> Hahahaha the child is angry!!

> Your host has left the livestream channel because he can't take his fans' teasing

> Mama won't tease you anymore!! Come back!!

> Heng-Heng, your image as a maiden top is cemented in my heart now. Resistance is futile!!

When the screen lights up again, it's Xia Xiqing's close-up face that appears.

> OMG Xiqing-*gege* is so pretty!!

> xqgg's face is too good-looking!!! All the beautiful bottoms to ever exist now have a face in my mind!!

> I love the mole on the tip of xqgg's nose. I wanna kiss!

"This pasta is pretty good. I really like cheese, so I asked for a little extra." Xia Xiqing holds the phone in his left hand and with his right hand holding the fork, twirls the pasta into a ball. The rich red sauce and a thick blanket of cheese on the pasta make it look delectable.

> So hungry! I'm going to make instant noodles!

> Oof, it's dinner time now. Sisters, let nom together!

> I'm having hotpot right now!!! It feels like a dinner date with Self-Study across time and space! I'm so happy!!!

> Xiqing-*gege*, I wanna see the inside of your ring finger!!!

> Yeah!! Me too!!

> I second it!!!

Xia Xiqing bites down on the fork and looks at the screen full of comments. He thinks for a moment, then flips the screen and aims the camera at the inside of his ring finger. "Can you see it?"

There's a pair of adorable wings tattooed on the inside of

his finger. But instead of a halo, there's a tiny crown above the wings.

> OMGGGG It's really a tattoo!!!

> Gosh, it's so cute!!! Somehow this drawing style feels inexplicably childish rofl

> Let me venture a bold guess. This is Zhou Ziheng aka Soul Painter aka Liddol Kiddo's masterpiece, right? LMFAO

> The style differs greatly from the drawing of the rose on Ziheng's finger! LOL it's defo drawn by Ziheng, then Xiqing-*gege* had it tattooed on his hand!

> I cry. I'm jelly again. Are these two men trying to give me diabetes?

> The point I'm making is that xqgg is on the losing end...to have to tattoo Zhou Ziheng's drawing

> Lmfao why are you focusing on that?! Don't bully my son!!!

> The couple tattoos are both so adorable! I'm ded!

Xia Xiqing turns the camera over to Zhou Ziheng, who has his head down as he eats his steak. The features under the cap are well-defined and handsome.

> Tbh Heng-Heng really does look very handsome and very alpha

> Of course. Even though his alpha persona has already fallen apart, he's truly exceptionally handsome!! Especially when he isn't smiling—so manly!!

As if sensing that Xia Xiqing is filming him, Zhou Ziheng lifts his eyes a little to look at him.

> OMFG the sheer lethality of this look!!

> No one can emerge unscathed from this gaze of Zhou Ziheng!!

> Damn, he's so manly! I take back my earlier words

"Are you filming me?"

There's a hint of a smile in Xia Xiqing's voice. "Yeah."

"What are you filming me for?" Zhou Ziheng can't help but smile too. He wipes the corner of his lips with a finger. "Only 'cause I want to. Do I need to pick a time?"

> Fark!!! The Double Alpha Moment I've been waiting for!!!

> I can just imagine the way Xiqing-*gege* looks as he raises an eyebrow!!

> I WILL ALWAYS LOVE DOUBLE ALPHA!!!

> How can these two be so many and gentle and adorable at the same time!!!

They eat and chat for almost an hour. Before they leave the restaurant, the waiter from earlier calls out to Xia Xiqing and gifts him an iris flower. Xia Xiqing accepts it with a smile, but this displeases Zhou Ziheng, who immediately frowns. His expression changes even faster than one can turn the page of a book.

> Oh damn, here comes the wolf!!!

> Caught off-guard!!!

The waiter thinks that Zhou Ziheng feels slighted, so he pulls another iris out of the vase on the counter and hands it to him. Xia Xiqing accepts it on Zhou Ziheng's behalf with a smile and thanks the waiter, then sticks the flower onto Zhou Ziheng's collar.

"Man." Zhou Ziheng takes the flower out of his collar to hold in his hand, and whispers to Xia Xiqing as they step out, "Don't smile at other people like that."

"I can't even smile? Why are you so fussy?" Xia Xiqing asks smilingly.

Zhou Ziheng, however, is getting anxious. "Don't you have any freaking idea how good you look when you smile?!"

Xia Xiqing remains rooted in place with a baffled expression, rendered speechless by Zhou Ziheng's words.

> Hahahahaha wtf what fantastic creature is zzh I'm dying!

> A compliment disguised as a scolding!!!
> lmfaoooooo don't you have any freaking idea?!!
> xxq: ??? Well then, thank you very much???

Zhou Ziheng keeps nagging Xia Xiqing the entire way, but Xia Xiqing simply pretends not to hear as he holds up the phone to film the various famous sights in the old city of Florence, like a serious and responsible tour guide. While he's at it, he also throws in a bunch of general knowledge of art. The landscape of Florence in the afternoon is radiant and enchanting. Red-tiled roofs of houses of varying heights glisten under the sunlight, as though they've been brushed over with a glossy layer of sweet syrup.

"Call me hubby." Zhou Ziheng bumps Xia Xiqing with his elbow. "Quick."

"Dream on."

"Come on, just once."

"Nope."

"Pretty please."

"I'll do it if you do it too."

"Hubby..."

Xia Xiqing pinches Zhou Ziheng's cheek in satisfaction and calls out sweetly, "Hubby!"

After strolling aimlessly, the two of them wind up back at the Cathedral of Florence. Xia Xiqing holds up the phone and introduces the fans to the grand, distinctive dome of the church, along with the magnificent "Gates of Paradise." When they walk over to the other side, they find a band doing an impromptu performance. Standing beside the keyboard, the lead singer is singing a classic Italian love song. The fans can't sit still upon seeing this.

> I want to hear Xiqing-*gege* sing!!!!
> Me too!!! xqgg, please!!!

> xqgg, please grant this humble wish of mine!!!

> xqgg look at me!!! It's my birthday today. Can you sing me a song??? Please!!

> Not again hahahahaha

Although this looks very much like a trick, it still works on Xia Xiqing nonetheless. "Really? Happy birthday."

> I want to hear *gege* sing!!!

Zhou Ziheng also starts to egg him on from the side. As if that isn't enough, he takes the chance to go up to the band after the lead singer is done with a song and communicates with them in English in the hope that they can let his lover sing a song. The band agrees readily and even starts clapping and cheering. Xia Xiqing has no choice but to brace himself and walk over. Zhou Ziheng takes the phone, moves a few meters away, and aims it at Xia Xiqing, who's standing in position in front of the keyboard.

Xia Xiqing adjusts the mic stand and smiles, deliberately avoiding Zhou Ziheng's camera as he lowers his head, and placing ten slender fingers on the keys of the keyboard, he quietly takes a breath.

In front of the church, long harmonious notes begin to flow from the simple sound equipment.

> OMG Xiqing-*gege* plays the keyboard!!

> Too cool, omg. xqgg's hands are too pretty!

His eyes are lowered. At the end of the last bar of the prelude, he starts to sing; it's an Italian song. The timbre of his voice, which is gentle to begin with, appears all the more stirring and rousing when coupled with the soothing rhythm of the music.

Zhou Ziheng can't understand the lyrics, but just standing quietly from afar watching him and listening to his voice alone is enough to make his heart stir.

Prendimi così, prendimi così dal niente.
(Take me away like this, take me away like this from nothing)
Tienimi così, tienimi così per sempre.
(Hold me like this, hold me like this for eternity.)
Notte prendi i sogni infranti,
(You take away the broken dreams in the midst of the night)
E fanne stelle scintillanti,
(And turn them into brilliant stars.)
Fammi guardare le mie rose
(So that I can see my roses)
Arrampicarsi fino al sole,
(Reach toward the sun.)
Ora che piove
(Now that it rains)
E l'alba verrà fino a me,
(And the sun will rise and come to me)
Sì, arriverà anche per me
(Yes, it will come for me)
E quando verrà lei mi dirà:
(And when it comes, it will say to me:)
Ero già qua, io ero già qua.
("I'm already here, I'm already here.")

His voice reverberates through the large open space outside the church, attracting the pedestrians and tourists passing by. Every one of them halts in their tracks to watch this beautiful young man from the East in silent appreciation.

As the last note falls, the flocks of white doves before the church suddenly disperse. Xia Xiqing lifts his head and watches them fly away freely into the clear skies of Florence.

Many people start to clap for him, and it's only then that Xia Xiqing comes back to his senses. Although he's a little nervous, he isn't the type of person to shy away from strangers, so he smiles with his head lowered and gives everyone a slight bow. Then, with his hands in his pockets, he saunters up to Zhou Ziheng's side.

"Your singing is so beautiful."

Zhou Ziheng's frank and sincere praises always have a knack for making Xia Xiqing feel good. He arches his eyebrow and says, "Of course."

"A pity that I can't understand it; I wanna learn Italian." Zhou Ziheng lets loose a long sigh. Then he suddenly recalls something, and asks, "There are a few phrases that keep repeating, like..." He attempts to pronounce the line in the lyrics. "*Ero già qua*, what does it mean?"

Xia Xiqing smiles, the expression in his eyes is clear and innocent as he gazes at Zhou Ziheng and answers slowly, "I'm already here."

Zhou Ziheng's heart suddenly skips a beat. The scorching heat of the midsummer light feels searing on his chest.

"Then...what does the *prendimi così* at the beginning mean?"

Just then, as if by mysterious chance, the church bell starts to toll again, like a foreshadow to the uncontrollable pounding of his heart.

Xia Xiqing extends a hand to him.

"Take me away."

E.07

Vanilla & Gunpowder

The third homeroom of grade eleven has a new transfer student.

It happens to be raining heavily that day, trapping Xia Xiqing, who was planning to climb the fences and skip class, in the classroom. He rests his chin in his hand and stares idly out the window at the downpour. The tightly-shut windows blend the scents of pheromones together into a peculiar smell, making him dizzy.

The homeroom teacher pushes the door open, adding another whiff of sandalwood scent to the mix as if a Buddha has entered the room. In the last row, Xia Xiqing stretches out both of his hands and sprawls over the table sleepily.

But in just that one instant, he straightens up.

This scent...so damn good.

It's the sweetest and most delicious scent Xia Xiqing has ever smelled. It's richer than the best vanilla cake in town, and having been soaked by the rain outside, it feels moist, and is at once both innocent and sensual.

The best part is that this is the glandular scent of an Omega.

Xia Xiqing, who's started to harbor wicked thoughts, cranes his neck twice from side to side and locks his eyes on the open door.

"I'd like to introduce a new classmate to everyone." The homeroom teacher pushes up the glasses on the bridge of his nose and turns to look at the door. "Come on in."

Before this, Xia Xiqing has always found their school uniform decent; its greatest failure is not in its ugliness, but in its blandness. White short-sleeved shirt with long black pants—nothing worth mentioning at all. But the moment the transfer student walks in, Xia Xiqing's exacting and demanding aesthetic meter shoots through the roof.

The newcomer seems about six feet and three inches, maybe more, and his long legs are wrapped in the black school uniform pants. But for an art student like Xia Xiqing, who comes with his own X-ray vision, he's no different from being fully naked. The newcomer is good-looking, with a slender figure and a tall stature, but the two steps he takes into the classroom are very prim and proper, not so much like a model walking a runway, but more like a soldier goose-stepping in Tian'anmen Square. The dude's side profile is also a true masterpiece—high nose bridge, high brows, and prominent bones; like a mixed-blood child.

The instant he turns around, Xia Xiqing can't help but arch his eyebrows and whistle inwardly to himself. Heaven must have, knowing his taste, specifically delivered this guy to his doorstep.

Most of his hair is wet, with water droplets pooling at the tips of his hair and trickling along his temples to his angular jawline, where they dangle as if they were about to drop at any second. His white shirt, drenched by the rain, clings to his body along with the humid summer air, barely revealing the muscular contours of his chest and abdomen.

With just one glance, Xia Xiqing has already sketched out in his mind how this person would look when he's sweating profusely under certain unspeakable situations.

As an Alpha, the ones Xia Xiqing likes best are not the weak, delicate Omegas. They don't appeal to him at all. He enjoys clashing and conquering. To put it bluntly, he likes the feisty ones.

"Hello, everyone. I'm Zhou Ziheng." He takes a piece of chalk from the homeroom teacher's hand and writes his name on the blackboard. His brooding, magnetic voice is like music to the ears. It reverberates throughout the quiet classroom, like a stone cast into the lake, stirring up ripples that barge straight into Xia Xiqing's heart.

The homeroom teacher adds, "Classmate Zhou here skipped a grade, so he's a little younger than everyone else. Everyone, please take care of him and help him integrate quickly into our Class Three."

Tch, the new kid is just a little boy. Xia Xiqing feels even more satisfied now.

Zhou Ziheng flashes a friendly enough smile and bows to his fellow students, "Nice to meet you, please take care of me."

Just as he's about to straighten up, a loud thud rings out as something falls to the ground. The clatter breaks the silence in the classroom. Zhou Ziheng straightens up and looks toward the sound along with everyone else. His gaze falls upon the seat by the window in the last row.

On that seat is a boy who can almost be described as

pretty. He looks apologetic as he raises a hand to scratch the back of his head in embarrassment and gives them a little smile. His voice is soft, like the only fluffy dry cloud that has escaped from the raining skies.

"Sorry, I accidentally bumped into it." He repeatedly bows his head and apologizes to everyone in a deferential manner. Finally, he lifts his head as his seemingly innocent eyes meet Zhou Ziheng's profoundly deep ones. "Sorry about that. Classmate Zhou."

The homeroom teacher coughs. "Be careful next time." Then he turns his head to Zhou Ziheng. "Oh yeah, just so happens that Xia Xiqing is the only one in class who doesn't have a desk-mate. You can take the seat beside him. Both of you are tall, so if you sit at the back, it won't affect the other students."

Xia Xiqing... Zhou Ziheng repeats this name silently to himself. He nods, then holding onto the bag hanging from his left shoulder, he strides over to the last row.

Bending to pick up his colored pencils one at a time, Xia Xiqing feels the heavenly aroma getting closer and closer to him with each breath he takes, its enchanting allure increasing in intensity until a pair of clean, white sneakers appears in his vision, and a lithe shadow envelopes him. A slender, spotless hand helps him pick up the last colored pencil from the floor, it's a red one. Xia Xiqing lifts his head and straightens up in his chair. He sees Zhou Ziheng half-crouching, handing him the colored pencil as if he's handing him a red rose in full bloom.

"Thanks."

Xia Xiqing reaches out to take it, using the opportunity to brush his finger against Zhou Ziheng's—a brief, light touch that barely lingers. But the other person barely reacts and merely gives a nod of his head before silently pulling out the chair beside Xia Xiqing to sit. He then quietly opens his school bag and takes out a black pencil case and a blue notebook.

He sits beside Xia Xiqing like this, the sweet scent of vanilla sending Xia Xiqing's heart fluttering.

"Let's begin the lesson. Take out the weekly test paper we didn't finish going through yesterday." The homeroom teacher cleared his throat. "Where did we stop yesterday?"

"Question thirteen!"

"No, we already finished question thirteen."

"I think we've moved onto the key topics?"

Although Xia Xiqing's heart is beginning to stir, he can tell that this Zhou Ziheng isn't someone who will rise to the bait that easily. The scent of pheromone on him is indeed sweet, but he's different from many of the other Omegas; he seems to be a little hard to get close to.

Could he have been hit on one time too many? After all, with the population explosion these days, high-quality Alphas and Omegas are creams of the crop that are in great demand. There are always many people falling over themselves to pounce on them.

Never mind if he's an Alpha. With the disparity in physical strength, he's unlikely to be at the mercy of the Omegas. But it's a different story if it's reversed. If an Omega were to encounter a pack of difficult Alphas, he would have nowhere to flee, and could only subject himself to their mercy.

So...he totally understands the Omega who radiates a do-not-approach aura; after all, it may be considered as a kind of self-defense. In this kind of rigorous mate-seeking environment, Xia Xiqing makes use of his natural harmless appearance to disguise his Alpha identity to get close to

✦ . 176 ‖‖

those hard-to-hit-on Omegas.

However...Xia Xiqing casts a sidelong glance at the person beside him. There doesn't seem to be that many Omegas who are this tall...or are there?

In order to establish a foundational friendship with Zhou Ziheng as soon as possible so he can have a basis from which he can launch a future attack, Xia Xiqing takes out his tried-and-tested feigning skill and pushes the test paper before him toward the middle where both desks meet.

"Let's look together." A sweet smile materializes on the face of this beautiful angel. So very amicable. So well-behaved.

Zhou Ziheng looks right at the face before him, without the slightest hint of evasion. He finds it weird and perplexing. This Omega who keeps making friendly overtures gives him the feeling that there's something amiss, but he can't exactly pinpoint it either. He has a pretty face and a fair complexion, with deep double eyelids and glistening black eyes, the corners of which gently slope upward. Zhou Ziheng's gaze slides along his exquisite, straight nose to its tip. There's a tiny little mole. He overlooked it earlier when he saw Xia Xiqing across the classroom.

The pheromone of this Xia Xiqing person is rose-scented, and a very intense scent at that. Although this scent isn't uncommon among Omegas, it differs greatly from all the roses he's smelled before. Zhou Ziheng can't exactly say what's so different about it.

"Aren't you going to look?" Xia Xiqing's full lips part slightly, like ripe, red berries, revealing a moist, vividly-colored, and faintly discernible tongue within.

Zhou Ziheng's Adam apple bobs imperceptibly. He flashes a smile. "I am. Thanks."

Naturally, when they look at the same piece of test paper, they have to sit a little closer...a little *more* closer. Xia Xiqing pretends to lean against Zhou Ziheng inadvertently, his right foot stepping on the side leg of his chair, and his elbow on his right knees popping up his pointed chin with his palm.

His pretty peach blossom eyes drift from the equations on the test paper to Zhou Ziheng's nape. The latter's head is bowed, and there are protruding vertebrae at the end of his smoothly-contoured nape.

Zhou Ziheng can sense him looking at his own nape. He's sure of it, but he doesn't say a word or look up. His eyes are fixed on the test paper. He can't understand why an Omega would have the bizarre fetish of staring at someone's nape. But this Omega seems very smart, Zhou Ziheng thinks to himself as he looks at the test paper filled with checkmarks for correct answers. He likes smart people. No matter what, smart people are always fun and interesting.

"Oh, right."

Looking as if he's just remembered something, Xia Xiqing puts his head down and rummages through his desk drawer. His back arches as he bends over to look. Zhou Ziheng finally takes his focused gaze off the test paper to glance at Xia Xiqing beside him. This posture stretches the white shirt on Xia Xiqing's back taut, completely outlining his protruding spine. His shoulder blades move in tandem with his movements, looking as if wings would break out of them in the next instance like a butterfly breaking out of its cocoon. Holding his breath, Zhou Ziheng's gaze follows the contour up and falls upon that slender nape of his. So much fairer and cleaner than the nape of many female Omegas.

The instant Xia Xiqing straightens up, Zhou Ziheng shifts his gaze away and back onto the test paper. His heartbeat is erratic and still stirs restlessly for a long while after that.

"Here you go." Xia Xiqing hands him a packet of tissue. Seeing as Zhou Ziheng isn't taking them, he pulls out a piece and stuffs it into Zhou Ziheng's hand. "Wipe yourself. Don't catch a cold."

Zhou Ziheng clutches the tissue tightly. "Thank you."

"You're welcome. We're desk-mates, yeah?"

The homeroom teacher is writing a tediously long proof on the blackboard. The heavy rain outside the window has yet to stop, but instead, seems to be getting heavier.

"The teacher said your name just now: Xia. Xi. Qing..." Zhou Ziheng enunciates each word, giving a special flavor that makes Xia Xiqing's already restless heart even harder to suppress. Unable to help himself, he licks his own lips.

Zhou Ziheng turns to him. "Which Qing character is it?"

Qing as in unclear, is what first pops up in Xia Xiqing's mind. He smiles, his expression is as gentle as an inopportune spring breeze. "Qing as in clear."

Zhou Ziheng nods twice. "Nice name."

"Ditto." The corners of Xia Xiqing's lips lift, although the smile has already taken on a different flavor.

Two people, each with their own agenda, arrived at some kind of tacit resonance by some fluke, like a flame leaping into the sea, or a glacier plunging into the lava.

Doesn't make sense. But very exciting nonetheless.

It's only during the evening self-study period that the rain outside subsides a little. Zhou Ziheng has been keeping his head down as he diligently works on the math questions. After going through two pages of rough calculations, he finally finishes his math homework. The person beside him has excused himself to go to the restroom ten minutes ago and has yet to return. Zhou Ziheng's neck feels sore, so he rolls it and leans back for a moment. The boy in the seat before him accidentally bumps into his desk, knocking over a bottle of red ink on the corner of Xia Xiqing's desk.

Zhou Ziheng thinks of Xia Xiqing's cordial and amicable manner earlier and hurries to pick up the glass bottle. He uses the tissue Xia Xiqing has given him earlier to press down on the ink before it spreads on the desk, using up an entire packet before he more or less remedies the situation. However, now his fingers are all stained with ink, the rose color seeping into the loops and whorls on his fingers. Zhou Ziheng decides to go wash his hands before the ink dries completely, and spray some more Omega pheromone perfume on himself while he's at it.

After raising his hand and asking the class leader for permission to leave, Zhou Ziheng leaves the classroom. He walks through a corridor and comes to the men's restroom at the far end. He's only just gotten closer when he hears a familiar voice coming from within. As a new transfer student, there aren't that many people whose voice he would find familiar. Desk-mate Xia Xiqing is one of them.

"I don't know why you're still pestering me." His tone has changed; even the timbre of his voice is different. It's completely different from the angelic, meek, and affable person Zhou Ziheng has seen earlier. This voice sounds impatient, blunt, and even pointedly sharp. "Or is my rejection not obvious enough? Isn't it a little unsightly of you to be hanging on me like this, hmm?"

The tone of this "hmm" twists and turns, sounding wicked to the max. Zhou Ziheng despises peeping and eavesdropping on others, but it seems pretty strange to simply leave like this now, as if he's afraid of Xia Xiqing or something.

Another person's voice comes from within. It's soft and

weak. One can tell that this is an Omega just from the sound of it.

"But I really do like you..."

"Oh, you like me, huh." Xia Xiqing mimics this person's tone as he repeats the words, then lets out a disdainful snort. "You like me, but you get tangled up with another person. Tch, your 'like' is really worth peanuts."

"Xiqing, I..."

"Get out." Xia Xiqing's voice grows frosty. It's decisive and to the point, as if he's unwilling to say another word.

Zhou Ziheng knows that if he doesn't leave now, it'll be too late, but his legs somehow refuse to listen. The next second, a skinny, pale guy with a sweet and soft raspberry pheromone scent walks out of the washroom. He quickly lowers his head when he bumps into Zhou Ziheng and leaves as though he's fleeing. Zhou Ziheng doesn't turn to look at him. He hears the sound of gurgling water from the washroom.

He walks in, and Xia Xiqing looks up from where he's washing his hands carefully, like a meticulous killer cleaning up the crime scene after a murder. His expression is frosty in the instant he lifts his eyes, but seeing the other person in the mirror, it suddenly changes. A hint of surprise flashes through those eyes, although it subsides very quickly. He smiles, turning back into that friendly desk-mate.

"What a coincidence." Xia Xiqing's voice is back to being gentle.

Zhou Ziheng stares at him in the mirror with a frosty expression and says nothing.

"You heard us?" Xia Xiqing keeps his composure, as though he isn't the one who said all those words earlier. He lifts his dripping wet hands to fasten the collar that was yanked open. One button at a time, as a drop of water trickles down his neck and comes to a stop at his protruding collarbone.

"I was going to continue pretending for a while."

Xia Xiqing turns and moves toward Zhou Ziheng one step at a time. Then he hooks the opened door with his foot and slams it shut. He places a hand on Zhou Ziheng's chest and pushes him against the door, his wet hand leaving a palm mark on Zhou Ziheng's white shirt, near his heart on the left. His hand is clearly cold, yet it's searing hot inside.

"I suppose you can tell," Xia Xiqing speaks bluntly with his utterly harmless face. "That I've taken a shine to you."

As he draws closer, Zhou Ziheng realizes that the earlier granular scent of an Omega on him is suddenly gone. On the contrary, in the rapidly shrinking pocket of air between them, he catches a whiff of an extremely pungent tobacco smell, mixed with a sweet-smelling scent of roses. So that's what his pheromones really smell like.

"I'm an Alpha. You guessed right." Xia Xiqing is frightfully direct. "I was only feigning being an Omega to get close to high-quality Omegas and make them mine."

As he speaks, his face draws closer, little by little. Misty eyes wander to Zhou Ziheng's lips. "For example, one of high quality such as..."

All of a sudden, Xia Xiqing furrows his brows slightly. That's not right. His granular scent is so faint.

Before he can finish the rest of his sentence, a tremendous force pushes him up against the icy-cold tiled wall before he can react. Zhou Ziheng's arms tighten around Xia Xiqing's waist, making it impossible for Xia Xiqing to resist.

He lowers his head and curls the corners of his lips slightly, and the scent of pheromones intensifies. The sweet scent of vanilla hasn't yet dissipated, but another scent that has been suppressed and concealed gradually emerges and envelopes Xia Xiqing. It's the lingering smell of gunpowder after a shot has been fired.

"What a coincidence." Zhou Ziheng grasps Xia Xiqing's chin and caresses Xia Xiqing's full, ample lips with his thumb, staining the corner of his lips with the rose-colored ink on his fingers. "I was also feigning."

The dynamic between Xia Xiqing and Zhou Ziheng has been staying within a very strange critical range. At first, they both thought they had taken a fancy to a top-notch Omega. Who would've known that both would turn out to be testosterone-charged Alphas the moment the veil was lifted?

This society is both normal and weird at the same time. The rapid expansion of the population has led the quality of genes to become more and more normally distributed, and high-quality Alphas and Omegas have become the minority. Under the huge pressure of choosing a mate for marriage and breeding, the Alphas, who originally stood at the top of the discrimination chain, have become the choice of many Omegas who want to improve their genes. Zhou Ziheng grew up in an environment where there were more O's than A's, and since elementary school, he's been harassed by a truckload of Omegas and even their parents. Unable to endure the harassment and unwilling to use his Alpha advantage to exert pressure on others, Zhou Ziheng's only option was to transfer schools. Because of this, he even tried to cover up his Alpha identity. At first, he wanted to pretend to be a Beta, but on second thought, he felt that Omega was the better choice to cut off unwanted attention. Besides, no Alpha would dare touch him anyway.

One pretends to be an O because he wants to harass others, while the other pretends to be an O because he's afraid of being harassed. What's more, they just happen to catch each other's eyes the very first time they meet. That's how strange this world is.

But how can two Alphas be together? No way.

Even so, neither of them plans to just drop it. Others only say that Alphas have the desire to conquer only when it comes to their own Omega. But for them, when two possessive Alphas meet, the thrill of their conquest is doubled.

In front of others, desk-mates Xia Xiqing and Zhou Ziheng will always pretend to be chummy. They put up a first-rate act, but they are always trying to trip the other up with underhanded means, both in the open and on the quiet.

During physics class, Xia Xiqing bends over his desk as he draws. Zhou Ziheng finds him particularly amusing. He acts like a floppy ragdoll day after day. When he's sitting at his desk, he's either sprawling or leaning, and never just sitting properly. He never pays proper attention in class either, but scores well on every test.

"I'll get someone to answer this question." The physics teacher stands at the podium and sweeps his eyes across the students. Everyone bows their head to avoid the teacher's gaze. "Well then...how about Xia Xiqing."

Completely immersed and absorbed in his personal creative endeavors, Xia Xiqing doesn't even hear the teacher calling him. Not long after, someone kicks his chair. Xia Xiqing turns to the perpetrator sitting beside him with a puzzled look and demands in a lowered voice, "What was that for?"

"Xia Xiqing? Why are you still not getting up to answer the question?

"Huh?" Xia Xiqing blinks. He sees the shadow of a smile on Zhou Ziheng's face, and when he turns his head, he sees the stern-looking physics teacher at the podium. Finally, he slowly rises to his feet, continuing his act even in the face of death. "Sir, I didn't hear you earlier."

The physics teacher has one hand behind his back and the other hand holding up a physics workbook, a pair of thick lenses sit drooping on the bridge of his nose. The tiny, astute eyes size up Xia Xiqing from above the frames. "Then tell me, what's your answer to this question?"

How would I know? Xia Xiqing is completely stupefied. He doesn't even know what question the teacher is asking about. He glances at the desk-mate beside him out of the corner of his eye. In any case, he was the one who tipped him off, so he might as well help him, right? In for a penny, in for a pound, as they say.

But Zhou Ziheng simply sits facing the blackboard, with his back straight as a ramrod, like an attentive, studious student. He doesn't even spare a glance at him.

No doubt this guy is doing it on purpose, Xia Xiqing thinks to himself. "Uh..."

The girl in front of him is kind enough to turn and remind him in a whisper, "The last multiple-choice question on page fifty-six."

Xia Xiqing is rather grateful, but he would've been even more grateful if she told him the answer as well. He bows his head and flips to the question. Xia Xiqing is actually pretty good at physics, but to ask him to do a question that requires calculation in such a short amount of time...

I can't afford to make a fool of myself. Rather than being watched by the entire class, he might as well humble himself before Zhou Ziheng and ask him for help. After some mental preparation, Xia Xiqing reaches out with his foot and kicks the leg of Zhou Ziheng's chair.

"Hey."

He has to kick twice before Zhou Ziheng turns to look at him.

"Hmm?"

Xia Xiqing signals to him with a look and points at the question. "What's the answer?"

Zhou Ziheng imitates him and props up his chin with his palm, then slowly enunciates his words one at a time. "Beg me."

Beg?! Xia Xiqing's eyes widen in a glare. *Are you kidding me? Beg him?*

Zhou Ziheng slowly lifts his eyebrow. "The teacher can't wait."

What rotten luck.

The physics teacher starts hurrying him. "Xia Xiqing, do you have the answer yet?"

Zhou Ziheng is still idly twirling his pen. It's been less than a minute, but Xia Xiqing feels as if it's been ages. The time stretches on, and each frame lingers for a very, very long time. He can't wait any longer.

Fuck this.

Zhou Ziheng finally compromises at the very last second and answers softly, "B."

Xia Xiqing tilts his head up and says with confidence, "I don't know. I was distracted earlier."

The physics teacher shakes his head in disappointment. "Does having good grades mean you can stop paying attention in class? Your attitude has been very problematic lately. You can't become complacent just because of your current grades. Learning is like rowing a boat against the current.

If you don't keep pushing forward, you fall behind." The teacher sighs after his big speech. "Sit down. Come to my office later during the break."

Xia Xiqing nods and sits. After the teacher turns his back to the class, he gives Zhou Ziheng the middle finger.

And so the feud between them is set.

The tide turns during English class on Friday morning.

"I'll ask a student to read this text next." The English teacher paces slowly on the podium. Eventually, his gaze lands on the last row.

"Zhou Ziheng, stand and read it for everyone."

On hearing this, Zhou Ziheng stands and picks up his English textbook with his right hand while bracing himself against the desk with his left. He begins to read, and Xia Xiqing, who's sitting beside him, turns to look at him with interest.

Good-looking. Pleasant voice. Long legs and a good figure. Has a brain to boot. No matter how he looks at it, this guy totally ticks all the boxes in his aesthetic checklist.

What a pity he's an Alpha. No fun.

After finishing the first paragraph, Zhou Ziheng suddenly senses an itch on the side of his thigh. He looks down and sees a slender, fair finger slowly tracing its way down along the seam of his pants. Just as he lowers his head, Xia Xiqing lifts his head to look at him. Their eyes meet, and Xia Xiqing flashes him a wicked smile with that innocent face.

Zhou Ziheng continues to read the text at an even pace with calm and composure. From the outside, there doesn't seem to be anything wrong, but he's very well aware that his heart is already descending into chaos.

That finger starts to become even more rampant. It wanders to his hipbone before turning to go upward. The fingertip moves slowly against the texture of the fabric, and where it passes feels hot, as though it's on fire.

Xia Xiqing enjoys this process of teasing. When he thinks about the last time Zhou Ziheng embarrassed him before the whole class, he feels even more exhilarated. Just as his finger is about to turn down once again, a hand grabs him by his wrist and forcefully pulls his mischievous hand away from Zhou Ziheng's straight, long leg.

What a good actor. Xia Xiqing shoots a glance up. Zhou Ziheng is still reading aloud calmly and seriously. Xia Xiqing's wrist is bony and thin, but Zhou Ziheng controls the strength of his grip just right. In fact, his grip could even be said to be loose. Ever since becoming desk-mates with him, Xia Xiqing is growing to realize just how strange this person is. On the surface, he seems aggressive and even a little cold, but he's always inadvertently revealing a great kindness that runs counter to his image. During the afternoon break on Saturday, Xia Xiqing was walking out of the school with his bicycle when he caught sight of Zhou Ziheng squatting behind the gymnasium, secretly feeding the stray cats. He can't bear to let the stray cats starve, just like he can't bear to grab his wrist with too much force?

Sensing that Xia Xiqing is behaving a little, Zhou Ziheng thinks he can let go of his hand now. However, the next instant, his own hand ends up being grabbed by Xia Xiqing. Long, slender fingers forcibly insert themselves between his own, turning a restraining grip into an ambiguous hand-holding with interlocking fingers. Zhou Ziheng tries to break free, but Xia Xiqing's strength is stronger than he expected, and refuses to let go no matter what.

Everyone in the class listens to Zhou Ziheng's reading in silence. Sweat gradually soaks through Zhou Ziheng's back, making his shirt cling tightly to his back, just like Xia Xiqing's persistent hand that he can't manage to shake off. He feels as though he's starting to hallucinate. The scent of roses is growing stronger and thicker, and it almost messes up his mind and screws up his eyes until he can't even get a clear look at a single letter before him.

In June, even the wind is scalding hot; so much that he feels like it will melt the glass windows and surge up to envelop him. To put a veil over this dangerous and forbidden moment; to turn the two hand-holding youths into everlasting amber.

As he finishes reading the last sentence, Zhou Ziheng feels vaguely relieved.

"Excellent. You may sit."

Xia Xiqing releases his hand the instant the teacher speaks, ending this wicked game as he looks up at the blackboard, pretending to be a well-behaved student. Zhou Ziheng sits. He can't say why, but his heart is beating a little abnormally. He opens his left palm on his knee under the desk, and looks down at it without a sound. The air conditioning cools the sweat on his palm, a side-effect of the hand-holding; the gaps between his fingers are red— rose-colored red. These are the marks left behind from being tightly held.

How strange. It's as if it's not this hand that was tightly grasped by Xia Xiqing, but instead, this heart, pounding violently from that oppressive sensation. It's at this moment that a crazy thought pops into Zhou Ziheng's head: *Wanna take a whiff of his acrid tobacco scent.*

Time passes very quickly, like a faucet someone has forgotten to turn off; once it's drained, it's gone. Their relationship is still peaceful on the surface, although they still pit themselves against the other in secret. Both have placed the other in a very special position in their hearts, but the way it seems to outsiders, neither of them gives a hoot about the other. As time passes, they come to establish a special kind of relationship.

The intra-school basketball game is the last activity before the holiday season begins. Although Zhou Ziheng is a transfer student, his reputation as the tallest Omega in history made him the focus of the basketball team. The captain of the basketball team is an always-grinning Alpha with a pair of fangs. He appears to be Xia Xiqing's relative. The scent of his pheromones is very unique—it smells of cedar. More than once, he's come to Zhou Ziheng to ask him to join the basketball team, but Zhou Ziheng is busy with the physics competition and always turns him down.

Not two days later, the basketball team's very quiet and gentle-looking manager also comes to persuade him. This guy is even more interesting. He looks like an Omega, but turns out he's a Beta, whose pheromone scent is so faint one can hardly smell it, almost like iced lime water.

Everyone has tried to persuade him, except one of the team's top players, Xia Xiqing, who simply refuses to beg him. Zhou Ziheng bumped into them once by chance in the cafeteria, where he saw the three of them eating together.

He passed by them with his meal tray, and heard Xia Xiqing retorting sarcastically, "What a waste of that height, right, Chen-Chen?"

Xu Qichen looked a little embarrassed. "Xiqing, don't..."

"Don't pay him any attention." Xia Zhixu didn't even bat an eyelid. "Or he'll drag you into it."

Zhou Ziheng glanced at Xia Xiqing, walked to the table behind them, and sat. As he dug in, he heard Xia Xiqing talk with a sting in his words about the basketball team, as well as those bullying jerks from the third-year basketball team. It suddenly occurred to Zhou Ziheng that Xia Xiqing also seems to show his real self in front of these two people. This made him uncomfortable; by that, he means his heart.

He thought that he was the only one who knew this person's true colors. But it was only then that he realized he isn't that one and only. What's even more ludicrous is that these two people are his friends, and yet he can't find a single proper identity to define himself. This ambiguity and lack of definition is comparable to torture.

Fellow desk-mates? Zhou Ziheng wonders if this is considered an appropriate relationship. But very quickly, he vetoes it. It isn't that it's inappropriate, but that he doesn't want them to be just...that.

The day of the basketball match between the second-year and third-year students happens to coincide with the on-campus mock test before Zhou Ziheng's competition. The head of the physics department organized all the potential talents together to participate in the mock test in the multimedia classroom. While heading to the test, Zhou Ziheng bumps into a red jersey-clad Xia Xiqing in the hallway. The contrast of red against the color of his complexion makes him glow under the sunlight. He's also wearing a red sports headband, giving him an air of rarely seen vigor and vitality; even his eyes are shining.

Such a shame that he isn't an Omega. Otherwise, he could've given birth to a beautiful baby. Zhou Ziheng is startled by this thought. He lowers his eyes and makes to walk away, but Xia Xiqing calls out to him.

"Hey."

Zhou Ziheng stops and turns to look at him.

"If we lose today," Xia Xiqing scowls at him with that face so exceedingly beautiful that Zhou Ziheng finds it a pity. "I'll never be done with you."

Maybe he thinks he looks like a little tiger right now? Zhou Ziheng is so amused that he almost burst out laughing. For some reason, the way Xia Xiqing looks as he puts on a show of power is simply too adorable.

"You won't lose."

In a rare moment, Zhou Ziheng's voice loses its usual aggressiveness that has been evident during all those times they butt heads with one another. It becomes low, with a hint of gentleness. Xia Xiqing's heart and senses come to a momentary halt as Zhou Ziheng's words tug his train of thought astray, back to the day when he saw Zhou Ziheng feeding the cats behind the gymnasium.

He finally remembers why he can't get that scene out of his mind. Because it was at that one dusk when he saw Zhou Ziheng crouching by the grass, when the bell in the school's abandoned clock tower chimed low and heavy, the sound reverberating through the twilight and sending a charge of electricity through his body. Just like now, this moment when he hears Zhou Ziheng speak.

This isn't an easy match. The third-year team is full of strong and sturdy Alphas. These guys are all skilled, but their conduct on the basketball court is just as shitty as their personalities. They belittle the Omegas in particular, and there are quite a number of Omegas in the second-year team. In the first half of the game alone they have two Omegas on the court, even though one of them is a fake.

Xia Xiqing is the small forward on the team, and as the small forward, his job is to score. If a basketball team dares to give the role of the small forward to an Omega, it has

to be because the captain is privy to the inside story of his disguise, but also because Xia Xiqing is indeed the most suitable candidate. Perhaps he isn't the small forward who has the highest scoring rate, but he's definitely the small forward who can play fancy enough to upset the other party's morale.

The match has only just begun when the ball is stolen by the center forward captain of the second-year team. It hasn't been long since the match started, and they are already getting off to a good start. The popularity of the double-Xia Duo was so overwhelming that even their third-year female seniors are switching sides to cheer for the two of them.

"Xia Xiqing! Fighting! Xia Zhixu! Go for it!"

"Xia Xiqing! I love you!"

"What? He's an Omega too!"

"I don't care! I want him!"

"They kinda look good together!"

"The captain's lawful waifu is right over there, kay, that Beta!"

Seeing the second-year team scoring one after another, the strapping tall third-year guys can't sit still anymore and start to assume the tactic of playing pickup games. They not only bump right into the other team, but starts to play dirty as well. A feint leads the defending Xia Zhixu to follow suit and jump, and when the other party is done shooting a hoop under the time difference, Xia Zhixu ends up crashing into him from the momentum and is consequently dealt a foul.

The power forward of the third-year team is an utterly disgusting Alpha. Even his pheromones smell of photinia, a scent that Xia Xiqing loathes the most. When he sees Xia Xiqing dribbling the ball, he comes charging over. Xia Xiqing thinks he's making a grab for the ball, but the guy fakes a fall and subsequently gets Xia Xiqing a whistle by the referee as well.

With all the dirty moves made, the other team's score gradually catches up. Xia Xiqing, now gasping for breath, has been hit several times in a row, and his arm is hurting.

"What business does an Omega have to be playing basketball?"

A third-year team reserve on the bench imitates the referee and lets loose an obscene whistle, "Just go home and make babies."

On hearing this, Xia Xiqing turns back and gives him a contemptuous look. "I can play on the court. Can you? Trash." With that, he intercepts the opponent's long pass, breaks into their penalty area at lightning speed, and lands a slam dunk with one hand.

"Hot damn, this burst of power!"

"Ahhhh, Xiqing-*gege*'s so cool, I can't!"

"Oh my gosh, he's so handsome! Xia Xiqing! The most handsome Omega ever!"

Both feet land on the ground. As Xia Xiqing gasps for breath, he pushes up a handful of hair, then smiles at the person on the bench and gives him the middle finger. This slam dunk greatly boosts the morale of the second-year team, but at the same time, it also further incurs the fury and wrath of the third-year team.

The cheers outside the court rise with fervor. Even Zhou Ziheng can hear it from his seat in the multimedia room on the third floor. It's clearly so noisy that it's affecting him from performing his best, and yet, it also increases the speed at which he's answering the questions.

When all is said and done, he still kind of wants to see the way Xia Xiqing looks when he plays basketball.

"Gosh, the class's finally over. I'm going to watch the

match." Two girls pass by, and one of them says in excitement. "The second and third years are duking it out, and there are a helluva lot of handsome guys in the second-year team. You know Xia Xiqing? He's super handsome! What a pity he's an Omega."

"I heard earlier that Xia Xiqing was badly thrashed."

"What?! How is that possible?"

To think that Zhou Ziheng currently feels the same as this girl. *How is that possible?*

"The third-year team is playing so dirty. They keep resorting to dirty tricks, and the referee is corrupt too. And now they're starting to body-check the other players on purpose. If this keeps on, they might really get injured."

"Oh no, I'm going to cheer Xiqing-*gege* on..."

The girls walk further away, and soon their voices move out of hearing range. Zhou Ziheng stares at his own paper. There's still a question left on the last set of problems. His heart slams against his chest as if it's in a hurry to break free. Zhou Ziheng takes a deep breath, puts his head down, and tries his best to clear his mind. It's just a basketball game, and getting injured in sports is a common occurrence. Besides, what does this have to do with him?

"Everyone, concentrate and make sure you check your work carefully when you're done writing." The teacher walks back and forth at the front of the room. "Don't make mistakes that you shouldn't be making."

After finishing the last question, Zhou Ziheng turns the paper over and starts to check from the first question. The cheers outside the window are increasing in intensity. He hears the shouts of Xia Xiqing's name from many of the spectators, and the face in his mind becomes clearer and clearer.

If we lose today...

The face that spoke such harsh words to him.

If he loses today.

A bird standing on the railing of the corridor outside the window suddenly flaps its wings and flies to the very center of the crowd. Standing in the middle with the ball in his hands, Xia Xiqing is facing a pincer attack by two people. His neck has turned red from the strenuous exercise, and his eyes dart back and forth as he tries to find an opening to break through the defense. He reaches out and fakes a pass to the center forward, and just as the two defending opponents are about to intercept the ball, they see only a flash of his arms before he's already under the basket.

The eyes of the opposing side's forward turn red when he sees Xia Xiqing barging in like this. Xia Xiqing lifts his feet and extends his arms, ready to do a layup, when he feels a violent bump to his back with such force that it almost makes him dizzy. He's flung toward the basketball stand and crashes to the ground, scraping his knees and the front of his calves. The referee blows the whistle, and his teammates rush over to help him up. Xia Xiqing clenches his teeth and forces himself up with his hands. However, his vision is still dark, and for a long time, he can't seem to recover from the impact. Most terrifying of all, he realizes he's sprained his ankle.

"Fuck..."

"We have to swap players." Xia Zhixu says decisively.

"Swap what? And who are you going to bring up?" Xia Xiqing frowns, his temper suddenly running loose. "We'll lose no matter who the fuck I swap with!"

A calm voice suddenly rings out from the crowd. "Says who?"

Xia Xiqing looks over in the direction of the sound. A tall figure appears in his vision, which is gradually regaining clarity.

Zhou Ziheng...

Walking over from the crowd, Zhou Ziheng pulls off his uniform jacket and tosses it at the red team's reserve area. Xu Qichen, who's sitting beside the reserve player, reacts quickly and tosses the red team jersey at him. He catches the jersey with his left hand, then grabs the hem of his tank top with his right hand and pulls it off.

Xia Xiqing's heart skips two beats as he looks at those muscles rippling along with his movements.

Zhou Ziheng swiftly puts on the jersey and raises his hand to the referee to signal a change of players. Xu Qichen helps the injured Xia Xiqing off the basketball court, and as Xia Xiqing brushes past Zhou Ziheng, he hears him speak.

"Though I was hoping you'd never be done with me." The corner of Zhou Ziheng's lips curls up. "But as I said, you won't lose. I won't let you lose."

There's something really wrong with his heart. Xia Xiqing bows his head, his sweat dripping onto Zhou Ziheng's trailing shadow on the ground. He can't control himself. The moment their hormones and pheromones collide, Xia Xiqing catches a whiff of the one and only scent of gunpowder.

The third-year players never expected the second-year players to be hiding such a tall reserve. Although it gives them the heebie-jeebies to look at Zhou Ziheng, they still have to keep up appearances. Anyways, it's just another Omega.

"Fuck. What the hell do the Omegas eat these days? Each one of them is taller than the last."

"So what if he's tall?" One of the point guards standing

on the opposite side refuses to concede. "When he's in heat, doesn't he still have to bow when you tell him to?"

Zhou Ziheng's angular jaw tips up slightly, and the light from the burning red sunset illuminates his face. He holds the ball in his right hand and dribbles it on the ground. "And so what if I'm an Omega?" His tall stature and aggressive face condense into an oppressive sense of pressure. "I can still beat you into submission all the same."

The whistle sounds, and everyone throws themselves into the battle. Zhou Ziheng is extremely fast. Before everyone has time to react, he's already run straight into the penalty area with the ball. The other side doesn't even have the time to defend.

"Get back on defense! QUICKLY!"

A running jump shot. *Score.*

"Oh, right." Zhou Ziheng smiles amidst the cheers. "I'd never bow to another."

Sitting on the bench waiting to be bandaged, Xia Xiqing quietly gazes at Zhou Ziheng. His height advantage almost overwhelms everyone present. All the other party's long passes are blocked off, and the worst thing is that they can't even block him, given his strong physical ability and explosive burst of speed and power.

"Is he really an Omega...?"

"What kind of godly Omega are all these second-year students...?"

"Shit, this is a massacre."

The battle in the second half of the game becomes more intense as it goes on. Because Xia Xiqing is bumped off the court bearing an injury, the second-year players are all angry and fight with even more viciousness. Under the leadership of the captain and Zhou Ziheng, they gradually close in on the score difference. There isn't much time left. The opponent finally gets their hands on the ball and is about to charge into the paint, when Xia Zhixu rushes over to defend.

Just then, Zhou Ziheng also happens to come over, but he suddenly pipes up, "Zhixu, who's the one that injured him?"

Xia Zhixu is confused for a moment, and the opponent almost seizes the opening to move into the paint. Fortunately, Zhou Ziheng comes right in and intercepts the ball.

"Number twelve."

"Got it." Zhou Ziheng turns around and dribbles. No. 12 is guarding the backboard. Zhou Ziheng was planning to score a three-pointer, but when he sees No. 12 standing under the basket, he changes his mind and charges right for the backboard.

When No. 12 sees him preparing to shoot a layup, he jumps and reaches out in an attempt to secure a rebound. But Zhou Ziheng is merely feigning. No. 12's feet haven't even touched the ground when Zhou Ziheng tosses the ball to another Omega teammate who's also under the backboard. The teammate is very up to speed and swiftly catches the ball to make a follow-up shot. Unable to control his body from the momentum going forward, No. 12 topples over to the ground.

"It's too late for the third-year players to catch up now."

"Did you see that? The second-year team is now gunning for No. 12!"

"Awesome! The second-year team is da bomb!"

In the last few minutes, Zhou Ziheng seems to be fixing his eyes on No. 12 alone, defending against him at the same time while winding him up, almost driving No. 12 berserk. When the game is about to end, the score difference is over twenty points; there's simply no way for the other team to catch up. The other side puts up a last-ditch struggle, but their long pass is intercepted by Zhou Ziheng, who's standing in the middle. No. 12 is standing before him, and yet Zhou Ziheng doesn't even seem to jump; he simply just stands as straight as a ramrod and holds the ball high in his hands. Just as No. 12 leaps up in an attempt to snatch the ball away from him—

The whistle sounds.

"Game over. Second-year team wins!"

Still maintaining his pose, Zhou Ziheng takes two steps back with the ball in one hand and slams the ball over to where No. 12 is standing. The impact is so forceful that the ball bounces high up in the air, startling No. 12 into taking several steps back.

THUD—Thud—thud—

The basketball bounces lower and lower and eventually rolls far away.

Zhou Ziheng shoots a contemptuous look over, lifts a hand to wipe the sweat from his temple, and walks off the court. He wasn't planning to celebrate with his teammates, but the team manager, Xu Qichen, forcibly drags him over.

"Let's take a picture together."

Injured member Xia Xiqing is also helped over by an insistent Xu Qichen. Xia Xiqing, who isn't planning to stand in the center, hops on one leg, and with the boys jostling around, he almost falls over.

"Hey, hey, geez..."

Suddenly, a hand reaches out from behind to hold him by the elbow. Xia Xiqing turns around and comes face-to-face with Zhou Ziheng. Strangely enough, the air of hostility about him seems to have vanished in an instant. Xia Xiqing can't figure out how someone can switch their aura so quickly. After holding him steady, Zhou Ziheng naturally comes to stand beside him.

ly. After holding him steady, Zhou Ziheng naturally comes to stand beside him.

Xia Xiqing turns his face away and hears Zhou Ziheng speaking in hushed tones beside him. "Your scent is about to change soon."

Xia Xiqing doesn't need the reminder; he's well aware of it himself.

"Look at the camera—"

Xia Xiqing lifts the corners of his lips and reveals his signature fake smile. "Yours too."

After the evening self-study session, Xia Xiqing sits motionless on the bench with his injured leg as though his butt is glued to it. The students around him have all left one after the other. Even Zhou Ziheng, who's slowly packing his bag, is getting ready to leave.

"Hey." Xia Xiqing tugs on his arm to stop him. "Don't go."

Zhou Ziheng's steps stall. He looks at Xia Xiqing. "What do you want?"

Xia Xiqing always looks good when he smiles. He answers matter-of-factly, "Take me back."

"Why?" Zhou Ziheng asks in all seriousness.

"No reason. Aren't you a good person?" Xia Xiqing grips tightly with his fingers. "Since you've already helped me win the game, you might as well help me all the way."

After being pestered for a long time, Zhou Ziheng finally compromises and takes Xia Xiqing home on his bicycle. As the wheels of the bicycle bump over the uneven road, Xia Xiqing feels his heart falling over and over again, and the shaking is making him dizzy. He finds the sweet vanilla scent on him particularly fragrant.

*Suddenly want vanilla cake...*Xia Xiqing thinks to himself, grabbing onto the back seat. *No. An ice-cream.*

There's a sudden jerk as they pass over a raised metal bar on the ground, which sends all of Xia Xiqing's earlier thoughts scattering. While still in a daze, he suddenly plunges into the wild gust of wind as they hurtle downhill without warning. The wind completely shoves Zhou Ziheng's vanilla scent onto Xia Xiqing behind him. The scent is so overwhelming that Xia Xiqing is practically engulfed by the sweet fragrance.

No, he still wants Zhou Ziheng.

Following Xia Xiqing's instructions, Zhou Ziheng rides into a quiet neighborhood and arrives at the foot of an apartment building. The streetlamps seem to be broken here; it's pitch-black all around.

"We're here." Zhou Ziheng brings his bicycle to a stop and props a foot on the ground.

"Oh." Xia Xiqing hops off the bike with one foot in the air. With his back to Zhou Ziheng, he thanks him and hops two steps before stopping. The moonlight illuminates his back, casting his whole body in a faint halo of light. Or perhaps that's just Zhou Ziheng's imagination.

"What's wrong?" Seeing Xia Xiqing standing still, he adds, "Oh. You can't go up, right?" With that, he parks his bike. "I'll help you walk up."

He walks over and takes Xia Xiqing's arm, but doesn't manage to move him.

"Hey..."

The next second, Xia Xiqing turns around and kisses him.

The tobacco scent on him can no longer be masked. It gradually intensifies, bringing along with it a stubbornness that draws out Zhou Ziheng's scent of gunpowder. The two scents intertwine. Together, their scents are truly intense, like a blazing fire, or a bomb that can go off at any moment.

Amidst the intensifying pheromones, Xia Xiqing clutches the front lapels of Zhou Ziheng's school uniform as the tip of his tongue boldly pries apart the other man's teeth. All those crazy notions in his mind egg him on, goading him into kissing Zhou Ziheng without care.

Zhou Ziheng's first reaction to this sudden assault is to push him away, but he soon remembers that Xia Xiqing is injured. His hands, ready to push Xia Xiqing away, come to rest on Xia Xiqing's shoulder instead of pushing him away.

Xia Xiqing gasps for breath. His face appears pale under the moonlight, but it's a pleasant sight to behold. The scent of roses is so thick and strong, and the contrast against the tobacco makes it smell all the more sweet and sensual. It overwhelms Zhou Ziheng, making him feel feverish in the head. He sees Xia Xiqing open his mouth slightly as if he has something to say, but ultimately, he says nothing. He simply turns away stubbornly and hops his way one step at a time to the apartment building. The moonlight eventually fails to catch up with his pace, as he sinks into the darkness.

I want you. These are the words he didn't say out loud. *Don't you want me?* He didn't say these words out loud either.

The tip of his tongue seems to be bitten. The faint metallic taste of blood permeates his mouth. Xia Xiqing looks down at the first step of the staircase and prepares to start hopping his way up. He really shouldn't be such a wimp, Xia Xiqing thinks to himself. But after a while, he thinks that he really shouldn't have done it at all.

With a soundless sigh, Xia Xiqing holds on to the handrail of the stairs and is just about to hop up, when he's stopped in his tracks by a forceful grip that pulls his whole body into a warm embrace. The scent of vanilla, the assault of gunpowder, the raging hormones of adolescence—all of these encircle him firmly, making him sink deeper into them.

Zhou Ziheng's hold on him is very firm. Xia Xiqing's heartbeat quickens. but he can somehow feel that in the body that's pressed close to him, the heart is beating even faster, as if it's pounding hard onto his own.

"I want to mark you so much." Zhou Ziheng suddenly breaks the silence.

Xia Xiqing's breathing hitches; the question he never did manage to ask has received an answer. He feels Zhou Ziheng's broad palm holding his nape, slowly caressing that patch of skin that can never be marked.

His voice is also slow and deep; the warm breath puffs on Xia Xiqing's ears as the scent of gunpowder gradually intensifies. "I want to bite it, want to open up your reproductive cavity, wanna knot inside you." The way he says the last part is both gentle and obscene at the same time. "I want to sully your rose scent."

Xia Xiqing scoffs. "You're crazy. I'm not an Omega."

Zhou Ziheng strokes his neck gently. "From now on, you can be an Omega only for me."

"Why aren't *you* the one..." Before Xia Xiqing can finish his words, he sees Zhou Ziheng bend down, lean over his shoulder, and hold down his head as he bites down on his nape.

"Ah..."

His teeth pierce Xia Xiqing's skin, and blood seeps out. The scent of roses is so sweet it makes him dizzy. Zhou Ziheng knows better than anyone else that it's impossible to mark Xia Xiqing, that his pheromones can't enter Xia Xiqing's body. But the instant he bites Xia Xiqing's nape, he still has the illusion of becoming one with him, beyond mere physical flesh. It's as if this soul in his embrace has penetrated its mortal body to dissolve seamlessly into his soul.

Xia Xiqing thinks that he won't feel any emotion other than pain. They are not a perfect match made in heaven. They are diametrically opposed to one another, a pair of natural-born opponents. But the instant he's pierced, he feels pleasure and thrill swamping him. The thick scent of gunpowder from Zhou Ziheng buries him in the ruins of desire. It's as if he's died once over. Agony and elation flood mercilessly over him, like the bout of rainstorm on that day when Zhou Ziheng first showed up. It trapped him in the classroom, forcing him to encounter Zhou Ziheng.

Xia Xiqing doesn't return to his senses for a very long time, even after Zhou Ziheng's teeth release their grip on Xia Xiqing's flesh. He's been marked—it seems like he really has been marked. His rigidly straight spine, trembling fingertips, and wildly pounding heart—from now on, all of these belong to Zhou Ziheng.

Zhou Ziheng's chest rises and falls gently; his lips are still stained with his own blood. He licks it away with the tip of his tongue, and just like that, gazes down at Xia Xiqing without a word.

Xia Xiqing's thoughts finally return from his shock. He lifts his eyes to look at Zhou Ziheng. Truth be told, he doesn't know what he should say at this moment, because he finally understands his own heart, which is why he's in even more of a fluster.

"I like you."

He freezes for a moment, his eyelashes fluttering in dazed confusion. He actually wasn't expecting Zhou Ziheng to say this. But Zhou Ziheng does it anyway, and bends gently to kiss the tip of his nose.

Xia Xiqing swallows. The kiss is too much for him to take.

He looks away as uneasiness and restlessness enshroud him.

"You..." He takes a deep breath and looks into Zhou Ziheng's profoundly deep eyes. "Didn't you say that you'd never bow to another?"

The tenderness in Zhou Ziheng's eyes is like the falling rain about to pitter-patter its way into Xia Xiqing's heart.

"That's right."

"Except when I kiss you."

E.08

Sweet Treats

During their honeymoon trip to Florence, Zhou Ziheng brings his camera along and records many of their memories along the way. When he returns, he spends a few days editing, trying to make a couples vlog. However, the whole time Xia Xiqing sits right beside him, staring at him like The Boss as he edits.

"No. This kissing scene must be cut out." Xia Xiqing scoops up a spoonful of ice cream and stuffs it into his mouth. "Do you want me to trend again?"

Zhou Ziheng frowns. "You will get on the trending list whether or not this segment is cut."

"How is that the same?" Xia Xiqing pokes Zhou Ziheng in the head with a finger, then scoops up another spoonful of ice cream and brings it to Zhou Ziheng's mouth. "How can the virality of the phrase 'Zhou Ziheng Xia Xiqing's vlog' and 'Zhou Ziheng and Xia Xiqing's Hot Kiss' be compared on the same level?"

Zhou Ziheng pretends to not understand. He bites down on the spoon in Xia Xiqing's hand and makes to yank it away, but Xia Xiqing smacks him on his head to snatch the spoon back. They engage in a tug-of-war for a while, when Zhou Ziheng suddenly releases his teeth. Xia Xiqing topples over backward from the momentum, and the quick-eyed Zhou Ziheng swiftly grabs him in his arms and drops a kiss on his mouth.

He sure has a lot of tricks up his sleeve. Xia Xiqing sets the tub of ice cream on the table, wraps his arms around Zhou Ziheng's neck, and breathes into Zhou Ziheng's ear. "Stop editing." With this one move, electricity surges through Zhou Ziheng's entire body. Still, in order to put out a satisfactory public display of affection, he cruelly turns down Xia Xiqing's "invitation."

"What the fuck? To think Zhou Ziheng shut me out of the study all because of a rotten vlog!"

Xu Qichen listens to Xia Xiqing's grumblings on the other end of the phone with a smile, and tries to calm him down. "Just let him do it. Once he's done, he'll no doubt come to keep you company."

Xia Xiqing presses his head against the study door from the outside and knocks his head against it. "Let—me—in!"

Xu Qichen can't stop laughing. *Why are these two so childish when they're in love?* "Xiqing..."

The voice on the other end suddenly gets louder. "Zhou Ziheng, if you don't let me in today, I'll fuck you until you can't get out of bed! I mean what I say!"

Xu Qichen says, "Err..."

A faint voice drifts out from inside the door, "Your buddy, Zhou Ziheng, has gone deaf and can't hear you!"

Xu Qichen says, "...Have fun there, guys. I'm hanging up."

Xia Xiqing turns two circles outside the study and decides to return to his own house and draw something to calm down. Zhou Ziheng coops himself up in his room and edits for two hours before he's done, and plans to release it at an appropriate time. After that, he logs into that renowned side account of his to browse through Weibo as a means to relax. As usual, he clicks into the Self-Study ship topic, and finds himself looking at a post.

@**Makenosense:**Did zzh and xxq break up? I always felt like they were just a publicity stunt...There's been no sign of them lately, and they don't update on Weibo either. Don't flame me. I'm just making reasonable guesses here

Despite the fact that he said not to flame him, there are still many replies from fans below his post.

@**sstarriest:** Did they date each other only for your viewing pleasure? Why do trolls like you exist? Our Self-Study is currently in the honeymoon phase, okay!

@**SelfStudyGirlFighting:** This mentality of yours is really hilarious, man. So the relationship is only legit if you post on Weibo?

@**HaveYouSelfStudiedToday:** Nine out of ten of those who say "don't diss me" are massive trolls. If you're such a pro, then why don't you go and be a stellar engine? The earth is depending on you to save it

Instead of setting a date, Zhou Ziheng decides to seize the opportunity and release the vlog today. In his anxiety to make the other party eat their words, he uses his own side account to post a new, fresh-out-of-the-oven couples vlog, syncing it to Bilibili simultaneously. The fans react as if they've won the jackpot.

@**TheOneAndOnlyMamaHengOnline:** Look at what I just saw!!!

@saturnandcameralstars: The caption!!! Couples vlog!!! Omgggggg I lived to see this day!!!

@snuffedout: crais heng-heng, mama is here to see you and my daughter-in-law asdfghjkl

@Juuuuun: AHHHHH HERE I COME!!! OMG I'M DEAD!

Zhou Ziheng's editing style is actually quite minimalistic, and the filter he uses is one of refreshing simplistic style, not that different from the colors of the original image. The vlog opens with Xia Xiqing at the airport, straddling the luggage with his head down, playing with his phone. He's dressed in a very casual burgundy tracksuit, with a black fishermen's bucket hat over his recently cropped hair.

"Little rose," says Zhou Ziheng from outside the frame.

> OMG little rose!!!

> Is that what it is, little rose?!?!?! Why is zzh's voice so hot!!

> Fuck! So exciting right off the bat! I'm dead!

Xia Xiqing lifts his eyes and subconsciously tugs his hat down, probably seeing the camera in Zhou Ziheng's hand. Then he plants both feet on the ground, holds on to his luggage, and strains to turn the luggage along with himself around so that his back is to the camera. Then he sticks a middle finger at the camera.

> xqgg is sooooo cute haha!!!

> We have here a little tsundere! Let's bully him together!!!

> Oh my god, why is xqgg's face so small? It's impossible to cover up my whole face when I wear a bucket hat, and xqgg looks so great in red, crais

> Didn't anyone realize that his middle finger is pixelated?

The camera focuses on Xia Xiqing's back for a moment, while Zhou Ziheng's bright and clear laughter continues to tinkle. "Grumpy Xiqing, being a tsundere on live."

> Hahahaha there goes zzh again!

> zzh aren't you gonna console your waifu?! Why are you still meme-ing!!

> Lmfaoooo this guy!

Very quickly, the scene changes, and a makeup-less Zhou Ziheng with a pair of black-rimmed spectacles appear in the frame. He also sports a recently cropped haircut and is dressed in a simple black t-shirt. He waves at the camera with a smile, then pans it over to his left side. His own dubbed voiceover speaks up, "I don't dare to say a word here, because he's sleeping."

Xia Xiqing's sleeping face appears in the frame, his head tilted toward the other side of the window. A small airplane blanket is draped over him.

> OMG!! xqgg's sleeping face is so gorgeous!!! His eyelashes are so long!!

> The bare faces of these two really puts us girls to shame

"He looks obedient and good when he's sleeping, but you can't wake him up, because he gets all grouchy."

> Lolololol so this vlog is a "Manual to Raise Xia Xiqing"?

> Loooooooool damn girl, that was good!!!

> This is the best comment ever hahaha

> zzh is so gentle T_T

The camera pans away, and Zhou Ziheng smiles at it. He frees a hand and attempts to pull Xia Xiqing's head over to his own shoulder, but his hand has only just touched Xia Xiqing when the latter frowns and dodges him. Zhou Ziheng then reaches an arm out to hold him by the shoulder and pulls him over. With his eyes still closed, Xia Xiqing struggles for a moment before he finally instinctively rests his head on Zhou Ziheng's shoulder, nuzzling against him for a bit as he settles into a comfortable sleeping position, and continues to catch up on his sleep peacefully.

> OMG this is so spontaneous and natural, crais I'm jelly

> This PDA really makes one jelly...

> Such bliss T_T

Still holding the camera, Zhou Ziheng zooms in closer until it focuses on the tip of Xia Xiqing's nose.

> OooohhhH!! Lemme do it! I wanna kiss the tip of his nose!

> It's my lips that have the first dibs!!

The scene changes again amidst the lively background music. This time, Zhou Ziheng is sitting on a bench, dressed in a mint-colored shirt and surrounded by a flock of doves. "Fortunately, I have my camera with me at all times." He looks into the camera and presses down on his bed hair. "My hair is all ruined from sleep." Then, he flips the camera around and pans around to film the surroundings. "This is Xiqing's alma mater. Beautiful, isn't it?"

> omgomg he brought his boyfriend back to his alma mater!!! Why is xqgg so sweet?!!

> Mah gawd! I'm so touched!! Although xqgg seems to be a tsundere, he's a real sweetheart!

> Man, this place is so pretty! I want to transmigrate into the dove beside Heng-Heng!

> Oh oh oh ohhhhh!!! This outfit of Heng-Heng's is the same as the one in the candid photo taken by that blogger from last time! I've connected the dots!

> Really!!! It's that photo of them kissing in front of Florence Cathedral!!! So this is that day!!

The scene changes, showing the back view of Xia Xiqing standing in a small kitchen. He's wearing the same blue-striped shirt and shorts as the one in the photo earlier that day. There's an Italian granny dressed in a lovely floral dress beside him. Xia Xiqing is bending down and helping the granny wash tomatoes. After washing a small basketful of them, he picks out a decent-sized one from within and takes a bite. Even though the vlog only shows his back, he very visibly shivers a little. He then turns around with a frown on his face and hands the tomato to Zhou Ziheng.

"So sour."

An arm reaches out from behind the camera. "So you give it to me instead?"

> Oh noessss now I'm sour! I'm just as sour as xqgg is now!!

> Geez, why is my ship so sweet?! What have I done to deserve such a beautiful perfect love?!

"It'd go to waste otherwise." Xia Xiqing turns back and talks to the granny in Italian.

"Are you going to chop? You'd better not. You don't know how to cook."

"I can learn." Xia Xiqing takes the carrot with his left hand and holds it down on the cutting board. He holds the knife in his right hand and moves it left and right trying to find an appropriate cutting position, unsure how he should start.

The camera keeps moving closer, and one hand reaches out to take away the knife in his hand. "Never mind, I'll do it. Hold this."

The camera shakes a little as the cameramen complete the handover. Xia Xiqing lifts the camera and aims it at Zhou Ziheng's side profile.

"Why are you filming? Don't tell me you're making a vlog to post on the internet."

Zhou Ziheng keeps his composure and shakes his head as he concentrates on cutting the carrot. "Nah, I won't post it."

"Alright, then."

> Hahahaha what a liar!!

> How can someone as smart as xqgg believe him so easily?!

> Because of LOVE~

Xia Xiqing doesn't film Zhou Ziheng dutifully as he ought to. Instead, he walks around with the camera, humming a little tune. It seems to be an English song.

> Whoooooooa Xiqing-*gege*'s singing is so, so, so good! Just casually singing like this sounds so good
>> I think I hear "I just wanna kiss you"!!!
>> I wanna kiss you too kyaaaaaaaa xqgg!!!!!

The picture suddenly shakes, and the camera pans down. A little blonde girl is holding onto Xia Xiqing's legs. She looks up with that rosy-cheeked little face of hers and chatters away in Italian. The camera moves in as Xia Xiqing squats. A long, slender hand reaches out from behind the camera and gently strokes the little girl's head. The background music suddenly changes.

> Oh!! The BGM is the song Xiqing-*gege* was humming earlier!! Heng-Heng is so attentive!
> xqgg is so cool when he speaks Italian! He sounds so good!
> Wails I'm so envious of this little girl!
> Me too!!! I want to hug Xiqing-*gege*'s thighs!! I want to be patted on the head by Xiqing-*gege*!

Not long after, the picture changes again to a dining table full of seated people. There's an impressive array of sumptuous Italian dinner dishes spread out on the table. Xia Xiqing is sitting on the left, getting pasta for the little girl. Zhou Ziheng says a phrase in English and looks at the camera, and everyone looks up in unison. The landlord grandpa even picks up his small glass of wine and raises it enthusiastically at the camera.

> So heart-warming! I love this vibe!
> And the present me is still envious of that little girl!

Zhou Ziheng sits and places the camera in the middle of

the table, aiming it toward himself and Xia Xiqing beside him. The little girl grabs a bottle of black pepper shaker and sprinkles a little on her own pasta.

Zhou Ziheng also wants some, so he says to her in English, "And some for me as well."

The little girl gets up to stand on her chair. At this, Xia Xiqing hurries to hold her steady by her calves. The little lass stretches out her arm, but can't reach Zhou Ziheng's plate. She's a stubborn one, however, and insists on sprinkling some for Zhou Ziheng herself. So, an amused Xia Xiqing can only pick her up and set her down on his lap.

"Now you can do it."

Zhou Ziheng pushes his plate in front of the little girl. "Please."

The little girl shakes her chubby little hand over it and covers the plate with black pepper.

"Hey!" Zhou Ziheng is between laughter and tears. He watches her unstoppable hand as he repeats "enough, enough." Xia Xiqing laughs too, but in her enthusiasm, she sends black pepper flying all over the air, making Xia Xiqing's nose itch. He turns his face aside and sneezes.

> Hahaha Xiqing-*gege* looks so adorable when he sneezes!!

> It has a family of three vibe!!! My sons!!! Mama wants to hold her grandchild!! Hurry up and make one for me now!!

> Ah so blissful. Just watching them puts me in a good mood~

The moment he sneezes, the granny immediately says, "Salute!"

Zhou Ziheng asks what it means in English, and the grandpa, who seems to understand some English, answers in heavily-accented English, "It means 'bless you.'"

Zhou Ziheng nods, and the grandpa asks, "Then what do

Chinese people say when someone sneezes?"

He thinks for a moment before answering in English, "Someone is thinking about you."

The grandpa's eyes light up with a look of marvel from the unexpectedness of it. "Chinese people are so romantic!"

> Really, it's so romantic when you think of it this way. Most people from the European and American countries say God bless you. Only Chinese people would say that someone is thinking about you when you sneeze~

> The Chinese language really is romantic sometimes!

> What's truly romantic is being praised as a romantic by an Italian hahaha

Zhou Ziheng smiles too and bumps his shoulder against the sneezer, Xia Xiqing. "Sorry, I presumed to think about you just now."

> Ooooohhh zzh is too good at this!!!

> Is this guy really someone who's never dated in his life?? How is he so good at this?!

> I can't do this anymore. Today is another day I shed tears over their beautiful love!

> I wanna sneeze too!!

Xia Xiqing shoots a glance at him after recovering from his sneezing, then pushes the black pepper-decorated pasta toward Zhou Ziheng. "Finish this up. If you can't finish it, you're not allowed to sleep."

The picture changes and Zhou Ziheng's face appears on the screen. He's leaning on the sofa with a look of relaxation on his face.

"It's already night now..." He squints his eyes at the small hanging clock on the opposite wall. "Ten-fifteen." He flips the camera over and focuses on the sketches on the opposite wall. "These are all Xiqing's previous works; he drew them while he was still in school."

He films them one piece at a time along the wall until he reaches Xia Xiqing's bedroom. The sound of running water can be heard from within.

"Oh, he's taking a shower."

> OMGGGGG AAAAAAAAH I WANNA SEE!!!!
> SCREAMS I WANT TO WATCH HIM SHOWER!!!
> xqgg I'm coming!!!!!
> xqgg is love!!!

Zhou Ziheng flips the camera over. "I know you all will say things like 'omggggg I wanna see,' and 'Xiqing-*gege* is love.'" He deliberately pinches his throat and perfectly imitates the behavior of Self-Study girls. But the next second, his expression turns stern again. "No can do." He extends his finger and makes a "no" gesture. "The internet isn't a land beyond the reach of the law."

> zzh you need to stahp!!
> Surf less net, browse fewer memes, Heng-Heng. Mommy is begging you
> Hahaha I'm going to make an emoji pack!

He strides over to the little balcony attached to the bedroom, but then, as if remembering something, he retraces his steps, taking the camera along with him. An extremely childish "kid drawing" appears on the screen.

"I drew this myself. It's a portrait of Xia Xiqing."

> LMFAOOOOOOOOOOOOOOOOO
> xxq: I look like this???
> Hahaha zzh, are you also harboring dreams of becoming an artist because you have one as a boyfriend?
> Heng-Heng, there are some things you really can't force lololol

The camera stays on the drawing for a very long time.

Zhou Ziheng still sounds very proud of himself. "I stayed up all night to draw it."

The scene changes the next second. The camera seems to have been placed on the small balcony, where it's pointed at a small, colorful swing seat on which Zhou Ziheng is sitting. As soon as he looks up, Xia Xiqing walks out of the bedroom wearing a loose T-shirt and a towel over his partially damp hair.

"Why didn't you blow-dry it?"

Xia Xiqing squeezes in next to Zhou Ziheng on that little swing seat and says matter-of-factly, "Why aren't you blowing it for me?"

> Omgomg Xiqing-*gege* is pouting!! Who can resist this?!!

> No one can resist it!!

> Too cute!!! Zzh, don't you want to do him??

> Hahahahaha don't you want to do him hahahahaha

Zhou Ziheng immediately grins like a silly fool. He cups Xia Xiqing's face and smooches him a bunch of times.

> Ahhhhhhhhhh I'm dead!

> I can't!!! RIP me!!!

> Mah gawd, my ship is so sweet I'm exploding!!!

"Why did you put the camera there?" Xia Xiqing points at the camera. "Aren't you afraid it will fall off?"

> Crap, so I was put right on the balcony??? Why do I feel like I'm teetering on the edge?

> Lmaoooo we teetering here?!

"It's fine. There's no wind here. It won't fall without an outside force." Zhou Ziheng grabs the towel on Xia Xiqing's head and meticulously dries his hair for him.

"You aren't filming this, are you?"

"I'm just filming it as a memento."

"As a memento..." A change comes over Xia Xiqing's

expression. He reaches out and hooks his arm around Zhou Ziheng's neck, then moves in and kisses him on the lips. He gazes at Zhou Ziheng with a pair of pure yet seductive eyes. "Why don't you leave a little something else as a memento?"

> Ohhhhhhhhhh we're getting into the after-dark segment! (ˆ‿ˆ)

> Ahhhhhhhhhhhhhh will I be able to see my ship rolling under the sheets while I'm alive?!?!?!

> hot damn hnnngh, who can stand Xia Xiqing's attacks?!!!

Seeing as the topic is going to veer off track, Zhou Ziheng hurriedly diverts Xia Xiqing's attention and smooches him all over the face until he's a little bewildered. "What are you doing?"

> Zhou Ziheng, mama wanna see the bedroom scene!!!

> zzh!!! You bad boy!! You have to listen to your waifu!!!

> Mommy won't allow you guys to change the subject!!!

> I really have to say that this distraction method is really darn hilarious hahaha (doesn't mean I don't want to see Self-Study's bedroom scene)

"Look, the stars are so bright!"

Xia Xiqing wipes his own face with the towel and looks up at the sky with Zhou Ziheng. "No shit, this isn't Beijing."

> Beijing: ...What have I done wrong *sound of arrow striking heart*

"I like to look at the stars." Zhou Ziheng wraps his arm around Xia Xiqing's shoulders and lazily stretches out his long legs, pushing off against the ground and swinging the tiny seat.

Very naturally, Xia Xiqing leans against Zhou Ziheng's shoulder. "Me too. You know of that 'Starry Night' painting by Van Gogh, right?"

Zhou Ziheng nods. "Of course."

"When he created that painting, he'd already been admitted into the Saint-Paul Asylum. I remember he wrote a letter to his younger brother who was sponsoring him at that time, and there was this line in it." Xia Xiqing looks up at the star-studded sky.

"'When I looked up at the stars in the sky, I often had the illusions of them being black dots representing cities and towns on a map. I ask myself, why are the shining specks in the sky not as accessible as the black dots on the map of France? We can take a train to Tarascon or Rouen, but we can't get to the stars.'"

He finishes with a smile. "I had an indescribable feeling in my heart when I saw it."

"What feeling?" Zhou Ziheng holds Xia Xiqing's hand.

"I also felt like that once." Xia Xiqing turns his head aside to look at him. "Do you understand what I mean? When I looked up at the starry sky, I also wondered why I couldn't get to the stars. But that was when I was still very young." He lowers his head. "The stars were the only light I could ever get in the darkness without having to plead for it."

Zhou Ziheng couldn't help but feel his heart clenched. He holds Xia Xiqing even tighter and kisses the top of his head.

"Do you know, the first law of thermodynamics, or in layman's terms, the law of conservation of energy..."

Before he can finish his words, Xia Xiqing pokes him in the side. "Here we go again."

Zhou Ziheng grabs hold of his hand with a smile. "According to the first law of thermodynamics, the energy in the universe can't be created or destroyed. So after we die, our physical bodies will be gone, but perhaps we will continue to exist in another form." He points to the stars in the sky. "They always used to say in the TV dramas that people will turn into stars after death, and it's true. Many, many years later, we may indeed become a part of a star, perhaps a small rock on it or something." He rests his head on Xia Xiqing's head. "So we can always go to the stars after we die, one way or another."

Xia Xiqing nuzzles against the side of Zhou Ziheng's face like a little kitten and looks up at the sky in silence for a very, very long time.

Seeing his silence, Zhou Ziheng asks, "Are you feeling a little sorry that you can't go to the stars until you die?" He smiles gently.

Xia Xiqing shakes his head and then nods again. "It's a little regretful, but..." He looks well-behaved and good as he tilts his head up. "I don't regret death itself. I just feel that... there are so many people in the world, so in all probability, I may not be able to become part of the same star as you. If we go to two different stars, we'll be separated by so many light-years." He sighs. "That's so far away."

Zhou Ziheng is stunned. He didn't expect Xia Xiqing to think about things like this. His heart swells, filled to the brim, like a small loaf of bread expanding in a warm oven.

"That won't happen." Zhou Ziheng strokes the side of Xia Xiqing's neck. "I've already drawn lots for us. It's the same star."

Xia Xiqing smiles and smacks his hand away. "Childish."

"That I am. I'm going to pester you even on the star."

"As you wish."

The vacation comes to an end. Zhou Ziheng takes on a new drama and doesn't return to Beijing for three or four months. After the filming ends, he takes a long break. He's been on the set for the entire course of the filming period, and including his vacation time, his fans haven't seen Zhou Ziheng for quite a number of months. This is even more so for Xia Xiqing. Other than going to the art gallery once in a while to try their luck, the fans have barely caught sight of Xia Xiqing in public.

So the Self-Study girls spontaneously start a topic on the net to bump the "Begging For The Reunion Of Self-Study" topic into the trending list by sheer force. Clicking into the topic displays various kinds of cute and silly stickers, fanarts, and video clips the fans made themselves. Because what else can they do? When the actual ship doesn't feed them, the fans can only sustain themselves.

In truth, it's also no fun at home for the two men at the center of it all. The paparazzi have been so close on their heels lately that they haven't been willing to head out. During the first two days of the break, Zhou Ziheng and Xia Xiqing cuddled at home and slept for the whole two days. Then, the next few days were spent watching movies and catching up on dramas. And after that, there was really nothing to do, short of holding a swimming competition in the living room.

Sitting cross-legged on the sofa surfing Weibo, Zhou Ziheng chances upon the Self-Study girls' trending topic. He springs to his feet, startling the napping Xia Xiqing.

"What are you up to?" Xia Xiqing rubs his eyes lazily and makes to turn over to continue sleeping.

But Zhou Ziheng forcibly turns him back again. "Wake up, baby." He shoves the phone right before Xia Xiqing. "Look, the Organization is summoning us!"

Xia Xiqing casts a glance at it and closes his eyes again as he attempts to yank Zhou Ziheng over to his side. "The Organization wants you to do me. Lie down."

Zhou Ziheng is momentarily rendered speechless. This won't do. He suddenly thinks of a good idea, so he promptly picks up Xia Xiqing and tries every means and way to coax him into waking up, then tries every means and way again to make him agree to drop into the fans group with him.

"If you can put this enthusiasm of yours for public displays of affection into acting, you will no doubt become an Oscar-winning best actor at six years old." Xia Xiqing can't help but grouse.

Zhou Ziheng pays absolutely no attention to Xia Xiqing's sarcasm and merrily logs into his Weibo side account. He taps open his fan group for a look; it's still abuzz with discussion threads of how to make Self-Study appear.

@HeatwaveFireworks: I miss Self-Study so much T__T I wanna see a fresh Xiqing-*gege*. I wanna see a fresh Heng-Heng!

@InkRain: What can two young lads in their twenties do all cooped up at home? Of course, it's gonna be something unmentionable. (੭ु˘ ੭ु⁾

@ThousandRiverMoonovo: Ohhhh I wanna see!!!

@SugarVinegarConvert: Me too!!! Livestream please!!!!!

Xia Xiqing tugs Zhou Ziheng's hand over and glances at his phone screen. He harrumphs. "See, what did I say?"

Zhou Ziheng pulls his wrist back. "There are also many of them who want to see the normal us, not just that...you know..."

"Oh, and you're feeling embarrassed now?" Xia Xiqing simply can't understand. "Then why aren't you the slightest bit embarrassed when you're thrusting it in, humph..."

Before he can finish his words, his mouth is covered by the red-eared Zhou Ziheng.

Xia Xiqing's eyes widen in a glare. Then after a while, he sticks out the tip of his tongue and licks Zhou Ziheng's palm like a little kitten. It's all too seductive. Zhou Ziheng pulls his hand away and lowers his head in an attempt to distract himself, but he unwittingly types an "ah" in the fans group's chat box and accidentally sends it out.

This one word causes a rippling effect akin to a stone tossed into a lake.

@hotspringsauce: AHHHHHHHHHHHHHH IT'S HENG-HENG!!

@Akira: Ahhhhhhh he dropped in!!!

@roseandbiscuit: AHHHHHHHH is it really Heng-Heng?!?!

@noicelesssugar: AHHHhhhhH Heng-Heng, mommy loves you!! Look at mommy please!!!

@nicknamesrrlyimpt: AHhhhhh!! My precious Heng-Heng, mama is here!!! Is my daughter-in-law besides you?? Mama misses her daughter-in-law!!!

The fans' enthusiasm resembles a marmot nest that has been poked. Meanwhile, the person in question, Zhou Ziheng, feels a little depressed; after all, this isn't at all a cool way to make an entrance.

Xia Xiqing looks at his own phone and laughs. "Are you a commander? Just one 'ah,' and thousands of Self-Study girls line up behind you."

Zhou Ziheng falls silent and sends a rose emoji into the group chat.

@beanieshy: Crais a little rose! Why is Heng-Heng so sweet?!

@PinkJellyGreen: Where's my little rose?! I wanna see my little rose!

A short while later:

@Tsing_Summer: Hiya, everyone

@SelfStudyGirlFighting: AHHhhhhhh the little rose is here!

@HaveYouShippedSelfStudyToday: The little rose's tone is so sweet!! Hiya~ Mama loves you!

@HasHenghengAppearedToday: xqgg pops up the moment zzh sends out a rose emoji. What is this divine pairing?!

"Hey, aren't you the one who wanted to show yourself in the fans chat? So why are you quiet now?" Xia Xiqing pokes Zhou Ziheng's side with his foot. "Say something."

"I haven't thought of what to say."

Xia Xiqing laughs so hard that he falls backward on the sofa. By this time, the fans are already in the groove of things.

@selfstudysisterhood: Heng-Heng, we wanna watch a livestream!!!

@GirlWhoLoveSelfStudy: Yeah!!! I want a livestream! A couple livestream!!!

@No1Cutie: Livestream!! Livestream!! Livestream!! [pleading]

By the time Zhou Ziheng returns to his senses, both of them have already been mass-tagged by the fans, who keep clamoring for a livestream in the chat. Zhou Ziheng was originally going to do a livestream anyway, and now, with the excuse of pampering the fans and giving in to their demands, he can go along with it and drag Xia Xiqing to do a livestream together.

Although Xia Xiqing is a bit proud and unyielding with his words, underneath all that, he's also the type to dote on his fans. So under Zhou Ziheng's coaxing and pestering, he finally relents.

"Just one hour. Any more than that, and I'll leave."

"No problem!"

Once the equipment is set up, Zhou Ziheng opens his livestream channel. The sudden surge of fans causes the screen and comments to freeze. Xia Xiqing takes the opportunity to run to the kitchen and grab a large tub of ice cream, then walks back to the living room to sit on the sofa while Zhou Ziheng sits on the rug and fiddles with the computer and camera.

"Whew, it's done..."

> OMG a close-up of Heng-Heng's beautiful face!!!

> Ahhhhh my baby's facial features really are superior!

> I see xqgg!!! He's sitting on the sofa in the back!!

> Hot damn, what did I see?! A matching set of couples lounge-wear!!!!

> You're right!! Sis, you've got good eyes!!!

> It's really a couples set!! Xqgg looks so good in that muted green!!

Zhou Ziheng picks up his glasses from the table and puts them on before saying a brief opening speech, "Good evening, everyone."

> Good evening, darlings!!!

> AHHHHhh Heng-Heng looks so so so so good with glasses!!

With his eyes on the screen, Zhou Ziheng reaches back and sets it on Xia Xiqing's knee, and kneads it. Xia Xiqing gets off the sofa and sits side-by-side with Zhou Ziheng on the rug. He raises his chin at the camera with a little spoon still in his mouth.

> Whoa, this tacit understanding

> I really love these intimate little gestures between them. So genuine and super sweet

> xqgg is really too good-looking X10086

Zhou Ziheng bends his leg and rests his arm on his knee. "I've been on set for a long time while filming, so it's been a long time, huh. I saw how everyone is so eager to watch us do a livestream, and it just so happens that we have nothing to do, so we'll satisfy your wishes." With that, he glances aside at Xia Xiqing. "Right, Xiqing?"

> I'm crying, how sweet. No matter what I see them do now,

✦ . 226 ‖‖

I find it all sweet. I can't take this anymore!

> I can watch their day-in-the-life every day for a lifetime!!!

"Don't listen to his nonsense." Xia Xiqing scoops another spoonful of ice cream. "Remind me again who was the one so bent on livestreaming that he spent half an hour pleading with me."

Zhou Ziheng is just about to speak when Xia Xiqing stuffs the ice cream into his mouth with a smile. "Zhou Ziheng, of all things to learn, why don't you learn the good things? When have you become someone who dares to do it but dares not to admit it?" With that, he even pats Zhou Ziheng's face. "You used to be so well-behaved."

> OMGGGGGGGGG

> xqgg totally has heng-heng under his thumb now hahahaha

> Just how much does zzh want to do a livestream lmfaoooo

> Please make your side account a premium account and update the profile to Public Displays of Affection Livestream Bloggers

> Public Displays of Affection Livestream LMAOOOOO

"In any case, this livestream is very sudden, so you should be prepared. This may really turn out to be a livestream without any meaningful content."

Xia Xiqing nods in agreement. "If there's any content you wish to see, leave a message in the comments. Who knows, I might like your idea."

> Dom CEO Xiqing, doting on his fans live!

> Wanna see both of you going wild in bed...[Underage Warning]

> Going wild hahaha. Bro, are you a werewolf in disguise?!

> Heng-Heng's gonna start spouting his fave phrase again soon!

Zhou Ziheng just happens to see that comment, and immediately says with a stern countenance, "The internet isn't a land beyond the reach of the law."

> Hahaha I knew it!!

> Standard outcome lmaoooo

> zzh, momma is begging you. Browse less net, read fewer fics!

> HAHAHA digging out his dark fanfic reading past again I see hahahahaha

> The tragic one is still Heng-Heng

> Why not get Heng-Heng to read a fanfic? Lolololololol!!

> Great idea!! What a marvelous idea to punish him publicly!! Girl, you're too good!

It isn't that bad at first, since only Zhou Ziheng is involved initially, but then, Xia Xiqing, while sitting beside him eating ice cream, is dragged into it as well. For a moment, the comments are all clamoring for them to read fanfics live.

What the heck is this development? Xia Xiqing is baffled, while Zhou Ziheng feels...complicated. On one hand, he finds it too shameful to read fanfics out loud in public, but on the other hand, he very much wants to see Xia Xiqing read it.

"Shall we read?" Zhou Ziheng asks tentatively.

Xia Xiqing frowns. "Who's we? Read it yourself."

Zhou Ziheng bumps his shoulder. "Ohhh, I knew you wouldn't dare."

"No, wait, what? Who wouldn't dare? I'm just too lazy to wallow in the same mud as you, kiddo."

> Ohhohohoho, what kind of divine nickname is kiddo?!!

> Why is my ship so sweet even when they are squabbling?!

> self-study is totally in mutual doting mode

"That just means you don't dare."

"And what if I dare?"

"Then do whatever you want!"

"Deal." Xia Xiqing puts the ice cream on the table and rolls up his sleeves. "Remember what you said."

Zhou Ziheng is so delighted on seeing his goading succeed that he almost bursts out laughing. He tries his best to hold it in. "Right. I mean what I say."

And so, because of this inexplicable competitiveness, Xia Xiqing agrees to read fanfics with Zhou Ziheng. The fans recommend several of the most ingenious fanfics in the fandom, and even tag both of them on the Weibo posts out of consideration.

> Truth be told, it's my first time recommending fics to the main characters themselves hahahaha

> You don't say lmfao

> I must be dreaming rofl. My ship is going to read fanfics to me on livestream!!

Xia Xiqing clicks into one of the tagged posts at random. This doesn't seem to be the first chapter. It's probably one of the chapters serializing on Weibo, and pretty popular too.

Zhou Ziheng glances at him. "That was fast. Don't you need to pick?"

"Whatever for? Everything the Self-Study girls recommend is the best."

> awww xqgg is too good at this!!

> OMG my idol praised me!!!

Xia Xiqing clears his throat, crosses his legs, and gets ready to read. "Xia Xiqing stands..." He almost bursts out laughing. "No, wait. It's so strange for me to be reading my own name."

"NG! One more time." Zhou Ziheng claps his hands and

pretends to clap the clapperboard. "Action!"

"Xia Xiqing stands before Zhou Ziheng. He reaches out with his long and slender index finger and lifts Zhou Ziheng's chin..." While reading from the phone, the incomparably professional and dedicated Xia Xiqing imitates the description in the text and lifts Zhou Ziheng's chin with his index finger. He gazes into the man's eyes and recites the dialogue in the text, "Don't you want to kiss me?"

Then, both men look at each other in silence for three seconds and burst out laughing at each other's faces.

> Hahahaha what kind of mega-shameful scene is this?

> Lmaoooo so embarrassing but sweet. I can't stop laughing

> The way Heng-Heng looks trying to hold back his laughter is so adorable!!

> This line is really too hilarious when it's read out!

"You're being too over the top!" Zhou Ziheng accuses him with a laugh.

"Who is? Not me for sure. That's how it was written. There's still a bunch more to come." Xia Xiqing flips through it, then sets the phone down on the table in mock protest, and says to the camera as he holds back a laugh, "I don't have any objections about the author's writing style except for one thing, and that is I'd never say such words."

Zhou Ziheng nods with unparalleled approval. "That's right."

"I'd generally force a kiss."

"Ahem!" His words cause Zhou Ziheng to cough incessantly.

> Lmaoooo @ Xiqing!!

> So manly!

> Force a kiss lololol. He really is all action and no talk!

> zzh got a fright lmfaoooo

Xia Xiqing turns and pats Zhou Ziheng's back, and at the same time says with a wicked smile, "Did you think of some not-so-pleasant memories?"

Zhou Ziheng steels himself. "Nah, it's pretty pleasant."

> Why are these two speaking in riddles now?!

> So zzh has been forcibly kissed by xqgg before!!! That must be it!! The innocent liddol kiddo!!

"I was the one who took the initiative for our first kiss. At that time, I went straight for...mmm! Mmm!"

Once again, Xia Xiqing's mouth is covered by Zhou Ziheng.

> Mad rush to cover his mouth hahaha

> The liddol kiddo has lost all his dignity as a top!

> Hot damn, so the first kiss was a forced kiss from xqgg!!! Xqgg OP!!! *voice cracks*

> OMG so the reality is 100x more exciting than fanfics!!!

In order to change the topic, Zhou Ziheng hurries to pick a fanfic to read as well. "Alright, I'm starting." He clears his voice. "Ever since he was a small child, Zhou Ziheng has liked his own *gege...gege?!?!*"

Xia Xiqing nearly spits a mouthful of water onto the screen. *The fuck is gege?* At this moment, sitting in his own office, Zhou Zijing sneezes.

"No, wait. How did I come to like my own older brother?!"

> Hahahaha zzh's totally shocked

> It's a brother complex setting, my son!!

> He's too honest hahaha brother complex right off the bat

"Huh?" It finally dawns on veteran netizen Zhou Ziheng. "Incest?"

> YUP!!!

> That's exactly it!!

Xia Xiqing casts a sideways glance at him in disdain. "Why

do you know all this?"

Zhou Ziheng takes it as a compliment. "I do, don't I?" He says, then adds, "Let's continue. The first time he met Xia Xiqing, his older half-brother of the same mother, Zhou Ziheng was only five years old. He stood timidly before the door and looked at that pretty and tall older brother, who was already in his youth."

By this point, Zhou Ziheng is suddenly a little unhappy. "Hey, aren't I a little too weak in here?"

Xia Xiqing smiles happily and sprawls over the table to look at him with his head cocked. "The fact is you are younger than me by five years. When I was in elementary school you were still sucking your thumb."

> roflmfaooooo
> The imagery of baby bundle Heng-Heng sucking thumbs is really too cute!!

Zhou Ziheng pouts unhappily and continues to read. "For many years afterward, his elder brother's cold and distant expression during their first encounter remains etched in his mind."

"Oof, this is quite realistic." Xia Xiqing suddenly butts in. "That was really my reaction when a younger brother suddenly popped up."

Your buddy Xia Xiuze lets out a sneeze online. Zhou Ziheng shakes his head and skips through several paragraphs, directly omitting the introduction as he searches for a dialogue to start performing. He grabs hold of Xia Xiqing by the right shoulder. "*Gege!*"

He really gets into character in one second, huh. The corner of Xia Xiqing's mouth twitches.

Zhou Ziheng furrows his eyebrows. The look in his eyes is complicated. "*Gege...* There's something I have to tell you."

> Holy moly, the oscar-winning movie star is in action!!!

> Fuck me, to think I get to see my idols acting out a fanfic in this lifetime!!! Fuckkkkkkk!!!

"What is it?" Xia Xiqing plays along.

"You..." Zhou Ziheng's Adam's apple bobs. He lowers his eyes. "Do you really like that girl from yesterday? She...she said she's your girlfriend."

Xia Xiqing raises an eyebrow. "So what if she is?"

> Omgggg xqgg is so alpha!!!

Zhou Ziheng's emotions spill over. He flings away the phone and grabs Xia Xiqing's shoulders with both arms. "I won't allow it!"

> Whoa!!! Damn! I'm getting goosebumps!

> Phone: What have I done wrong?

"What has it got to do with you?" Xia Xiqing pries his hands away.

"Of course it has to do with me! I—I won't let you date her! You can't even be friends with her!" Zhou Ziheng gets all worked up and suddenly pulls Xia Xiqing into his arms. "You're mine! Mine and mine alone!"

The impact makes Xia Xiqing's chest ache. Seeing as Zhou Ziheng is so immersed in his role, Xia Xiqing has no choice but to play along, so he goes with the flow and moves to push him away. "You're insane. Let me go."

But Zhou Ziheng only tightens his grip. "I'm not insane! I'm very sane!" Even his voice is starting to tremble, and his fundamental professionalism as an actor allows him to switch the lines back to the original text he's just read, "Don't you ever think of leaving me! I like you. Can't you tell that I like you?!"

"You..."

"You know it very well! You know it better than anyone

else that I like you with all my heart and soul, that I like you more than anyone else in this world." Zhou Ziheng hugs him and says, "*Gege*, I can't stand watching you smile at other people. I really can't bear it. Didn't you say before that what you do is always for my own good?" He grabs Xia Xiqing's shoulders and looks into his eyes. "Please, I beg of you. I feel terrible. I think about you like crazy every day. Can you..."

Xia Xiqing can guess what the upcoming dialogue is. He lowers his eyes. "No."

Zhou Ziheng suddenly kisses him, catching him off-guard. Xia Xiqing is truly startled, and all of his shock is genuine. The kiss is savage, but very quickly, his lips move away. Xia Xiqing shoves him.

"What are you doing?!"

Zhou Ziheng wipes the corner of his lips and pants heavily. "You belong to me alone. *Gege*."

Xia Xiqing is completely intimidated by Zhou Ziheng's acting skills. When he thinks about how the two of them have just kissed on live camera, the blood rushes to his face, and his ears burn. He grabs a cushion from the sofa and slams it at Zhou Ziheng. "If I let you mess around again, I'll write my name in reverse!"

Zhou Ziheng smiles like a rascal as he takes the blows from the cushion. "Qingxi Xia. Sounds nice too."

After Xia Xiqing is done throwing all the cushions, he looks at the screen, which by now is bombarded with so many comments from the fans that it's barely readable.

> KYAAAAAAAAAAAA A FORCED KISS!!!! I'M SO DED!!!!

> I'm dead, I'm dead, this time I'm really dead!!

> OMG showing off their love AND acting skills on live-stream!!! The acting slew me!!! And look at that sexual tension between Self-Study!!!

> YELLLLSSSSSSSS I'm going crazy! I'm screaming!! I'm running wild!!! MERRY CHRISTMAS TO ALL SELF-STUDY GIRLS TODAY!!!
> That last line really is epic!!! Wtf all hail Heng-Heng!!
> This marmot is screaming again from her coffin today: brother complex's the best!!! Self-Study's THE BEST!!!
> Fck, that really was a forced kiss just now!!! Fckkk, did any sharp-eyed sisters get a clear look?! Did zzh use his tongue?!?!?!
> Triple ask from the soul: Did he use his tongue? Did he??? Use his tongue?????

Good heavens, what kind of fans are these? Xia Xiqing is truly regretting it now. No doubt they will make it onto trending again this time.

He didn't expect Zhou Ziheng to smirk as he boasts, "I did."

As if that's not enough, he proceeds to bump Xia Xiqing's shoulder and leans in next to his ear.

"Did you feel it, *gege*?"

E.09

:

Revenge by Hickeys

ummer is just around the corner.

S   These days, Zhou Ziheng is guest-starring in a new film by Director Kun Cheng. It tells the story of what happens after three delinquent youths in the hutongs of Beijing accidentally pick up a backpack containing drugs. Zhou Ziheng plays a police officer in this film.

Kun Cheng knows Zhou Ziheng all too well, so he goes straight to the point when he comes looking for the actor. "You'll be playing a policeman. The uniform will look damn handsome on you. Your part in the film will take less than two days to shoot. And it's right in Mao'er Hutong."

Zhou Ziheng agrees readily.

After the release of the film, Zhou Ziheng once again makes it onto the trending list: #Zhou Ziheng in Police Uniform.

As the responses are so overwhelming, Zhou Ziheng is even invited to the promotional events, despite being clearly just a cameo. Many sponsors also take advantage of the hype to hand out olive branches, which is how Zhou Ziheng is caught off guard and starts getting busy again. Xia Xiqing isn't very satisfied with this situation.

"What?" Leaning on the sofa, Xia Xiqing kicks the cushion by his leg to the ground with a look of displeasure. "We agreed that you'd accompany me to Osaka, and now you're going to stand me up after I already bought the tickets and booked the hotel."

Zhou Ziheng sits ingratiatingly on the sofa and sets Xia Xiqing's calf on his lap, then grabs his hand toward him and smooches it several times. "But I have no choice; I'll go to you immediately once I'm done filming. Or you can wait for me, I'll reschedule the flight and we can go to the airport together?"

Xia Xiqing wants to kick him. As soon as he bends his knee up, he remembers that Zhou Ziheng's back injury from filming has yet to heal, so he shifts his leg away and slumps back in resignation. "Okay, but, don't you movie stars have work schedules? First come, first serve, right? I was the one who booked you first."

Lying on his back like this exposes his slender white neck to view. His Adam's apple bobs as he speaks, making Zhou Ziheng want to touch it. Zhou Ziheng leans over in Xia Xiqing's direction, but he's only just reached out to him and has yet to make contact when Xia Xiqing raises his head, bumping the tip of his nose against Zhou Ziheng's fingertips.

Xia Xiqing lowers his eyes to look at his fingers, then chomps down on them. Zhou Ziheng merely smiles and doesn't make a sound. He brushes a finger across the bridge of Xia Xiqing's nose.

"It can't be helped. This magazine suddenly came calling,

and my sister-in-law said that it's a huge leap for my fashion resources, so she insisted that I accept it."

He sprawls over Xia Xiqing's body like a large dog and pins him down firmly, cupping Xia Xiqing's face and squishing it until it's all out of shape, then plants kisses on him.

"I promise you there won't be a next time, really. Babe, wait one day for me, and we'll take the plane at night, alright? I saw that there's a flight before dawn! I'll get Xiao-Luo to change the reservation!"

"You! You're crushing me... Get up."

"I'll get up if you forgive me!"

"Are you getting up or not?"

"Are you forgiving me or not?"

Seeing Zhou Ziheng's aggrieved expression, Xia Xiqing's heart softens, but he still stubbornly refuses to concede. "I won't forgive you if you don't get up."

"Oh, my..." Zhou Ziheng's expression changes. "Oh my god, my lower back hurts so much."

Xia Xiqing is startled, thinking that he really has hurt his lower back from the movement. He hastily reaches out a hand to touch it. "Where? Are you okay? Told you not to move so much, but you don't listen!"

Zhou Ziheng's initial scrunched-up face immediately blossoms into a smile. He shamelessly moves in closer to Xia Xiqing. "I knew you'd dote on me. My back will stop hurting if you forgive me."

I must have spoiled you too much, that you've now learned to play tricks. Xia Xiqing meant to fly into a rage, but the words are right at the tip of his tongue when he gets another idea. He holds back his temper and pinches Zhou Ziheng's chin with a smile. "Sure, I forgive you."

"Really?" Zhou Ziheng is delighted. "I knew it. Our Xiqing

dotes on me the most."

"Ain't that the truth?" Xia Xiqing wraps both arms around Zhou Ziheng's neck and nuzzles the latter's chin with the tip of his nose before gradually sliding to his jawline and below his ear, his breaths hot as he says. "Really."

The sudden teasing short-circuits Zhou Ziheng's brain. It's only when the tip of Xia Xiqing's moist and warm tongue sweeps across his earlobe, taking their couple earrings into his mouth, that Zhou Ziheng's back suddenly stiffens. Hot air spills over, like a tightly shut glass door to the sauna that has just been opened.

"Xiqing..."

"What are you calling my name for?" Xia Xiqing's tone is clearly unfeeling and cold, but in Zhou Ziheng's ears, it's coated in a layer of warm, sticky honey. Xia Xiqing gives up pestering Zhou Ziheng's ear, seeing as it can't withstand a single puff of air. Instead, he looks up into Zhou Ziheng's eyes. "Calling my name means you want to do me."

This is too blunt a sentence, even more so than digging out his heart and putting it on display. Xia Xiqing is too much. Zhou Ziheng doesn't avert his gaze, but he subconsciously licks his dry lips. His throat feels itchy.

"Don't lick your lips in front of me." Xia Xiqing drops a light peck on the corner of Zhou Ziheng's lips. "Lick me."

He draws out the sounds as he says the last two words, a little habit typical in his native dialect. A single "me" is so captivatingly uttered that it draws away all of Zhou Ziheng's soul. Zhou Ziheng finally caves—he has no wish to hang on anyway—and leans down to kiss him deeply. The instant his lips lock onto Xia Xiqing's, all his senses are amplified. Each lick and nibble hit his sensitive nerves right on target. Zhou Ziheng's heart rate lies in Xia Xiqing's hand, giving him free rein to speed it up, slow it down, or even bring it to a temporary pause.

The sound of water is particularly conspicuous in the spacious living room. Xia Xiqing presses his knee up against Zhou Ziheng's groin and teases him in a saccharinely sticky voice in between kisses.

"You sure get hard fast, as expected of a little wolfhound."

Zhou Ziheng bites down on his lower lips and reaches out to rub the bulge between Xia Xiqing's legs. "You're pretty perky yourself."

With this touch, Xia Xiqing doesn't even try to suppress his moan. His voice is wanton and a little raspy. Zhou Ziheng finally succumbs. He pins Xia Xiqing and starts to undo his leather belt, but Xia Xiqing seems unwilling, and insists on rolling over to straddle Zhou Ziheng as he slowly takes off his own belt. He holds it in his hand and cracks it a couple of times. Finally, he grabs Zhou Ziheng's hands and ties them with the belt, looking very much like a proud cowboy.

"Xiqing, what are you doing?"

"Making love." Xia Xiqing lies over his chest and kisses the side of his neck. "Can't you tell?"

He licks and sucks the skin at the side of Zhou Ziheng's neck until a deep red mark appears on it. It's only then that he stretches out his tongue to lick it with satisfaction, and moves on to search for the next suitable territory. After a few more rounds of this, Zhou Ziheng finally realizes what he's doing.

"Hey, you can't leave any marks...I have to strip tomorrow for the magazine shoot." Zhou Ziheng lifts his hand and rests his bound wrist at the back of Xia Xiqing's neck to caress his head. "Behave. "

Xia Xiqing bites down on Zhou Ziheng's shoulder. "You're

the one who should behave."

He leaves obvious teeth marks. Xia Xiqing licks and kisses his way down. As he holds down Zhou Ziheng's struggling body, he leaves one mark after another on it. It feels so much like a tug-of-war that Xia Xiqing feels excited.

Those fair, slender hands peel away Zhou Ziheng's sweatpants. Xia Xiqing blows a puff of air onto Zhou Ziheng's firm and solid lower abdomen, and licks the dip of his groin with the tip of his tongue, wetting it. He can hear Zhou Ziheng gasping, and he can feel his own growing desire. This is too much of a torture—what a way to sacrifice himself along with the enemy. But he's always been a self-destructive player, the kind playing for the excitement of bloodlust and carnage.

It's only until Xia Xiqing is satisfied with his "masterpiece" all over Zhou Ziheng's body that he releases him. Almost instantly, Zhou Ziheng flips him over and pins him down from the back, pressing Xia Xiqing's entire body against the carpet, unable to move.

Zhou Ziheng takes in a small piece of soft flesh on Xia Xiqing's nape into his mouth and gasps as he strips off his and Xia Xiqing's pants. In a rare moment of roughness, he presses down Xia Xiqing's head onto the carpet. "Why do you love to tease me so much?"

Even his voice is all wrong. So, so wrong. He's panting too hard—hot and scalding.

"You know...you're like a rapist right now." Xia Xiqing turns his face around with difficulty and smiles. The sweat trickles down his temple. "Do your fans know this is what you're like?"

Zhou Ziheng takes the lubricant under the coffee table and uses it to expand Xia Xiqing's opening, all the while nibbling at the hollow part of Xia Xiqing's shoulder. "I imagine they're thinking about stuff more intense than this."

"Is that so...? I like it a little more intense too." Xia Xiqing's voice undergoes a slight change as the expansion progresses. He turns his head as if to ask for a kiss, and Zhou Ziheng generously kisses him, shutting up that blunt mouth of his.

The moment he enters, Xia Xiqing lets go of the kiss and starts moaning. Saliva trickles down along the contours of his pretty lips. This position allows Zhou Ziheng to penetrate particularly deeply, his scorching hot shaft going on a rampage as he pounds into Xia Xiqing, making Xia Xiqing shrink forward in retreat. But Zhou Ziheng grabs hold of his shoulders and pins him down onto the soft carpet to stop his movement.

Lust that has been relieved is like a floodgate opened, flowing freely between searing hot back and chest and spilling over the exit of the body, making his head tingle with numbing pleasure. Xia Xiqing usually doesn't like to cry out loud, but today, he intentionally goes wild with abandon as he moans, so much that Zhou Ziheng can't control himself and slams hard one thrust after another into the deepest recess of that wet and hot tunnel. Only when Xia Xiqing's whole body goes limp from the fucking does Zhou Ziheng scoop him up and flips over to set him on his own body, letting him sprawl limply over him. Zhou Ziheng holds him in his embrace, kissing him as he continues to thrust into him.

He knows that he has a photoshoot the next day, but Xia Xiqing's fooling around causes Zhou Ziheng to toss his professional ethics out of the window as he gives in to his animal instincts and blazes through the night.

He initially thought that Xia Xiqing would be too lazy to get up when he wakes up early in the morning, but to his surprise, Xia Xiqing follows him up from the bed when the alarm goes off. He's clearly so tired and sleepy that he can barely open his eyes, yet he insists on getting up even with his stiff joints and aching back.

"Why don't you sleep a little longer?"

Xia Xiqing is like a soulless teeth-cleaning machine as he closes his eyes and mumbles incoherently, "I'm going to the photoshoot too."

Having finished shaving, Zhou Ziheng is now wiping his face, as he asks in astonishment. "Whatever for?"

"Why?" Xia Xiqing carefully rinses his mouth and looks up at him. "Can't I?"

"You... Once I'm done with the shoot, I'll go to the airport with you—"

"I want to see you make a fool of yourself." Xia Xiqing gives him a wicked smile and kicks Zhou Ziheng, who is already done washing up, out of the bathroom.

And it works. Zhou Ziheng looks thoroughly embarrassed from the moment he steps onto the set. He quickly grabs a staff member and asks, "Can I not take off my clothes for this photoshoot?"

"Oh, there are two sets. You'll be fully dressed in one set, but you'll have to take off the top for the other set," the staff member patiently explains to him.

However, the hickeys on Zhou Ziheng's body extend all the way from his neck to his lower abdomen, and he can't cover up all the marks whether he's clothed or not. Meanwhile, Xia Xiqing is like a smug boss as he sits on the makeup artist's couch and munches on chips, staring at Zhou Ziheng in the mirror.

Zhou Ziheng frowns helplessly as he looks at Xia Xiqing, only to see the latter raise his eyebrows at him, the bag of potato chips in his hands makes crackly sounds.

"Ziheng, your neck..." The styling director is gay and is one of the best stylists in his field, very much sought-after across the entire entertainment industry. On seeing those red and blue marks on Zhou Ziheng's neck, he tuts a few times. "You sure are enjoying your couples life."

With that, he looks at Xia Xiqing in the mirror, who returns a demure smile.

"What are we going to do? Even a concealer won't be able to cover it up." The makeup artist is troubled. "Or do we do some post-processing?"

The styling director shakes his head. "This photographer hates excessive post-processing. There are too many marks, post-processing will definitely wear down the skin texture."

In the end, the entire gang comprising of the photographer, photography assistant, styling director, makeup artist, and costume designer, all crowd into the small dressing room to discuss the hickeys all over Zhou Ziheng's body for close to an hour. Zhou Ziheng feels as if his sense of shame has been trampled to the ground, worn down to the point where there's nothing left of it.

The most ridiculous thing is that the perpetrator himself is also participating in this public execution, discussing it animatedly with all the others.

"I think it's better to just change the theme," Xia Xiqing proactively proposes.

"Turn it into a theme about promiscuity?" The styling director is all for it.

"...Seconded." Xia Xiqing holds out his hand, and the two men high-five in tacit understanding.

"Let's not be so direct," the photographer has only just said this when his hand is grasped by a grateful Zhou Ziheng. Just as he's about to express his strong approval to his savior, the photographer adds, "Although this is the theme, let's not spell it out. The concept can still be the same as before, just don't cover up those hickeys. Keep them all."

And so, the hickeys all over Zhou Ziheng's body become the new element of focus of his magazine photoshoot. He sits on the office chair, wearing a pair of gold-rimmed glasses, his hair all combed up with a few strands intentionally styled to hang off the side of his forehead. He has on a pair of black suit pants with black leather shoes, but there isn't a single inch of fabric on his upper body. Traces of lovemaking extend all the way into the waist of the pants, no doubt leaving one's imagination free to run wild.

Although the pure-hearted little puppy Zhou Ziheng remains bashful, his excellent professionalism allows him to see this suggestive, lust-laden photoshoot to the end. Xia Xiqing has to concede that although he initially did this as a prank, he's still very much titillated as he watches the entire process of Zhou Ziheng's photoshoot from the sidelines.

Once the job wraps up, the two immediately depart for the airport. Just before boarding the plane, Xia Xiqing hurriedly switches on his phone and secretly logs into Zhou Ziheng's side account on Weibo.

@ihatelenzlaw: Remember to buy the new magazine this time~! There's a surprise!

E.10

:

Love Me, Love My Dog

I t rained in the morning.

Rainy days are particularly suitable for sleeping, so Xia Xiqing, nestling under the quilt, turns over to hug Zhou Ziheng's waist from behind and continues to lie in bed. But just as he's about to fall back into dreamland, Zhou Ziheng's mobile phone starts to vibrate incessantly.

Xia Xiqing shoves Zhou Ziheng impatiently. "The phone... so damn noisy..."

A dazed, half-awake Zhou Ziheng reflexively reaches for his phone and picks up the call. Only then is Xia Xiqing satisfied. He burrows his head against the back of Zhou Ziheng's warm neck and falls asleep once again.

In his dream, he vaguely hears Zhou Ziheng saying something, he sounds pretty worked up, but a short while later, all is silent again. And so, in such a daze, Xia Xiqing continues sleeping for god-knows-how-long.

By the time he wakes up naturally, he's the only one left

on the bed. He looks at his phone for a moment, then gets out of bed to wash up. As he heads downstairs, he hears a child's voice, but he assumes it's from the television.

"Ziheng," Xia Xiqing says as he descends the stairs. "What are you watching? Is there any cold beer left at home? I want one."

There's no one in the living room. The sound seems to be coming from the study. Xia Xiqing follows the sound, and just as he reaches the door, a child suddenly appears and wraps his arms around both of his legs. The child's eyes are blindfolded with a tie, and he tilts his head up, giggling, as he shouts, "Gotcha!"

Startled, Xia Xiqing jumps and presses back against the door. "Where did this child come from?"

On hearing Xia Xiqing's voice, Zhou Ziheng, who's been hiding under the desk, crawls out on all fours and sits on the office chair wearily. He clutches his collar and fans himself with it. "My older brother's."

"Your older brother?" A surprised Xia Xiqing takes off the tie on the little guy's face. "This is mine, right...?"

"I'm just borrowing it for a while." Zhou Ziheng swivels the office chair around, then claps his hands at the little guy and opens up his arms. "Come here, Xiao-Yin."

Xiao-Yin runs over and hugs Zhou Ziheng, saying in an adorable voice, "Uncle, I want to eat candy."

Zhou Ziheng taps once on his nose. "You can't have anymore. Your mommy says you can only have three pieces per day."

"Xiao-Yin?" This doesn't sound like a name for a boy, so Xia Xiqing asks, "What's his given name?"

"Auntie's asking you!" Zhou Ziheng holds the child's hands and swings them. "What's your name? How old are you?"

On hearing this, Xia Xiqing goes over and gives Zhou Ziheng a kick in the knee. "You're the one who's the auntie!"

"You're scaring the child." Zhou Ziheng can't stop laughing, but he pulls Xia Xiqing's hand over to plant a few kisses on it, acting like a pampered child as he begs for mercy.

After teaching him a lesson, Xia Xiqing squats to stroke the little guy's face. "Tell *shushu*[7] your name."

The little guy is unexpectedly gutsy. "Then, will you give me candy?"

"Sure." Xia Xiqing grabs hold of his little chubby hand and kneads it. To his surprise, it feels amazingly good to touch. "Shushu will give you as many as you want."

Xiao-Yin's eyes light up. "My name is Zhou Nianyin, and I'm..." He cocks his head and thinks for a moment. Eventually, he gestures a "three" with his hand. "Three and a half years old!"

"Wow, good for you!" It's all too easy to be led off-track by a child. Xia Xiqing can't help but imitate the tone of a child and speak to him in a babyish voice too. "Shushu will give you candy later." Having said that, he looks up at Zhou Ziheng. "What a good-looking child!"

"My child will look even better." Zhou Ziheng rests both hands on Xiao-Yin's head and smiles childishly as he reaches out a leg to touch Xia Xiqing's waist. "Why don't you make me one?"

Xia Xiqing rolls his eyes at him. "I'll make you a hammer." Having said that, he adds, "Why don't *you* make *me* one? The child will be beautiful with my genes."

"Yeah, yeah." Zhou Ziheng picks up Xiao-Yin and sets

---

7 "Shu(shu)" is an honorific title or suffix that is used for any man who's at least one nominal generation older than the speaker. Literally, it means "uncle," but it is used regardless of familial relation.

him on his lap. He holds onto him with one arm and frees the other hand to grab Xia Xiqing's wrist, and rubs it. "Our Xiqing is the best-looking of all. No one can compare."

Xia Xiqing keeps staring at Xiao-Yin. As if suddenly remembering something, he looks at Zhou Ziheng. "Xiao-Yin's name is really well-chosen. Zhou Nianyin, 'thinking of Yin,' which is your sister-in-law."

"Right." Zhou Ziheng grabs Xiao-Yin's fleshy hand and strokes Xia Xiqing's face with it. "In the future, our child can be called Zhou Nianqing[8], with Nian as the generation name. Sounds good too."

For some reason, hearing this suddenly makes Xia Xiqing's ears burn. He lowers his eyelids and curses in a small voice, "Lunatic."

Xiao-Yin imitates him and parrots Xia Xiqing in that adorable voice of his. "Lunatic."

Xia Xiqing bursts out laughing on seeing this little nephew mimic his cursing. He brushes a finger lightly across the tip of Xiao-Yin's nose. "Little one."

Thinking that Xia Xiqing doesn't like what he's saying, Zhou Ziheng immediately corrects himself. "Then, how about Xia Siheng? Thinking of Heng. The child will take after your surname. It sounds nice too."

On hearing this, Xia Xiqing promptly stands up, turns his back to Zhou Ziheng, and covers his ears. "What nonsense are you spouting...?"

Xiao-Yin also mumbles inaudible sounds as he gets off Zhou Ziheng's lap. He also covers his ears, rambles something incoherent to himself, and toddles behind Xia Xiqing.

"You two sure look like a pair of uncle and nephew."

---

8 This name would mean "thinking of Qing."

Since they're almost out of snacks and food in the apartment, they decide to take Xiao-Yin out shopping while it's not so crowded in the morning. They both don sunglasses and masks and put a large sunhat on Xiao-Yin before driving to a supermarket, one of a chain that sells imported foods.

"You guys really are dressed alike." After parking the car, Zhou Ziheng picks Xiao-Yin up with one hand and wraps his right hand around Xia Xiqing's shoulder. Xia Xiqing takes a look at himself. It's true. He's dressed in a blue T-shirt and a black fisherman's hat, while Xiao-Yin is dressed in a blue short-sleeved shirt and wearing a small black hat as well.

"We look like a family of three." Zhou Ziheng reaches over with the hand on Xia Xiqing's shoulder and strokes the side of Xia Xiqing's face. "Right?"

Xia Xiqing swats his hand away. "Right, my foot."

Shopping in supermarkets isn't really a common occurrence for Xia Xiqing. Places like this reek too heavily of the secular world and humanity, and are pretty much the place he used to hate the most. Every single person he used to brush past was a part of a family or couple; he was the only one who was alone. Meanwhile, Zhou Ziheng, as an actor himself, also rarely goes shopping in supermarkets on his own, albeit for different reasons.

Xiao-Yin, who's been placed in the child seat of the shopping cart, points with his little finger at everything he sees. When he sees the chocolate and candy shelves, he exclaims out loud in excitement, like a jubilant little sparrow. As soon as he gets worked up, Xia Xiqing will put boxes upon boxes of candies and chocolates into the shopping cart. Zhou Ziheng can't bear to watch any longer and grabs Xia Xiqing's wrist.

"Hey, hey, no more."

"I want! I want!" Xiao-Yin wriggles around on the shopping cart. He grabs Xia Xiqing's finger with his little hand and pouts. "Shushu, I want more."

"Alright, alright. One more box." Xia Xiqing is no match for the little one and picks a large gift box of candy to put into the shopping cart.

Zhou Ziheng shakes his head. "And to think I wondered whether you'd like kids. I didn't expect you to spoil him this much."

"Let him eat them if he wants, they're just snacks..." Seeing the smile on Xiao-Yin's face, Xia Xiqing's heart expands like a bulging hydrogen balloon that would soar in the next second.

"His mother doesn't allow him to eat too many snacks." Zhou Ziheng moves the chocolates around in the full cart. He can't help but sigh. "If my sister-in-law sees this, she'll no doubt reproach me." He then points at Xiao-Yin. "You mustn't tell your mommy, okay?"

Xiao-Yin nods repeatedly, like a little baby chick. He wraps his chubby little hands around Zhou Ziheng's long, slender index finger. "Shhh! Don't tell mommy."

Leaning over the side of the shopping cart, Xia Xiqing is so amused by Xiao-Yin that he can't stop laughing. He keeps stroking Xiao-Yin's head and doesn't take his eyes off of him. Zhou Ziheng rarely sees Xia Xiqing like this, and deep down feels a little unhappy. He presses down the brim of his hat and clears his throat.

"Aren't you liking him a tad too much?"

Xia Xiqing raises his head. "And what about it? He's your nephew."

Zhou Ziheng feels very justified in his jealousy. "So what if he's my nephew, is that reason for you to like him so much?"

"Why not?" Xia Xiqing smiles and arches his brows. "If you want, you can also like *my* nephew this much." He says, then starts laughing incessantly, leaving Zhou Ziheng helpless.

They buy some more necessities, then during checkout, they go their separate ways, as Zhou Ziheng goes off to get the car while Xia Xiqing takes Xiao-Yin along to pay.

"Shushu, can I eat this candy now?" Xiao-Yin pulls out a pack of gummy candy through the gap of the shopping cart.

Xia Xiqing grabs his little hand. "In a while. Let's give the lady the money first."

"But I have no money..." Xiao-Yin feels around in his little pocket for a long time, then spreads out his tiny little hands.

Xia Xiqing can't keep the corners of his mouth down, and replies in a gentle voice, "But I do."

The cashier instantly recognizes Xia Xiqing and exclaims in a quiet voice, "Xiqing-*gege*?"

Xia Xiqing lifts his head and smiles politely at her, then proceeds to take out the groceries in the shopping cart.

"It's really you?!" The girl is suddenly very excited. "Oh my god, to think I'd see you in person!"

A little startled, Xiao-Yin hides behind Xia Xiqing and grabs the leg of his pants with his little hands. Xia Xiqing reaches behind with his hand to pat him on the head. "It's okay."

The cashier calms herself down a little. Her hands shake even as she scans the codes. The man himself is really so good-looking that she can't get enough of it. It takes a while before she suddenly remembers the child's presence, and can't help but ask, "Xiqing-*gege*, whose child is this?"

Xia Xiqing pays the money and picks up the shopping bag, while his other hand reaches out to hold Xiao-Yin's.

He looks up at the cashier and smiles. "My nephew. Isn't he cute?"

"Cute!"

"Thank you!" Xia Xiqing squeezes Xiao-Yin's hand. "The lady says you're cute."

Xiao-Yin feels a little embarrassed. He twists his little foot round and round, and says slowly with his hand still hanging onto the hem of Xia Xiqing's shirt, "Thank you."

Xia Xiqing leads Xiao-Yin into the car, and also gets in the backseat. They have no child seat, so he has to watch over Xiao-Yin at all times, too busy to talk to Zhou Ziheng. This situation continues until mealtime. Xiao-Yin is a strange one, too. He doesn't eat when his own uncle feeds him food, instead insisting on having Xia Xiqing feed him, then takes one bite after another with relish.

Zhou Ziheng can't help but put down his bowl and says to Xiao-Yin in all seriousness, "You can't keep pestering Xiqing-shushu."

With a small grain of rice stuck on his mouth, Xiao-Yin stares wide-eyed with those black, grape-like eyes of his and enunciates each syllable with force, "I want Xiqing-shushu."

Zhou Ziheng is between laughter and tears. "You can't want him!" Then he turns his face to Xia Xiqing with a somewhat aggrieved expression. "Why does everyone want to fight me for you?"

Xia Xiqing picks up a small spoon and feeds the kid another mouthful. "Who's fighting you? Your ego is off the charts."

"Then stop feeding him and let him eat by himself."

"If I don't feed him, am I supposed to feed you instead?"

"Sure, feed me. Come on."

Xia Xiqing is so amused he laughs. "You sure live up to the

name, kiddo."

Now used to having two uncles accompanying him, Xiao-Yin becomes all the more boisterous. Both very busy men spend a whole day at whole playing games with the little darling, including eagle, hen, and chicks, as well as hide-and-seek. Xia Xiqing even lies on the floor to draw with him.

"Xiqing-shushu, you're drawing it wrong." Xiao-Yin grabs the crayon in Xia Xiqing's hands. "Like this..."

Zhou Ziheng pinches Xiao-Yin's cheeks. "You're really something, to get an artist to learn to draw from you." He then looks at Xiao-Yin's previous "masterpieces" and can't help but shake his head in lament. "The children of the Zhou family are truly abstract artists."

But he also finds it strange. Xia Xiqing has never been one for patience, but is particularly attentive to Xiao-Yin. This is entirely beyond Zhou Ziheng's expectations. When the three of them sit together to watch Peppa Pig, Zhou Ziheng can hardly bear to go on, but Xia Xiqing watches along with the little buddy with great relish.

"Xiqing-shushu, Peppa is a good friend of mine."

"Really? Your friend is so cute."

"You are a good friend of mine, too!"

"How nice. If that's the case, I'm also Peppa's friend."

Looking at the big guy and the little one in silence, Zhou Ziheng suddenly feels a little sad. He suddenly thought about Xia Xiqing as a child. How adorable and lovable must Xia Xiqing have been? Does he also want to have a cute child to take care of and love, to make him the world's most blissful baby? But no matter how he guesses, Zhou Ziheng knows very well that he can never share in his experience.

After a whole day of playing, an exhausted Xiao-Yin falls asleep leaning against Xia Xiqing's arm. Xia Xiqing gently sets his little head on his own lap and pats his little body, and watches his adorable sleeping face.

"Since you like children so much, let's adopt one in the future." Zhou Ziheng suddenly pipes up.

Xia Xiqing's hand pauses in mid-air. Eventually, he shakes his head. "Forget it."

"Why?"

He doesn't answer. Zhou Ziheng is just about to keep probing when the doorbell rings. He goes over and looks at the camera—it's Jiang Yin.

"Sister-in-law, you're finally here." Zhou Ziheng opens the door and leans beside it. "You're done with work?"

"Yeah. Thank you for all the trouble. Where's Xiao-Yin? I'll take him to mom and dad's."

Jiang Yin changes her shoes and walks in. In the living room, Xia Xiqing reaches out a hand and waves at Jiang Yin, greeting in a soft voice.

"Yin-jie."

"Xiqing." It's only then that Jiang Yin sees the little one lying beside Xia Xiqing's legs. "He likes you that much, huh?" Then she looks pointedly back at Zhou Ziheng and smiles. "As expected of Ziheng's nephew."

"Hurry up and take him away." Zhou Ziheng folds his arms before his chest. "At this rate, your precious son is going to encroach on another man's territory."

"Oy, the stink of jealousy."

Jiang Yin picks up Xiao-Yin, and Xiao-Yin opens his eyes. Still a clingy one, he reaches over to pull Xia Xiqing's hand. Xia Xiqing smooches his little cheek.

"See you next time, little cutie."

Only then does Jiang Yin take her son and leave Zhou Ziheng's house. Once the child is gone, the house suddenly quiets down. The drawing tools all over the ground have yet to be cleared away, and it's a mess all over, but no one wants to move. Xia Xiqing reclined on the sofa. After Zhou Ziheng closed the door and comes over to sit beside him, he shifts over to lean against Zhou Ziheng's shoulder.

"Tired?"

Xia Xiqing shakes his head.

"Why don't you want to adopt a child?" Zhou Ziheng grabs Xia Xiqing's hands and locks fingers with him. "Too much trouble? Or too much of responsibility?"

But instead of answering the question, Xia Xiqing throws out another: "Do you think I can take good care of a child?"

The tone in which Xia Xiqing says this doesn't seem like a question; rather, it's more like a rhetorical question from a lack of self-confidence. Zhou Ziheng instantly understands. He's worried that he won't be able to properly take care of a child.

"You can. You're very gentle."

Xia Xiqing says with a bitter smile, "But I don't even know what a good parent is like." The setting sun softens his silhouette. "People from broken families always pine for a perfect one, but when the day comes, most of them become the kind of people they hate the most. This kind of vicious circle is entirely fatalistic."

"You won't. I know." Zhou Ziheng kisses the top of Xia Xiqing's head. "You were so gentle with Xiao-Yin earlier, so I know you'd be a good father. He's not even your child, yet you are so gentle and patient with him, and you adore him from the bottom of your heart."

"That's because he looks like you." Xia Xiqing explains bluntly. "He looks very much like you when you were a child."

These words are like a pitch that strikes Zhou Ziheng right in the heart. "So you like Xiao-Yin so much because he looks like me?"

Xia Xiqing lifts his head and smiles a little. "Yeah, I thought that when I saw him for the first time. It felt like I went back to the time when I saw you in that park."

I want to place all the beautiful things in the world in your hand and to give you all of my tenderness, no matter how scarce it is. With this thought in mind, Xia Xiqing leans back against the sofa and stares at the ceiling, speaking in a daze.

"Zhou Ziheng, I realize that I really do love you very much."

Zhou Ziheng's heart clenches.

"I'm taking 'love me, love my dog' a bit too seriously. Your little nephew, your parents, your family, and friends— I like them all. The foods you love, the movies you love, the songs you love... When I eat, watch, and listen to them now, I think they're all great. I like them too." He shields his eyes with the back of his hand. "I kinda feel like I'm slowly losing myself."

Slowly turning into you, into another Zhou Ziheng.

Zhou Ziheng never expected him to say these things. He leans over and kisses Xia Xiqing on the lips, then kisses the palm of his hand.

"A misconception." He takes Xia Xiqing's hand and looks into his eyes. "You are you. You have always been." Then, he suddenly smiles, looking a little childish, yet gentle to the max. "It's just that I've hidden you away, and I won't ever return you in this lifetime."

Xia Xiqing doesn't snap out of his thoughts for a very long time after that. He remains in a trance until Zhou Ziheng touches his face and drops a tender kiss on his cheek.

"What's the matter? What are you thinking about?"

Xia Xiqing smiles and reaches out to caress Zhou Ziheng's hand. His long, slender fingers slip through the gaps between Zhou Ziheng's fingers. "Then you must know that when people go to a higher altitude, like Tibet for example, they get altitude sickness, right?"

Zhou Ziheng doesn't understand this sudden change of subject, but he still nods, "That's right."

"Then, do you know what happens when people who live at high altitudes come down to the plains?" Xia Xiqing gently rubs the tips of Zhou Ziheng's fingers against his own, his pair of beautiful eyes sparkling with tender starlight.

"What happens?"

"They get drunk on oxygen." Xia Xiqing wraps both arms around Zhou Ziheng's neck. "I'm a little drunk on oxygen right now." Every word he says is sincere and earnest, laced with a tinge of imperceptible vulnerability. "You won't ever know what it's like for a person who lacks love to all of a sudden receive too much of it."

The child who's longed for a piece of candy since he was young is so overwhelmed by the sudden shower of candies that he's dazed and at a loss.

Zhou Ziheng kisses him on his lips and embraces him as if he's embracing a child. "What are the symptoms of one drunk on oxygen?"

Xia Xiqing feels puzzled by his question, but still, he answers, "Dizziness, languidness, as if you are drunk on wine. Sometimes, there will be chest tightness and erratic heartbeats."

"Is that so?" Zhou Ziheng tousles his hair and hangs close to him like a large well-behaved hound. "Then, I'm also drunk on oxygen. From the very first day I met you, I've been drunk. To this day, I've still yet to recover from it."

He grins like a child as he nuzzles the tip of his nose against Xia Xiqing's.

"What am I to do? You have to save me."

E.11

Invaluable Team-up

In order to boost interest two days before the broadcast of *Survive and Escape Season 2*, the production team once again invites the previous cast of guests from the *Werewolves of Millers Hollow*. They want to use *The Werewolves of Millers Hollow* game to drive up the premiere ratings of the program, and to preemptively commandeer the popular discussions.

The guests, who are already familiar with the routine, arrive in the studio. The broadcast has only just begun when the channel is packed with program fans and Self-Study girls who've come to watch. The screen freezes for a long time before it begins to move again.

> Ahhhhhhhh xqgg I missed you!!

> Heng-Heng, look at mama! Mama is here!!

> Everyone looks so good this time! Zhixu's coiffed hair is so stylish!

> Did Xiao-Xiao dye her hair? The rose color looks so nice! As expected of the head of the Self-Study girls!

> Is Xiuze eating chips hahahaha! So adorable! Why is everyone from the Xia family so cute?!

Everyone takes their seat based on their previous positions. Player 1 Xia Zhixu, Player 2 Xu Qichen, Player 3 Ruan Xiao, Player 4 Yang Bo, Player 5 Xia Xiqing, Player 6 Shang Sirui, Player 7 Zhao Ke, Player 8 Xia Xiuze, Player 9 Zhou Ziheng. After they are all seated, the program director, acting as the game master, starts to deal out the cards. Everyone's expression is very entertaining to watch.

Xia Xiqing turns over his card for a look. "Can't carry this time. How boring."

Xia Zhixu glances at him with disdain. "Since when have you carried before? With me around, you won't be able to carry."

Xu Qichen smiles. "Can't you two try to get along?"

Zhou Ziheng shakes his head. "They've been feuding for twenty-five years."

> Hahaha I can watch these four sitting here chatting for an entire year!

> Wait for me, I'm joining you! I really love the group crosstalk of these four. Too cute!

> Feuding for twenty-five years lmaooo it'll be fun if they are paired up as lovers later

"Night falls. Please close your eyes."

The room dims, and everyone closes their eyes as the lights turn an eerie shade of dark red.

"Cupid, please open your eyes."

Xia Xiuze opens both eyes.

> Whoa, the younger bro is Cupid in this game

> So curious who he will pair up as lovers

"Cupid, please pair up the lovers."

Xia Xiuze stares at the camera and almost without hesitation, gestures a 5, then a 1.

> Hot damn, he paired up xqgg and Zhixu!!!

> LMFAOOOOO way to go Xiuze!

> So, this game is basically the Three Musketeers of the Xia Family? Lolololol

> Lmfaooo nooooo! What good does it do you to make me laugh myself to my death?!

"Cupid, please close your eyes." When the game master walks over to Xia Zhixu and Xia Xiqing and pokes each of them respectively, the voice of God once again sounds, "Lovers, please open your eyes."

As soon as Xia Xiqing opens his eyes and sees Xia Zhixu, he rolls his eyes dramatically. Xia Zhixu mimes himself flipping the table and standing up, mouthing, "I quit this game!"

> Hahahahahah how to continue!

> You know what they say about tempting fate ROFL. Who would've thought that the two feuding for twenty-five years would end up as a pair of lovers?!

> xqgg: I'm gonna self-expose and take my lover down with me

> Hahhaha self-expose and take down his lover

"Werewolves, please open your eyes and confirm your associates."

Xia Zhixu, Ruan Xiao, and Shang Sirui open their eyes. Xia Zhixu makes an OK sign at the camera.

> Wheeze, that shot of Zhixu is so handsome!

> The most pro player on the werewolves team is a part of a human-werewolf pair. This is so exciting!!

> Feels like this human-werewolf pair is going to carry

> I think so too. Unless Ziheng and Screenwriter Xu can ferret them out

"Werewolves, please choose your victim."

The three of them look at each other. Xia Zhixu signs a 3. Ruan Xiao is momentarily taken aback. Then she uses her palm and makes the gesture of slicing her own throat with a perplexed expression on her face. Shang Sirui is rather stunned too. Xia Zhixu nods and pats his own chest.

> Damn, isn't Zhixu a little too two-faced to be selling out his teammate right at the start?

> Won't this be too obvious? The others won't suspect him of having been paired up as a lover?

> Killing off one of their own to defraud the potion is too exciting!

Ruan Xiao thinks it over. So far, they've rarely offed themselves to scam the potion out of the witch, so perhaps it may really work this time. After all, there are too many pro players in the good guys team right now. It's not a big deal to take a gamble, and they will win big if it succeeds. Therefore, she nods her head and faces the camera to point to herself.

> He really convinced Xiao-Xiao

> I wonder who the witch is. If they manage to get their hands on the potion, it's big casualties for both the good guys and the werewolves

> No wonder fangs-*gege* is a Xia, the way he plays dirty and fierce

"Werewolves, please close your eyes."

"Seer, please open your eyes."

As soon as the words are spoken, Xu Qichen opens his eyes and looks at the camera.

> Screenwriter Xu is the seer!

> Feels like Screenwriter Xu is going to carry this round. Screenwriter Xu, fighting!

> Xiya sama, I'll forever love you!

> Is Screenwriter Xu really Xie Xiya?

"Seer, please choose the person whose identity you wish to check."

Xu Qichen holds out his hand and signs a 5.

> Poor Xiqing-*gege*. He keeps being the first to be verified and paired up as the lovers

> And the only reason he isn't the first to be killed is that his lover is in the werewolves team hahaha

"This means good guy, this means bad guy. This is his identity." The production crew gives him a thumbs up. Xu Qichen nods with a calm and composed expression.

> If I were in his shoes, I'd also check xqgg's identity first. He's the biggest uncertainty of everyone here

"Seer, please close your eyes. Witch, please open your eyes."

On hearing this, Zhao Ke opens his eyes.

> Zhao Ke-*gege*!! Damn, no doubt they will be able to scam the potion out of him!

> What I'm thinking is that the werewolves team will be momentarily basking in the joy of having scammed the potion that they probably won't guess that Zhixu has been paired up as the lovers

"This is the victim tonight." The game master signs a 3. Zhao Ke looks at Ruan Xiao with a frown. "You have a bottle of antidote. Do you want to save her?"

Still frowning, Zhao Ke considers it for a few seconds. Eventually, he nods with awe-inspiring righteousness.

> Hah, he still saved his wife in the end

> If he didn't, Xiao-Xiao will no doubt beat him up later when she finds out that he's the witch lololol

> My desire for self-preservation caused me to be scammed out of a potion

"You have a bottle of poison. Would you like to use it?"

Zhao Ke makes a cross with his hands before his chest and closes his eyes.

"It's now daytime." The narrator pauses. "The sheriff's election campaign will now begin. Players who wish to run for sheriff, please raise your hands."

"Player 1 Xia Zhixu, Player 2 Xu Qichen, Player 5 Xia Xiqing, Player 6 Shang Sirui, and Player 7 Zhao Ke are in the running for sheriff. Please make your speeches now, starting with Player 1 Xia Zhixu."

> Xia "No-Matter-What-I've-Got-To-Be-Sheriff" Xiqing

> The two lovers haven't even figured out each other's identity, and they are already running for sheriff, hhh. So unrestrained. As expected of the Xia family

Xia Zhixu clears his throat. "I'm up first. I joined the campaign just to get in some words. I always feel like I might be the first one to be killed off, so I figure I should take the opportunity during the sheriff campaign to get some words in. I'm a good guy. I'd also suggest the seer verify Xia Xiqing's identity later. A thorough identity check must be conducted on the dirtiest player of the game; otherwise, there'd be no way to continue playing."

The words have only just left his mouth when Xia Xiqing glances at him. The two exchange a look. Xia Xiqing instantly comes to the conclusion that Xia Zhixu is a werewolf. Only a human-werewolf pair in which the other party or himself is a werewolf would be so eager to get the seer to verify his own lover's identity. On one hand, he can use this method to drop a hint to his lover about his own werewolf identity. On the other hand, he can waste one of the seer's identity checks.

It's a human-werewolf pair again. Xia Xiqing feels mentally exhausted.

> Hahahaha selling out his lover right at the start

Xu Qichen casts a glance at Xia Zhixu before calmly starting his own campaign speech. "I'm the seer, and there's a pleasant surprise from my verification last night. Give me the sheriff's badge, and if there's anyone after me claiming to be the seer, I'll tag them as a werewolf; I won't even need to verify. I repeat, there's a pleasant surprise from my verification last night. Once I get the sheriff's badge, I'll out the werewolf; over."

Xia Xiqing says with a smile on his face, "Chen-Chen's so bold. I'm a seer too, and I've verified Xia Zhixu to be a werewolf." With that, he looks at Xia Zhixu. "Are you going to expose yourself or not? If you do, no one will get the sheriff's badge for this round."

> Xia "Will-Die-If-He-Doesn't-Threaten-His-Own-Lover" Xiqing

> Lmfaooo xqgg is at it again. It's so emotionally tiring to be his lover rofl

> Xia Zhixu: Careful that I might really self-expose and take you down with me

Xia Zhixu's expression changes dramatically as he slaps his palm on the table, startling Xu Qichen so much that he whips his head around to look at him. But Xia Zhixu laughs, shrugs, and silently mouths "It's a pity I can't self-expose."

> Pretty sure Zhixu really wanted to self-expose and take down xqgg for a very brief instant hahahahaha

> Xia Zhixu: The desire to win made me put down my personal enmity

Seeing Xia Zhixu's reaction, Xia Xiqing shrugs too. "Okay, I lied. I'm not the seer. I just wanted to see if I could trick a werewolf into exposing himself. Seems like he's a mentally strong one. Frankly, I'm an eyes-shut villager, so I don't have much information this time. I feel like the way Chen-Chen said there's a surprise with his verification is a little unlike when he played the seer in the past. But then again he's very firm, and he's always very firm every time he plays the good guy. On the other hand, I have no idea if there'll be others claiming to be the seer later. I'm not, so I shall pass on first. I'm just here to see if I can trick others and muddy the waters."

> xqgg understands Screenwriter Xu all too well

> Feel like Xiqing-*gege* and fangs-*gege* are both trying to deduce each other's identity

After he's done, Shang Sirui takes over. "I'm a villager or higher. I also find this seer speech a little strange. If there's no one else claiming to be the seer, everyone can consider giving me the sheriff's badge. I have a good identity who can carry everyone. That's all for now, I guess; over."

Zhao Ke says, "I'm a strong special character. Initially, I wasn't planning to fight for the sheriff's badge when the seer revealed himself, but he wouldn't report the identity of the person he verified, so I still don't trust him. It's better for a special character like me to get ahold of the sheriff's badge instead. I have information on hand. Everyone can cast their votes for me; over."

"The campaign speeches conclude. Player 1 Xia Zhixu and Player 5 Xia Xiqing withdraw from the election. Players who are not running in the election, please proceed to vote." The program crew takes a look at the vote results. "Player 3 Ruan Xiao, Player 4 Yang Bo, Player 8 Xia Xiuze, and Player 9 Zhou Ziheng voted for Player 2 Xu Qichen. Player 2 Xu Qichen is hereby elected sheriff. Last night was a peaceful night."

Xu Qichen ponders it over for a moment. "Let's start with Ruan Xiao and have the speeches given in ascending order."

> The sheriff sure knows how to choose!

> His first choice is the werewolf who offed herself to scam the potion the night before. Screenwriter Xu is truly awesome! His sixth sense is amazing!

"I'm the first to give my speech, huh..." Ruan Xiao's expression is one of distress. "It was a peaceful night last night, which means the witch used the potion. There's no new information right now. The sheriff said there's a pleasant surprise with his verification, so does that mean said person is a werewolf? Then we'll go for the werewolf this round, I guess. Let's not get sidetracked with what we say. When the time comes, just go for the werewolf. I'm on the sheriff's side. I'm a villager and above; could be a villager, could be a special character. Feel free to guess; over."

Yang Bo speaks next. "Ah, I'm an eyes-shut player again, so there's nothing I can see from my perspective. All I can do is to hear the sheriff verify identities first. I voted for the sheriff and not the other special character during the election, mainly because the sheriff said there's a pleasant surprise from his verification. I'm waiting for it, and I hope he won't disappoint us. The two who didn't claim to be special characters have both withdrawn from the election, and in my mind, that cements their identity as the good guys. Then, all those not running for sheriff voted for the present sheriff. It's possible the werewolves are pretty scared and afraid of this sheriff. I'm just making wild guesses here. If we can go after the werewolf this round, then let's do it. I'm a good guy; over."

> Whoa, feels like Yang Bo has improved a lot

> Yeah, he no longer hedges even if he's speaking as a

villager. It's terrific

> Omgggggg it's Xiqing-*gege* next!

Xia Xiqing already understands that he and Xia Zhixu are a pair of human and werewolf lovers. In that case, he can only play according to the way a human-werewolf pair ought to play. The more he can get the good guys team and werewolves team to tear each other apart, the better.

He leans back in his chair and smiles relaxedly. "I ran because I was planning on muddying the water by gunning for the badge, but on second thoughts, such a way of playing might cause others to tag me as a werewolf and come after me, so I withdrew from the election."

The moment he says that, everyone bursts out laughing. Xia Xiqing makes a special point of hissing fiercely at Zhou Ziheng in a hushed tone, "What are you laughing at?"

> OooOOoOhhHHH a public display of affection!!!

> Ziheng:??? Everyone is laughing, why can't I?

Xia Xiqing shifts his gaze to Xu Qichen again. "But I don't think the sheriff is necessarily the real seer. If the seer card falls to a player who doesn't really know how to play this game, then who knows, maybe he didn't run for sheriff because he didn't suss out a werewolf, and someone might have just pretended to be the seer right then. Of course, it's all just reasonable doubt on my end. I'll hear what the sheriff has to say about his identity check later. I hope there's really a pleasant surprise. Then there's the peaceful night, which means the witch's antidote is gone. If I'm the werewolf, I'll definitely kill the sheriff in the next round. The sheriff must make good use of his special privilege and explain who he will check in the next few turns. I'd suggest..."

He looks around before locking eyes on Shang Sirui. "... Verifying Shang Sirui's identity next round. He said earlier that he has a good identity that can carry everyone, and the only identities that can carry this game are either the witch or the seer. Yet you don't dare to claim to be a special character, this in itself is a little contradictory. Maybe you are a werewolf who wanted to pretend to be a seer but lost the courage to, and gave up midway. Of course, this is just my own two cents. The sheriff doesn't have to listen to me. It's OK even if you want to verify my identity; over."

> Wow wow wow he ferreted out a werewolf in no time at all. Xqgg is so awesome!

> xqgg's ability to pinpoint a werewolf is so OP! Actually, if xqgg isn't one of the human-werewolf lovers, the good guys team would be truly godly!

Seeing as he's been named, Shang Sirui smiles, unperturbed. "You may verify my identity, no problem at all. I'm not afraid of being checked, but why am I afraid to claim to be a special character? Anything can happen in a slaughter-of-city game. If I speak up, that means I'm a werewolf? I don't think that's how you play this game, right?" He pauses for a beat, then changes the subject. "Besides, everyone is certain the seer is who he claims to be. But my opinion is that this seer identity is not set in stone yet. When Qichen played special characters in the past, his speeches were not like this. I'll listen to his speech later. If we have a werewolf identified, then, by all means, gun for him. There's no need to waste time talking about other things. If there isn't, then we can see if any werewolf shows their tails. I'm a villager and above, over."

> Is ssr trying to convey a message to his own werewolves teammates hahaha. Pretend to be a seer, guys!

> Claiming to be a seer against Screenwriter Xu in this round is basically suicidal. I think Screenwriter Xu is currently trying to

trick the werewolves into exposing themselves

> Agree with that. Screenwriter Xu didn't manage to ferret out a werewolf with his identity check. He's probably listening to the speeches now to try to trick one out

Zhao Ke continues after Shang Sirui without preamble. "I'm a special character. It's a pity I didn't get the sheriff's badge this time. The sheriff didn't report the result of his identity check, but all those not running in the election still voted for him. Who knows, perhaps it's his werewolves teammates voting for their fake seer friend. Just a wild guess. If there's someone else claiming to be the seer, I'll take a closer look. Perhaps the badge will have to be ripped up. I'm really a special character. Special special special character; over."

> A special special special character who got cheated out of his potion by his girlfriend!

> Xiao-Xiao is trying so hard to hold back her laughter!

> Short-lived special character, Zhao xiao-Ke!

"My turn." Chewing bubble gum in his mouth, Xia Xiuze grins as he speaks up. "Why do Zhao Ke's earlier words sound like he's sending a message to his werewolf friends? It's like he's saying, 'you guys, hurry up and claim to be the seer, fight the sheriff for the badge.'"

> Ohhohoho, our adorable baby Cupid is starting to muddy the water!'

> Baby bro is so adorable! He's like a chibi version of xqgg!

> This older sister here is waiting for you to grow up!!

"For now, I'll side with the sheriff. It can't be helped if there's really a seer who didn't run for sheriff. In any case, I won't be the scapegoat. I'm a bonafide good guy, but I don't have much information to give, so I can only listen to the outcome of the seer's identity check first; over."

Finally, it's Zhou Ziheng's turn. He's always very serious when he's playing a game, and when he's not smiling, he looks cold and unapproachable. "There's no need to look at me, guys. I'm not claiming to be the seer."

The moment he says that, everyone breaks out in laughter.

> Hahahaha Zhou Ziheng's dry humor

> Heng-Heng is so manly! Especially when he wears all black and doesn't smile

"I'm a good guy, but I'm not the seer, so I do believe that Xu Qichen is the seer. If he's a werewolf pretending to be the seer, there's no need for him to resort to speaking in such vague terms. I'm more inclined to believe that he's trying to draw speeches out of everyone." Having said that, he looks at Xia Zhixu beside him. "So, even if Zhixu says he's the seer later, I won't believe him. If he is, he wouldn't have withdrawn from the election earlier. If the seer doesn't speak, we basically have no useful information this round. The witch used up the potion, so it's perfectly normal even if the witch doesn't reveal his or her identity, and I don't really believe Zhao Ke is the witch. As for the rest, I'll wait for the sheriff's speech; over."

> Feels like Heng-Heng is giving Zhao Ke a hand

> Heng-Heng thinks to himself: this childhood friend of mine really makes one worry. Is he just asking to be killed?

Xia Zhixu taps the tabletop with both hands. "It's finally my turn." He pauses dramatically for a moment before speaking up again. "I'm the seer. I verified Xu Qichen to be a werewolf last night; werewolf sheriff."

With that, he even makes a point to wink at Xu Qichen, his fangs looking all arrogant and adorable. Xu Qichen is a picture of calm as he looks back at him wordlessly.

> Lolololololol fangs-*gege*'s fancy method of courting death!!

> Screenwriter Xu: Go on, keep acting

Seeing Xu Qichen like this, Xia Zhixu immediately reaches out to rub his hands. "Nah, I'm just joking, Mr. Policeman. I was wrong, I'm not the seer, I was just talking rubbish." Everyone laughs at how chicken he is. "When I ran for sheriff, I just wanted to get some words in. I always feel like I'd be the first to get killed off, but luckily, I lived. Can you feel my desire to survive?" He arches his eyebrows at Xu Qichen, who turns around and pulls his hand away.

Xia Zhixu continues, "Anyways, I find the speeches of those who went before me very interesting. Xia Xiqing wants to verify Sirui's identity, while Xiuze is low-key suggesting that Zhao Ke is a werewolf. Xia Xiqing, Sirui, and Zhao Ke don't really believe the sheriff, while Xiuze and Ziheng vouch for them. The others are just hedging it. Just the fact that they vouch or didn't vouch for the sheriff has already put them in different camps. In any case, I'm pretty much sure that Zhou Ziheng and Xia Xiqing aren't lovers in this game."

> The Xias really play dirty hahahaha

> He even wants to pass the buck to Ziheng lmao

"I hope the sheriff has a werewolf identified. If so, there's no need for us to fight over it. If not, then there must be a werewolf among the three who claim to be special characters: Ruan Xiao, Shang Sirui, and Zhao Ke. I think the sheriff can check the identity of the special characters in the next round. This is a slaughter-of-city game. It's safer to sacrifice someone who doesn't claim to be a special character, and whose speech isn't all that good; over."

Xu Qichen doesn't give his speech immediately. Instead, he keeps silent for a moment, sweeping his eyes across everybody at the table. "Let me give my statement for the next round of identity checks. I'll first check Ruan Xiao's identity, and if I survive the second time, I'll check Xia Zhixu's identity."

> Screenwriter Xu is really awesome! As expected of a pro player!

"The reason for checking Ruan Xiao's identity is because she's the one and only person not running for sheriff, but who doesn't claim to be a villager either. If I recall correctly, she said she could be a villager or a special character. I'm purely running on intuition here by wanting to check her identity. As for Xia Zhixu, it's because I'd like to eliminate the uncertainty and ascertain if this pro player is my team-mate or a werewolf if I make it to the third day." With that, he looks at Xia Zhixu. "The amount of characters you have claimed to be in this game is too many. Feels like you are a werewolf, and yet you are not."

Xia Zhixu shrugs and smiles brightly.

"I said earlier that my check on the first night turned up a pleasant surprise. Everyone, take my lead for this werewolf: Shang Sirui."

The moment he says that everyone's eyes shoot toward Shang Sirui. The expression on Shang Sirui's face, however, barely changes.

"There's nothing else to say. Vote out the werewolf in this round. I'll observe the outcome of the voting. If I die after checking Ruan Xiao's identity tonight..."

He's yet to finish his words when Shang Sirui smacks the table. "Boom!"

The narrator's voice sounds. "The werewolf has self-exposed. After his last words, we will be moving directly into the night."

> SSR really self-exposed!

> xqgg must be thrilled to bits now, having taken down one

werewolf and one special character. He was just trying to trick San-San earlier, I can't believe San-San really self-exposed

"I'll say a few words to my fellow werewolves. Leaving aside killing the sheriff first, Zhao Ke should be the witch. Off him in the round after this. Ruan Xiao feels more like Cupid to me. In any case, we will be able to figure it out through the process of elimination. My life for a sheriff. The odds of us werewolves winning is still very much in our favor."

Shang Sirui leaves, and the set darkens once again. Everyone closes their eyes.

"Werewolves, please open your eyes."

The narrator has only just said the words when Ruan Xiao and Xia Zhixu both open their eyes. Without a pause, they choose Player 2 Xu Qichen.

> There's only one hidden werewolf left in the werewolf team, and he's also one of the lovers

"Werewolves, please close your eyes. Seer, please open your eyes."

Xu Qichen opens his eyes and chooses Ruan Xiao. As expected, he gets the answer he's looking for.

> Screenwriter Xu is really good, but it's really a tough fight this time. No way he can carry

"Witch, please open your eyes. This is the victim tonight. You have a bottle of antidote; would you like to use it?"

Zhao Ke shakes his head helplessly. He already knows that it's the seer who will leave this round, but he's already used up his antidote, so there's nothing he can do. When the narrator asks about the use of poison, he shakes his head once again.

"Witch, please close your eyes. It's now daytime." The narrator's voice pauses. "The one who died last night is Player

2 Xu Qichen. No last words. Please hand over your sheriff's badge."

Xu Qichen clutches the sheriff's badge, looking hesitant. He seems to cast a look at Xia Xiqing, but eventually, he lifts his hands and makes an X with them.

"The sheriff opts to tear up the sheriff's badge. The game continues."

> I seriously suspect Screenwriter Xu has guessed that xqgg has been paired up as the lovers!

> Feels like one can't just give the badge to players like xqgg even if he's one of the good guys hahaha

> Luckily he didn't hand him the badge, or it's a lost case

"Make your speeches now, starting from the left of the deceased."

Ruan Xiao sighs in resignation. "So I'm the first to speak again. That was such an exciting round. The sheriff seemed to have already predicted he would die, and every word he said was all carefully thought through. But I don't think Shang Sirui's last words at the end are necessarily true. He said Zhao Ke is the witch and asked his fellow werewolves to kill him off, but I somehow feel like he's giving Zhao Ke a hand here. We don't have a seer now anyway, so I'll listen carefully to Zhao Ke's speech again later. As for me, I may be Cupid, or I may be a villager taking the blow for Cupid. It's a slaughter-of-city game, so it's very common to claim to be someone else. Everyone can make a guess for themselves; over."

> Feels like Xiao-Xiao can't survive this round

> Zhao Ke has yet to name the person he saved. I feel like he will help Ruan Xiao out

Now that Ruan Xiao is done, it's Yang Bo's turn. He ponders it over carefully. "Shang Sirui spoke to his teammates when he left, and the ones he mentioned may all be questionable. I was thinking, why not vote someone out among those he mentioned? But then, Ruan Xiao's speech earlier sounded very much like a good guy. In that case, I'll listen to Zhao Ke's speech. I also find the people who threw shade at the seer earlier dubious, over."

> XQGG I LOVE YOU!!!!!

"Oof, everyone is so focused on Shang Sirui's last words. Why isn't anyone focusing on the sheriff's speech before Chen-Chen left?" Xia Xiqing taps on the tabletop with his fingers—his usual habit when he's pondering over a strategy. But of all those present, only Zhou Ziheng notices this subtle gesture.

"I'm an eyes-shut player, but based on my understanding of Chen-Chen, I can kind of guess what happened on the first night. I think it's very likely that he didn't verify the identity of a werewolf. He probably verified the identity of a good guy, and so this bout of verification was wasted. Moreover, the way he plays has always been steady by comparison. I reckon it was me or Ziheng he checked on the first night. But of course, that's another story. It's not important who he checked, what's important is that he didn't find a werewolf. That's why he didn't say explicitly when he was running for sheriff; he wanted to listen to the speeches and figure it out from there."

> Wow, as an eyes-shut player, xqgg is even more formidable than those with a third eye

> This guess is really way too accurate for comfort. Are you sure there's no script?

"Actually, I suspected Shang Sirui when he ran for sheriff, so I tricked him on purpose. He didn't self-expose then, which means he didn't self-expose because he couldn't take the pressure. Then, why did he self-expose after the sheriff's speech? Because the sheriff's statement on his identity verification process was too accurate—he found out the identity of his werewolf teammate." With that, he turns aside and smiles sweetly at Ruan Xiao, "Am I right, Werewolf Beauty?"

> what a tease I cry

> OMG this smile!! I'm dead! RIP me!

> Everyone, take a look at zzh's expression. Truly a maniac who can't keep his eyes off his wife!

"What's more, the last words Shang Sirui left were too cunning. He included two people, and I don't believe that both are really special characters. One of them must be the fellow werewolf that he's carrying." Then, Xia Xiqing sprawls over the table. "Of course, all of you don't have to agree with my train of thought. In any case, I'm an eyes-shut player. I think Shang Sirui self-exposed because he was afraid that Chen-Chen would verify Xiao-Xiao's identity. He wouldn't even let Chen-Chen finish his sheriff's statement. It's too obvious. Oh man, feels like I'm gonna have to carry this game as a villager."

> xqgg is so so so so cute!

> If the little rose is really a villager, he might actually carry for real this time. A pity he isn't

Once Xia Xiqing is done with his speech, Zhao Ke begins his. "I'm indeed the witch. I saved Ruan Xiao on the first day. Actually, I don't fully agree with Xiqing's logic. I think it's also possible that Shang Sirui did so to smear Ruan Xiao's identity; that's why he intentionally chose that time to self-expose. What's more, he deliberately spoke to his werewolf teammates, and I'm now suspecting if Xiqing is his fellow werewolf instead. Xiqing's trying too hard to slander Ruan Xiao, but then it's all the same no matter what role

Xiqing plays. I can't be certain for sure. I won't vote Xiqing out this round, but of course, I won't vote for the person I saved either."

After this, he pauses for a moment before analyzing, "I think the possibility of werewolves offing themselves in a slaughter-of-city game is very small. After all, they can't know for sure that I'm the witch, so the honey-trap is almost too perfectly played. How can there be such a coincidence? One of the werewolves who pretended to be a special character already left, and I think there are still werewolves around. For some reason, I feel like Xiuze is just here to muddy the waters. He keeps changing tune, and it doesn't feel like he's helping the good guys."

Xiuze is rather pleased to be suspected. "Ruan Xiao-jiejie said she's the Cupid, but she wouldn't make a definitive statement of it. Feels like she doesn't really have the confidence, huh. When Sirui-*gege* left, he spoke about Zhao Ke-*gege* and Ruan Xiao-jiejie, and it just so happens that Zhao Ke-*gege* saved Xiao-Xiao-jie on the first night. I keep feeling like there's something fishy here. The more I think about it, the stranger it feels."

"I agree with my brother more. Of the two special characters, one must be fake. I'm more inclined to think it's Ruan Xiao-jiejie. We can vote her out this round; it's unlikely that she's Cupid. She didn't even mention the couple she paired up; it's really too unlike a Cupid's speech."

> Younger bro: I'm the real Cupid! Don't steal my identity!

Xia Xiuze signals the end of his turn, and it's finally time for Zhou Ziheng to speak. "I've been at the back in both rounds, and it makes me rather happy to listen to the performances. Let's talk about Xiqing first. Although I'm not fully certain that he's one of the good guys, his reasoning is basically the same as mine. Adding on to what Ke-*zi*[9] said, it's not entirely impossible for the werewolves to off themselves in a slaughter-of-city game, especially if they are gutsy enough. Besides, there has to be one pro player on the werewolves team."

> Heng-Heng's really too good at this!!

> Goodness me, to think the Self-Study husband and husband pair can figure out the werewolves despite being eyes-shut players. Big brain!

"In that case, I can basically deduce the werewolves' identity. Shang Sirui, Ruan Xiao, and Xia Zhixu after me—three werewolves in all. Who knows, perhaps Xia Zhixu is the one who suggested offing Ruan Xiao."

> Hot damn, Heng-Heng too OP!!!

"If Ruan Xiao isn't the werewolf, then most likely it's Xia Xiqing who spoke out against her, with Xiuze being the other possibility. But I'm more inclined to believe the former. Let's try voting out Ruan Xiao this round. It might be risky, but I think this is the only way to gain on the werewolves; over."

Now that the werewolves' identity has been pointed out, there's a variety of interesting expressions on everyone's faces. Contrary to expectations, Xia Zhixu doesn't feign.

"Why am I suddenly shoved into the werewolf team? Just because I'm a pro player? It's hard to say if Xia Xiqing is a werewolf lynching his fellow werewolves to save himself, isn't it? Oh, wait. Zhou Ziheng is a pro player too. You're not selling out your own teammates to protect yourself, are you? There's no need to stoop so low, is there? Those are your teammates by blood, buddy." After muddying the

9 In this context, "-*zi*" is being used to make a diminutive nickname.

waters, Xia Zhixu pretends to realize the truth. "Oh, I get it now. You must have been paired up as the lovers, that's why you betrayed your werewolf teammates. So this round is a human-werewolf pair again, huh? Never mind it, let's just vote out Ruan Xiao first. We'll suss out the lovers in the next round and deduce their identities one step at a time. I'm not afraid, anyway."

> Zhixu: Hurry up and vote my teammate out. In any case, I'm a human-werewolf pair wahahahaha

"The speeches of all players have concluded. Next is a vote for the player to be cast out of the game." The narrator looks at the voting result and continues, "Player 1 Xia Zhixu, Player 4 Yang Bo, Player 5 Xia Xiqing, Player 8 Xia Xiuze, and Player 9 Zhou Ziheng voted for Player 3 Ruan Xiao. Player 7 Zhao Ke voted for Player 8 Xia Xiuze. Player 3 is out of the game. No last words. The game continues. Night falls. Please close your eyes."

The lights in the room dim once again, and music starts playing. The remaining six players close their eyes.

"Werewolves, please open your eyes."

The one and only werewolf opens his eyes and grins smugly.

> Fangs-*gege* sold his teammates out one by one
> Xia Zhixu is really so handsome hnnnn...

"Werewolves, please choose a victim."

Xia Zhixu chooses Zhao Ke without hesitation and closes his eyes. The narrator reads out the lines for the seer according to procedures, then moves on to the witch. Zhao Ke opens his eyes.

"Witch, this is the victim of the werewolves. You have a bottle of antidote; would you like to use it? You have a bottle of poison; would you like to use it?"

Although Zhao Ke can't see who died, he can guess that the werewolves have no doubt killed him. He has to use the poison this round. With this thought in mind, he signs an eight to poison Xia Xiuze to death.

> Ke-zi is really gunning for baby bro as always

> Actually, Ke-zi isn't a fool. Baby bro is indeed not in the good guy camp, but he isn't a werewolf

"Day breaks." When all the players open their eyes, the narrator continues. "Two people died last night. Player 7 Zhao Ke and Player 8 Xia Xiuze. The game continues. Make your speeches now, starting from Player 5 Xia Xiqing."

Xia Xiqing sweeps his eyes across the remaining players at the table. "The game isn't over, which means there's still a werewolf left. Ziheng's analysis earlier is on point. He said that there's definitely a pro player on the werewolves' team, and look at how rare it's been for us few pros to survive until the end? If I were a werewolf, I'd have self-exposed myself a long time ago. Would I still let the sheriff say so much?"

> Well, that certainly is true lmfaoooo

> If Xiqing-*gege* is the werewolf, he would've played much better this round

"The way Shang Sirui self-exposed was too amateurish. If he wanted to self-expose he should have done so earlier and taken as many down with him as possible. Earlier, I thought Xia Zhixu is a werewolf for sure, but the way he claims to be one feels a tad too merry, so it somehow doesn't feel like it. But after the last round of speeches, I changed my mind again. My gut feeling tells me that Ziheng is the werewolf."

> He's finally going for his hubby!

> This round will decide the winner! If one of the lovers is voted out, the game will end

"He's terribly calm every time he plays a werewolf, and

he'd attempt to smear every single one of us both explicitly and implicitly. I'll vote Zhou Ziheng out this round."

Zhou Ziheng's expression remains calm as usual. He even smiles at Xia Xiqing.

> Hnnn our Heng-Heng is so sweet

"I've been waiting for the lovers to appear, and now I finally get it. Xiqing has definitely been paired up as one of the lovers. I can now be sure that you're a human-werewolf pair." Zhou Ziheng's tone is confident and sure, but very quickly, he starts to ponder over it again. "But who have you been paired up with? Let me gather my thoughts. If you're a human, then you may be paired up with Zhixu. If you're a werewolf, then it's possible you're paired up with Yang Bo..." As he says that, he frowns. "No matter who you are paired up with, I will surely vote you out this round. You're definitely the lovers. You seemed to be on the good guys' side earlier, but you have also been helping the werewolf teams deduce who the special characters are. You want to wait for the werewolves and special characters to kill each other until the end, when you can pick off the remaining ones. I don't care which of you is his lover, but the remaining player must follow my lead and vote him out."

Neither Xia Zhixu nor Yang Bo says anything as they look at Zhou Ziheng in silence.

"Xiqing is too obvious. We don't need to care who his lover is this round at all. Vote him out, and the game will end. Be sure to vote him out with me. That's all."

Xia Zhixu is so relaxed during his turn that it surprises Zhou Ziheng. "Sure, I agree with voting Xia Xiqing out. This is the one thing I want to do the most! Come on, guys, vote Xia Xiqing out this round. There's really nothing else to say. The one who doesn't vote him out is the werewolf."

"You're done?" Yang Bo finds it a little hard to believe, but Xia Zhixu nods in all seriousness. "Yeah, I'm done. Go on ahead with your speech."

"Hmm..." Yang Bo is obviously quite hesitant.

> Whoa, this is too hard. All three of them are pro players. If I'm there live, I'd be stumped too

> Who would've guessed that the survivors, in the end, are three villagers and a werewolf?

"I'm a bit confused now. Why does it feel like Ziheng and Zhixu are the real lovers joining forces to vote Xiqing out? Then...if Xiqing is a villager just like me, won't we lose if we vote him out? Isn't Zhixu a tad too enthusiastic about going along? If he's one of the lovers, surely he won't be that happy to see his lover die? What kind of flimsy relationship is that?"

> Hahahaha flimsy relationship. Can we not be so precise hahahaha

> He's really been taken in by Zhixu. Zhixu wanted to smear Ziheng!

"Ziheng and Zhixu are really too much like a team. Let me think about it."

He contemplates for so long that it exceeds the time limit. The narrator says, "Time's up. Please start to vote for the player to be cast out of the game."

The scene is so chaotic that even the public voting is a mess. As Yang Bo points at Zhixu, he looks on with a dumbfounded expression as Zhixu, who said he would vote for Xiqing, votes for Ziheng instead. Ziheng sticks to his guns and points at Xiqing, while Xia Xiqing points at Ziheng with a cheeky grin. After seeing the voting results, Xia Zhixu and Xia Xiqing stand up simultaneously in a rare moment of solidarity and give each other a high-five.

"Player 9 Zhou Ziheng is out of the game. The game ends! Cupid team wins!"

Little buddy Xia Xiuze looks as happy as a little sparrow as he comes running out from backstage to his older brother and Zhixu's side. "AHHHHH, WE WON!"

> So it really is the Three Musketeers who wins lolololol
> The Three Musketeers are da bomb!!
> Y'all, look at Ziheng's expression!

By the time he heard Yang Bo's speech at the end, Zhou Ziheng already guessed that the lovers are Xia Zhixu and Xia Xiqing, but it was already too late. He's both miffed and amused. To think these two foes would work together to play such a good game.

"Not bad, huh. The two of you really had me fooled."

Xia Xiqing circles to Zhou Ziheng's side and leaps to sit on the table before him with both legs swinging restlessly. He pokes Zhou Ziheng in the forehead. "That's the point."

"Little liar." Zhou Ziheng grabs his hand. He may be scolding him, but the smile on his face is tender. "Running with another man behind my back."

Xia Xiqing takes hold of Zhou Ziheng's hand as well and locks fingers with him. The victory puts him in an excellent mood. He laughs. "Tch, is Xia Zhixu a man?"

This just happens to land in the approaching Xia Zhixu's ears. "What did you say?!"

Just as he's about to throw a fit, Xu Qichen returns to the room. "Xia Zhixu, amazing acting skills you got, huh! Get over here!"

Zhou Ziheng clutches Xia Xiqing's hand as they both look over at the other side of the room, gloating at Xia Zhixu's misfortune. Xia Xiqing even turns toward him and raises an eyebrow, like a proud little villain.

Zhao Ke, who's just managed to coax his wife backstage, yells, "Guys, wanna get hotpot together tonight?!"

"Yeah!"

E.12

Their Story Goes On...

Weibo Mini Segment Part 1

After Zhou Ziheng's application for graduate studies is approved, he accepts a new movie that features a boxer. Every day, he heads to the boxing gym with his gym bag to learn boxing from a trainer. Xia Xiqing, on the other hand, has been busy with the fall exhibition. He finally finds some free time to ask Zhou Ziheng to watch a musical with him, but Zhou Ziheng turns him down.

Renaissance: Not watching the musical, come watch me box

Little Rose: What's so good about watching you box? Not going

With that, he tosses the phone into the pocket of his suit.

Renaissance: No wait. How can you say I don't look good while boxing??

Renaissance: I'm wearing a boxer's outfit, okay?!

Renaissance: And headgear!

Renaissance: And gloves! Boxing gloves!

Renaissance: In red. They are all in red, and they look good!

Xia Xiqing's assistant takes out the documents for him to sign. Hearing his phone vibrating frantically, he can't help but ask, "Umm...Xiqing, you seem to have a lot of messages."

"Oh, it's nothing." Xia Xiqing takes his phone out to unlock it, and a preview of the latest message pops out on WeChat.

Renaissance: I even strip when I get hot!

Pfft.

The assistant feels more and more perplexed on seeing Xia Xiqing squatting on the floor laughing, without any regard for his image.

At nine-thirty that night, Xia Xiqing heads to the boxing gym based on the address given on WeChat. It's in such a remote location that he drives around a few times before finding it. He heads up the buildings and follows the instructions to the entrance of the boxing gym. It's pitch black inside. Xia Xiqing hesitates for a moment before dialing Zhou Ziheng's phone. He reaches out to push the glass door open, trying to find the light switch in the lobby.

"Hello?" It takes a while for the call to get through. Xia Xiqing looks around. "Where are you? I'm here. Why aren't there any lights out here?"

Suddenly, a person hugs him from behind. His arms wrap around Xia Xiqing's body as he lowers his head to kiss him from his nape to his chin.

"The lights are broken." Zhou Ziheng's voice envelops him from behind.

Xia Xiqing breaks away from him. "And still you call me

over?"

"How should I have known that you'd come at night?"

Zhou Ziheng is still wearing boxing gloves. He lowers his head and bites down on the velcro of the gloves to rip them open, then takes them off. His slightly sweaty hands take hold of Xia Xiqing's. The entire process of removing his gloves hasn't escaped Xia Xiqing's eyes, and his heart thumps. For whatever reason, he suddenly finds it a little hot in here. His throat feels parched too. So he removes his suit jacket, hangs it over his left shoulder, and loosens his tie with his hand as he follows Zhou Ziheng in. Even though the outside lobby is pitch black, Xia Xiqing still feels very reassured to be led by his hand.

"How's your training going?" There are lights inside after they enter the training area. Zhou Ziheng steps one foot on the edge of the boxing ring and lifts his leg over the rope. "Not bad. The coach says I have some talent."

How can you not have talent? Xia Xiqing is tempted to say, but then, he figures he can't let the guy get too smug. He walks over to the side of the ring, puts both hands on the rope surrounding the ring, and looks at Zhou Ziheng, who's wearing a red boxing tank and shorts.

"Show me some moves?"

Zhou Ziheng says with a smile, "You and me? Don't you have a black belt in Taekwondo?"

Xia Xiqing finds it amusing. "It's not the same."

"It's fine. As long as you can fight." Zhou Ziheng walks over to his side. They look at one another across the rope. "Our Xiqing-*gege* is the best. He's not only handsome, but he can fight too."

This mouth of his is really sweet today. The corners of Xia Xiqing's lips lift. He remembers a phrase from the internet:

"Smoochykins, I'd suggest you..."

All of a sudden, Zhou Ziheng grabs him by the chin and leans down to kiss him. The tip of his tongue wanders aggressively, attacking him until Xia Xiqing feels his scalp tingle and his brain short-circuit. It lasts for only a brief moment, before Zhou Ziheng releases him and sees those pretty eyes staring at him wide-eyed. Finding it exceedingly adorable, he licks the corners of his lips and laughs.

"What are you doing?" Xia Xiqing returns to his senses. "You startled me..."

Zhou Ziheng grabs the lower edge of his boxing tank, strips it off smoothly with one hand, and tosses it to a corner of the ring. The smooth contours of his sculpted muscles appear even sexier under the overhead lighting of the ring. He wraps his arms around Xia Xiqing's waist through the rope and plays dumb.

"Didn't you call me smoochykins?"

Xia Xiqing is momentarily rendered speechless.

"You said smooch, so I did. See how obedient I am."

Weibo Mini Segment Part 2

After practicing boxing for two whole months, Zhou Ziheng's body grows visibly more sculpted. After all, this sport is the most effective for training and strengthening the shoulders and chest muscles. Xia Xiqing is delighted to be fed such a feast for the eyes. Not only that, he even peels off Zhou Ziheng's clothes and draws a whole stack of human figure sketches while Zhou Ziheng has yet to start filming.

Coming out of the shower, Xia Xiqing sees Zhou Ziheng

sitting on the bed with his back to him. Zhou Ziheng just happens to be picking up a new muted green pajama top, and as he pulls the shirt on, his movements stretch the muscles on his back and shoulder blades taut. The way they ripple is inexplicably sexy, as if he was oozing hormones.

He wears his pajama pants very low, with the deep dimples of Venus on his back exposed. Xia Xiqing rarely sees it from his angle of view. For some reason, he suddenly imagines the perspective of a bystander standing at the side, watching as Zhou Ziheng thrusts the back of his waist to and fro on top of him. Those dimples rock in tandem with each thrust, imbued with scalding passion and lust.

Xia Xiqing shakes off the water droplets on his head and walks over to pounce on Zhou Ziheng, pinning Zhou Ziheng—who's sending a WeChat message—under him. Zhou Ziheng is not the slightest bit annoyed, and grins broadly as he rolls over to hold Xia Xiqing in his arms.

"What are you doing?"

Then, he sees Xia Xiqing spreading his legs apart to straddle his lap. The water on his hair drips down, and Xia Xiqing shakes his head again, scattering water all over Zhou Ziheng.

While Zhou Ziheng is wiping his face, Xia Xiqing bends the fingers on his right hand and taps twice on Zhou Ziheng's chest. Zhou Ziheng doesn't get it, and grabs his slender hand.

"What was that for?"

Xia Xiqing falls on top of him and presses his hand against the left atrium of his heart. He grins like a child. "I want to go in. Open the door for me."

Zhou Ziheng presses his arms against Xia Xiqing's waist and reaches under the hem of his silk pajamas to stroke the skin on the side of Xia Xiqing's waist with his fingers. He feigns a deep expression. "No can do."

"I can."

"You can't."

Even though Xia Xiqing, who's having this childish conversation with him, rather enjoys this too, he still prefers to play it straight. His fingers nimbly and skillfully undo the buttons on Zhou Ziheng's pajamas, and as he does so, he smirks. "I gave you the chance, and you wouldn't take it, so don't blame me for barging in to loot."

"Oh, you want to loot? But there's nothing else in here other than you."

"Such a sweet mouth," Xia Xiqing looks at his lips. "Let me have a taste."

Zhou Ziheng may be fighting back verbally, but he's beyond lazy to keep up with his act, and doesn't offer up even the slightest bit of resistance. The kiss sets his body on fire. Xia Xiqing's slender hand caresses him from his jaw all the way to his hair, as if caressing his heart. His kiss is tender, yet scalding at the same time. The tip of his tongue throws Zhou Ziheng's breathing into disarray. His body grinds against Xia Xiqing in tandem, clinging to that thin, velvety layer of fabric.

When they let go of each other, Zhou Ziheng feels as though he's just downed a huge glass of hard liquor. His heart is pounding terrifyingly fast, but Xia Xiqing is still smiling, and with his tousled hair and flushed face, it looks as though he's the one who's drunk. He teases Zhou Ziheng with his eyes, then lowers his head and continues to undo Zhou Ziheng's buttons.

Zhou Ziheng tries his best to calm his breathing, but his fingers already can't help but start caressing Xia Xiqing's nape. Even his voice is lower, "Not sleeping in the middle of the night is going to make you lose your hair, *gege*."

Xia Xiqing is running out of patience, as he can't manage to undo the last few buttons no matter how he tries, so he simply rips them off with brute force. With a "pop," the buttons go flying and fall onto the floor. Hearing the sound, he looks innocently at Zhou Ziheng with his lips slightly parted.

"Oh, my hair hasn't fallen out, but your buttons did."

This one's simply too wicked. The fire in Zhou Ziheng has already set half of his body aflame. He cranes his neck in an attempt to kiss him, but Xia Xiqing leans back in evasion as he taunts him.

"What's the matter? Aren't you the particularly reserved one? So tuck yourself in and sleep, little buddy."

Zhou Ziheng continues to lean in, in an attempt to kiss him. "You tore my clothes up. I want compensation."

"That's easy. I'll buy ten more for you." Xia Xiqing slides his fingers gently across the grooves on his chest and exerts a little force as if he's attempting to put out a cigarette. Then he bends his knee and rubs it suggestively against a certain sensitive part. His voice is soft and slow, "Is ten enough?"

"Not enough." Zhou Ziheng wraps his arms around Xia Xiqing's body and flips over, with his hand cradling the back of Xia Xiqing's head, pinning Xia Xiqing. He lowers his head to kiss the exposed side of Xia Xiqing's neck, all the way to his ear.

"Even ten times isn't enough."

Weibo Mini Segment Part 3

On Qixi Festival, the Chinese Valentine's Day, Zhou Ziheng takes out the present he's meticulously prepared and hands it to Xia Xiqing, then stretches his hand out with an excited expression.

"Where's my present?"

Xia Xiqing looks at him, perplexed. "Who in the world demands presents like that?"

The liddol kiddo instantly turns hostile. "No can do. I want it. You didn't prepare it, did you? You don't love me anymore. Give me back my present."

Xia Xiqing hides the gift. "Who in the world demands presents back like that?"

"True..." Zhou Ziheng quietly draws his hand back, but midway through, Xia Xiqing grabs it and slips on a diamond ring. Zhou Ziheng is taken aback by surprise.

"A ring! Are you proposing to me? When?! I want to write the wedding invitations myself! I'll call Ke-zi right now and ask him to be my best man!"

Xia Xiqing is momentarily tongue-tied. It's hard for him to back down now. He wonders if he should kneel first and think later. Of course, there's no concealing the truth given that he didn't buy a pair of rings.

"Didn't you say we were getting married? Why is there only one ring?"

Xia Xiqing shrugs. "Technically, you're the one who spoke of getting married. As to why there is only one ring, it's because this one is custom..."

The phone rings and Xia Xiqing gets up to answer the call. Zhou Ziheng sulks alone by himself, questioning how he could've gotten only one custom made. He eventually wanders his way to Xia Xiqing's alcohol cabinet.

By the time Xia Xiqing returns after finishing his call, he

finds Zhou Ziheng hugging a half-empty bottle of vodka, sitting on the floor with his long legs stretched out in front of him.

Vodka again. They might really have an affinity with this liquor. Xia Xiqing walks over and drags Zhou Ziheng over to the sofa in the living room as though he's dragging a corpse. He sits on the carpet and pats him on the cheeks.

"Hey, we finally get to spend Qixi together, and you go and drink yourself to sleep? If you don't wake up, I'm going to splash you with water."

Zhou Ziheng suddenly grabs his hand and gives him a silly smile, his face flushed. "Thank you all for attending the wedding of Xia Xiqing and me!"

Xia Xiqing says, "...You are really drunk."

He attempts to lift Zhou Ziheng's upper body, only for Zhou Ziheng to hug him around the waist.

"I'm not."

"Okay, okay, you're not. That's what all drunk people say. Get up. Your clothes are all wet. Go change."

Xia Xiqing grabs the edge of his shirt in an attempt to take it off for him. At first, Zhou Ziheng won't cooperate, but after some coaxing, he obediently stretches out his arms to take it off. He even goofily leads Xia Xiqing's hand over to his tummy.

"I'll let you touch my abs."

"Good for you. It's even better than a washboard." He stands up, picks up the dirty shirt, and makes to walk away. "I'll get you your pajamas."

"I don't wanna!"

Fine then. A drunk Zhou Ziheng's temper is far bigger than anyone else's. In no time, he yanks Xia Xiqing over and pins him on the carpet with his entire body.

Xia Xiqing feels as if he's performing in a special Qixi program—boulder-crushing on his chest. "Cough, cough...I'm dying... Oh no..."

As if he's gotten some signal, Zhou Ziheng straightens up his upper body and stares at Xia Xiqing's face. Finally able to catch his breath, Xia Xiqing sucks in big gulps of air. His neck is already flushed. He's only just managed to get a breather when Zhou Ziheng kisses him without warning, while his hands grope willfully all over him.

"Hey! Hmm...what the hell has gotten...hmm...mmm..."

Zhou Ziheng's kiss spreads to the side of his ear. He nibbles his soft, delicate earlobe and says in all seriousness, as if right on cue. "Time to head to the nuptial chamber to consummate the marriage."

Xia Xiqing pushes him away by the chest and stares at Zhou Ziheng's drunken, glazed-over eyes. He licks the corner of his lips. "That fast?"

Zhou Ziheng blinks, and in this momentary lapse in concentration, Xia Xiqing rolls over to pin him underneath. He spreads his legs apart to straddle Zhou Ziheng and slowly pulls off his belt, his tone flirtatious.

"Not gonna have some fun first?"

Xia Xiqing reaches over to pull Zhou Ziheng's right hand toward his own face, the other man's fingertip poking at his own soft, gentle lips. He slips that long, slender ring finger little by little into his mouth, as the tip of his tongue swirls around it. Just as Zhou Ziheng's breathing grows heavier, Xia Xiqing pulls the finger out.

"Hmm?" Zhou Ziheng looks at his own finger with a frown, turning it over and over again. Then, he lifts his head and sees Xia Xiqing with his tongue out, a sparkling diamond ring on the tip of it.

He holds it up with his hand to the living room light and examines it carefully. "This is the first piece of jewelry I ever designed in my life, and to think it ends up disdained." Xia Xiqing then slips it onto his own index finger. "I might as well wear it myself."

"Give it back to me!" Zhou Ziheng yanks his arm and pulls him down to his own chest.

Xia Xiqing nips his nose gently. "Why? You think it's good stuff now that it's snatched away from you?"

"Give it to me. It's mine!" Drunk Zhou Ziheng is beyond stubborn.

"Be reasonable, okay? You're an adult now, aren't you?" Xia Xiqing hides his hand behind him. "Convince me, and I'll give it to you."

"I'm an adult." Zhou Ziheng holds the back of Xia Xiqing's head in place and kisses him.

"I can fuck you until you're convinced."

Mini Extra 1: Happy Birthday, Xia Xiqing!

Xia Xiqing flies to London a week before his twenty-sixth birthday to attend a very important art exhibition. To prepare, he's gone into seclusion for nearly two months. Zhou Ziheng wanted to tag along, but it's nearing the end of the semester, and he has a pile of deadlines waiting for him. Since he can't get away, he can only wait for Xia Xiqing back home like the good boy he is.

He never asked for Xia Xiqing to return home on time, but there are six out of ten messages in their daily WeChat conversations asking him about his return flight. It's even more pitiable than simply pleading with him outright to return early, like a golden retriever guarding the house back at home.

The deadline for a Very Important Paper at hand is just two days before Xia Xiqing's birthday. Zhou Ziheng burns the midnight oil before he finally ticks the big headache off his to-do list. This is then followed by the preparation of the birthday surprise. He knows his fans have missed him very much since his semi-retirement, so he livestreams the entire process as he puts his birthday plan into motion.

On the nineteenth of December, he heads out alone to make purchases. Early the next morning, he calls Xia Zhixu, Xu Qichen, and Zhao Ke over to help him decorate the house.

"Let me see if the livestream is on." Zhou Ziheng runs over to adjust the camera, aiming it at Xia Zhixu, who's working on the balloons.

Xu Qichen enters the livestream on his phone. "Yep, the comments are out in full force too."

> OMG whose legs are these?! *drools*

> Looks like fangs-*gege*~

> Heng-Heng, mama misses you so much!

> Heng-Heng, I love you!!!!!

Zhou Ziheng tidies his hair while facing the camera. "Man, I've been so busy lately that my hair has grown so long. Oh right, y'all have to promise me not to run to his Weibo account and divulge the secret, otherwise, I won't stream anything ever again. All the surprise will be gone." He then mumbles to himself. "Though I think he probably has no time to go on Weibo. He hasn't even replied to the messages I sent him yesterday."

He's wearing a cream-colored beanie, with his long bangs

showing a little from under the edge of the hat. There's a pair of black-framed glasses sitting on his nose, making him look younger.

> Heng-Heng is so boyish today!

> So it's true, going to school will make you retain that bookish air~

> OH, I see the Christmas tree~ It's huge!

"Oh yeah. This is the Christmas tree I bought a few days back." Zhou Ziheng walks over to the Christmas tree next to the floor-to-ceiling window. This tree is much taller than him, with all kinds of gift boxes, bells, and stars hanging on it. "I decorated it myself. Actually, every gift box here contains real gifts inside, but I'm not going to tell him."

At this point, Zhou Ziheng smiles smugly. "Some people really know how to pick the right day to be born. Just take a break for two days after their birthday, and they get to celebrate Christmas. How blissful."

> OMG, this pup is going to make me die of sugar. seriously. Geez

> THIS IS INFURIATING ME TO HELL AND BACK!!!

> Fuck, y so sweet?!

> T_T our little artist is truly the apple of our Heng-Heng's eye

> FFFFF

"I spent a long time gift-wrapping them, and they're tough to wrap, so I won't be opening them to show all of you. But just so I know what's what when he opens them..." Zhou Ziheng reaches out and picks up one of them, showing the bottom to the camera. "I wrote hints underneath. See."

A few small words are written at the bottom of the box: *AirPods Case.*

> Ohhh, so Heng-Heng will give such practical gifts too, huh?

Hahaha

> Why do I find it kinda funny hhhhh

> Eh, mind if you tell us which brand~ I wanna get the same one!

"This?" Zhou Ziheng puts the gift back on the tree. "I knitted it myself."

> Oof, my bad, sorry to impose

> Fuck

> Why did I even come in here?! Why would you lure a dog in only to kill it?

> Gosh, I just imagined the 6'4" Heng-Heng holding two needles to knit a smol, tiny, little AirPods cover. I'm dying from the cuteness!

> Crais, I'm so jelly. When will it be my turn to experience such sweet love?!

"Actually, I realized that it's very interesting to do craftwork. There are weaving rules in the process, and as long as you follow the rules, you can basically get the results you want. This aspect is very much like solving a math problem."

> Hahahaha as expected of a science nerd

> No. You're a talented one. Unlike me, I can't get the result I want

Zhou Ziheng crouches again and takes out a black gift box from under the tree. "This is the scarf I knitted for him. I knitted this secretly in the lab, since he would notice if I knitted it at home. Sneaking around like this...I even had to bribe my fellow lab mates with hush money. It was so hard."

> hahahahaha hush money!

> Really too adorable!!

Zhou Ziheng moves his phone elsewhere, and passes by the living room on his way. In passing, he films the other three guys who are decorating the place. It just so happens

Xu Qichen accidentally lets go of the balloon he was blowing, and the balloon goes flying as it hisses out air right into Xu Qichen's face, startling him into seeking refuge in Xia Zhixu's arms out of reflex.

> oh my god my adorable Screenwriter Xu

> There's an abundance of food being handed out in this livestream. Single dogs, please enter at your own discretion

"There are actually gifts hidden in the sofa too." Zhou Ziheng reaches under the sofa cushion and pulls out a long gift box. "This is a custom-made watch. Next up, the stairs. Look here."

The camera shows a gift box placed on each step of the stairs, the size of which gradually increases with each step all the way up until the very last gift box, which is almost as tall as a person.

"This is a physiotherapy chair." Zhou Ziheng pats it. "It's tough for Xiqing when he paints, and he often suffers from a sore neck and sore arms, so I went and ordered one of these from overseas. Hopefully, it'll be of use to him." He circles around the gift and mumbles under his breath, "If it doesn't work, I'll still have to do it myself."

> *swoons* I'm gone

> Go ahead and keep it up, I can still take it T_T

Gifts and surprises of all sizes are hidden in every corner of the house. These are all presents Zhou Ziheng started to collect and prepare as early as six months ago. If he sees something nice, no matter where, he would buy it at the first opportunity so he can give it to Xia Xiqing. But it's never enough. Xia Xiqing always deserves the best.

That afternoon, Zhou Ziheng spends the whole afternoon doing another livestream of him making a birthday cake.

He's learned and made several attempts beforehand, but to ensure that everything goes without a hitch in the last round, he makes a special trip that takes him more than halfway around Beijing to the studio of the Le Cordon Bleu pastry teacher, to dedicate all his energy into making the final product.

"I can't show you all the final product, but I'll take photos and post it on my side account afterward. You can go and take a look for yourselves when the time comes."

By the time he leaves the studio, it's already nine-thirty. With the fruit of his labor in tow, Zhou Ziheng drives home and chats with his fans along the way, his phone set before him.

> Crais Zhou Ziheng looks so hot when he drives

> But is xqgg really unable to come back today? I saw someone posting photos of him at the art exhibition earlier on Weibo

> Oh, man. What a pity. But it's probably alright to be a little late. It's a celebration every day for these two

Zhou Ziheng glances at the screen at the red light and smiles. Just as he's about to say it doesn't matter, he sees a message from Xia Xiqing—

> Babe, I may not be able to return tonight. Flights are delayed due to heavy snow here. But I definitely can make it home tomorrow in the daytime. I love you.

Although Zhou Ziheng has already mentally prepared himself, he still can't help but pout when he sees this message.

> What's with that cute expression earlier?!?!

> Ahhh, is it because xqgg can't make it back?

> Oh noes, Heng-Heng, come here into mama's arms for a hug!

"We're finally here." Zhou Ziheng drives into the

neighborhood and directly into the underground garage. It's already eleven at night. He picks up the cake and closes the car door, still holding his phone in his other hand. "I'm going home now."

> Omg, are you going to end the livestream when you reach home? Nooooooo

> Crais, I still wanna chat for a little more

> Don't end the livestream so fast!

"I won't. I still have to sort out some stuff after going back, so I can keep the livestream open." Zhou Ziheng placates everyone and sets the cake temporarily on the ground.

He takes out the access card to swipe the elevator of the underground garage that leads right to his house. A chime rings out, and the elevator door opens. Zhou Ziheng enters, still holding his phone camera up, then swipes the access card again.

"I feel like a mega cake now." Zhou Ziheng lets out a silly smile at the camera. "Being in the dessert room the whole day truly turns one into a cupcake boy."

The elevator ascends slowly.

> Hahahahaha cupcake boi

> Why is this tol boi so cute?!

The blinking number on the digital panel switches from B1 to 1.

"It's a good thing he's not coming back tonight, since I haven't had time to change my clothes or cut my hair. Tomorrow morning, I'll..."

To his surprise, the elevator doors open once again. He swallows back his unfinished words in shock. Xia Xiqing stands before him. Not even his coat can hide the chill he brings with him, or how flustered he's been in his rush to hurry back.

"Xi...qing?"

The comments go wild with elation.

> OMG WHAAAAT?! Xqgg is back!

> I knew it!!! He was lying! What a love liar!!

> I wanna see Xiqing-*gege*!! Quick, lemme see Xiqing-*gege*!

"Um...Well, about that, I..." Zhou Ziheng suddenly panics. He forgets to hold his phone up. The entire screen is filled with his panicked face. "He's back. I've got to go. I didn't expect him to be back so fast. See you next time. I'm logging off."

> ????? Didn't you say you'd stream for a little longer

> He's so happy the moment his wife is back that he can't even hold up the phone properly!

> Are we just tools to you?!

> How cold of him!

Zhou Ziheng hastily turns off the livestream so nervously that he accidentally drops the phone on the ground. He bends to pick it up, when he hears a chuckle from Xia Xiqing, as he bends over to pick up the phone before him. With a teasing smile on his face, Xia Xiqing straightens up and hands the phone to Zhou Ziheng.

"Scared you, huh?"

Zhou Ziheng is about to reach out to take it, but Xia Xiqing draws his hand back and takes a step forward until the cold tip of his nose almost touches Zhou Ziheng's. Zhou Ziheng can almost smell the base notes of the perfume emanating from his neck—the scent of burnt sandalwood in the snow.

Xia Xiqing lifts his eyes and looks at the still somewhat dazed Zhou Ziheng, saying in a very soft voice, "You miss me that much, huh?"

The elevator door slowly closes, and the four sides of the

mirrored interior reflect their intimately close bodies back at them.

"You lied to me again." Zhou Ziheng leans down to kiss him, but Xia Xiqing nimbly takes half a step back, sticks his hands into his coat pockets, and shrugs.

"How should I know that you'd fall for it again?" Then he cocks his head and stares at the box in Zhou Ziheng's hands. "Is that for me?"

Zhou Ziheng sets the box down.

"Where did you go to buy a cake in the middle of the night that you'd only be back now...?"

Before he can finish his words, Xia Xiqing is pushed by the tricked little wolfhound against the elevator's wall. Both of his hands are held up above his head by Zhou Ziheng's hand.

"Hey, mmm..."

The forceful kiss cuts off the words he didn't get to say. Unlike before, this is a full-on invasion. The tip of the tongue launches an offensive the moment he's caught unprepared. The pleasure from being trapped in space is like a tidal wave charged with electricity, that instantly engulfs every cell in his body. He shivers under the shackle that is Zhou Ziheng. But how can Xia Xiqing possibly hand the initiative on a silver platter to another person? He pushes Zhou Ziheng's legs apart with his knee, about to make his move.

Suddenly, the ascending elevator jerks to a stop. The lights go out, and this small, narrow space suddenly turns into a sealed, soundless black box, trapping both of them inside. Zhou Ziheng stops what he's doing and releases his grip on Xia Xiqing's wrists. He reflexively takes him into his arms and whispers, "You didn't do this, did you?"

Vexed, Xia Xiqing shoves him, but doesn't manage

to shove him away. "You think I'm mad? Would I not be scared?"

Only then does Zhou Ziheng realize he's misunderstood him. He buries his head into Xia Xiqing's neck and nuzzles against it. "Don't be. I'm here."

"Go and press the emergency button." He bosses Zhou Ziheng around, but Zhou Ziheng remains unmoved, so he tugs at Zhou Ziheng's hand. "Did you not hear me?"

At this moment, Zhou Ziheng is utterly overwhelmed by the scent emanating from Xia Xiqing. This scent with cool undertones oozes out from his skin to gently permeate the air, twisting into an invisible hook that uproots the desire at the bottom of Zhou Ziheng's heart, until it can no longer be concealed.

"Have you heard the story of the boy who cried wolf?" He bites Xia Xiqing's collar with his teeth and pulls it open, then drops tender kisses on the collarbones beneath.

"...What about it? You think...I'm that kid who lied?" Xia Xiqing's fear doesn't recede; instead, it blends with the aroused desire into a certain kind of gluey emotion. That sticky, syrup douses his face—suffocating and sweet.

"Hmm, lying will always get you punished." Zhou Ziheng chuckles and reaches into Xia Xiqing's coat to hold that lean waist. "So he eventually..."

Xia Xiqing senses a small bite on the side of his neck.

"...End up being eaten by the wolf."

Zhou Ziheng tears off a sticky note on the cake box with the pickup time written on it, and reaches out with one hand to stick it to a corner at the top of the elevator. At some point, Zhou Ziheng has pulled out the tie behind Xia Xiqing's coat, and peeled the coat off as well. It's way too dark here, and Xia Xiqing can't overcome this fear. No matter how much he wants to take the initiative, his hands can't stop trembling.

"Ziheng…" From his term of address alone, he's already conceding his ground. "Call them to come and repair the elevator. We'll go home first, alright?"

Zhou Ziheng kisses his way up from Xia Xiqing's collarbone to the corner of his lips, then takes his burning earlobe into his own mouth. "No. I won't call them. They can't save you."

Zhou Ziheng tenderly and cruelly kisses Xia Xiqing's cheek and the corner of his eyes, as his fingers undo the buttons of his cardigan one at a time.

"Only I can save you."

Having said that, he moves Xia Xiqing's hands behind his back and uses the waist-tie of the coat to tie him up.

"What are you doing?" Xia Xiqing's body has gone weak all over. He can't tell if it's out of fear or pleasure. In the darkness, he can't see anything; all he can hear is Zhou Ziheng's searing hot breath when he speaks.

"Do you…" Zhou Ziheng puts his hand on Xia Xiqing's belt buckle with a smile. "…Know what desensitization therapy is?"

Xia Xiqing can feel the belt pulling away little by little as it scrapes against his waist. But he can't resist; he can't move, and it's not entirely because he's bound. His strength has been drawn away; he has no chance of resisting.

"Deleting files is always less thorough than overwriting them." Zhou Ziheng kneels with one hand holding Xia Xiqing's waist, and his other hand unzips his neat and tidy pants. "So let us overwrite your memory of the darkness, on your birthday. Then you won't be afraid anymore."

Xia Xiqing attempts to dodge, but all of him has been

bound; he can't even hold onto the back of Zhou Ziheng's head with his own hands. The only thing he can do is feel. He can't see how Zhou Ziheng pulls down his zipper, but he can hear it. He senses the wet tip of Zhou Ziheng's tongue licking its way down from his lower abdomen, like a beast enjoying a sampling before a sumptuous feast. Xia Xiqing grows semi-hard just from the sensation of his hot, damp breath on him. He hears the sound of his pants sliding down to his ankles. The cool air tickles the skin of his groin.

The next moment, he's tightly enveloped by a hot, wet mouth—it's even more thrilling than being caught in a choke-hold.

He's very well aware of the extent of his own desire, so he bites down on his lips for fear of whimpering out loud. Zhou Ziheng's tongue swirls around his tip and even licks maliciously at that tiny hole. It isn't a tongue now, but the slithering, winding serpent in the Garden of Eden, that arouses his greed and burrows into the crevices of his heart to wreak havoc. Even the fissures in his bones are making a viscously lewd sound as they creak.

"Ziheng..." It's only when he opens his mouth that he realizes just how weak and soft his voice has become, having been doubly assaulted by fear and pleasure. "Release me. Let's go back first, can't we..."

Zhou Ziheng forcefully grabs his thighs, the force of which indicates his refusal. His long, slender fingers caress Xia Xiqing's scrotum, fondling it with pious devotion. This snake has burrowed its way into his bones, making him itch to the point of burning up. All he can see when he opens his eyes is the vast darkness, and every single move of Zhou Ziheng when he closes them—every suck, lick, swallow, and arousal is crystal clear.

Teeth begin to clatter noisily in advanced celebration of this extraordinary healing treatment.

"Ah, ah, Ziheng, deeper..."

In the end, fear is no match for bestial instincts. Xia Xiqing has given up struggling. Hedonism has always been the creed he believes in. His legs tremble with wild abandon, while his tightly-bound arms scrape against the wall. Until Zhou Ziheng picks up speed and takes him in deeper, until Zhou Ziheng's hands make their way into his shirt to pinch his erect nipples, taking his cock deep into his throat again and again.

He cums in Zhou Ziheng's mouth, way faster than he expected. Zhou Ziheng obviously didn't expect it, either. Even though he can feel the muscles of Xia Xiqing's thighs tensing up and Xia Xiqing's rapidly heaving chest, he didn't anticipate the extent to which Xia Xiqing would get aroused, so he chokes hard on the semen.

Xia Xiqing, having ejaculated, leans back against the elevator's wall and gasps heavily for breath. When he hears Zhou Ziheng coughing while still kneeling before him, he feels the urge to laugh. "Serves you right."

Zhou Ziheng holds back a cough and chides, "How conscienceless."

"I never have had a wonderful thing like a conscience." Having just climaxed, Xia Xiqing's voice is husky and devastatingly sexy. He can't see clearly before him, so all he could do is kick off his pants by feel. He then lifts his right leg slightly and pokes Zhou Ziheng with his shod foot, which just happens to reach past his open legs, to press against his lower abdomen.

With his hands still bound, Xia Xiqing chuckles and exerts a little force as he steps on it.

"So, what's the second course of treatment, Doctor Pervert?"

Zhou Ziheng grabs hold of Xia Xiqing's ankle and runs his hand up along the contour of his calf, caressing his skin as he comes to the back of his knee. He lowers his head to kiss Xia Xiqing's thigh, then yanks him down into his arms.

"Are you scared?" He gently pats Xia Xiqing on the back and kisses his sweat-soaked nape tenderly.

But Xia Xiqing doesn't give in. "Untie me first and talk properly, or you'd look more like a pervert."

"Alright." While still holding him in an embrace, Zhou Ziheng's arms circle around to undo the tie, then kisses him.

"Bitter." Xia Xiqing scrunches up his face and spits several times.

Zhou Ziheng finds it amusing. "I don't even mind. To think you yourself would disdain it that much."

Xia Xiqing suddenly says that he wants to eat cake, so Zhou Ziheng has no choice but to take the cake out.

His luminous watch glows in the dark. Zhou Ziheng says, "I suppose we still have to stay here past midnight even if we call for help now."

"Then light up the candle for me."

Flickers of candle flame light up. In no time, the warm, gentle light fills up the dark, narrow space. Xia Xiqing can even see himself in the mirror on every side.

"It's quite pretty."

"I made it myself."

Xia Xiqing laughs. "Good for you huh." He takes a bit of frosting with his index finger. "Let me have a taste." But instead of putting his finger into his mouth, he wipes it on Zhou Ziheng's lower lips, then wraps his arms around Zhou Ziheng's neck to lick and kiss him, before licking his lips in satisfaction. "Very sweet."

And so he uses the same trick to dab cream on the tip of Zhou Ziheng's nose, cheeks, chin, and even earlobes and cleans it up little by little. The faint light from the birthday candles allows him to take back some of the control.

"Sure, go ahead and ravage the cake I made you." Zhou Ziheng says that, but his breathing has already become unsteady from the teasing.

"Not only do I want to ravage your cake," Xia Xiqing undoes his jacket and reaches in with his hand to press Zhou Ziheng's lower back. "I want to ravage you too."

He sits up and fumbles in his own coat before fishing something out of his pocket, and tosses it to Zhou Ziheng. Zhou Ziheng takes a look by the candlelight—it's lubricant.

"Hey," Zhou Ziheng is both miffed and amused. "What are you doing, carrying this around?"

"Saw it in the duty-free store. The packaging looked nice, so I bought it."

Xia Xiqing says it casually, but Zhou Ziheng finds him adorable and pulls him over to kiss him over and over again. The fluffy aroma of cream lingers on both of their bodies. As they kiss, their bodies grow hotter. In the dark night, desire licks at the back of the two men as they entangle with each other until breathing becomes difficult. A thin film of sweat separates their cheeks as they cling together, the spray of their breath moistening each other's eyes.

"Relax, babe." Zhou Ziheng unscrews the lubricant and squeezes it into his palm. The moist, sticky liquid wraps around his fingers as he probes into the entrance, opening and closing like a flower petal as it takes him in. Xia Xiqing squirms impatiently in his embrace, leaning on his shoulder as he endures it and gasps for breath. A whimper escapes, and he diffidently bites down on the shoulder, his saliva soaking Zhou Ziheng's beige sweater.

"Hurry—hurry up." Xia Xiqing's voice is weak with lust and desire. He kneels on the ground with his legs spread apart, or rather, he's practically sitting on Zhou Ziheng's fingers. But when Zhou Ziheng actually speeds up the expansion, he grows limp in Zhou Ziheng's arms, pecking his lips like a small animal. Even his breaths are quivering, "Mm... mmm, ah."

Waiting is truly a torment, so he takes back control by taking out Zhou Ziheng's rock-hard cock from inside his pants.

"So hard..."

He licks his palm wet like a kitten, then wraps around the shaft, sliding it up and down in tune to the frequency of Zhou Ziheng's expansion. He feels it growing bigger in his hand and hears the sound of Zhou Ziheng sucking in a breath, and this gives him a sense of accomplishment far more than anything else.

"Does it feel good?" Xia Xiqing kisses his chin. "Come in, okay?"

Zhou Ziheng lets out a long breath and says in a hoarse voice, "Beg me."

"Beg what of you?" Xia Xiqing licks the tip of Zhou Ziheng's ear, his voice wanton and soft. "Beg you to fuck me in the elevator? To slam me into the mirror and fuck me until I drool? Or beg you to fuck me until I can't walk...so that I can only let you carry me home where you can throw me onto the bed and continue to screw me?"

He intentionally sucks in a breath right beside Zhou Ziheng's ear and laughs out loud. "How do you want me to beg you?"

"You really are..."

Zhou Ziheng's last shred of inhibition is broken down. Blood surges to his head, and he grabs Xia Xiqing by his waist, forcing him to kneel on the ground while he holds his own rock-hard cock and enters from the back a little at a time.

"Ah...!" Xia Xiqing senses his body being opened up inch by inch. Pain and pleasure fill up his entire body.

Zhou Ziheng reaches forward with his right hand and grasps his long slender neck and pushes, forcing Xia Xiqing's lowered head up, into raising his head up. "Didn't you want to look in the mirror?"

The candle flames illuminate the mirror, offering a panoramic view of his trembling shoulders, flushed face, and forced-open lips—courtesy of the thrusts.

"Does it look good?"

Xia Xiqing laughs. He reaches out with his tongue and licks Zhou Ziheng's fingers, putting on a brave front as he says with a smile, "Of course...I'm good-looking, to begin with...ah, AH!"

The watch on Zhou Ziheng's wrist reads a minute to midnight, the glowing numbers looking particularly vivid in the darkness. He straightens up to push himself even closer, his huge tip pressing hard against Xia Xiqing's sensitive glands. He hears Xia Xiqing's moans grow more urgent and shrill. Xia Xiqing's pried-open mouth can't hold in his saliva, so it has no choice but to drip down into his hand and onto the straps of his watch.

"Ah, ah...There. Feels so good...A little lighter, Ziheng, Ziheng..."

The numbers change from 23:59 to four neat os.

Zhou Ziheng holds Xia Xiqing's waist and speeds up,

gasping as he says, "Happy birthday, *gege*." He takes Xia Xiqing's chin in hand and makes him look carefully at himself in the mirror. "Look. Xia Xiqing's last second at the age of twenty-five and first second at the age of twenty-six are all spent in intimate union with Zhou Ziheng. How will you be able to leave me in the future?"

Xia Xiqing shivers all over on hearing these words. He barely has the strength left to hold on, so when he's picked up, he clings on to Zhou Ziheng, back to chest. He cranes his head around to kiss him deeply until he loses all his strength. Amidst the hot turbulent waves of climax, he completely loses his lead, letting Zhou Ziheng wash him away over and over again, pushing him to shore and yet dragging him down.

"I love you, Zhou Ziheng..."

"I know, babe." Zhou Ziheng kisses him on the shoulder. "Don't steal my words. You have to let me say them first. Thank you for coming into this world. Thank you for encountering me, for accepting me, and for loving me." He tenderly wraps his arms around Xia Xiqing, as warm current envelopes his body. "I love you, Xia Xiqing. Your birth is the best gift I've ever received."

It's just the same for him. More than all the blessings and celebrations in this world, the most precious gift that Xia Xiqing has ever received is Zhou Ziheng. Xia Xiqing wonders just how great of a man he must've been in his last life to be able to meet this little guy in this one.

They end this absurd birthday "union," and the task of tidying up naturally falls on Zhou Ziheng alone. In the end, he even sprays the perfume in Xia Xiqing's luggage all over the elevator in an overt attempt to cover it up. Only when he feels that there should be nothing amiss does he dare to press the emergency button.

Xia Xiqing flops on Zhou Ziheng's shoulder, staring at his burning red ears. He blows a breath on one. "I don't see you being shy earlier when we were doing it. Your on and off switch is really weird."

"Hush, quiet."

"Little pervert."

"..."

But he's only just pressed the button when the lights of the elevator unexpectedly turn back on by themselves, and an ascending symbol reappears on the display screen.

"What's, what's going on here?" Zhou Ziheng says with a start.

Xia Xiqing picks up his coat from the ground and puts it loosely on his shoulders. "Fulfilling your perverted plan, I guess."

"It wasn't me!" Zhou Ziheng denies anxiously.

"Let's hurry back. My back is sore as hell. I want a bath."

"I'll go with you!"

"Sounds like you want me to die."

It's not until the afternoon on the next day that the anxious fans waiting on Zhou Ziheng's side account finally receive a photo of Xia Xiqing wearing a birthday hat, making a wish to the cake.

@LitteRoseFallingIntoTheRedPond: OMG, a fresh new Xiqing-*gege*! Happy Birthday, Little Rose!

@MyBelovedIsAnArtist: Happy Birthday, my precious! After another adorable year, you'll become even more handsome! Love ya!

@UniverseNo1Cutie: Heng-Heng's cake looks so cute! But even so, we won't forget your crime in abandoning us last night!

@MyBabyHeng: The cutie who personally bakes a cake even has to take on the role of the photographer! Please start the livestream and tell us about the wonderful things that happened last night~

@MyIdolNameIsCensored: Ohhhhh, I can vaguely catch a glimpse of a hickey...

@PerhapsYouAreMyLittleRose: Happy birthday! But why did the cake look all smushed like that? It looks like it's been raked by a cat's claws

Unexpectedly, Zhou Ziheng replies.

@ihatelenzlaw: Even worse, it's been ravaged

What's better is that Xia Xiqing also replies ten minutes later.

@Tsing_Summer: What? You say it like you were the one ravaged

@ihatelenzlaw: Bring it on

Mini Extra 2: The Proposal

Ever since becoming a graduate student, Zhou Ziheng rarely seems to break out of his seclusion, but the popularity of Self-Study, the national couple, never once wavered. Self-Study girls also never lose their zeal just because the two main leads are no longer in business. On the contrary, they jokingly labeled them "underground romance."

However, it's still inevitable for traces of them to be dug up. Just the other day, Zhou Ziheng's graduation thesis was somehow posted online, causing quite the uproar.

@LaughNGetFlayed: I know all the words, but put them together, and I don't understand a thing...

@HeavenForbids: Heng-Heng is truly an ace student. Ps,

Physics really looks hard. Brain-ded

@ShowbizNo1Cutie: I'm sorry, my IQ is giving my idol a bad name.

@SmartCookie: Didn't anyone read the end of the thesis?! Friendly tip: Highlighting the acknowledgments section!!!

@Sisisi: Thank you SmartCookie!! The acknowledgment is too sweet, omg! Self-Study girls crying like babies!

Guided by this comment, many people shift their focus from the thesis itself to the acknowledgments section of this graduation thesis. Many of them also make a point of posting screenshots of this paragraph on the internet, and for a time, it's widely reposted and circulated.

Finally, I would like to thank my boyfriend, Xia Xiqing, who once said, "Someone who cares about the flows of wind and water, the conversion of night and day, the birth of the universe…How are they not romantic?" I hold these words close in my heart, for they give me the courage to advance in this field of unknowns, to explore why the stars shine, and how the universe changes. I am forever grateful for his company.

A paragraph like this may seem simple, but it's incredibly touching when placed in such a position. The world thinks they've witnessed the origin of this romance, but no one knows how they really began. No one knows that it's because of Xia Xiqing that Zhou Ziheng continued with his acting career, and no one knows how, one night under a virtual starry sky, Xia Xiqing told Zhou Ziheng in his own way that he's not a lonely individual whom no one understands, that Xia Xiqing is the one whose soul resonates with Zhou Ziheng's.

Very quickly, "Zhou Ziheng Thesis Acknowledgment" makes it to the top of the trending list, becoming the most talked-about topic nationwide.

@NaturalBornAlpha: OMG, how can there be such a sweet guy? I'm so jelly. I really am, crais

@DoYourBestToday: Once again, I've witnessed a divine love. Why aren't you guys married yet? What are you waiting for?! GO GET MARRIED!

@AWishADay: Praying for me to get married this year.

@Ihavealilrose: I'm really crying today as I lap this all up T_T this perfect love is killing me.

A couple days after the frenzy over the acknowledgment passed, a new hot topic appears. This time, it's a set of photos posted on Weibo by a passerby.

@Tinayang:I was truly lucky to see Xia Xiqing at an art exhibition in LA today. At first, I thought I was mistaken, but he really stood out in a crowd of foreigners, and my friend even said she saw his work on exhibition. Once I was more or less sure, I mustered up the courage to take a photo with him, and he was actually really nice! His work is really awesome too. It has that all-encompassing feel that is very impactful when seeing it in person. I'm so happy. So here they are, I'm sharing them with everyone.

She attaches three images. The first is a painting on exhibition by Xia Xiqing, which features a vast universe with the silhouette of a figure in the center, of what looks like the upper half body of a person drawn with flowing modernist lines. It isn't an exact human shape, but a relatively abstract expression. He seems to be suspended in the universe, with a glowing planet as his chest, while below the planet is an illusion of red quicksand and a tight tangle of lines. The overall style is very special, and the theme vast. It is wholly different from his earlier works.

The second image is a photo of Xia Xiqing with this passerby. In the photo, he even makes a special point of pulling down his mask to reveal his delicate, gently smiling face.

The last image is a photo taken by this passerby of Xia Xiqing in all his artist charm, giving a live explanation of his work.

Without a doubt, this set of photos shoots right to the top of the trending list. Originally, the exhibition Xia Xiqing participated in was a niche art exhibition that usually receive relatively little attention, but because of this chance encounter, it unexpectedly ends up in the limelight.

@Imcuteright: A fresh new Xiqing-*gege*! Im ded! Xiqing-*gege* I love you!

@eggyolkpastrywithouteggyolk: This guy's face really is something...

@Redbeantaro: Is this painting a portrait? That's Heng-Heng, right? Xiqing-*gege* never painted in this style before. He's amazing!

@Waterfall: As expected of an artist. That artistic impact is really all too real. But there's one thing I've been curious about. Is this a two-way painting? I accidentally looked at it upside down just now and realized that it seemed a little different. The outline of the person isn't so obvious when you look at it upside down, and when combined with the red brushstrokes beneath the planet, it looks like rose petals escaping from some kind of vessel

@SelfStudyGirlNo1: hot damn, big brains in the comment section! I just checked, and I'm stunned! Too damn powerful! I'm getting goosebumps. It really looks like roses!

@iloveartists: So, if you look at it upright, it's Heng-Heng with a little planet in his bosom roaming the universe, but look at it upside down, and it's a rose breaking free of its shackles to dash toward the universe! Holy moly, this is too romantic!!

@loveselfstudy: I'm no longer worthy of being called a

shipper of this divine couple! What have I done to deserve such divine love?!

At this time, one of the two parties at the center of the whirlwind is still on a flight from LA to China, while the other is too busy discussing details of a surprise with Xia Zhixu, Xu Qichen, and others to bother about anything else or know what is happening on the internet.

"Do you guys think it will work? Do we throw the confetti when he steps through the door? Wait, no, maybe I'll just skip it. I'm afraid of startling him..." Zhou Ziheng is so nervous that he's getting anxious. He repeatedly rehearses with a few close friends before eventually grabbing Xia Zhixu to go over the scene. "Pretend for a moment you're Xiqing."

Xia Zhixu's eyes droop. "I refuse to."

"Just for a moment." Zhou Ziheng darts out, then walks toward him with a feigned air of composure. "Xiqing, I've something to tell you. Stand there first and don't move..."

"Cut!" Zhao Ke waves. "Damn it, my dear Heng-Heng. What kind of phrasing is this? What do you mean 'stand there first and don't move'? Are you about to go out and buy oranges?"

Xia Zhixu laughs so hard he has to crouch. Zhou Ziheng, on the other hand, turns his head toward Xu Qichen with an innocent expression, but even Xu Qichen can barely hold in the smile on his face.

"Sorry, Ziheng. This looks like it really won't do..."

"Executing Plan B!" Zhao Ke shouts out the slogan in order to boost morale. "My package plan is finally going to be implemented! Yes!"

Zhou Ziheng suddenly hesitates. He's been secretly preparing for this proposal for many months, procrastinating from spring to summer, but to date, he still can't be sure if

Xia Xiqing even wants to get married. Who knows? Perhaps his thoughts are still the same as before—fearful and with an aversion to such contracts as marriage.

Xia Zhixu can tell that he has something in mind, so he pats him on the shoulder and says, "How about this? The hotel has already been booked anyway, and he has to eat when he lands, so you guys go ahead first. You can probe him about it during the meal. If the timing is right, you can say it."

Xu Qichen concurs. "That's right. Zhixu and I will be there too. Don't worry. If worse comes to worst, it'll be just a meal. You have a lifetime ahead of you."

Zhou Ziheng nods and nervously heads upstairs to change his clothes, but after changing in and out of several outfits, he still can't find a suit he's satisfied with. Eventually, he simply puts on a white button-up shirt and suit pants and, bringing along the surprise, he drives to the hotel he booked in advance. He's been lying low for so long that the paparazzi seem to have given up on him, so he enters the hotel without many disguises.

But to his surprise, within half an hour of him entering the hotel, the hotel lobby is completely surrounded by a crowd of fans and reporters. He calls Jiang Yin and asks, "Sister-in-law, what's happening?"

"I should be the one asking you that. Why did you go outside? Don't you know that the two of you have been on the trending list for the last couple of days?"

Zhou Ziheng is utterly confused. "I don't...I haven't used Weibo for six months already. I've even stopped using my official account for a few days."

"It's all good. Nothing bad." Jiang Yin comforts him. "It's just that everyone rarely sees you make an appearance, so they all went to look at you. I'll get someone to pick you up later. Everyone will understand if it's a private trip."

"You can't pick me up! I...I have something important to do today."

Jiang Yin is puzzled. "What important thing do you have to do? I'm telling you, you better not get Xiqing there too, or else the situation will really get out of hand."

Zhou Ziheng abandons himself completely to despair. He sits on the top floor of the restaurant and pulls out a square box of crimson velvet from his pocket.

The proposal he's been planning for so long is about to be cut off by the enthusiasm of the outside world, before he even knows if he can pop the question. A massive gloom hangs over him, like a dark cloud that can't be dispersed. And yet, it's right at this moment that Xia Xiqing calls him on the phone. Zhou Ziheng puts his emotions in order before answering.

"Hey, Xiqing."

"I just got off the plane. Are you done with the thesis revision? Let's eat together."

If he hadn't said it, Zhou Ziheng would've almost forgotten the excuse he prepared for the surprise. On hearing Xia Xiqing's totally oblivious tone, Zhou Ziheng recalls what his sister-in-law had said earlier.

"I...I actually booked a restaurant, but it's now all a mess. There are so many people outside that I'm stuck here."

Xia Xiqing is a little confused. It's only when he comes out pushing his suitcase that he realizes there's a huge crowd of people at the airport. "Aye, seems like my itinerary has been leaked too."

Hearing Zhou Ziheng's sigh, Xia Xiqing feels both amused and sorry for him. The two of them are like little people floating on the sea but trapped on two separate pieces of driftwood, desperately flailing about as they paddle toward each other.

He's just about to speak when he receives another call. Xia Xiqing takes a look—it's Xu Qichen.

"Ziheng, I'm going to take another call. Why don't you go home first? We'll eat there."

With that, he cuts off the call and puts on his earpiece as he walks through the VIP passage. Dejected, Zhou Ziheng puts his phone into his pocket along with that little square box. The ride that Jiang Yin called for has already arrived downstairs. Zhou Ziheng leaves the restaurant under the escort of bodyguards and gets into the car.

Xiao-Luo, who's sitting in the passenger seat, turns around. "Ziheng, where to now? Home?"

"Yeah."

Zhou Ziheng thinks of how he's been secretly learning jewelry design from scratch all these months. He has not one artistic cell in him, but when he thinks of how his own ring is designed by Xia Xiqing himself, he decides he simply has to design the most beautiful wedding ring personally. For this reason, he even went abroad to select gemstones and have them crafted by hand.

But it still doesn't seem to be the right time to give him this ring. It isn't just because of this unexpected disturbance, but also because he isn't sure if Xia Xiqing is ready. Or rather, whether he himself is ready to accept a failed outcome.

But he can't wait even a day longer. He wants this person to be with him forever, never to be separated.

Just as the car manages with some difficulty to drive out of this crowded area, Xiao-Luo suddenly receives a call. "Hello, oh, yeah, yeah. Ziheng's here. Do you want to talk to

Ziheng? Huh? Ok, sure. I get it. Bye."

Immersed in his own thoughts, Zhou Ziheng doesn't take any notice of Xiao-Luo's peculiar behavior, nor does he realize that the car is no longer heading in the direction of home. He merely hangs his head and looks down at the written and rewritten proposal in the notes app of his phone, reciting them word for word in his mind.

Maybe next time, Zhou Ziheng decides. Then he looks up and realizes that they've come to an unfamiliar, remote place, at what looks like a private tarmac.

"Where is this place?" Zhou Ziheng asks.

The car comes to a stop. Xiao-Luo leaves the passenger seat and sees Xia Xiqing at a distance, so he raises his hand to greet him. Zhou Ziheng gets out of the car too, his face full of shock the instant he sees Xia Xiqing. He's completely befuddled as he walks toward him.

Watching as he walks over, Xia Xiqing plants a kiss on him, and even tousles his hair. This kiss baffles Zhou Ziheng even more. "Why did you bring me here?"

"This isn't the destination." Xia Xiqing points to the private plane behind him and drags Zhou Ziheng aboard.

"Where are we going?"

"Guess." Xia Xiqing laughs. "Don't you have lots of ideas?"

These words turn Zhou Ziheng's ears red. He doesn't know if Xia Xiqing is merely teasing him or if he knows something, but he decides to feign ignorance and follow Xia Xiqing onto the private plane. He doesn't want to let the cat out of the bag so early, or all his earlier preparations will have been for naught.

Xia Xiqing had a long plane ride earlier. Now, after he boards this plane, he pulls Zhou Ziheng along and heads right for the bed in the private cabin. Zhou Ziheng sits at the edge of the bed and watches in confusion as Xia Xiqing sits on his lap and wraps his arms around his neck. The scent from the perfume he's personally mixed for Xia Xiqing oozes out from his body and stirs up ripples of lust the moment it comes into contact with the heat. Xia Xiqing nuzzles the tip of Zhou Ziheng's nose with his nose, his lips playing fast and loose with its approach. His voice is a little hoarse too.

"Missed me?"

He's wearing a pair of glasses, the lens of which has fogged over with a layer of hot mist. It partially obscures his eyes, which are burning with a naked desire.

It's at this moment that Zhou Ziheng suddenly feels that all his earlier dilemmas have been smoothed over. As long as Xia Xiqing is here, he doesn't need anything else.

"Do you want me?" Xia Xiqing takes off his glasses and kisses him, though it's merely a fleeting peck on the lips. But in the next second, when he parts from him, Zhou Ziheng wraps his arms around his waist and kisses him. Tongues intertwine, crushing all of their longings into the ashes of burning desires.

Xia Xiqing responds passionately to Zhou Ziheng's sincerity, as pleasure and emotions commandeer the interlocking of limbs. It's only been a few days since they last saw each other, and yet his chest feels as though a large hole has been dug out. It's only in this moment when they embrace each other again that this hole is filled, and everything returns to the right track.

"Deeper...Ziheng." His body rises and falls like waves, his lean waist bending into a beautiful arc with every thrust into him. "Mmm...Ziheng, I want more..."

Zhou Ziheng kisses the reddened corners of his eyes and tirelessly whispers his love for him, over and over again, with incomparable tenderness. The corners of Xia Xiqing's lips lift in a smile, all of him spread wide open like a rose in full bloom, no longer concealing its frail and delicate stamen.

"I love you, Ziheng." The sweat on his hair damps his face as he endures the torment of lust and pleasure. He sits on Zhou Ziheng's lap, burying his head by the side of his ear, his panting breaking his words into fragments. "I...I want to be with you...forever."

Stunned, Zhou Ziheng freezes. But Xia Xiqing smiles sweetly and wraps his lips in a kiss.

They sleep in each other's arms, and by the time they wake up, they've already arrived at their destination. Zhou Ziheng wakes up with a mess of bed hair, while Xia Xiqing rummages through his suitcase for a pair of long pants.

"I'm not sure if it'll fit you..."

"It's...it's alright. I'll just wear mine." Zhou Ziheng remembers the ring box in his pants and hastily picks it up from the floor to put it on. "It isn't dirty anyway..."

"Right," Xia Xiqing teases him with a smile as he tugs at the waist of Zhou Ziheng's pants. "It's not, but you are."

Zhou Ziheng still has no idea what is going on even as he descends the plane. This place has an abundance of sunlight. He squints his eyes and asks, "What is this place? Why aren't you telling me anything?"

A car is already waiting for them outside. Everything has already been properly arranged. Xia Xiqing tugs Zhou Ziheng along and gets into the car before continuing, "Saipan Island."

"Why the sudden vacation?!" Startled, Zhou Ziheng looks on as the car drives forward. Sure enough, it doesn't take long before he catches sight of the seaside scenery. "This is way too spontaneous."

"Don't you already know the kind of person I am?" Xia Xiqing chews on his bubble gum and blows out a large bubble. It bursts with a pop. "Besides, who said I'm here for vacation?"

"Then why are we here?"

Xia Xiqing doesn't answer Zhou Ziheng. He merely turns to face him with a smug smile. "Guess."

How can Zhou Ziheng possibly guess what Xia Xiqing is thinking deep down? This guy is a tougher nut to crack than a hundred thesis papers.

The driver finds a place to stop the car. Xia Xiqing thanks him and pulls Zhou Ziheng out of the car. This place doesn't seem to be a tourist site, but rather, an ordinary building along the street. Before Zhou Ziheng can get a better look, Xia Xiqing drags him inside. Strangely enough, many people here are looking at them, all of them men and women in pairs.

"What is this place?" Zhou Ziheng looks puzzled as Xia Xiqing pushes him down into the chair before the reception desk. "Why are we here?"

Ignoring him, Xia Xiqing takes out a stack of certificates and visas from his backpack and hands them to the woman at the counter. He then says to her in fluent English, "Hello, we're here for our marriage license."

"What?!" Zhou Ziheng blurts out in shock. "Marriage?"

The eyes of the female staff at the counter dart between the two men's faces. "Uh... Have you decided?"

Xia Xiqing says with a smile, "Don't mind him. He's been thinking about it for the better part of a year. He's just too keyed up to react right away. I'm not tricking him into marriage."

With that, Xia Xiqing turns and moves closer to Zhou

Ziheng, then reaches out a hand and rummages through his pockets. Zhou Ziheng dodges him.

"Hey, what...what are you doing?"

In the end, Xia Xiqing fishes out the little square box and pops it open to show the female staff with a small wave. "See, this is the ring he designed for me. Pretty, right?"

"I..." Zhou Ziheng is speechless.

"You dare to deny it?" Xia Xiqing stifles a laugh and points at Zhou Ziheng's mouth, then hands the box to him. "What are you waiting for? You've been hiding it for so long that it's all warm now. Put it on for me."

Zhou Ziheng freezes for a second, still unable to believe everything even now. It all feels like a dream. With trembling hands, he takes out the ring that he's kept a secret for a very long time, and puts it on Xia Xiqing's finger. Xia Xiqing presses his fingers together and holds them up to the sun for a good look.

"Yup. It's really pretty. Thank you."

Then, as if he's been cued, he slips off the ring on Zhou Ziheng's ring finger which he had personally designed for Zhou Ziheng for last year's Qixi Festival—also known as the Chinese Valentine's Day—and puts it on again.

"Perfect."

Xia Xiqing holds his hand and places their overlapping hands on the table to take a photo, just enough to reveal both of their rings. He then smiles at Zhou Ziheng, "And what about those lines you prepared? Little Movie Star?"

Zhou Ziheng is completely dumbfounded at being asked this by Xia Xiqing. He's prepared on the sly for so long, even rewriting his proposal several hundred times for fear that Xia Xiqing wouldn't agree to his request. But now that the moment is before him, he can't even think of a single sentence. He really is too nervous. How could he have anticipated that Xia Xiqing would be so straightforward, that he would skip over all the processes and throw him a shocking fastball outright?

"I...you...are you willing..."

Looking at the way he's stammering, Xia Xiqing pinches his face with a laugh. "I don't really feel like having the additional title of fiancé or something. Too troublesome. I want you to be my husband, to be with me for the rest of my life." He kisses Zhou Ziheng's face. "I know you have a lot of concerns; you're afraid that I still can't walk away from my past. But I love you, Ziheng. There's nothing more important to me than being with you." The corner of his lips curves up. "I'm not afraid to tell you. I've even fantasized about who I should invite to crash the wedding."

Zhou Ziheng suddenly feels that he really is an over-thinker. All along, he's been underestimating Xia Xiqing's resolve and courage. He's also underestimated Xia Xiqing's love for him.

"Thank you."

"What do you mean by 'you.' Call me hubby!" Xia Xiqing takes the marriage certificate and waves it at Zhou Ziheng. "It's all legal now."

On the way back to the hotel, Zhou Ziheng is still feeling dizzy, but Xia Xiqing remembers what Xu Qichen has told him about the buzz on Weibo. At long last, he opens up Weibo and finally sees that most reposted screenshot of the thank you acknowledgment.

Not long later, Xia Xiqing makes the trending list again, simply because he shared that Weibo post, with an addition of the hand-holding photo he's just taken.

@Tsing_Summer: This guy wrote his acknowledgments

too early, it should now be changed to: "I would like to thank my husband, Xia Xiqing." Oh well, let's see how it goes for his master's degree graduation.

Mini Extra 3: Ziheng & Xiqing's Qixi Festival 2021

Zhou Ziheng's new movie is a romance-themed arthouse film. As the main lead, he has to participate in a promotional roadshow with the production team on the day of Qixi, or also known as the Chinese Valentine's Day.

What he doesn't know is that Xia Xiqing has gotten his assistant, Xiao-Luo, to help him get a roadshow ticket. On the day itself, he wears a low-profile ensemble of black overalls and army-green baseball cap, with a black mask thrown in to complete the disguise. He then waits until the other fans and audience have more or less entered the venue before entering.

On stage, Zhou Ziheng is gentlemanly and mature; his deep, rich voice manly, and his words gentle. Completely different from the guy last night who acted like a spoiled child before bed and a vicious beast in bed.

The roadshow has reached a Q&A segment, and the fans in the audience raise their hands enthusiastically, some even standing up. On seeing Zhou Ziheng looking toward the audience, Xia Xiqing immediately slides further down in his seat and pulls his cap lower.

There's a little girl sitting beside him, likely brought here by her mother sitting to her right. The girl looks at Xia Xiqing and whispers, "*Gege*, are you too tall to sit in the seat?"

Xia Xiqing turns to her and smiles. "*Gege* is playing hide-and-seek with the *gege* on stage."

A male fan who's been chosen stands up excitedly. "Hi, Ziheng!"

"Hello." Zhou Ziheng smiles at him and teases, "I didn't think I had male fans too."

"You do!" The fan takes a moment to calm himself. "Ziheng, this is your first time acting in a pure-romance movie. We all like it very much. The character you played in this movie, Chen Luo, is more of the bashful type, totally different from the roles you played before. Is this a new challenge of yours?"

Zhou Ziheng smiles as he holds the microphone with one hand and puts the other into his pants pocket. "Yeah...

"Indeed. My previous roles tended to be characters who harbor a lot of bitterness and resentment. However, the role this time is more like a boyish character who's a little shy, and even a little childish."

Xia Xiqing laughs at the word "childish."

"But I wouldn't say that it's a challenge...I think this role suits me pretty well."

That's right. Xia Xiqing agrees. *In reality, this guy is pretty shy when he's being pursued and confessed to. He's basically playing himself.*

"Then, can I ask what makes you decide to play Chen Luo?"

Surprisingly, the director beats him to the answer, "I remember Xiao-Zhou telling me that the reason he joined was that someone told him he should star in some aesthetically pleasing romance film at his age, or he might not get his chance by the time he eventually decides to do one, and end up having to take on idol dramas geared toward older audiences."

Everyone bursts out laughing, and the audience clamors to ask for the identity of the person who said that.

"Well..." Zhou Ziheng feels a little embarrassed.

A female fan's voice booms out, "Was it Xia Xiqing?!"

Zhou Ziheng can't keep the smile off his face and replies vaguely in tacit acknowledgment, "It is if you say it is."

"Why isn't he here?!"

"He's probably in Beijing."

Time passes quickly, and the Q&A segment comes to an end. After the special guests sing the theme song, it's soon time for the closing segment.

The host says, "Today is a special day too—Chinese Valentine's Day. We have prepared a cake, so let's ask the team to cut it."

After waiting for so long, Xia Xiqing finally sees the appearance of the cake on stage. He rises to his feet and bends over at the waist to pick up the large bouquet of flowers behind the last row. With a grand total of a hundred and eleven red roses, the massive bouquet completely shields his face and upper body from view.

Amidst a chorus of exclamations of surprise, Xia Xiqing strides onto the stage. Still completely oblivious, Zhou Ziheng cuts the cake with his back turned.

"Ziheng."

On suddenly hearing a familiar voice, Zhou Ziheng turns around in astonishment, only to have a bouquet of roses thrust into his arms.

Xia Xiqing hugs him as if he's a fan and whispers into his ear, "Happy Qixi. I love you."

"Xi..."

"We'll talk tonight. I'll be waiting for you." His voice is so dripping with seduction that it freezes Zhou Ziheng in place.

Having finished all that, Xia Xiqing walks off the stage with big strides, the back view of his long legs stealing the attention of many fans who turn to watch.

To his surprise, when he returns to his seat, Xia Xiqing finds the little girl reserving his seat for him with her hand on it. "*Gege*, you're back!"

"*Gege*, are you not playing hide-and-seek anymore?" The little girl asks anxiously. "Why did you go up there?"

Xia Xiqing's smiling eyes peek out from under the brim of his cap.

"*Gege* went to concede defeat."

Spring Festival

2022 New Year

Xia Xiqing initially thought that he would have to spend the Lunar New Year alone this year, he even thought of returning to Wuhan to have some fun at his eldest nephew's place. But he never expected Zhou Ziheng, who's supposed to be filming for another half a month, to wrap up in advance—just in time for New Year.

"If you want to go back to Wuhan, I'll go with you!"

Zhou Ziheng's voice over the phone carries with it a wintry vibe, as well as the delight of having finished his work. As usual, he's acting like an oversized puppy, one that can't hide his emotions in front of Xia Xiqing.

Xia Xiqing is on his way home from the gallery. He turns the steering wheel absentmindedly; Zhou Ziheng's voice from the incoming call is on speaker. Xia Xiqing enjoys having this tiny space saturated with Zhou Ziheng's voice—

it fills him with a sense of security.

The streets are less crowded as the Spring Festival draws near. Red lanterns and golden string lights hang from the trees on either side, adding to the festive atmosphere.

"Don't you have to spend time with your parents in Beijing?"

Xia Xiqing stops before a red light as he speaks. A young mother holding the hand of a six or seven-year-old boy walks past on the sidewalk. The child is all decked up in red, like a little red packet, while his mother carries a small red paper lantern for him. It's a heartwarming sight.

"I think they're having a community celebration at the compound that day. They told me about it a long time ago. Besides, there's still my older brother, his presence alone in Beijing is enough. What, you don't want me to spend New Year with you?"

Xia Xiqing laughs. "Don't give me that. Don't you know very well whether I do or not?"

The light turns green, and he drives his car forward with a smile at the corners of his lips. "Hurry back, we'll book a flight for the twenty-ninth."

"Sure, I'll be there tomorrow—wait for me!"

Zhou Ziheng indeed returns to Beijing as fast as he can, and furthermore, heads over to Xia Xiqing's gallery to give him a surprise, all bundled up in layers upon layers.

"So soon?" Xia Xiqing is rather surprised. "I was going to go pick you up."

"I caught the earliest flight back, didn't even sleep." Zhou Ziheng leans naturally against Xia Xiqing, resting his chin on the crook of Xia Xiqing's neck. "I missed you so much."

Zhou Ziheng's height is truly very conspicuous, and the two of them attract even more attention as they stand together in front of the most popular work in the exhibition. Xia Xiqing has no choice but to take him by the wrist and lead this giant, praise-seeking hound back to his office. The two of them spend several hours there playing the lovey-dovey game, during which Zhou Ziheng renews his vigor in another equally physically exhausting way.

Of course, he's always been a frisky one in the face of Xia Xiqing's titillations. Except, the price of doing it in winter is a little too high, since it's a tedious task to put the layers upon layers of clothes on one at a time. Thus, Xia Xiqing shamelessly and brazenly has Zhou Ziheng do it for him.

The next day, they get on a flight back to Wuhan.

Xia Xiqing hardly ever goes back to his hometown for Lunar New Year, unlike Xia Zhixu, who would return to Wuhan with Xu Qichen every year even though he's taken up residence in Beijing for work. As Xia Xiqing no longer has many relatives in this place who he can sit and have a New Year's Eve dinner with, they take a cab to Xia Zhixu's house immediately upon arrival.

On the way there, he talks on the phone with Xu Qichen, who happens to be in the midst of a blissful trip to the supermarket with Xia Xiqing's eldest nephew.

"To think I was afraid of coming at a bad time and disturbing you guys at your deed," Xia Xiqing quips jokingly.

Understanding dawns on Xu Qichen on the other end of the line, and he says with one part embarrassment and one part propriety, "No one does that kind of stuff in the middle of the afternoon."

Upon hearing this, Zhou Ziheng chimes in, "Why not? He's exactly that kind of person."

The corner of Xia Xiqing's mouth lifts into a smirk as he turns his head to glare at Zhou Ziheng. This glance of his, however, seems less of a reproach than a come-on.

As they get out of the car, the driver looks hesitant, as if he wants to say something. Xia Xiqing notices this and says, "You're not wrong, sir—he is an actor. Happy New Year, may you have a prosperous one."

With a look of enlightenment, the cab driver grins happily and extends his own New Year's greetings, "Then, may this handsome lad star in even more productions in the coming year!"

Xia Xiqing laughs and turns around before saying, "Enough of that. If you get even more scripts to shoot, I just might turn into a stone statue from all that waiting around. Might as well throw some money in and join the production."

Zhou Ziheng can't help but laugh too. "Why are you always thinking of being the bank-roller?"

"Well it's gratifying—I can do whatever I want."

Xia Xiqing presses the doorbell and hears Xu Qichen's voice: "Come on up, Xiqing. We're making dumplings!"

This is the first time they're visiting Xia Zhixu's house. Knowing his manners, Zhou Ziheng has with him a fruit basket he bought downstairs. But when the door opens, the first one that runs out to welcome them turns out to be a little white Pomeranian.

"So cute!" Xia Xiqing squats to hug the puppy as he looks up at Xu Qichen at the door. "Chen-Chen, you guys have a dog now?"

"Oh, no." Xu Qichen is wearing a beige sweater that gives him a gentle appearance. He explains, "This is a friend's dog. Their family went on a trip, and we just happened to come back, so they left their pets here with us."

He's only just said this when a chubby orange cat strolls leisurely over to them. It rakes its claws on the ground and stretches by way of a greeting.

Xu Qichen introduces, "This little Pomeranian is called Cotton Candy—don't you think it looks like one?" Then he picks up the orange cat and waves its paws at them. "And the kitty is called Tangerine."

"Which friend?" Xia Xiqing picks up Cotton Candy and enters the apartment with Zhou Ziheng. "Do I know them?"

Tangerine is too heavy, so Xu Qichen puts it down again. "Song Yu. You know him, I think. You even said he was handsome back in school."

This sentence immediately triggers a certain someone. Xia Xiqing throws a subconscious glance at Zhou Ziheng. "No, I..." he starts to play dumb, "did I say that? Why don't I remember... You must've remembered it wrong, Chen-Chen."

"Who did you say remembered wrong? Our Chen-Chen has an excellent memory." Xia Zhixu, who's similarly wearing an apron, appears with a large tub of dumpling filling, stirring it as he walks. At the same time, he also takes this opportunity to stir Xia Xiqing up. "Did you forget? Back then, you said Song Yu was tall as well as handsome. Only too bad that he was a tad too fair and not buff enough. It'd have been better if he had more muscles."

Furthermore, Xia Zhixu adds, "Oh, right, did you see? He's very muscular now. His figure is amazing."

Xia Xiqing only wants to make him shut up. "I'm not interested. No one is better than my Heng-Heng," he says as he takes Zhou Ziheng's arm.

Zhou Ziheng, however, asks the other two, "Is he really very handsome? More handsome than Zhixu?"

"As expected of my good buddy." Xia Zhixu smugly sets down the filling in his hands and walks over to give Zhou Ziheng a brotherly hug. "He really is handsome, though."

Xu Qichen explains, "They're not the same type, I guess. Zhixu is more of a sunshine boy, while Song Yu is...too aloof. He does have an exceptional air about him though."

"Alright, enough with the praise."

"Chen-Chen, let's stop talking and wrap the dumplings."

Presenting a rare moment of a united front, uncle and nephew pipe up in perfect unison.

On the contrary, Zhou Ziheng is relieved upon hearing Xu Qichen describe Song Yu as aloof. He knows Xia Xiqing won't like him. A taciturn enigma can probably only be handled by the kind of little angel who can melt anything.

By all logic, wrapping dumplings should be a task well suited to Xia Xiqing—after all, he can work wonders with large sculptures as tall as ten meters. But surprisingly enough, he turns out to be rather bad at it, and ends up tearing the skins of several dumplings in a row.

Xu Qichen coaches patiently from the side, "Xiqing, don't stuff so much filling, just this little bit will do. Then fold it. Put both hands together and use this area between your thumb and index finger. Pinch it, and it's done. Easy-peasy." As he speaks, he finishes wrapping a pretty little dumpling.

"So dumb." It's a rare opportunity for Xia Zhixu to mock Xia Xiqing. He comes over and swiftly wraps a dumpling right in front of him. "You don't even know how to do this, and you call yourself an artist. I think Ziheng has spoiled you so much that you don't know how to do anything."

Xia Xiqing grabs a portion of dough to smash into Xia Zhixu's face, but Zhou Ziheng grabs his hand first.

"Uh-uh, no wasting food." Zhou Ziheng says as though he's reminding a child.

Xia Xiqing can only put the dough back. He flashes a genial smile at the temporarily victorious Xia Zhixu, "Just you wait." Then he turns to Xu Qichen, who's wholly absorbed in wrapping dumplings. "Chen-Chen, do we have any playing cards at home?"

"I think so..." Xu Qichen finishes wrapping one and pinches all the sides of the dumpling again to ensure that the filling won't spill. Only then does he look up to give Xia Xiqing the directions: "In the second drawer of that beige chest."

Zhou Ziheng suddenly lifts his head. "What a good memory you have."

Xu Qichen smiles at him. "I'm just average, can't be compared to you."

"And there they go, flattering each other." Xia Zhixu arranges the dumplings and grins as he watches Xia Xiqing look for the cards, even his little fangs are exuding an air of provocation. "What, still thinking of getting one up on me? I'm telling you, that's not possible in my house."

Xia Xiqing sneers, "Really? Xia Zhixu, how many years has it been since you evolved into an actual human being? And you dare to challenge me? Without your uncle, I, you'd still be all alone right now."

This call-out is instantly effective on Xia Zhixu, who subconsciously glances at Xu Qichen. However, the latter is so engrossed in wrapping dumplings that he's oblivious to everything else.

"Just you wait. We'll see who loses more."

"Why compare losses? So inauspicious. Obviously my wins will trump yours."

Zhou Ziheng is similarly engrossed in his great undertaking of wrapping dumplings like Xu Qichen is, except that his duty is to roll out the wrappers. As someone who's diligent in everything he does, he takes his job rather seriously, rolling each dumpling wrapper with such an intensity until they're all the same size and roundness.

Even Xu Qichen can't help but exclaim, "You're so good at this, they look just like the machine-made ones they sell at the store."

Zhou Ziheng feels very satisfied. It even surpasses the joy he feels when he wraps up filming at a production. This is his first time rolling dumpling wrappers, and it turns out to be a great success. On the other spectrum, Xia Xiqing and Xia Zhixu begin to give up. Eventually, one runs off to pet the cat, while the other goes off to play with the dog. The atmosphere, however, grows a lot more harmonious.

"It's been such a long time. Come to think of it, I'd hardly said more than a few words to Iceberg Song. Does he have a girlfriend now?" Xia Xiqing holds Tangerine in his arms and scratches its chin while idly asking for gossip.

"No, but he has a boyfriend." Xia Zhixu teases Cotton Candy with the bone-shaped toy in his hand.

"Huh?" Xia Xiqing is a little surprised. "I couldn't tell at all. I thought he had no worldly desires. So who's it?"

Cotton Candy barks a few times before Xia Zhixu finally relinquishes the toy. He answers in a casual tone, "Yue Zhishi. The little mixed-blood cutie in junior high level. You remember him, right? Super large eyes and little curls."

"Ohhh..." Xia Xiqing recalls him, but then he realizes something amiss. "Wait, no. Isn't he Song Yu's younger brother? There was a lot of buzz about it in third year of high school."

"It's not like they're related by blood." Xia Zhixu claps his hands and gives him a quick rundown, "In any case, Song Yu has been infatuated with Yue-Yue since they were young, and

Yue-Yue only has eyes for his ge, so the two of them got together after Yue-Yue went to university. Yue-Yue is basically Song Yu's child bride."

Xia Xiqing sits cross-legged on the ground. "How nice," he sighs. "If only Zhou Ziheng was my child bride too. He must have been super adorable as a child—Little Mister Prim-and-Proper."

"You wish." Xia Zhixu clicks his tongue. "It may sound like a breeze coming from my mouth, but they had to go through a lot of hardships before they ended up together."

However, Xia Xiqing is already starting to let his imagination run free as he conjures up happy childhood times with little child bride Zhou Ziheng. He isn't listening at all.

Though it isn't long before he shakes his head. "Better not. He can't be my child bride."

"Why?" Xia Zhixu starts to play with Tangerine.

Xia Xiqing doesn't answer. He picks up the whining Cotton Candy and asks Xia Zhixu where the dog food is. Turning around, he sees Zhou Ziheng's focused back, and thinks about how adorable the guy is.

It's exactly because he has such a happy family that he grew up to become a serious, adorable angel with a righteous sense of justice. If he had been Xia Xiqing's child bride, who knows, he might even have ended up getting beaten up with him.

"Xiqing!" Zhou Ziheng happens to turn around with an extra ball of dough in his hand. "Can you sculpt this into me?"

Xia Xiqing is leaning against the wall as Cotton Candy gobbles up its meal by his feet. He smiles, "Man, I can't even wrap dumplings."

Zhou Ziheng puts on a very regretful expression.

"I'll try."

It takes Xia Xiqing only one second to concede.

Before their meal, Xia Xiuze calls on video chat for nearly an hour, for the primary purpose of seeing his older brother. Although Xia Xiqing calls him annoying, he still can't help but ask after Xia Xiuze and who he's having New Year's Eve dinner with tonight. Sounding utterly unbothered, Xia Xiuze tells him that he's getting together with his classmates for dinner, and even goes on about a number of unimportant incidents that happened over the last month in great detail. Xia Xiqing appears impatient, but still he listens to everything his little brother says.

"Ge, my classmate is calling me. I gotta go!"

"Go on. And no drinking," Xia Xiqing adds casually.

"I won't. Don't worry!" Xia Xiuze makes sure to raise his voice and extends his holiday greeting to everyone else in the room, "Happy New Year, everyone!"

Zhou Ziheng responds with a smile, "Happy New Year, Xiuze."

The words have only just left his mouth when he receives a call from Pei Tingsong.

As soon as Zhou Ziheng connects the call, he hears a small voice from the other end say, "Ready, and..."

Suddenly, six men crowd onto the screen and start to sing together:

On every street, big or small,
The first greeting from the lips of all,
That everyone encountered hears:
Wishing you a Happy New Year,
May you have a Happy New Year...

What surprises Zhou Ziheng most of all is that there's actual vocal harmonization.

After a round of singing, Ling Yi holds up a hand and clenches a fist in the air. "Out."

The six men clap in unison as they say, "Happy New Year!"

Overwhelmed, Zhou Ziheng wonders if he should sing a couple lines back to return the favor. However, Xia Xiqing leans over first, and notices that they seem to be still in stage costumes.

"Yo, heart-throbs, you guys still have to work on New Year's?"

Fang Juexia, who's at the very front, nods, "Yeah, the New Year's Eve Gala. We'll be going on stage shortly."

It appears that a senior is walking past off-screen, and the Kaleido members all bow in greeting, "Hello senior, Happy New Year!"

"Then, will you guys be heading back after the show?" Zhou Ziheng asks.

"Depends, I guess," Pei Tingsong says with a smile. "We're planning to fleece a meal out of Qiang-ge."

"That's right!" Ling Yi nods. "We must have hotpot today!"

Lu Yuan gives him a big thumbs up. "I approve—"

"You approve of everything he says." Jiang Miao glances at him with a smile.

He Ziyan wraps an arm around Jiang Miao's shoulders. "Hey, I approve of everything you say too."

Fang Juexia notices the flour on Zhou Ziheng's shoulder. "Hey Ziheng, are you guys making dumplings?"

Zhou Ziheng nods, "That's right. Me, Xiqing, Screenwriter Xu, and his boyfriend—we're spending the New Year's together tonight."

"What, am I just Screenwriter Xu's boyfriend?" Xia Zhixu jokes as he walks over to greet them. "Happy New Year, heartthrobs!"

Xu Qichen comes over too, half of his head popping out on the screen. "Hello, good luck with the performance! We'll be watching you guys on TV."

"Why do I suddenly feel nervous now?" Pei Tingsong clutches his chest.

The guys on the screen suddenly look back behind them, before turning around again.

"Qiang-ge is calling for us," Pei Tingsong says. "We have to go."

"Alright, good luck!" Zhou Ziheng hurries them on.

"We're turning on the television now," Xia Xiqing says with a smile.

After hanging up, they turn on the television and wait for the New Year's Eve Gala to start. In no time, the living room turns lively. The four of them worked to put together an entire table of dishes, and once the dumplings are brought out, a festive New Year's Eve atmosphere immediately takes hold.

Kaleido's program is near the beginning, and can be considered part of the opening. The four of them put on a decent show of showing their support before the television, and Zhou Ziheng even records a video to send to Pei Tingsong, like a parent would.

"This dumpling is so good." Xi Xiqing pops another piece into his mouth.

Xu Qichen tells him, "I added aspic in the filling. It's very juicy, right?"

"This fish is delicious too."

"Eat more greens, Chen-Chen."

"Oh, right." Xia Xiqing remembers something and walks over to the sofa to pick up his coat. "I bought fireworks on the way here. Let's go downstairs at midnight to set them off, just like when we were little."

Xia Zhixu mocks him, "Fireworks are not permitted in the city now, or are you still stuck in your childhood?"

"You think I don't know that?" Xia Xiqing fishes out two small boxes and shakes them with raised eyebrows. "That's why I bought the incense version."

Xia Zhixu's eyes droop. "What, sparklers? Won't it be embarrassing for the four of us to wander around outside with these? Even the kids are going to laugh at us."

He really hit the nail on the head.

It's almost midnight, and there are many people downstairs. The four of them each clutches a lit sparkler in their hand, but even the kids next door are holding much more impressive sparklers than what they have.

"Mommy, look! Those four shushu are so funny." A child tugs his mother's hand.

Xia Xiqing walks over and points his sparkler at him. "Hey kiddo, you should be careful what you say eh, or else you'll be punished and won't grow up tall."

The child immediately hides behind his mother.

Zhou Ziheng says with a laugh, "Xiqing, don't scare the child."

"Will you say something nice?" Xia Xiqing teases the child. "You see that *gege*? If you say something nice, you will grow to be as tall as him."

The child looks to Zhou Ziheng and falls for the bluff. He behaves himself and says to Xia Xiqing, "*Gege*, you're so handsome. You'll earn a lot of money next year."

"That's more like it." Xia Xiqing pats his head with a smile and takes out two pieces of chocolate from his pocket. "Here, Happy New Year."

He walks back and, after a minute of back and forth

bickering with Xia Zhixu, all of a sudden someone in the neighborhood starts counting down. Their group of four also joins in on the shouting.

"Three! Two! One!"

In an instant, countless fireworks promptly go off, blooming brilliantly in the night sky, looking as if they're close enough to touch.

"Happy New Year, Xiqing." Zhou Ziheng hugs Xia Xiqing and drops a kiss on the top of his head.

Xia Xiqing lowers the hand holding the sparkler and leans into Zhou Ziheng's embrace. "I love you, Ziheng," he says quietly.

Then he lifts his head and moves closer to Zhou Ziheng's ear, where he breathes, "Let's spend all our New Years together in the future."

2023 New Year

On the fifth day of the Lunar New Year, Zhou Ziheng encounters a stray cat as he's out jogging around the community. The devious little thing runs straight at him, falling at his feet and gazing guilelessly at him.

The kitty is a black and white piebald, dusty and dirty on the surface, but quite handsome upon closer examination. More precisely, the fact that the cat has a small black dot at the tip of its nose endears it particularly to Zhou Ziheng.

Thus, it is by this strange twist of fate that Zhou Ziheng ends up taking this kitty home.

Xia Xiqing has yet to rouse. Upon hearing Zhou Ziheng

open the bedroom door, he instead flips the covers up over his face, then turns around to continue sleeping.

"Wakey-wakey," Zhou Ziheng says as he collapses onto the bed, reaching into the covers to grope for Xia Xiqing's face. "It's time for breakfast."

"Too cold." For all that Xia Xiqing complains, he catches Zhou Ziheng's hand between his cheek and pillow, warming it for him. He doesn't sound completely awake yet, voice soft and sticky as he mumbles, "Five more minutes..."

Unlike Zhou Ziheng, Xia Xiqing doesn't have the energy to stay up till three and then get up at seven to go out jogging. He thought Zhou Ziheng might give up, but instead he burrows into the covers, kissing Xia Xiqing from face to ear to neck. Unable to endure it, Xia Xiqing flips them over to straddle over Zhou Ziheng, taking his face firmly in hand.

"Are you a dog? Why are you slobbering over me so much?"

Zhou Ziheng smiles. "But at least you're awake now. Get up, get up; I found your son downstairs!"

Xia Xiqing figures that he must not have woken up after all. "What? My son?"

Zhou Ziheng just looks earnestly back at him. When Xia Xiqing sets gaze upon his so-called son, the little beast actually meows at him.

He chuckles at the little piebald kitty. "Look at the smoky voice on you!"

"I already gave him a bath. The vet said that he's pretty healthy—no injured limbs or anything." Zhou Ziheng waves a cat wand in front of the kitty, then nudges Xia Xiqing with an elbow. "Let's give him a name?"

"What name, though..."

Xia Xiqing considers it for a moment. It's the fifth of

the Lunar New Year today, and, as the saying goes, the fifth welcomes...

"How about Caishen?" Traditionally, Caishen, the Chinese god of wealth, is worshipped on the fifth day of the Lunar New Year. Xia Xiqing scratches beneath the kitty's chin. "Caishen—what a lucky name."

Zhou Ziheng isn't sure if he wants to laugh or cry. "Isn't this name...a little too ambitious?"

The kitty doesn't seem to mind, instead focused on playing with Xia Xiqing's pajama sleeve.

"Good point." Xia Xiqing strokes the cat's head. "What about Hongbao?"

If nothing else, "red envelope" is a much humbler name for a cat. Hongbao meows in response.

"Look, he agrees."

Smiling, Zhou Ziheng puts his arms around Xia Xiqing. "He's saying, 'How slapdash!' Aren't you, Hongbao?"

Hongbao meows cutely.

"How is that slapdash?" Xia Xiqing pinches Zhou Ziheng's chin. "This way, you'll always have a red envelope during New Year."

Zhou Ziheng buries his face in between Xia Xiqing's shoulder blades, wheedling, "If I forgo my red envelope, then could I have something else instead?"

"Enough is enough! I don't think my back could take anymore." Xia Xiqing gives him a shove, but Zhou Ziheng doesn't budge.

"You don't have to move. You can just lie there."

"Stop it."

"I love you."

"Sweet talking won't work—I won't fall for it!"

But in the end, it's Xia Xiqing who capitulates.

"Even the cat saw it." Covered in sweat, he complains without actually resisting. He's left without the energy to even smoke.

"He doesn't understand."

"Nonsense."

In the corner, Hongbao swishes his tail and meows.

Zhou Ziheng only rests for a few days at home, but his job is unavoidable even during public holidays. Late at night, he's given notice that he's needed to help publicize his new movie. During the interview, the host asks him about any new gains over the New Year, and he doesn't even think before he answers.

"I gained a kitty, a neighborhood stray that I took off the streets. He's only been home a few days. He's very cute."

The livestream audience goes wild in the bullet comments, all of them clamoring for cat pics. Zhou Ziheng just smiles, saying, "Please give the kitty a little privacy."

> hahahahaha

> stingy! won't even show cat

> Heng-Heng: Leave the kitty alone, please and thank you.

Meanwhile, Xia Xiqing is painting at home and, unable to bear the begging from his fans, has started up his first livestream of the holidays.

"What am I working on? It's still the unfinished oil piece from before." Xia Xiqing adjusts the camera and picks up his palette knife, sitting before his canvas and chatting as he paints. "Red envelope money? Why would I get any money from that? I've been part of the older generation since I was little, so I've always been the one giving out the red envelopes."

He tilts his head, touches up a detail, then leans back.

> so hard-working, both of you working even through the

holiday season

> I just came from Ziheng's stream. Ugh, it's so hard switching between streams. I wanna watch them both.

> me too!

Xia Xiqing turns to dip his brush, but he suddenly finds Hongbao winding up for a leap right up onto the table, tail sweeping perilously close to Xia Xiqing's paints. He hurriedly picks Hongbao up, wiping his tail for him.

"You sure know where to play around."

> Eh? Since when did Xiqing have a cat?

> kitty, such an adorable kitty, come closer kitty...

> damn, is there a possibility...

> you must have just come from Ziheng's livestream!

> Zhou Ziheng, you sure have got game...

> so this is a confirmation that they've been cohabiting, right???

Xia Xiqing has yet to notice the bullet comments. Instead, after cleaning off the cat's tail, he catches hold of the cat's paws and picks him up, introducing him to everyone.

"This is my son. You can call him Hongbao." He takes Hongbao to the camera, fitting himself into frame as well. "He was pretty pitiful, with nowhere to stay over the holidays, so a little angel brought him home. I never figured him to be a cat person, but he really likes this one. I don't know why, but he never gets tired of taking pictures or cuddling with him..."

> ahhh so cute

> "a little angel" ugh what a sweet nickname

> I think I've figured it out, Hongbao has a beauty mark on his nose.

At this comment, Xia Xiqing pauses. He turns to little Hongbao, and the little kitty quite cooperatively turns his head back to meet Xia Xiqing's gaze.

"Huh, he really does."

Hongbao gives a long series of meows and chirps.

> what's he trying to say?

> how has he not hurt his voice yet

> do you think Hongbao is only meowing so nicely because he knows he has an audience XDDD

Xia Xiqing chuckles. "He's saying happy New Year, right, Hongbao?"

Hongbao turns his nose and swishes his tail.

—Of course not, I'm filing a complaint against you.

—This couple is too affectionate, always paying attention to each other as if I'm not even here.

—Give the kitty a little privacy!

Afterword

To the cutest Self-Study girls of the world:

We have finally come to the official end of this novel.

I know that most readers don't want it to end, but it's not realistic to keep on writing either~ A very sincere thank you to every adorable reader who's accompanied me over the course of the entire novel. The emotional support and encouragement all of you have given me isn't something I can describe with mere words alone. They are so very precious to me.

My original intent in writing this novel was to focus on the impact of the family environment on people, because it had a great influence on me. Of course, I might not have fully expressed my original intent, but that was the starting point of the two protagonists. No doubt these two protagonists are not all that realistic, perhaps even too ideal, but nevertheless, the difference in their personalities is largely due to the difference in the families they were brought up in.

In fact, I think what many readers have discussed about the two main characters is even more complete than what I have to say. I'll just start with their families.

Zhou Ziheng's character design is perfect. To put it bluntly, as someone did, he's a Jack Sue. Actually, I didn't really want to write a perfect persona because it's tough to do it well; it's all too easy for it to be untenable or too two-dimensional. But in order to create a contrast against Xia Xiqing, I decided to go ahead and write such a character. Most of his goodness stems from the fact that he has a very ideal family. A lot of writing and effort have gone into making the different facets of his personality hold up, whether it's his intellect, his profession, his acting talent, and most importantly, his personality. I hope he's at least a rounded character, albeit not a very realistic one. I've come across comments that Zhou Ziheng's manner of speaking is very fake, that guys like this don't exist in reality. In fact, they do. There's a *shixiong*[10] from our laboratory who speaks this way. *laughs*

As for Xia Xiqing, he's too controversial. He can be described a man who steps on many people's landmines. I'm an author who treats my characters as my dear sons, so I can't really accept them getting scolded by others; that's why my trigger warnings keep increasing the more I write, lest everyone come and yell at him. Perhaps there are people who find it melodramatic and think that his experience is too exaggerated, but we have to know that there are countless children in the world who are suffering domestic violence right this very moment and are even losing their lives as

10 In some contexts, terms related to the more traditional models of apprenticeship are still used. Here, "shixiong" is an honorific title or suffix for any male student who's ever studied under the same master or teacher as the speaker, but only those who started studying before the speaker did.

a result. This is a harsh reality that won't change simply because you don't know about it.

I have also seen a comment saying that those with avoidant personalities are not worthy of being loved. At the time, I felt like I was quite the failure to have failed to convey to this reader what I wanted to express—that everyone deserves to be loved. No matter how different you are from a so-called "normal person." Whether you are depressed, bipolar, or if you have an avoidant personality disorder, you all deserve to be loved.

Of course, I've seen a lot of criticisms too. I'll definitely work harder in my writing and strive to keep improving. These two protagonists seem unrealistic to many people, but in my heart, they truly exist. Toward the end of the novel, I felt like I was more of a recorder than a creator. They are the ones making their own stories, and I merely write them down.

And then, the physical book happened, and I've already signed on for a North American Unabridged version in Simplified Chinese. Thank you, everyone, for going all out to give me confidence.

I've started a new novel in my author's profile specifically for the new Self-Study pairing's extras. You'll see it when you click on my profile. The online cover was designed by a reader, and I've already asked for permission.[11] Remember to read them~ Self-Study girls never graduate! Self-Study never comes to an end~ They will continue to live happily ever after in some parallel universe. Thank you, everyone, for loving them. (I'm shedding tears again at this point. Way to

---

11 The first part of this paragraph refers to things that occurred on the online novel publishing platform on which this novel had originally been published, http://www.jjwxc.net.

go, me.)

I'm a person who loves to express ideas through words, because I think that since they've already been written, I might as well use words as a vehicle to communicate with the readers. Whether it's the beauty of the integration of art and science, or the definition of what is normal, or the influence of family—I hope to be able to convey it. But these are not what I want to express the most in this piece of work. At the end of the day, I hope that everyone can feel how good it is to be alive, as Xiqing did. As long as you live long enough, you will definitely meet someone who was born to love you.

Everyone is born to be loved.

Hope I can still meet all of you again in the next novel.

A super long-winded Chu-Chu
2019.03.05

Rose and Renaissance

Copyright © ZHI CHU

Via Lactea